Published by Pendelhaven 2022

Pendelhaven
121 2ieme Bourbonniere
Lachute, Quebec, Canada
J8H 3W7
www.fateofthenorns.com
www.pendelhaven.com

Based on the Fate of the Norns world created by Andrew Valkauskas

Cover artwork by Erwan Seure-Le Bihan

Editing: Erik Growen

ISBN 978-1-988051-12-3

Published in Canada
Printed in the USA

RAGNAROK
FATE OF THE NORNS
GRONLAND
SVALBARD
FINNMARK
HALOGALAND
THE NORTH SEA
ISLANDIA
TRONDELAG
JAMTALAND
POHJOLA
NORRLAND
HELSINGLAND
KALEVALA
MIRKVID
SOGN
FAROE
UPPLAND
THE GREAT SEA
HORDALAND
SVEALAND
ROGALAND
ALBA
VESTFOLD
RANRIKE
STRATHCLYDE
ORSE SEA
GOTALAND
NORTHUMBRIA
HIBERNIA
JUTLAND
ZEALAND
SKANE
BALTIC SEA
THE GREAT ISLES
BALTIC TRIBES
WESSEX
FRISIA
SAXONY
WENDLAND
BRITTANY
FRANCIA
BLACK SEA

I dedicate this book first to my wife, who's tolerance and support made it possible.

I also dedicate it to all who sift through the history written by the winners to realize that the losers often had a point.

I dedicate it to tolerance and the realization that we are all human and our basic natures are the same and do not change. From that start we can perhaps find peace and brotherhood.

I also dedicate it to the people of the Ukraine who at the time of this writing struggle to survive against a foe that strikes at civilian targets without honour or remorse. Evil leaders and power brokers make wars, common soldiers and civilians suffer for them on both sides.

I also thank Andrew and the gang at Fate of the Norns Ragnarök for their help and comradery. I may not see you chaps often but I am fond of you all. Food, Fire, Flax, Friends.

Table of Contents

Chapter 1: A Mixed Blessing

Munin screeched, black wings spread wide, eyes glaring at the seven burly men in tunics and trews forming a half-circle before her. The woman, on whose golden-haired head Munin perched, whimpered. Her pretty features were pale and drawn with terror.

"A bit of extra sport. Ten skatt says I can pluck the raven from her head." A huge blond man hefted a throwing axe.

"Too easy a bet. You're the best with a throwing axe of any of us, Obasi, and you know it. Still in all, you hit the bird. I'll give you ten skatt for a drumstick," said a man to Obasi's right.

Munin squawked louder but didn't move.

"Right then, black chicken for dinner it is." Obasi made ready to throw the axe.

The woman's head was secured through a hole in a heavy plank of wood by her braids which were tacked away from her head.

"STOP!" Sigurlina's voice riveted the crowd like a breath from the grave. The pretty, blond teen drove through the common room using her staff to thrust men twice her weight out of the way. A chill emanated from her, and it was almost like she absorbed the light from the flickering torches and fires that illuminated the great hall. Ice crusted the outer surface of the heavy wool cloak that hung from her shoulders. A black skeleton, armed with a staff, flanked her, pushing men to the side. Sigurlina and the skeleton moved to stand beside the raven.

"Thank Frey," whimpered the woman Munin stood upon.

"We're here now, Eir." A trace of warmth entered Sigurlina's voice as she spoke to the woman, then her gaze turned to ice as she scanned the men before her.

"Get away, witch. This has nought to do with you." Obasi hefted the throwing axe in a threatening manner.

Sigurlina's eyes flashed, and the great hall of Orkney seemed to grow colder. The men and women sitting and standing on the wooden platform that surrounded the dirt floor in the middle of the hall paused in the activities of life, mending nets, weaving cloth, grinding grain, and watched the scene in silence. Only the howl of the storm, which shook the walls and forced the cold of Fimbulwinter into the great hall, could be heard.

Sigurlina remembered how her mother and grandmother had dealt with men like Obasi and tried to emulate the posture of those, now passed, Seithkona. She pulled herself to her full height, taller than half the men in the room, and fixed her eyes on her opponent. "I choose to make Eir my affair, so she is my affair! You had best learn this, Obasi. I take what I take, and I protect those I choose. I am Seithkona."

Over half the guardsmen that stood by Obasi drifted away from him.

Obasi took half a step back. "All I see is a silly little girl with a stick. Run along and let the men get back to our sport. She's only a thrall."

Sigurlina glared at him. "Skeleton, at…" She stopped herself mid-sentence. A frigid smile

1

spread across her face.

"Obasi, you do not know how lucky you are that I have arrived." The voice was deep, resonant and came from immediately behind Obasi.

Obasi spun around and found himself staring directly into the throat of Audun Bear Friend. Obasi looked up into a wide face framed by wild, red hair and a thick, bushy beard. A snow-encrusted cloak was wrapped around the huge man's left arm. He fingered the hilt of his battle-axe with his right hand.

"I am one of Jarl Erik's guards. To attack me is to attack the Jarl himself." Obasi stepped back and felt a chill run up his spine as he neared Sigurlina. The chill was worse than staring up at the big man.

Audun looked to the other men in the crowd. "Has anyone attacked him?"

The crowd of men collectively shook their heads.

"What in Niflheim is going on here?" demanded a new voice. It belonged to a handsome, late-teens man with a well-trimmed beard and a lean, muscular build. Snow and ice adhered to the heavy, blue cloak he wore. Fjorn pushed into the area around Eir. His hand strayed to his sword when he saw the bound woman. "Who has done this?"

"She's only a thrall. We were having some sport, my Lord." Obasi spoke with a tremor in his voice.

"Obasi, I ordered you to leave her be." A short, clean-shaven man with boyish features and brown hair that peeked out from under a cap helm moved to stand beside Eir. Chain mail could be seen through the gap in his wool cloak. A long sword rested in a shoulder sheath at his back. His voice was soft but intense and so sharp it could cut meat.

"Just because she's your playmate doesn't make her a freeman. The wench spilt my mead and needed to be punished." Obasi looked down at Jolnir, but a tremor in his voice made a lie to the larger man's bravado.

"One of them pushed me. I couldn't help it," whimpered Eir.

"Silence, thrall!" snapped Obasi.

Jolnir's hand strayed to his sword hilt. Fjorn's steady voice stilled the action short of the blade being drawn. "Obasi, you have been told before. My father and I decide who is punished and how in this hall. This is our responsibility, given us by Jarl Erik. You show my house dishonour to ignore our laws."

"My Lord, she—."

"NO! When Jarl Erik left you and your fellow guardsmen here to reinforce our garrison, he placed you under our seat. To dishonour us is to dishonour the Jarl. I will not have Erik Bloodaxe dishonoured in my father's hall."

"Yes, my Lord." Obasi fell to one knee and looked down, but his face reddened with rage.

"Audun, please unbind Eir. Obasi, we are fresh back from patrolling the gates. I think we need an extra patrol outside the palisade. I'm giving you the duty. Sigurlina, your slender friend

2

should accompany Obasi with orders to bring him to safety in case the cold becomes too much for him."

"My servant would be happy to oblige." Sigurlina's smile was as brittle as ice.

"I... But the evening feast will be starting soon," objected Obasi.

"So it shall," Jolnir added his words to Fjorn's.

"As you command, my Lord." Obasi half snarled at Fjorn then left to get his cloak.

Audun finished lifting the board from around Eir's neck as tears dried on her cheeks. She threw herself into Jolnir's arms. "I was so scared."

Jolnir held the slender beauty and gently stroked her golden braids. "Shh. It is over. You are safe."

Eir pulled a little away, and the two kissed. "Thank you." She turned to the others. "Thank you all. And you..." she faced Munin. "Extra liver and kidney tonight for you, my brave bird."

"Good bird, good bird." Munin nodded her head.

"Jolnir, a word before my father comes to table." Fjorn's voice was firm.

Jolnir nodded and moved to stand by the Karl's son.

"Can you control your men?" Fjorn spoke softly.

"In battle, yes. When I am present, yes. You can't think I would ever--."

Fjorn shook his head. "I know you care for Eir. That's part of the problem. Obasi is trying to strike at you through her. Jolnir, I love her too. She is the kindest person I have ever known. She stood with me when my mother succumbed to the dark sadness after the first year of Fimbulwinter. I... I am with Sigurlina now, but for years, I pursued her, and I will always have a warm place in my heart for her."

"Then it is good you found Sigurlina. I'd hate to have to challenge a friend to a blood duel." Jolnir was grim-faced.

"And I'd hate to face you in real combat. The bruises from the wooden training swords are bad enough. I'm telling you my feelings so that you know what comes next is for noble reason. If you cannot keep Obasi in line, I'm going to send Eir up island to keep her safe."

Jolnir's soft features flashed through anger to resolve, then he sighed. "It is good she has a friend like you. I'll keep Obasi in line. He knows he is no match for me with a blade. Will your father reconsider selling Eir to me?"

Fjorn shook his head. "He made her father a promise. Only to the man that swears oath to her will he surrender his right, and that right will be her dowry. It was a promise made to protect her that now does the opposite, but it is binding for good or ill."

"True, I must have the Jarl's permission before I can give her my oath, or I must leave the royal guard." Jolnir shook his head.

Not for the first time, Fjorn wondered how a man that looked so soft could rise so high in the king's guard. When he and his companions returned from the raid on Winchester, he'd found that Jarl Erik had left fifty swords from his personal guard to reinforce the Orkney defence. In the weeks since his return, Fjorn had come to see the new defenders as a mixed blessing. Most were warriors and acted as such. Some, like Jolnir, were true men of honour and added to the household guard's training. Others, like Obasi, hated being in a 'backwater harbour town' and fermented strife wherever they went.

"I'm sure permission will only be a matter of asking." Fjorn slapped the other man on the shoulder. "We should have a hot drink while we wait for dinner."

Jolnir smiled. "Wouldn't you rather spend time with your lady? Sigurlina is one woman I wouldn't want annoyed with me."

Fjorn glanced at Sigurlina, who was helping Eir slice liver for Munin by the hall's central fire pit. With her staff set aside and the skeleton on patrol, she looked nothing more than a slender maid, pretty with a clear complexion, but no more extraordinary than that. "You'd never guess the force within."

"The Norns have plans for you. A team like yours doesn't just happen, my friend," said Jolnir.

"Maybe?" Fjorn shifted uncomfortably, remembering a promise made during a battle at his father's gate not long ago. "Audun wants to take ship as soon as the storm breaks."

"That could be trouble. I--."

A blast of cold air caused the torchlight to dance against the hall's walls. A hulking figure in a thick cloak moved into the common area. A second figure, the size of a child, moved to the first one's side. The smaller figure threw back her hood, revealing a rich head of dark, brown hair. She hung her cloak on a peg on one of the support pillars unveiling a body that was anything but childlike, clad in a snug, blue dress.

"Speaking of trouble, here's Ragna," quipped Fjorn as Sigurlina rushed from the fire to hug the small woman.

"Would we want her any different?" Audun walked up from the shadows.

"Diwon seems to be keeping her occupied. You have to admire the old man's stamina." Jolnir gestured towards the hulking man that had entered with the diminutive woman.

"I wish Sigurlina didn't talk to her so much. I... well. When I first met Sigurlina, she hadn't even been kissed. Now... she knows things. I mean, only in theory, but still." Fjorn blushed crimson.

Audun and Jolnir laughed and slapped Fjorn on the back hard enough to make him stumble forward.

The hulking man with Ragna doffed his cloak revealing that he was of late middle years with a beard that had yet to surrender the last of its gold to silver. He had a warrior's build and moved with an economy of motion that spoke to years of training. His thick, gold-streaked, silver hair fell to his shoulders, and a band of cloth covered the space where his left eye should have been.

"I hope Diwon is in the mood to tell a tale." Fjorn watched as the big man bent down and kissed Ragna, then pulled Sigurlina into a one-armed hug. Diwon spoke, but the words were lost to the distance. Sigurlina blushed.

"A skald that wants to share the audience. Are you ill?" Jolnir looked at Fjorn, amazed.

"I'm wise enough to want to learn from the best. Diwon can tell a tale like no other. His voice can trick the mind and make a man believe that day is night and black is white. It's as if he took a quaff of Fjalar and Galar's mead from the source."

"He does have a gifted tongue." Hearing his own words, a blush rose to Jolnir's cheeks. The other men failed to notice.

Munin flew across the great hall and came to rest on Diwon's shoulder. The big man laughed, then, taking Ragna's hand, moved to join Fjorn and the others.

"Hail, my friends. 'Tis a storm worthy of icy Jotunheim out there. Am I early for the feast?"

A herald's voice filled the hall. "Announcing Karl Geldnir Storm Rider of Orkney. Let all gather for the feast."

Fjorn's father walked to his seat at the middle of a table at the end of the great hall just before the private chambers. Geldnir was an older man with a bald head and a heavily muscled upper body. The cane that supported his left side was gnarled oak. Fjorn had seen the old Karl fell men with a single blow of that staff, despite his crippled leg.

Fjorn moved to Sigurlina's side. "My lady." He offered her his arm and escorted her to their places at the table to the right of the Karl. Jolnir took a seat to Geldnir's left; his men fell in beside him.

"There was an incident," Geldnir commented when Fjorn settled himself.

"I dealt with it, father." Fjorn tried not to flex his knuckles.

"I saw." Geldnir laughed. "I was about to take action when that raven appeared. Well handled. I'm glad you saved me the trouble. From you, the Jarl will put off any insult as the brashness of youth. From me, he expects more." Geldnir dropped his voice. "Make sure all know that you have powerful friends. All of you. So long as you are together, none would dare assail you. Together you can sleep easy. On that note, where is your wolf?"

As if on cue, the door opened at the far end of the hall admitting a weather-beaten, muscular man with dark-red hair.

"Vidurr prefers to keep his own company. I think crowds bring back memories," explained Fjorn.

"As long as his sword and his teeth are in your service, my son, he can spend his days baying at the mo... I miss the moon, but baying at whatever he wants to bay at."

Vidurr made a per-functionary dip of his head to the front of the hall, pulled a wooden bowl from his pack and lined up to get stew and bread with the rest of the household.

Eir deposited a small portion of salt pork on the board of each of those at the head table.

5

Another thrall followed her, filling tankards with weak mead. A small piece of bread and a few boiled root vegetables were added to each board.

"I've been using that bag you brought to increase our supply of honeycomb. It won't be long before we'll be drinking better mead than this troll's piss. Wonderful thing that bag," remarked Geldnir as the meagre feast wound down.

"Lord Geldnir, good people one and all. Might this poor skald share with you a tale to reward the hospitality of my hosts?" Diwon stood in the middle of the floor in front of the high table.

"Speak good skald. As if any could stop thee," Geldnir chuckled.

Diwon bowed, lifted his arms dramatically and gestured for all to pay heed. The fire itself seemed to settle. No knot popped, no torch sizzled out of turn. Even the most talkative in the room fell silent.

"I will tell you a tale of fair Asgard. A tale of woe, and a tale of doom. A tale of a father's grief and a God's rage.

"As you all know, Odin Allfather has drunk deep from the well of knowledge. To know 'tis a noble thing, but to know too much can be a weight too heavy for even the strongest to bear. Imagine, if you can, the burden of knowing the days to come, of seeing the twists and turns of fate, but being unable to turn destiny aside. Of being constrained to watch helpless as all you have wrought is overthrown.

"When the sun and moon still shone in the skies, Asgard was a noble realm, and Great Odin knew joy. He was husband and father and had a father's pride, especially in his son Baldur. Baldur, fairest of the Gods. Baldur, like a day when honeysuckle drifts upon the wind, and the sun kisses the cheek and soothes winter's ache from the bones. Baldur, whose voice was as the babbling stream rushing from the winter's melt."

Fjorn could swear that he could smell honeysuckle and feel the warm kiss of the sun on his skin. Most of his mind appreciated the story, letting it carry him away, but a small part watched Diwon, noting his posture, the subtle drop of tone, the cadence of his voice, which rose and fell like the babble of a flowing stream. Fjorn was a student at the feet of a master, hungry to learn all that master could teach.

Diwon looked directly at Fjorn. His blue eye seemed to sparkle as a smile touched the old skald's lips.

"Baldur was fairest and beloved of his mother and father. So beloved that when dire prophecies threatened Baldur, Odin rode to the halls of Hel to consult volva seers. So the all-father passed from the living worlds to discern the future of his beloved son. In this way, Odin learned that Baldur would be slain by treachery and be consigned to the frozen realm of Niflheim. The All-Father concealed this prophecy from Frigga. Sadly, the Norns care little for the comfort and joy of Gods or men and so did take it upon themselves to shatter fair Frigga's illusion of peace. As Frigga, mother of mothers, queen of the Aesir, slept, a dream came to her that Baldur would be slain. Waking in a panic, she swore that her dream would not stand. She would brace against the Norns themselves, so her beloved son should not know death before her. So, he would not become the plaything of Hel. Frigga traversed the nine realms extracting a promise from all to never do the Good God Baldur harm.

So loved was Baldur that all in existence agreed to this pledge. Nought would harm Baldur by deed or omission. Nought would still the warm spring breezes or bring sorrow to Odin and Frigga with his passing." Diwon's voice dropped and seemed to hold a hitch as if sorrow sought to emerge, and he fought it back. The fire flickered. The coiling smoke almost shaped itself into images of spring. Diwon's voice continued.

"But Odin was not satisfied and wished to test the pledge. Thus, he gathered the Aesir, and they all did cast things at Baldur and watched them twist away lest they scratch the Good God. It became great sport to so carry on.

"All was well, but destiny is tricky and has many tools, not the least of which are treachery and deceit."

Sigurlina felt a shudder run up her spine as Diwon's voice took on a timbre as cold as any shade's. She watched the skald. A trick of the fire cast shadow onto his face and made his eye glow like a red coal. She swallowed. She'd faced draugar and held her courage, but for that moment, she would rather have faced all the armies of Hel herself than Diwon. He continued in a voice equal parts the cold of anger and the fire of rage.

"A beast stood among the Gods. One Odin called brother and gave every courtesy. One who supped with the Aesir, sharing their bread and mead, while in his dark heart, he plotted their fall. Loki, in envy of what the Aesir had wrought, sought to destroy them. His desire was to suck all joy from the world and cast everything into shadow.

"And so, Loki, the trickster God, did take the form of a Goddess and travelling to Fenslir, Frigga's hall, did so speak to Frigga."

Diwon's voice became wheedling with an irritating undertone.

"Great Frigga, great mother, are you truly certain that Baldur is safe? Did all take oath that they would do him no harm? I only ask so that I might stand in his defence should the need arise, for I too love him."

The old bard's voice lightened, becoming softer, not truly feminine, but there was no mistaking his intent.

"Dear lady, I assure you. All in the nine realms do love Baldur. All have sworn to do him no harm," answered Frigga.

The voices shifted back and forth with the speaker as if two occupied the body of the single skald.

Loki spoke. "I rest assured that it is so in Asgard, home of the Aesir Gods."

Frigga replied. "Yes, all in Asgard have so sworn."

"Have all in Vangard, home of the Vanir Gods, so sworn?"

7

"Yes, all in Vangard have so sworn."

"Have all in Alfgard, where the Lios Alfar dwell, so sworn?"

"Yes, all in Alfgard have so sworn."

"Have all in Svartalheim, where dwell the Svart Alfar, so sworn?"

"Yes, all in Svartalheim have so sworn."

"Have all in Nidavellir, the Dvergar's realm, so sworn?"

"Yes, all in Nidavellir have so sworn."

"Have all in Muspelheim, where the fiery Muspel Jotuns roam, so sworn?"

"Yes, all in Muspelheim have so sworn."

"Have all in Jotunheim, home to the icy Rime Jotuns, so sworn?"

"Yes, all in Jotunheim have so sworn."

"Have all in Niflheim, Hel's frozen realm, so sworn?"

"Yes, all in Niflheim have so sworn."

"Have all in Hvergelmir, where serpents rule, so sworn?"

"Yes, all in Hvergelmir have so sworn."

"Have all in Midgard, the realm of mortal men, so sworn?"

"And here did Frigga pause. All in Midgard save a little shrub that grows upon the mighty oak, have so sworn. I forgot the mistletoe as I travelled the realms, but it is such a small thing. I see not how it could pose a threat."

"You have been most thorough, Great Mother. Baldur is truly blessed," said Loki hiding poison behind a honeyed tongue.

"And so, as the Aesir feasted, Loki slipped away and made his way to Midgard. He walked across the realm of man until he came upon a mighty oak. Nestled in its branches, was the humble mistletoe."

"Oh, plant evergreen that braves the winter's winds when most have hidden their leaves in slumber, I greet thee," flattered Loki.

The mistletoe nestled on its branch and replied to Loki, for despite all, Loki is a God and has a God's power. "I am glad to be appreciated for something, good traveller."

How Loki must have smiled at the sullen tone of the little herb. "What vexes thee, strong one that braves the winter's chill?"

"I am snubbed. When great Frigga roamed the realms asking all that they pledge safety to her son, she passed me by. I, who need him least, because I don't hide my leaves away when the cold winds blow. I, who would have given my word without hesitation, had I been but asked. But no, she deemed me less worthy than the grass in the meadow. She begged the oak to never lend its limbs, roots or leaves to tool of harm against Baldur. But me? She couldn't even bother to address me. I waited for her words, and they never came, then she walked away."

Loki shook his head and made a tutting sound. "Fair, brave herb that faces the winter's dark, I hear your words. What insult was given you! How shameful that the Aesir should treat you thus when you bravely hold the memory of spring through the cold months. They owe you much. Even now they gather all manner of things to Asgard to have sport, casting them at Odin's son. How unfair that humble rocks should see the golden halls, and you are denied."

"I have heard the stories, as I hold here against the wind and the storm while the other plants do sleep." The white berries on the mistletoe grew red with rage.

"This is not right. Come; lend to me your longest shoot. I will take you to Asgard, where you might see the golden halls of the ever-living.

"It is not known if the mistletoe came swiftly to Loki's hand or if it took more twisted words, but in the end, it surrendered its longest shaft. A stick shorter than an arrow.

"Loki, in his mischief, was good to his word and brought the mistletoe shaft to Asgard. There he sharpened its end and wove enchantments around it. From that flimsy stick, he forged a spear, and enchanted it so that it would never miss its mark. A weapon of doom forged for a single purpose.

"A merry day came to Asgard. All the Gods were deep into their horns; the mead flowed like a river. All was jest and dance. Many of the Aesir had gathered on the field of Idavoll and were making sport of casting things at Baldur; laughing when the items would turn away at the last, missing the God of light and warmth.

"Hod, the blind God, Baldur's brother, stood at the edge of the group."

"Good Hod, why do you not join in the sport?" asked Loki, who walked up beside the God of all things cold and dark.

"Your jest is in poor taste, Loki. I cannot see to cast a stone. My brother has seen to that." Bitterness oozed off of Hod.

"I am sorry. I did not think. But come, if I direct your hand, surely you can join in the sport. Nought can strike Baldur. You can do no worse than the rest. Have a pitch; it will lighten your mood."

A rare smile came to Hod's lips. "Thank you, Loki. Your courtesy does you credit."

"Take this trifle." Loki placed the mistletoe spear into Hod's hand. "Now, face this way." Loki turned Hod to face Baldur. "Now over your shoulder and throw."

"It was a moment that lasted an age. Mighty Odin looked about and recognised the march of doom. His foreknowledge, once shadowy and indistinct as prophecy often is, became crystal clear. The malignant spear flew from Hod's hand even as Odin screamed, "NO!"

"Bound by Loki's enchantments, the spear sped true, striking Baldur and piercing his heart. Loki saw the rage in Odin's face and fled as the Allfather raced to his son's side, embracing his beloved child as the life fled his form, and his spirit was swept into Hel's frozen realm.

"In his rage, Odin wrested the hateful spear from Baldur's side and cast it away with all his might.

"So powerful was the arm of the Allfather that the thing of wood, wound with the spells of doom, burst free of Asgard's borders and sailed across the nine realms to split the very oak that housed the mistletoe from which the spear was made."

Diwon's face was grey as if some old wound had opened. He sighed, and stillness filled the hall. He waited, letting his audience hear themselves breathe.

"Odin, Allfather, had lost his favoured son. All was bleak and icy winds did blow, chilling Odin's living heart. His grief was that of all fathers, but worse, because for him, there was no hope of reunion before all should end in Ragnarok. Tears flowed from his eye, and all the nine realms heard his cry.

"At Frigga's bidding, Hermond rode to Niflheim to treat with Hel, ruler of the frozen realm, Queen of the cowardly dead, daughter of foul Loki. Hel, the heartless maiden whose form is half corruption, did grant a boon from the frozen depths of her twisted soul. She said that if all in all the realms wept for Baldur, she would release him.

"Thus, once more, Frigga sought out all that is. The mistletoe wept for the use it had been put to. Frigga found Loki, who claimed his foul deed was an accident and cried false tears in hopes he could turn Odin's wrath. All things wept for Baldur until, in Jotunheim, Frigga came upon Thokk, a haggard old giantess living in a cave of ice. The Great Mother begged the hag to shed a tear, but the Hag replied, "I will weep only dry tears for Baldur. He was a disappointment while he lived, and after death, nothing has changed. Let Hel keep him. Have you wept for Ymir, your own blood, whom Odin slew? Have you shed a tear for Thrym, whom Thor laid low? Go, I have no tears for Aesir."

"And so, Frigga turned away broken-hearted, not knowing that the hag was Loki be-spelled and that those tears she needed were in truth already shed. Too late to make a difference, the Aesir came to know this. Now Baldur sits upon an icy throne at Hel's right hand. All the world weeps for his return. A father grieves for the loss of his son that will stretch beyond the end of the worlds."

Diwon's voice stilled. The light from the fire and torches dimmed. Fjorn nodded, noting how the old skald had moved so that his body subtly blocked the light reaching the head table. The room exploded into applause, and someone thrust a horn into Diwon's hand.

The old skald sipped at the horn and moved to the wooden platform at the side of the hall.

Fjorn heard Sigurlina snuffle beside him and turned to see a tear trickling down her cheek.

"What's wrong," asked Fjorn.

"I... I feel sorry for Odin. He must have really loved his son." Sigurlina smiled. "Diwon is very good."

"That he is." Fjorn looked at the form of the big man fading into the shadows at the edge of the hall. "Very, very good." Signalling Eir over, he bent close to her ear. "Take Diwon a horn of mead from the barrel I keep in my private chamber."

"The good mead, my Lord?" Eir sounded surprised.

"Let us just say, I'm not taking any chances." Rising, Fjorn escorted Sigurlina towards the rest of their friends, who had formed a little group around Diwon.

#

"ᚠᚨᚦᚺᚠᚱᚲᚷᛈᚺᛏᛁ᛬ ᚲᛗᛪᛊᛏᛒᛖᛗᛨᛁᚻᛈᛪ," Sigurlina looked at the runes scraped onto the back of an old goatskin with a charred stick and made the sound she'd learned that went with each rune. Fjorn sat beside her on his bed in the small, private room his station as the Karl's son afforded him. The floor beneath their feet was wood. A lamp flickered in a sconce on the wall.

"Good. Now try putting them together." Fjorn used the charred stick to scrape four Runes on the goatskin.

"Ken Is Segul Segul." Sigurlina struggled to match the sounds to the letters. "K...i... s...s... Kiss. Kiss."

"Good." Fjorn proceeded to match his action to his text. Sigurlina's hands rested against his chest as he stroked her back. Pulling away, Sigurlina reached down and undid the clasp on Fjorn's belt.

"Really," breathed Fjorn.

Sigurlina blushed prettily. "I..." She looked down shyly, then kissed him and grabbed the sides of his tunic, helping to pull it off over his head. She stepped back to admire his lean, well-muscled form. "I think I want this. I... It's a thing of life. I've seen too much of death."

"So, it isn't me?" remarked Fjorn.

"Of course it's you. It's many things. I..."

Fjorn kissed her to erase the frown his words had put on her face.

"I will pledge myself to you," Fjorn stated when the kiss broke.

Sigurlina rested in his arms and was reaching for the tie on his trews when the curtain door jerked aside.

"Fjorn, your father commands your... Oh..." Ragna smirked from the doorway. "I could say it took a while to find you."

Sigurlina pulled away, blushing. "Ragna..."

"Just remember what I told you about lily root." The diminutive woman winked. "Unless you want to trap him that way."

"I'd never!" gasped Sigurlina.

"Wouldn't be able to say that if I'd come a little later." Ragna's smile widened.

"Ragna, why are you here?" Fjorn didn't manage to keep the annoyance from his voice.

"Your father has ordered the crew of the Apenhet to the council chamber. That's all I know. Your father sent me to find you two. I didn't have to think too hard to figure out you'd be here. Audun is collecting Vidurr."

Fjorn practically leapt from the bed and scrambled to pull on his tunic.

"Not bad, Siggy. Pity you saw him first," Ragna commented towards Sigurlina.

"I.. I." Sigurlina stammered, a blush tinting her pale cheeks.

Fjorn rolled his eyes as he buckled his belt. "We should go." He turned to grasp Sigurlina's hands. "For now."

Sigurlina blushed deeper and looked to the floor with a shy smile. Ragna nodded vigorously behind Fjorn's back. When Fjorn led the way out of the room, Sigurlina shot Ragna a smile and a wink.

Fjorn stopped at the council room door where Vidurr and Audun waited. Glancing at his companions, he could see they were as confused as he was. Taking a deep breath, he pushed open the door, stepped into the room beyond and froze mid-stride.

Jarl Erik Bloodaxe loomed over the map table that filled the centre of the room. Karl Geldnir sat staring at his monarch with Kadar, his bondsman, at his side wearing a suit of chainmail bearing the royal crest. Erik was a robust warrior with dark hair beginning to grey.

Kjorn swallowed, gazing at his king.

"You lost the Horn!" Erik stated in an angry voice.

Fjorn bowed before speaking. "Yes, your Majesty, but we did take it from Hakon and sink a good portion of his fleet." Fjorn felt sweat bead on his forehead.

Erik's lips trembled, then he let out a guffaw and moved to pull Fjorn into a bear hug. "That you did, boy. By the Gods. When I heard the news, I couldn't believe it. I would have paid good skatt to have seen Aethelstan's face when he came back to Winchester and twice as much to have watched what he did to that bastard Hakon." Erik pushed Fjorn roughly away, but the smile stayed on the Jarl's face as he pointed forcefully at the younger man. "You have a price on your head in Wessex; the rest of you as well." He expanded the gesture to include the crew of the Apenhet. "Nicely done, all of you. Nicely done!" Erik grinned. "That's three smiles for a Jarl to your credit. You're making a habit of it, Fjorn."

Fjorn stopped himself from breathing a sigh of relief and tried to match his king's jovial tone. "I can but try, My Jarl."

"All of you come around the table. We have much to discuss," ordered Jarl Erik.

The crew of the Apenhet took places standing around the table. Audun looked down at the map that was rolled out. It depicted Northumbria through to the Orkney Islands. He recognised his handiwork.

"Kjorn, fetch the keg we brought and horns for all, including yourself. We can drink while Fjorn tells the tale. I'd like to hear a skald's account. Epically one who was in the thick of it. Way the rumours tell it, you stormed Winchester and carved a trail of blood to the treasure hall, then summoned a hundred Kraken to cover your escape. This after singing the dead back to life along the coast of Northumbria after a jotun set it to light with flaming spears." Erik snickered and took a long pull from the horn in his hand. "I'll mention before you start, King Cuaran has sent word that you are welcome in Jorvik as his honoured guest. In fact, that is part of why I am here, but later. When the drink has had a chance to chase the chill from my bones."

"I thought you were going to Islandia?" remarked Vidurr with an indifference bordering on insolence.

Erik's face soured, then, with a deep breath, he shook it off. "I am. My ship is harboured on the far side of the island. I left the Queen to govern most of my guard in my absence. By the way, girl." Erik gestured towards Sigurlina. "She says to tell you 'dear as sister' that she is proud of you and to remember your arrangement."

All eyes turned to Sigurlina. She bit her lip before speaking. "The Queen is my friend. Please, Jarl Erik, tell her I appreciate her courtesy and will honour what we discussed."

The Jarl smiled at Sigurlina. "And so we have the truth of it. Even a jarl is nought but a messenger for beautiful women. I will carry your greeting."

Sigurlina blushed crimson and looked at the floor. "Thank you, My Jarl."

Erik turned his attention to the group, "In any case. I saw no reason to undo the good of your scheme, Fjorn. The seas are still dangerous, and sadly, Hakon still has ships aplenty. So, by all accounts, I was never here. I came by the landward gate under the premise that I was with Kjorn, who was coming home from bearing your dispatches. You will all keep this council. I like the idea of Hakon chasing his tail looking for me."

"Isn't this an unnecessary risk?" asked Geldnir.

"Less risk than staying on ship. The Queen, well. A dark moon brings out the worst in her." Erik sighed heavily. "Best for us both if I leave her be for a day or three."

"Oh," Geldnir nodded. "We will keep your secret as long as you need."

"She'll be fine by the time I cross back to our port," remarked the Jarl.

Ragna released a little 'humph' sound, shook her head and rolled her eyes.

Vidurr nodded. "My Elsa was the same. Take up trapping. I always checked the line when the moon was dark. Better for both of us. Though I'd give all even to fight with her again." The ulfhnednar hung his head.

Audun shook his head. "One reason I stay single."

"What?" asked Fjorn and Sigurlina in unison.

"Be happy you don't know," remarked Geldnir.

By this point, Kjorn had returned with a keg under his arm. He filled horns for everyone and passed them around.

"Now, Fjorn, wet your throat and recount your exploits. I'm certain your exaggeration will not be so grand as those I've heard, and your telling will like put Kjorn's to shame." Erik turned to Kjorn. "You're a stalwart sailor and guardsman, but as a skald; Bragi was not kind to thee."

"As you say, My Jarl," Kjorn nodded.

"Well then, Fjorn. Tell your tale."

Fjorn took a long swallow of mead before speaking. "I'll start with when we left Alvaldshes...." Fjorn spoke in the sing-song voice of the skald, mimicking actions, making a story of his recent exploits and those of his friends.

Diwon entered the room, but none took notice. He stood in the corner nodding in places as the tale was recounted. Geldnir listened as attentively as the Jarl and smiled at the skill his son demonstrated.

"As the horn of the kraken sank into the sea, the ships parted, and Halla Sea Born guided the Apenhet through the gap. Then ship and crew vanished into the cold and dark of Fimbulwinter while behind them the harbour of Winchester burned, and kraken swarmed Hakon's ships."

Erik drained his horn. "Well told. I'll forgive you losing my horn. Surprising you made it out alive. Bit of luck they had. What did you call the fire sprite? Oh yes, a skui, to hand, but you used what the Gods gave you."

"Your Majesty, I promised the smugglers I would speak on their behalf. They would have pardon in exchange for the aid they lent us." Fjorn pressed his case, hoping the Jarl's favour would carry it.

Erik nodded. "Done. It sounds like they are fair enough blades. I need every blade I can get."

"Thank you, Jarl Erik." Fjorn bit his lip. "I know you want to keep your presence a secret, but there is another matter."

"Fjorn, the Jarl has been very gracious already," cautioned Geldnir.

"There is no harm in the asking." Erik held his horn out to be refilled. In the corner, ignored, Diwon filled a horn from the Jarl's keg and sipped its contents.

"The boon is not for myself. Your guardsman, Jolnir, wishes to wed."

"Really?" Erik sounded surprised.

"He has a great affection for one of my thralls, Eir. I am oath-bound not to release her to any, save the one she takes oath with," explained Geldnir.

"And is this Eir a pretty girl?" asked Erik.

"Lovely," Fjorn and Geldnir responded in unison.

Erik sighed and puffed his cheeks. "Yggdrasil has many branches. I will grant my leave, if both desire to take the oath, fully knowing to whom they swear. The problem is, none may know I was here. Still..." Erik stroked his beard. "I will leave a writ that grants my leave that you may execute upon your return. I will be well away by then. Take Jolnir with you. ...He should be good for this task."

"Task?" repeated Fjorn.

"I am not here simply to praise thee. Before I sent you after the horn, there were rumours that the White God's church was searching for something. Some kind of weapon that would ensure victory to any that held it. Supposedly, the Romans brought it to the Great Island. Geldnir, fetch in your pet monk. He might know what this thing is."

"I'll get him," offered Audun.

"Knock and wait to be summoned before you bring him in," ordered Erik. "I need skin

14

and ink to write the grant for Jolnir."

Geldnir extracted a shaved goatskin, stylus and inkpot from under the map table.

Audun left the room.

With an expression of extreme concentration, Erik scratched out Runes in a spidery script. After several minutes he sat back and looked at his clumsy, handy work. "You have your letters, don't you, boy?" Erik asked Fjorn.

"Yes, My Jarl. My father saw to it."

"Good. If you would rule, you must have open eyes. It is more important to be able to read so that no scribe can replace your words with his own, but to write is useful as well. A ruler who doesn't know his letters is like a warrior with only one arm. It can be done, but you are always at a disadvantage."

"I will remember that, My Jarl," agreed Fjorn.

"Good. Now getting back to your exploits."

As they waited, Erik grilled the others on details of liberating the horn of the kraken. In minutes Audun knocked on the door.

Jarl Erik lifted a hood from a peg on a support post and donned it, pulling it down so that hid his face. He then stepped back into a corner of the room and assumed a posture like a guardsman. "Question him about the weapon, then dismiss him."

"Come," ordered Karl Geldnir.

Audun entered with a slender, bald man dressed in a patched robe. A simple wooden cross hung from a leather thong around his neck. Vidurr curled his lip at the sight of the man.

"Hello, Agathe," greeted Geldnir.

"My Karl. I am told you wish my counsel." Agathe inched away from Vidurr. He glanced around the room and swallowed. "Am I to die this day?"

"Why? Have you done something to earn death?" asked Fjorn.

"I am loyal in the things of this world to your house, Karl's son." The old monk looked directly into Fjorn's eyes.

"Then you have nought to fear from me in this world." Fjorn made himself smile to try and ease the fear he saw in the monk.

"We have a question about the White God. In the stories you tell of him, is there a weapon that would give victory to any who held it?" asked Sigurlina.

The Godi smiled. "There is the jawbone of an ass that Samson used. That is a great story. I could--"

"Where is it supposed to be?" demanded Geldnir.

"Lost in the holy land. If it still exists. Samson was a long time ago."

"Something else, something that might be around here?" insisted Fjorn.

"The true teachings of the White God are of peace. He was the lamb sacrificed for our sins who suffered on the cross, wounded by spike and spear..." the monk trailed off, looking

15

speculative.

"What is it," demanded Fjorn.

"The Spear of Longinus. When the Romans hung the White God's son on the cross, one of the legionaries thrust his spear into our... I am sorry; my Lord's side."

"Like Odin gaining the runes," remarked Audun.

"But this is re...." Agathe looked at the room full of Pagans. "Of course, you believe your stories are real as well. In any case. They say that whoever holds the spear will be victorious in battle. It was lost centuries ago, but rumour has it that it may be on the Great Island. There is a story amongst the Celts that–," explained Agathe.

"Thank you. I'm sure we can find a Druid or Bard to tell us the tales of the Celts. This spear sounds an interesting weapon," remarked Diwon.

All present simply accepted the one-eyed stranger being there and speaking as an honoured guest. Fjorn shook his head as he tried to think. A glance from the older skald and Fjorn's thoughts slipped away.

"That will be all, Agathe. You have proven yourself useful. You may return to your prayers." Geldnir smiled at the monk who hurried from the room.

"I wish he'd get over thinking that I'm going to kill him," remarked Fjorn.

"He doesn't understand our ways. You have garnered quite a reputation, and there was no love between you before you left. He will, in time, come to see you as you truly are," soothed Geldnir.

"That information was worth the trip." Erik removed his hood and stepped up to the table. "My spies tell me that the Crusaders think they know where this spear is. I need you to get there first and take it."

"Where should we start looking? The Great Island is vast," commented Audun.

"My spies tell me that the Crusaders are looking in Northumbria, close to Jorvik. That is another reason I am sending you. King Cuaran will greet you with open arms and aid you in return for past kindness to his people."

"I will assemble a crew. Can I draw from your guardsmen?" Fjorn looked Erik in the eye and saw his own face some twenty years on.

Erik smiled. "Take those you need."

"Will I get to kill Crusaders?" asked Vidurr.

"I would not insult you by asking you here if that were not the case. Kjorn has all the details. Now we had best get on our way." Erik stood and walked from the room, with Diwon following behind. Diwon paused by Fjorn and whispered. "The trick is to listen to their voice and then match the rhythm so that they start to think your words are their thoughts. Practice, you'll make a skald of yourself."

16

CHAPTER 2: SAILING WITH DEATH

Sigurlina yawned and rubbed sleep from her eyes. The Apenhet, provisioned and ready to sail, sat in the harbour. Torches burned along the gunwales of the small longship, and the fore and aft lanterns were lit. With the storm passed, stars twinkled in the skies. The red glow from Muspelheim's fires marked the horizon, and the dancing lights of the Bifrost Bridge shimmered to the north. The cold nipped at her despite her thick cloak, and blocks of ice could be seen floating in the harbour. Munin cried from above. Sigurlina held out her arm, allowing the raven to land. She carefully tucked Munin under her cloak.

"What does she say?" asked Audun, who stood beside Sigurlina.

"It's clear to the harbour mouth. How long will it take us to reach Jorvik?" Sigurlina looked up at her big friend.

"Two, two and a half days to the Humber River, maybe longer. It all depends on the wind. Then the inland voyage. At least this time if a storm blows in, we should be able to make port." Audun hugged himself against a remembered chill.

"They're as fine a pair as I've ever laid eyes on, but onboard, there's no place for them. I'd have told you before, but too much happened too fast, and we needed her." Kjorn's voice came out of the night.

"Do you want to tell them to dress and act like men when they're on board? The Crusaders don't have shield maidens; it makes them careless. Sigurlina and Ragna are a secret weapon as long as Hakon's people see them as women." Fjorn stepped out of the shadows with Kjorn at his side. Both carried sea benches. Kjorn had changed from the royal mail into warm seafaring clothing.

"But tradition--," objected Kjorn.

"We're at war. A war to preserve our way of life, and the right to choose the very Gods we worship. I'll take victory over tradition and trust the Aesir to understand." Fjorn's voice was adamant.

"What are you two talking about?" asked Sigurlina.

"We're going a Viking. There's no place for a woman on board a raiding boat." Kjorn stated his case.

"You're not leaving me behind!" Sigurlina's cheeks reddened. The black skeleton that stood in the shadows to one side, watching to be sure no enemy attacked the party, stepped closer to its mistress at the tone in her voice.

"I never said that." Kjorn eyed the skeleton warily.

"I can't stop being a woman! So, what did you mean?"

"Do you see what you started, Kjorn?" Fjorn rolled his eyes. "Siggy, what he means is the tradition. Normally, if a woman wants to go a Viking, she dresses in men's clothing and lives as a man for the duration of the raid. It prevents problems on board. But we are not going a Viking.

We are searching for a treasure, and our enemies think anything with bosoms is harmless."
Fjorn saw a scowl cross his lady's face and rushed to add. "More fool them! But it worked to our advantage in Winchester. I don't want to surrender that advantage."

Sigurlina bit her lip. "It's like the men who want to study Seith."

Audun stared at Sigurlina. "I haven't heard of this. I know that few men study Seith."

"Seith is woman's magic. Even great Odin had to take on the woman's role when he studied. Dressing as a woman, weaving, spinning, grinding grain, doing women's work and holding a woman's place. Only in this way can a man learn the secrets of the Seithkona. Once trained, she can go back to being a man if he chooses. There was a Seithkona in my village growing up. She was as tall as her husband and had to shave each day. She also had the most beautiful dresses and jewellery. It took three Crusaders to kill her when they attacked."

"So, you understand?" said Kjorn.

"I guess if you want me to dress like a boy--."

Fjorn cut her off. "No! I have said why I want you to dress as you are. Having you travel as a woman also makes a statement about our peaceful intent. We are not going a Viking on this trip. We are seeking the spear. You and Ragna are women, and that is that. I have spoken as captain."

"So, you did notice." Ragna sauntered out of the shadows. One of Jarl Erik's guards carried her sea bench.

Fjorn took a long, slow breath. "Where's Vidurr?"

"Last I saw, he went wolf and left with Jolnir to track down Obasi. Having Jolnir aboard, I understand, but why bring Obasi?" Audun sneered a little at the second name.

"Two reasons. One, to keep him where I can watch him. Two, to keep him away from Eir. I don't trust him." Fjorn replied in a voice that hardly carried.

"Ah." Audun and Kjorn nodded in unison.

A minute later, Obasi appeared carrying his sea bench. He had dressed in a chain mail coat with a cap helm that didn't hide the scowl on his face. Vidurr and Jolnir flanked the reluctant guardsman carrying their sea benches.

"We should board." Fjorn led the way onto the Apenhet, where six oarsmen waited, ready to cast off.

Hours later, Vidurr sat the ice watch. "Port three lengths," he called as they moved past an iceberg.

"Port three lengths," Audun's voice called back from the stern. The Apenhet shifted subtly to starboard.

Vidurr scraped a wet stone down the length of his sword as he continued to scan the murk.

"Quiet night?" Sigurlina approached the bow.

"Hmm." A brief upcurling of Vidurr's lips invited the girl to stay.

Sigurlina settled in the bow. "Ragna snores," she gave by way of explanation.

"I know," Vidurr sighed. "We all know."

A companionable silence descended between the pair as the dark ocean slipped by. Vidurr didn't know if the girl came by it naturally or from her years living with the dead, but he welcomed her company. Unlike most, she didn't clutter the air with empty words. She was like the silence of the hunt, where one spoke only when needed. She could fill a little of the hollow space inside him and seemed to know when the void left by his family's murder at the hands of Crusaders was threatening to swallow him.

A dim light shone in the distance. Vidurr focused on it and sniffed the air. "Light to port." He sniffed the air again.

"Light to port. I see it." Audun called back from the tiller.

Sigurlina stood on the gently rocking boat and parted the folds of her cloak. Munin looked up groggily from her perch on Sigurlina's arm. "Please fly over and see what that light is. And be careful."

"Yura bitch!" squawked Munin.

"What?" Sigurlina glowered at the raven.

'You woke me up. I was warm and....' Munin's mental voice trailed off as she looked at her mistress's expression. 'I'm sorry.'

"You should be," Sigurlina spoke aloud. "Now, go have a look at that light."

"Good bird?" Munin spoke aloud.

"Yes, good bird." Sigurlina's expression softened as she petted the feathers on the raven's head.

"Good bird, good bird." Munin leapt into the air and vanished into the darkness.

"She has never spoken to you like that before," commented Vidurr.

"I think she's still adjusting. One day she was a girl, then she's a spirit, then she's a raven. Now that she's had time to think about things, it's all catching up with her."

"I understand. The first time I changed, I ran into the woods and didn't return to the village for nearly a moon. It is easy to let the fur...or feathers take control."

Sigurlina closed her eyes. "Munin says it's a ship, and there's someone on board. I'll wake Fjorn."

"Hmmm." Vidurr nodded.

Sigurlina moved to where Fjorn slept, huddled in his cloak at his oar station and knelt beside him. She was tempted to kiss him but knew that would not sit well with the crew, so she shook his shoulder.

Fjorn stirred.

She shook him again. "Fjorn, wake up. There's another ship."

Fjorn became a blur of motion as he came to his feet, hand on the hilt of his sword. "Where?"

"Port," Sigurlina pointed. "Munin says it's riding low in the water and that there are at least two, maybe three, people aboard. She says only the aft lantern is lit and that it's hard to see. She didn't want to get too close."

Fjorn looked at the distant light then bellowed. "Stations. Arm yourselves, but no action without my command. Audun, set course to come alongside that vessel. Sigurlina, we'll send your slender friend aboard first. If he isn't attacked, we'll follow."

"I'll tell him." Sigurlina moved to where the black skeleton sat pulling on an oar.

"Is it a good idea to look for trouble? We have a mission from the Jarl," cautioned Kjorn as he came alongside Fjorn.

"I don't know, but I know that a ship at sea without torches, in times like these, means they are in a bad way or hiding. If they were hiding, they would not have any lights at all. We'll see what is what. If there's trouble, the wind is at our stern, and by the time they tack around and hoist sail, we'll be well away."

Kjorn nodded his approval and slapped the younger man on the shoulder hard enough to make him stumble. "We're finally making a sailor of you."

The Apenhet cut through the water until a deeper shadow against the gloom took shape. The ship was three times as long as the Apenhet, but, aside from a single lantern hung from the stern, there was no sign of life.

"Reef sail and back oar," ordered Kjorn. The oarsmen obeyed, and the Apenhet stopped beside the larger vessel.

"Lines away," called Kjorn.

Four seamen threw hooked lines over the gunwale of the strange vessel and, grunting, pulled them to its side. The gunwale of the larger ship was charred and rode barely above the gunwale of the Apenhet.

"She's low in the water," commented Audun as he left the tiller oar.

"Might be treasure." Ragna pushed her way in amongst the men.

"Sigurlina, if you please," called Fjorn.

No sooner had he spoken than the skeleton, with a torch sticking out of its ribs and a staff in its hands, leapt onto the larger ship. There was a splashing sound as it landed.

Ragna sighed. "Just couldn't be skatt. My luck!"

Vidurr moved to join the group.

A child's scream came from the other ship, followed by whimpering and a babble of Anglic words. The skeleton's head flew over the gunwales and landed on the Apenhet's deck.

"Cast off, hoist sail," bellowed Fjorn.

"Wait, wait," called an old woman's voice in Orse. "Harr, sheath your sword or, by Lady Hel herself, I'll see you in the coldest recesses of Niflheim." There was the sound of a wheezing intaken breath, then a dark figure hobbled to the edge of the larger ship. "We mean you no harm," spoke the old woman's voice.

"Hold." Fjorn bellowed to his crew as he moved to look at the old woman.

"You killed, I mean, undid, I... you know what I mean, my skeleton," blurted Sigurlina.

"A misunderstanding, child. Please, captain, our ship is sinking, and we are adrift."

Fjorn studied the old woman's features in the torchlight. She looked almost grandmotherly, except she was dressed in black. Her grey braids snaked out from under her heavy, black hood.

"There is a child aboard," added the woman.

"This feels wrong." Sigurlina silently formed her next words in her mind. 'Munin, fly over and see what more you can see.'

Munin climbed out from under Sigurlina's cloak and leapt into the air.

"What aid do you require?" asked Fjorn.

"Passage to a friendly landing. Whom do you serve?" The old woman's voice was soft, soothing, as if she was accustomed to allying people's fears with her words.

Fjorn noted the skaldic tricks of tone and timing in her speech. His hand tightened on his sword hilt. "We sail for Erik Bloodaxe, Jarl of Norveig. Who is your Lord or Lady?"

The old woman smiled. "I am Daldis, and my mistress is the Lady Hel, though in Midgard, I keep faith with King Cuaran through Karl Baleygr."

Munin let out a frightened squawk and sped back to the Apenhet.

"There's a draugar on that ship!" shouted Sigurlina.

"Cast off," Fjorn bellowed needlessly as Audun cut the tiller hard and Kjorn worked to hoist the sail.

"Wait, please!" Daldis's eyes focused on Sigurlina. "Seith sister. I am an Angel of Death. I swear by Lady Hel and upon Gungnir and Mjolnir that you and your companions will come to no harm from any aboard this ship. Please, hear me out."

Sigurlina stared for a long moment.

"That is a potent oath." Audun held the tiller but took no further action.

"Fjorn, I think we should hear her words." Sigurlina sounded hesitant.

Fjorn stared at Daldis. "Why do you travel with a warrior of Hel's army?"

"My lady sent what aid she could when I was set adrift by Crusader scum."

"Fjorn, it's a draugar. Big, scary, undead warriors. Remember the last time?" chimed in Ragna.

"Does your oath bind the draugar?" asked Fjorn.

"It binds me, for I was sent to serve, mortal. At this time and place, we have no conflict." A voice that sounded like a rusty blade drawn over a whetstone came from the sinking vessel. It sent a shudder up the spine of all who heard it.

"Sigurlina, with me. Audun, Kjorn, be ready to cast off." Fjorn motioned for Sigurlina to follow him and, taking a torch, stepped across to the other vessel.

Water sloshed on the deck almost knee-deep, and everything was charred. The shadowy form of a child huddled near the bow on some crates piled up to be above the water. The draugar, with its burnt countenance and glowing blue eyes, stood to one side. It was dressed in rich robes and held a sheathed sword. Jewels gleamed on the scabbard.

The chill in the water threatened to cramp Fjorn and Sigurlina's legs.

"Sigurlina, get the child to the Apenhet while I speak with our new...." Fjorn eyed the old woman and draugar. "Acquaintances."

Sigurlina moved towards the child.

"What happened?" demanded Fjorn.

Daldis sighed and looked mournful. "The short of it is, betrayal."

"We are sinking." The draugar's voice was as chilling as the water.

Fjorn shuddered. "If you will be oath-bound to peace, you may board my vessel. Is there anything you wish to take?"

Daldis looked over the sinking ship. "Let what little those thieving Crusaders missed go with Baleygr as it was intended."

The draugar moved to take off the sword it wore over its shoulder, then paused, looking towards where Sigurlina carried a boy of about eight across the flooded deck. The draugar kept the sword.

Fjorn moved to steady Sigurlina as she boarded the Apenhet. Daldis followed, leaving Fjorn and the draugar on the sinking ship.

Fjorn steeled himself and gripped the draugar's arm. The contact chilled Fjorn's hand. "Do you swear by your mistress, Hel, that you will bring no harm to me and my crew?"

"I have so sworn, and so do swear again," replied the undead warrior.

"By what name are you known?"

The draugar paused as if recalling something half-forgotten. "In life, I was called Harr."

Fjorn couldn't be sure, but it seemed like a shadow of pain crossed the scorched features of the creature.

"I am Fjorn. Keep thee the obligation of the guest, and you are welcome with my crew."

The draugar dipped its head in acknowledgement. Together they leapt onto the Apenhet.

No sooner had Harr's feet touched the deck than blades were drawn. Ragna raced to the bow and turned, glaring at the draugar.

"Sheath your weapons. Harr is a guest. To strike him without provocation is an insult to my honour," called Fjorn.

"This is madness," snapped Kjorn.

"If I be mad, I will be mad with honour," returned Fjorn.

"I will not sail with a devil," snapped Obasi.

"Then feel free to swim!" Fjorn glared at his crew. "It is my order, and I am captain. Free the lines so that the other ship doesn't pull us under. Set sail. Mistress Daldis, Harr, join me at the tiller. Ragna, heat some stew for our guests." Fjorn turned to Harr. "Do you eat?"

"There is nought of meat or drink in Niflheim, but I remember what it was to cup a warm bowl in my hands on a cold winter's day."

"So shall it be." As he spoke, Fjorn watched the sinking ship retreat into the distance. The dot of light from its lantern lowered on the water and then vanished.

"The old Karl's ship was a noble one. I could feel her fighting to stay alive for us. She is a great spirit. Now she too is free," remarked Daldis.

Sigurlina watched where the ship had sunk and half-imagined that she saw a ghostly vessel rise into the air and speed towards the Bifrost Bridge. She whispered, "That can't be. Ships don't have spirits."

"Don't tell that to a sailor, my young Seith. They will tell you different. Better say that not all ships have been gifted a spirit by their captains and crews," remarked Daldis.

Fjorn moved to stand beside Sigurlina. "She served you well. If you would, Mistress Daldis, please come aft. Sigurlina, if you could find some blankets so our guests may warm themselves."

Soon after Fjorn, Sigurlina, Audun, Kjorn, Vidurr and Jolnir sat in the Apenhet's stern around Daldis and Harr. Fingers caressed weapons, but no one drew blade. Ragna huddled in the bow with the boy, Sigurd, who was wrapped in blankets and seemed to sleep. Daldis and Harr cupped bowls of steaming stew, though Harr never raised his to his lipless, skeletal mouth.

"Mistress, you said you were brought to the boat by betrayal?" prompted Fjorn.

The old Angel of Death nodded and began to speak. "I lived in the village of Rauoa, on the southern border of Northumbria, under the seat of Karl Baleygr. The forces of Aethelstan were a constant threat, but my Karl was strong, and King Cuaran reinforced us with fresh troops. At great cost, we held the murdering horde at bay. Then Forni came to our village. When Baleygr took the seat, his brother, Forni, had run off. Now he returned clad in the black robes of a Godi of the White God. He tried to preach to the people, but we had all seen the hypocrisy and dishonour of the Crusaders, and none would listen. Still, my Karl made his brother welcome. It was a blood tie. He could do no less. I had my suspicions, but what could I say. It was for me to see to those who left life behind, not interfere in the ways of Karls."

It was Fjorn's turn to sigh. "I can guess where this story goes, but go on."

"A morning came when the Karl did not wake. I was called to tend to his body. More fool Forni that he did so. I have lived with death for many years; I know poison when I smell it. My Karl reeked of it. It is called Old Man's Friend; it slows the breathing, so it would seem the victim suffered the straw death.

"Forni stood over me as I dressed the body. That day all mourned as Baleygr was carried to his longship. Sigurd, Baleygr's son, was next in line for the Karl's seat, but he is but a boy of eight summers, not a man who can lead a village in war. Forni thrust himself forward and took the seat. Many said that we should send to Jorvik and let the king decide. Still in all, they would let Forni sit as steward until the king could pass his judgment and the funeral was complete.

"Baleygr's final ship was prepared, and all were gathered in the great hall to sing his praises. Forni slipped from the hall. I followed him. If only I had been quicker. I lost him in the streets. I only know what he did from what came next."

"He opened the village gates and let in Crusaders," finished Fjorn.

"Not only that. If it had only been that, we might have still prevailed. I realised too late the extent of Forni's herb lore. All were at the great hall, and all were deep in their horns, for Baleygr was much loved. Forni had blended herbs into the mead barrel. When his Crusader minions swept through the gate, all but the night watch were unconscious. The invaders slew those that stood against them and despoiled those who slept, stealing weapons and armour. They unmanned any who shared Baleygr's blood and might hold claim to his seat.

"I hadn't drunk of the mead." Daldis smiled shyly and seemed to blush. Fjorn could see a hint of what, long years before, had been a comely maid. "It gives me gas."

"I barely reached Sigurd before the Crusaders came to his room. Waking him, we raced towards the docks."

The old woman trembled, and her voice was colder than the icy waters around them. "The mongrel scum were despoiling Baleygr's funeral ship. Looting it like common thieves. Hiding behind barrels stacked on the shore Sigurd and I bided our time. A Crusader ran past us and had words with the leader of the ruffians on the dock. They all raced into the village. I hoped to take one of the small fishing boats, but they were gone. I can but hope that some of our village escaped and took what ships they could find before we reached the docks.

"Sigurd and I ran to the only ship left, Baleygr's final vessel. It was soaked in oil, but still sound. We boarded and cast off the lines. The ship didn't move."

"No wonder," remarked Kjorn.

"I tried to raise the sail, but I am no sailor. In the end, I prayed to Lady Hel for aid. Harr came. It was like Baleygr's corpse was bathed in blue fire, then it sat on its byre. Sigurd screamed. I do not blame the boy, but it did cause the Crusaders to look our way. They raced up the dock towards us. Harr, who had possessed Baleygr's body, pushed us off and hoisted the sail. The wind caught us, and we sped towards deeper water."

Daldis shook her head. "I dared to hope then. Sadly, it took but minutes for the Crusader scum to cluster on the docks with bows and pitch. They filled the sky with flame, and while most fell short, some found our deck. The oils set to aid Baleygr's final journey caught, and the ship burned. Harr doused the flames as best he could while I held the tiller until the flames on the gunwale burnt through the ropes that secured it, and the oar vanished into the sea. I thought that we would roast alive, but slowly, the fires died. And there we were in a scorched boat with no oars or tiller, taking on water. Harr dropped what remained of the sail. The sea current had caught us and wouldn't let go. We left the Crusaders for the mercy of the waves. I counted it a good trade."

Sigurlina moved to the old woman's side and hugged her. "We are friends."

Taking a shuddering breath, Daldis let the younger woman hold her.

"Friends," agreed Fjorn.

"Why did you come?" Audun stared at Harr.

"I go where my mistress, Hel, commands and do what is her will. She wished for Daldis and Sigurd to escape. Thus I was sent." Harr stared at Audun with the blue, flickering flames that were the draugar's eyes. His tone seemed strange, holding an undertone of regret in the harsh rasp.

Audun nodded.

"We sail to Jorvik. We can take you there, though...." Fjorn paused to consider his next words.

"I will depart at your first landing. My duty here is fulfilled." Harr stared over the dark ocean.

"I have a gift for you, good captain. For the kindness you and your crew have shown us." Daldis rummaged in the leather pouch on her belt and extracted a bone pendant. "You will know when and where to use it."

Sigurlina gasped. "That is a Hel's Favour. It helps clear the path to Valhalla or Muspelheim. My Grandmother told me about them."

"Very good, child." Daldis placed the pendant in Fjorn's hand. "I sense this crew will have use of it before the Yule. And this other gift I give thee. When the day comes, as it does for all, call me. I will come if I am able."

Fjorn closed his fingers around the bone pendant. "Thank you, lady."

"I have warmed myself. Now I would sleep." Daldis rose. Sigurlina rose with her and helped her to a place in the bow.

"Wind's dying," commented Kjorn.

"I will take an oar," offered Harr.

Fjorn looked at the undead warrior. "If that is your wish. Aft station port."

With a nod, Harr moved to the empty oar station.

"I never thought I'd see the day," Kjorn looked at Harr and shook his head.

"Strange times," agreed Audun.

"Wake me if anything happens," Fjorn returned to his blankets.

CHAPTER 3: TROLLING FOR TROUBLE

Sigurlina pulled on an oar as Obasi shovelled fish stew from a wooden bowl into his mouth. The wind had died, leaving a strange calm that she could see worried Audun and Kjorn.

She kept pace with the oarsmen and was pleased that her arms didn't ache with the effort as they had during her last voyage.

Obasi finished his stew tossing his bowl and spoon unwashed into his sea bench. Stretching, he looked over the water, then sauntered to Sigurlina's side. "I am finished, witch."

Sigurlina yelled, "Pause."

The oarsmen lifted their oars from the water and stopped. Obasi, half scowling, sat and took the oar from Sigurlina. "Stroke," he yelled as Sigurlina scrambled out of the way. Moving down the centre of the ship, she came to the tiller oar where Kjorn sat watch. The old sailor sniffed the air obsessively.

"What is it?" Sigurlina sat beside him.

"The air's too still, and my knee is aching something fierce. I don't like it. I don't like it one bit. If I couldn't see the stars, I'd have no doubt that we were in for a blow."

"Sky port." Audun's voice came from the bow where he sat the ice watch.

Kjorn looked behind himself and swore. "Freya's tits!"

Sigurlina followed the line of his gaze. Behind them, it was like a dark wall devouring the stars. It had already blotted out the light of Muspelheim's fires on the horizon.

"Wake Fjorn," ordered Kjorn.

"I'm awake," spoke a pile of blankets on the opposite side of the stern.

"Storm's coming in fast." With Kjorn's words, a gust of wind swept over the deck, making the brazier in the middle of the ship rise up in a pillar of sparks.

"All hands, brace for a storm," ordered Fjorn.

Those oarsmen that slept were woken by their comrades.

"Sigurlina, you and Ragna empty the cauldron. See to it that everybody eats, then stow the cooking gear and brazier. Make sure the coal and kindling chests are secure and put an extra oiled hide over them. Kjorn, how far to the–."

"Shore lights, forward starboard," bellowed Audun's voice from the bow.

"Thank Idun," breathed Kjorn.

"Hoist the white shield. Make for that light. Put your backs into it." Fjorn moved to his rowing station. Sigurlina rushed to take the oar of an oarsman that Ragna was pushing a bowl of stew on.

The Apenhet sped towards the distant lights as the wind began to gust. The wall of black continued to fill the sky. A fine spray of ice could now be felt on the gusts. The deck was becoming coated and slippery.

"Fjorn, I need you here," called Audun.

"I've got it." Sigurlina appeared beside him.

"Pause," called Fjorn.

Sigurlina took his oar then yelled, "Stroke."

Fjorn rushed to the bow, passing Ragna, who was stowing the brazier.

"Look," Audun pointed to the light on the shore.

Fjorn squinted through the gloom. "Thor's swollen nuts!" Hulking shadows moved across the light that he could now identify as a bonfire. Listening carefully, he could make out the sound of screams. "Crusaders?"

"Only if they're growing them extra-large." Audun shook his head.

Vidurr moved up between the other two men, howled and transformed into a pony-sized red wolf, pinning Fjorn between himself and the ship's railing.

"Vidurr," complained Fjorn through a face full of fur.

Vidurr sniffed the air. The wind gusted, then died, then gusted and died. The sea became choppy as the dark clouds to the stern rushed closer.

"Do we risk landing?" asked Audun.

Vidurr howled again, taking on his human form.

"Trolls. I'm not sure how many. I also smelt roasting meat, human or pig."

"Probably human." Audun began tracing runes on his battle axe.

Fjorn looked to the stern and bit his lip. The cloud was almost upon them, and the gusting wind had turned into a constant pressure against his face. "I won't face a storm at sea if I can help it." Moving amongst his crew, he issued orders in a quiet voice. "Douse all lights. Take down the white shield. Prepare your weapons. Audun, that big shadow on the coast, looks like a spit of land. If we steer to the port side of it, the spit should hide us from the village."

"I'll tell Kjorn to steer to port," the big navigator moved to the stern of the ship.

Fjorn stared at the distant fire, then moved down the middle of the ship, checking that the crew was battle-ready.

"What is it?" asked Jolnir when Fjorn drew near.

"Trolls," Fjorn answered.

"How many?" whispered Jolnir.

"No way to know. They can't have been there long. They're still cooking the villagers. There may even be survivors. Hopefully, the trolls are wounded. We don't have a choice. Either way, that storm is bearing down on us."

"Pause," called Sigurlina's voice from the rowing station beside Jolnir. "Shipping Oar. Jolnir followed her example. "Stroke," called Sigurlina. "Fjorn, I may have a way to learn something about the trolls."

"Munin can do a flyover, but I don't want her getting close. It's too dangerous. Trolls will eat anything, and she's as much part of the crew as anyone." Fjorn's voice was firm.

Munin landed on the young captain's shoulder. "Pretty bird, pretty bird." She began grooming the hair around Fjorn's ear.

Sigurlina rolled her eyes. "Honestly, do you really think I would do that to Munin? I can almost hear the dead in that village. I just need a moment to call one over then we can ask it. While I do that, Munin can fly ahead and, keeping her distance, see what she can see."

"Witch," muttered a voice from amongst the rowers.

Munin hopped over to Sigurlina's shoulder. The young Seith's eyes stared far away. "Yes, I like him too, and no, you can't watch. Honestly! Now fly ahead and meet us at the beach. Stay away from anything that moves."

"What do you need to contact the dead?" asked Fjorn.

"Just some quiet." Sigurlina moved to the bow.

The shore grew nearer even as the oarsmen slowed. The fire on the shore raged, and the silhouette of the trolls came into clearer focus against it. Hulking creatures like gigantic, overly-muscled men with bulging bellies and legs like tree stumps. The thickness of their over-long arms warned of their incredible strength.

Sigurlina sat in the bow, trying to ignore the noise around her and the freezing sleet falling on all sides.

"Come to me. Come to me. Speak thee now. Come to me," she chanted under her breath.

The shimmering form of a man of middle years appeared before her.

"How many trolls attacked your village?" whispered Sigurlina.

The shade looked confused, then the image of a skeid with a full crew came to Sigurlina's mind.

"About the same as one of the big trading ship's full crew," verbalised Sigurlina.

"Eighty more or less," remarked Audun.

"How many are in the village now?" asked Sigurlina.

The shade projected the image of a kravi. The figures of the crew were wounded.

"Twenty-five or so, and they're wounded."

The shade nodded.

"Are there survivors?"

The shade leapt up and down, visible only to Sigurlina, and gestured wildly towards the shore. Sigurlina got a mental picture of a woman and two children tossed into a great hall that had been converted into a barn containing a collection of farm animals.

"Relax, we will help. Do the trolls know we're coming?"

The shade looked confused and then lunged at Sigurlina, trying to force its way into her body.

Sigurlina steeled her will and pushed back. The shade tried again, its eyes becoming two red, glowing points of light. Sigurlina reached into her belt pouch and grasped the two blue stones that were her Grandmother's final gift to her. She felt her will strengthen.

"By Hel, by Freya, by Odin and Surt, I command thee leave this living realm. Your time is past. Remember the death that took you."

The shade seemed to scream, then vanished from Sigurlina's sight.

"Nicely done. I honestly think you could have dealt with him without my gift." Sigurlina's grandmother's voice sounded in her mind; then, the presence was gone.

Sigurlina rose shakily to her feet and faced Fjorn.

"Are you alright?" asked Audun, who stood by Fjorn.

"I almost forgot what it was like dealing with the ones that wouldn't leave. He had a strong will. I'll be fine before we reach shore."

The fire in the village vanished behind the shadow of a spit of land.

"Trolls aren't as dangerous as I've been led to believe if that village killed sixty of them before it was taken," remarked Fjorn.

"I… I don't think they did. It's just an impression, but…No, I can't say more," remarked Sigurlina.

"We know what we have to face. You've done more than enough." Fjorn squeezed her arm.

Sigurlina smiled at him. The Apenhet lurched as its bow drove into the frozen, pebbly beach. Everyone leapt ashore, and the oarsmen hauled the Apenhet up the beach while Ragna retrieved and uncovered the bow lantern. She set it on a large stone away from the waves. Fjorn spent that time in furious thought.

"What's the plan?" asked Ragna as the others gathered around the lantern. Harr and Daldis took a position at the outer edge of the group. A deeper shadow swept out of the black sky and landed on Ragna's hood.

"Get this black chicken off of me," hissed Ragna.

"Yura bitch," commented Munin.

Sigurlina held out her arm, and Munin perched on it, vanishing into the warmth under her mistress's cloak.

"Munin says a palisade surrounds the village with two great halls and some smaller houses and shops inside the wall. From what the shade showed me, I think the villagers used the smaller hall as a barn. The buildings form a rough square. There's a court surrounded by the buildings. Two trolls are guarding the door to the smaller hall. Munin says that from the sound of things, there are a bunch of trolls in the other hall having a party, but she can't say how many. The trolls have built the fire we saw on a barren outside the gate. They've spitted two people on polearms. Ten of them are feasting around the fire. There is a trampled path moving inland from the village. Munin didn't follow it very far."

"I've fought trolls. You want three or more warriors to each of them," remarked Vidurr.

"There are likely still villagers in the smaller hall. Trolls like their meat fresh. Would that there were sun. Trolls turn to stone in sunlight. I'm told large fires also work," offered Daldis, who stepped towards the lantern.

"I don't know how to get to the villagers. Even if we do, will they be fit to fight? And how do we arm them?" asked Fjorn.

"I can take over one of the trolls." Harr's voice was as cold as the winds of the incoming storm. He moved to Daldis's side.

"You can't..." began Ragna.

Fjorn held up his hand. "Why would you help us?"

"My lady has not forbidden it, and you have shown me respect. Also, I do not like trolls." The glowing blue dots that were Harr's eyes seemed to intensify.

"If I can see inside the barn, I may be able to shadow step into it. I could heal the wounded, get them ready to fight," offered Sigurlina.

Fjorn bit his lip. "Ragna, do you speak troll?"

"A little."

"Can you get them angry enough to chase you?" asked Fjorn.

A vicious smile spread across the small woman's face as she made a sound reminiscent of an ox being castrated by the repeated slamming together of two rocks. "Just a song I picked up about the size of their--."

"It will do. Daldis, you and the boy will stay with the ship. I'll take two of the oarsmen; I think it's time to revive an old family tradition. Sigurlina, if you could summon another of your slender friends, it would increase our numbers. Everyone else, this is the plan," stated Fjorn.

#

Harr waited at the edge of the light from the troll's fire. A large, leather hide sack from the Apenhet lay in the snow beside him. Seven trolls capered about the flames while three sat nursing leg wounds, and two lay passed out in the snow. One troll ripped an arm off a human corpse suspended on a pike by the fire. The barren before the gate was ten strides across.

Harr let the intermittent squalls of sleet cover him with an icy sheath. The wind surged and flowed through the dead trees. The cold was nothing to Harr. There was nought of warmth in him to freeze. There was nothing of passion in his acts, simply duty in his service to Hel and honour. Even this act, done of his own accord, was driven by a muted hatred of the animals that danced before him. His brother, felled by trolls when the sun still burned in the sky, would be avenged. It was a debt he never paid in life that now, in death, could be set right.

Several of the trolls had arms supported in crude slings. Kegs littered the ground. While Harr watched, one troll hoisted a keg and drained it like a man would drain a horn.

A troll lurched and fell to the ground. Its fellows laughed and pelted it with whatever was to hand. A troll, with its arm in a filthy sling, staggered to the edge of the fire's light and hoisted the blood-spattered tunic it wore. There was the sound of water flowing.

Harr rolled to look at his victim, gestured with his hand, and hissed, "Mine."

The troll shook its head and gurgled. The blue glows that were Harr's eyes blazed as he repeated, "Mine."

The troll lurched back. It punched itself in the head and bellowed, pounding its chest, then stumbled towards Harr. Harr lay in the snow concentrating on his puppet. Reaching down, the troll carefully picked up the large hide sack and carried it into the village.

#

Ragna watched from the edge of the firelight. The black skeleton lay in the snow beside her.

"Why do I let them talk me into these things? I mean, really. I could be at Orkney with the royal guard to pick from, but noooo. Here I am lying in a snowbank about to become troll bait. It just isn't fair." Ragna whispered to the skeleton.

The skeleton turned its empty eye sockets to her, and even through the dark and lack of a face, it looked incredulous. It lifted a skeletal hand, which was a deeper shadow in the night, and stared from it to Ragna.

"Oh, well, of course, sorry." Ragna watched a troll that had left to relieve itself lurch through the palisades' open gate into the village carrying a large sack.

"That's it!" Leaping up, Ragna danced and waved her arms while bellowing a song in trollish.

"Oh, hard as a rock, but not everywhere.

"Dingle dangle, is that a worm there?

"All the trolls they have mossy hair.

"But they're lost in the brush down there.

"For a momma troll, it just isn't fair.

"Can't tell the difference, though the boys don't care."

Ragna stopped singing and bolted into the gloom as the five male trolls that were around the fire bellowed and ran after her, while the four female trolls laughed and kept drinking.

The first troll to reach the edge of the clearing ran groin first into the black skeleton's staff. The troll fell, clutching itself. The second troll stumbled over its fallen comrade, landing face-first in the snow, giving the skeleton time to stand and block the third troll's blow.

The fourth troll limped into the fight, swinging a club as large as a tree trunk, catching the skeleton a glancing blow that shattered the left shoulder and sent the left arm to lay in the snow. Releasing its staff, the skeleton lashed out, grabbing the object of Ragna's song, driving bony fingertips into the troll.

The skeleton's last thought, before it was shattered, was that, given proportions, the song did make a valid point.

The trolls milled around clutching their wounds, then the sound of badly accented trollish reached their ears.

"Dingle dangle, is that a worm there?"

"Troll wedding day, and they still couldn't tell.

"Shrivelled on an ice block, a gift from Hel."

Drunk with mead and battle, the five male trolls roared and chased the voice. The two with leg injuries quickly fell behind their comrades.

Ragna used the lead the skeleton had bought her to guide the trolls along a trail leading from the village where pounding feet had flattened the ice and snow. She raced along the trail, slipping and sliding as fast as her legs could carry her. Three of the trolls were closing the distance.

Ragna passed between two large trees, and a rope sprang up from the ground. The three fastest trolls ran belly first into the rope, falling onto their backs with a crash.

Kjorn and three oarsmen sprang out of the snow on one side of the trail, while Audun and three oarsmen appeared from the other. They charged the trolls, driving blades into the drunk and befuddled beasts. Audun slammed his axe into the chest of a troll, releasing the enchantment he had put on the axe. A hole the size of a man's head blasted out of the troll, spraying gore in all directions.

The two remaining trolls came limping up the trail. The shattered end of the skeleton's arm waved back and forth below the last troll's tunic. They skidded to a stop staring at the humans massacring their comrades.

Vidurr, in his wolf form, pounced from the frozen trees, hamstringing one of the newly arrived trolls, which fell to its knees. Jolnir and Obasi leapt out of the snow. Obasi threw an axe that buried itself into the standing troll's calf.

Bellowing, the standing troll swung a war hammer one-handed. Vidurr leapt back but caught part of the blow, which drove him into a snowbank. Shaking his head, Vidurr came to his feet and ran three-legged back to the fray.

Jolnir closed with the troll that could still stand. The small man danced in and out of range of the war hammer, leaving precise wounds on the hulking beast.

The trolls roared in rage and frustration.

Vidurr leapt at his foe, closing his wolf jaws on the throat of the troll he had hamstrung. Obasi chopped down with his blade severing the standing troll's leg at the knee.

The surviving troll, of the three that had run into the rope, scrambled to its feet and charged towards Vidurr. Kjorn, Audun and the oarsmen raced after the troll.

Vidurr twisted his jaw and pulled. Blood poured from the troll's throat, coating the wolf. The injured leg healed as Vidurr used Ulfhednar magic to absorb the troll's life force.

Jolnir shifted his focus from the troll with the missing leg to the one barrelling towards them. Slipping under its guard, Jolnir thrust, opening the arteries in the beast's groin. Blood painted the snow red as the troll fell onto the ice trail.

The troll with the missing leg collapsed. Vidurr moved to lap up the beast's blood, completing his healing.

"That is what I call a good start," said Kjorn as the humans gathered together.

"But only a start," cautioned Jolnir.

Ragna emerged from the trees rubbing her throat. "I'm just glad it's over. Trollish isn't easy to sing in."

Audun chuckled and laid a massive hand on her shoulder. "We all appreciate your pains."

A wind carried a wall of sleet down onto them.

Obasi sneered at the others. "The storm is thickening."

The wind whipped over the snow, adding biting ice crystals to the freezing sleet.

"It's only starting. We should go. We need to secure the village." Audun strode to the dead trolls further up the trail. He pulled a short sword, which one troll had been using as a boot knife, free. "Take any human weapons. If Sigurlina is successful, the villagers will need them."

Nodding, the others liberated the works of man from the beasts they had felled, collecting several bags of skatt, as well as flints and steels. Vidurr led the way back to the barren in front of the palisade gate.

#

The possessed troll knelt and opened the sack it had picked up. Sigurlina crawled out, took a breath and scowled. "Thank you, and you stink."

The troll grunted.

Sigurlina hid against the side of the larger great hall and scanned the common area formed by the buildings. Two trolls lounged by a second fire in front of the smaller hall. One of them used a pike as a cane whenever it stood or walked. The other had a bandage wrapped around its head, covering one of its eyes, and its face seemed deformed even for a troll.

A crash followed by gruff, angry voices came from inside the larger great hall.

"We can't stay here," said Sigurlina.

The possessed troll grunted.

"Get them to open the doors on the smaller hall. If I can get to the survivors, I can get them ready to fight." Sigurlina focussed her thoughts. The shadows cast by the fire seemed to deepen. Sigurlina flitted into a pool of darkness, vanishing from sight.

The possessed troll walked up to the smaller hall's twin doors which were barred with a long sword pushed through brackets that had been mounted halfway up the doors' length. The other trolls turned to look at the possessed troll and grunted something. The possessed troll pointed to his mouth. One of the guard trolls stood, pulled out the sword holding the doors closed against each other and opened one of the doors.

Sigurlina cast her spell, stepping from the shadow she was in into the long shadow cast by the fire against the hall's door. Her head swam from the energies of Svartalfheim as she huddled into the darkness. The guard troll passed her. Sigurlina reached out, barely touching the broad muscles of its back, purging the taint of Svartalfheim from herself into the beast. The troll paused and started to turn, but a drunken babble from outside the barn distracted it. A moment later, the door closed, plunging Sigurlina into darkness.

Kneeling, she opened a pouch on her belt and made a pile of kindling on the floor.

"Munin, as soon as you can see, find a perch and watch the door," ordered Sigurlina.

A muffled, "Good bird," issued from under the seithkona's cloak.

"Who's that?" whispered a woman's voice.

"Shh...A friend. Just wait." Sigurlina struck flint to steel, igniting the tinder, which she used to light a candle.

Munin flew up and perched on a roof support facing the door.

"Put it out. They'll see," hissed the woman's voice.

In the wavering candlelight, Sigurlina could see the hall contained maybe fifty people bound hand and foot. Many were unconscious, and they huddled amongst cows, pigs, sheep and chickens. The hall stank of waste.

"I'm here to help." Sigurlina moved to the middle of a group of injured people and focused her power. A light dew seemed to rain down on the injured, and several who were unconscious awoke. She cut the ropes binding a man's hands, then passed him the blade. "Free yourself then the others."

"Are you from Jorvik?" asked a woman whose features were near skeletal in the flickering candlelight.

"No, we were sailing by and saw the trolls' fire." Sigurlina moved to the middle of another group of people.

"How many warriors do you have?" demanded an elderly man who was being freed of his bonds.

Sigurlina performed another healing, then took a deep breath. "Fifteen."

"Against that hoard of trolls," gasped a matronly woman in a blood-stained tunic.

"I'd hardly call twenty wounded trolls a horde," remarked Sigurlina.

"There were..." A heavily muscled man who was missing his left hand scrambled to his feet. "All that noise. They left the wounded and moved on." The man gritted his teeth and flexed his remaining hand as if he clutched a sword. "Maybe my boy still has a chance. I'm Gaut, chief man of this village."

Sigurlina moved down the barn and did another healing. By now, most of the first group were free of their bonds.

"I'm Sigurlina. We need to retake the village before we worry about the trolls that have left. There is a storm coming in."

Gaut squinted at her in the gloom. "Who do you follow?"

"I follow Jarl Erik Bloodaxe. My captain is Fjorn, son of Geldnir, heir to the seat of Orkney."

The man looked stunned. "Hakon's bane is here? Then you must be Sigurlina Shadow Walker, the Seithkona."

Sigurlina buried her surprise that people would know her name and stepped further down the 'barn's length. "I am she. Have your people cut everybody free and collect those who need more healing in the middle of the hall. We'll need to get weapons to help with Fjorn's plan."

#

Fjorn and two oarsmen came up to the back of the palisade. A gust of wind showered them with sleet.

Hefting a length of rope, Fjorn threw it over one of the spiked logs of the palisade. The loop caught, and he began pulling himself up. Topping the barrier, he looked over the village, then dropped down inside. First one oarsman, then another followed. They huddled in the dark, listening. Fjorn crept forward, staying to the shadows. The oarsmen followed.

They came to the great hall. The sounds of raucous laughter and guttural conversation pushed through the wall.

Fjorn scanned the common. By the smithy was a wagon piled with scrap metal. In front of the smaller of the halls, two wounded trolls lounged, passing a keg between them. Fjorn gestured to one of the small, square houses that formed a gapped formation across the commons. Fjorn and the oarsmen sprinted to the cover created by the house and hid behind a pile of logs stacked against the wall.

They waited in the dark under the eaves. The palisade broke the worst of the wind, causing the sleet and the snow to fall straight down. Pale orange light from the fire in the barren outside the gate reflected off the snow.

Fjorn felt the cold creep into his feet and fingers and silently wished for things to move forward.

A troll lumbered across the commons with a bag hoisted onto its back. It ducked into the shadows cast by the larger of the great halls, then emerged without the bag and lumbered up to the two trolls guarding the smaller hall's door.

"Gumple dumple is ta voton wogot." Fjorn vaguely heard a woman's voice singing, followed by the bellow of troll voices.

Fjorn waited. The door to the smaller hall opened. One of the guards entered the building. The newly arrived troll and the remaining guard were quiet. The guard troll started for the gate as the enraged troll voices continued. The newcomer grabbed a keg. The guard troll punched him in his injured arm. The newcomer howled, and the two trolls began to scuffle.

Fjorn and his men scuttled to the cart in front of the smithy and hoisted its pole. Grunting, they man-hauled the cart to the larger great hall and jammed it against the door. When Fjorn glanced over, he saw that the second guard troll had emerged from the smaller hall with a battered human figure on the end of a rope and was trying to break up the fight between the other two trolls.

Fjorn led his men behind the larger great hall and pulled a bag of tinder from his pack. Laying a metal plate on the icy ground, he set the tinder and struck sparks from his steel. A spark took in the kindling, and, after a couple of gentle breaths, the fire licked up. Pulling more wood from his backpack, he built the flames. The oarsmen removed their packs and pulled out two

35

ship's torches. They lit the torches from the fire and then circled the great hall setting the dry under-thatch ablaze.

Fjorn battled the treacherous footing in his haste to set the fire in as many places as possible on the great hall. The thatch was being a problem. Every time the fire grew, it melted the overburden of ice and snow, which reduced the flames to a smoky, smouldering mess. He took comfort in the sound of coughing and hacking from inside the hall. Over that din, there came a resounding boom.

"Thor's swollen nuts!" Fjorn sprinted to the hall's door to see the blade of a battle axe pull back into the hall, leaving a gap, as wide as his forearm was long, in the planks of the door. Smoke poured out of the opening.

The axe struck again, opening up another panel in the door. The two oarsmen joined Fjorn with weapons drawn.

"Try to keep them in the building. Let the smoke do our work for us," ordered Fjorn.

The door planks shattered and were wrenched into the hall by meaty hands. Two trolls crowded against the cart, which was waist-high to them. Other shadowy forms moved behind them.

"Help," called Fjorn as he stepped back from the doorway.

\#

Vidurr crouched in his wolf form at the edge of the barren in front of the palisade's gate. He could smell his comrades from the Apenhet as they positioned themselves for the attack. Four drunken female trolls still lurched about the fire in front of the gate. Two male trolls still lay in the snow. As he watched, one of the dancers stopped and kicked her fallen comrade. The drunken troll responded by clumsily swatting at her. The other females laughed and clapped.

Beyond the fire, Vidurr saw points of orange light through the open gate. One of the dancing trolls lurched close to him. Vidurr pounced onto its back, sinking his teeth into its neck. Audun, Kjorn, Obasi, Jolnir and six oarsmen sprang out of the darkness. The female trolls turned to face their foes. Two tripped in their drunkenness, measuring their length on the icy ground. The two trolls, lying in the snow, groaned and sat up groggily. The others stumbled towards the comparative safety of the village.

Kjorn reached the troll Vidurr was biting and drove his long sword into the beast's side. The troll roared in pain. Audun caught up to a troll that was stumbling to its feet by the fire and swung with his battle axe. The enchanted blade connected with the troll's leg. There was a booming sound. The leg shattered, the foot and ankle breaking away. With a violent shove, Audun sent the troll sprawling into the fire, where it screamed and hardened into stone.

Ragna slipped out of the dark and moved to block the gate. Wind whipped ice and sleet through the frozen air, coating everything in ice. A troll nearly twice her height ran towards her from the fire. Ragna stood motionless in a slush puddle, a perfect target. The troll raised its club, ready to crush the human. At the last moment, Ragna stepped aside. The troll swung, the momentum causing it to slip sideways on the icy bottom of the slush puddle. For a moment, the troll stood, arms windmilling helplessly. Then with a screech, its feet flew out from under it. The troll's legs went up, and its head went back. For a second, it seemed to hover at the level of Ragna's chin before it dropped into the slush puddle. A wall of dirty water and ice went upwards, soaking Ragna. Spitting water out of her mouth, she drove her short sword into the troll's neck.

Jolnir dropped low, sliding on the icy ground, and slashed his blade across the backs of a third troll's legs. The troll fell, bleeding, to the ice. Jolnir pressed his attack.

Obasi and the oarsmen fell on the male trolls dispatching them as the drunken beasts tried to lurch to their feet.

#

Sigurlina heard the trolls howl in the confines of the 'barn'.

Gaut looked at her in the flickering candlelight. He held a heavy piece of wood pulled from an animal pen in his remaining hand. The other humans were similarly armed with improvised weapons.

Two of the villagers leaned against the 'barn's door. The wooden shafts that held the hinge sections together had already been knocked loose. The men were the only thing holding up the twin slabs of wooden planks that made up the doors. The bar the trolls had used to hold them shut would fall into the barn with the rest of the door.

"NOW," commanded Sigurlina.

They dropped the door. The survivors surged into their village, ready for vengeance.

The two guard trolls circled the possessed troll in the common. The guards were bellowing something. The roof of the other hall smouldered in several places. There was no guessing if the fire would fully catch. However, smoke poured out of the cracks in the hall and the fires granted enough light to see.

One of the guard trolls circled to the possessed troll's back while the other troll kept the possessed troll distracted. Sigurlina focused her will and stepped into a shadow, emerging from a shadow behind the guard troll who was behind the possessed troll. She slammed her palm into the troll giving it the malaise that svartalfheim had imparted to her, then drove her dagger into its back. The troll howled and spun around as Sigurlina stepped away, barely managing to dodge the greatsword the beast wielded.

Villagers surged forward, pummelling the guard trolls with whatever came to hand. Catching her breath, Sigurlina stepped into a shadow emerging from a shadow behind the other guard troll. She brushed the guard troll's back with her fingers, then drove her dagger into the back of its bad leg. The possessed troll grabbed the pike out of the guard troll's hand, reversed it, and brought it down into the beast's neck. Blood spilt out, painting the snow and ice as the troll fell. The remaining troll swung its greatsword like a scythe, cutting one of the villagers in two at the waist. The villagers huddled back. The troll swung again, targeting a burly young man.

The possessed troll used the pike it held in its good hand to parry the greatsword. The wooden shaft split. The remaining guard troll reversed its swing. The greatsword bit into the possessed troll. Blood fountained up, spraying in all directions.

Sigurlina drove the hilt of her dagger between the guard troll's shoulder blades and put her weight against it. The dagger tore down the flesh and dislodged, dumping Sigurlina onto her backside in the filthy blood-stained snow. The guard troll turned and kicked her, lifting her off the ground and slamming her into the side of the 'barn'. Sigurlina heard a loud crack and felt pain blossom along her side. She crab-walked into a shadow and enhanced it to hide herself.

Gaut lunged past the combatants to the fallen guard troll, pulled the short sword it had in its belt, as a dagger, free and drove it into the back of the guard troll's bad leg. The guard troll spun in place, dropping to hands and knees. A woman plunged a dagger that the possessed troll had, as a belt knife, into the neck of the remaining guard troll and started sawing. Seconds passed as villagers swarmed the guard troll, stabbing and beating at it until the head came away and rolled to look up at the dark sky with lifeless eyes.

Sigurlina rose painfully to her feet and scanned the area. Ragna, dripping wet and filthy, danced around a troll that lay in a puddle of slush blocking the village's gateway. Her short sword would dart in, stabbing the beast, then the diminutive woman would jump back before a counterblow could be struck.

Fjorn and two oarsmen stood in front of the larger great hall's doors. Smoke billowed out of the doorway. As she watched, a polearm thrust over the smith's cart that blocked the door, catching an oarsman in the belly. Fjorn sidestepped a spear thrust, then leapt onto the rubbish in the back of the cart and slashed into the huge arm that held the spear.

"Take what weapons you can and go to the other hall." Sigurlina gasped as she fell to her knees on the compacted ice and spoke in a painful whisper. "Come hither servant, durable symbol of our ending. I summon thee black one." The ground bubbled as a black skeleton rose from it, holding a staff that was a mirror to Sigurlina's own.

"Kill trolls, protect humans. Go to the other hall." Sigurlina sat in the slush, exhausted from the magic and her wounds.

"Help!" called Fjorn across the common.

The villagers huddled back from Sigurlina as their pretty, young saviour became a thing of terror that could summon the dead.

Sigurlina's gaze fell to the horrified townsfolk.

"Go, if you are armed, go, and one of you bring me my staff. Now is the time to battle." Her voice dropped, "You can be afraid of the witch later." She rose to her feet and stumbled towards the larger great hall.

#

Obasi thrust his sword towards the back of the drunken, supine troll, only to have the beast roll out of the way. Roaring, the troll slammed a fist the size of a small cauldron into one of the oarsmen shattering his chest. Obasi thrust again, catching the troll in the shoulder as it lumbered to its feet.

The troll roared and shook itself, then slammed into the ground with a pony-sized wolf on its back. Vidurr bit into the troll's neck as the other oarsmen brought home their blades.

Ragna danced around the troll in the puddle, stabbing it every time it started to rise. Audun pounded towards her over the icy ground, battle axe raised to strike. When he tried to stop, he pirouetted on the icy ground as he careened towards the troll. His feet caught on a slush-buried root. He fell forward, brandishing his axe two-handed above his head. The axe came down with the full weight and momentum of Audun's huge form behind it, cleaving the troll's skull in two. The axe handle broke where it attached to the blade, which lodged in the troll's head. Audun landed in the puddle, sending another shower of dirty slush and troll blood over Ragna.

Ragna spat water out of her mouth and looked skyward. "Why is it always me?"

"Get the weapons. We aren't finished yet," ordered Kjorn.

Audun pushed himself out of the freezing slush. He could see smoke billowing out of the larger great hall's open door and Fjorn battling to keep the trolls within the building.

#

Fjorn was driven back by a pikestaff thrust, and a troll pushed out of the burning hall tossing the cart to one side, spilling scrap iron over the common. The beast sucked in a lung full of clean air and focussed on Fjorn, aiming a savage axe blow at the young captain's head. The blade descended then stopped against the edge of a bejewelled sword. Harr, half coated with ice, the blue coals of his eyes blazing, stood beside Fjorn.

"My troll died." Harr pressed the battle against the hulking brute before him.

More trolls exited the hall. These seemed to be less drunk or injured than the ones at the town's gate. Fjorn landed a blow on a troll armed with a spear as it pushed its way out of the hall. A black skeleton appeared, slamming its staff into the troll attacking Fjorn as three more trolls lurched out of the smoke. Four villagers joined the fray, armed with liberated weapons. The trolls surged forward, pushing onto the common.

Stumbling, Sigurlina stopped short of the battle. Focusing her will, she opened a vortex that sucked the energy of the trolls' spirits to herself, using it to heal her wounds and restore her strength. A boy appeared at her side carrying her hawthorn staff.

Audun charged up to join the battle, dripping wet, with a long slender blade of blue energy in his hand. Almost as big as the trolls, he evaded a huge club and drove the rune blade home in one of the beasts.

The oarsmen distributed weapons to the townsfolk as Vidurr, and the rest of the party, joined the fray. Vidurr caught a mace to the side while Kjorn took a spear to his good knee. An oarsman caught between two trolls and was crushed to death. Fjorn fought one troll while another towered behind him, club raised. The black skeleton charged forward, driving its staff into the troll's jaw. The massive club came down, shattering the skeleton. Sigurlina snatched her staff from the boy and raced into the fight, striking the back of the troll's neck. When the troll turned, Fjorn drove his long sword into its back, piercing the beast's heart.

The villagers drove against the trolls, as the wind picked up, and the storm hit in earnest. In minutes the battle was over.

CHAPTER 4: OUT IN THE COLD AND THE STORM

Fjorn looked at the wounded. Clearing his throat of the smoke that still billowed from the hall, he sang:

"Youth to the Gods golden apples of grace.

"Indun's power heal mortals of faith."

Three verses later, the wounded could be moved into the 'barn'. Snow and sleet pummelled down, and the wind howled.

"Jolnir, please collect Daldis and Sigurd from the Apenhet. Everyone needs to be out of this weather."

Jolnir nodded. Blood spattered his clothing, and his sword-blade was notched in several places. "Yes, Captain."

Harr walked to Jolnir's side. "I will come with you."

Jolnir looked at the draugar. An imperceptible shudder ran down the stalo's back. "If you insist."

Harr stepped towards the gate, and Jolnir fell in behind him.

"The hall is ruined. What are we going to do?" asked a woman who moved to Fjorn's side.

Fjorn looked at the other hall. "I'd say we all have hall enough to weather this storm. Better here than on a ship anyway. Make yourself useful. Pile as much firewood as you can find by the door before the weather fully closes in."

"Yes, my Lord," the woman replied and left to do his bidding.

Fjorn noticed that Sigurlina was sorting through the items carried by a troll. He glanced around and saw that Ragna was doing the same.

"Audun," called Fjorn.

"He took your crewmen and went to search the trolls' bodies," said a woman who paused from shovelling snow onto the smouldering thatch of the great hall. Gaut could be seen organising the able-bodied people to put out the fire.

"Thank you," said Fjorn.

"Thank you, Son of Orkney. We owe you our lives." She turned to stare at Sigurlina. "Tell your witch woman, I also thank her."

Fjorn smiled. "You can tell her yourself."

"I... She commands the dead. I... Please tell her thank you from me." The woman returned to dumping snow on the hall's thatch.

Fjorn shook his head and moved to where Sigurlina had finished looting a troll's body. "Anything?"

"A flint, steel and a bag of skatt, but... It might be nothing," she smiled wearily at Fjorn.

"What?"

"I've searched three trolls. They all had skatt struck in Wessex."

Ragna walked to Fjorn's side, her clothes were soaking wet and filthy, and she was hugging herself. "The skatt I found was from Wessex too. Every troll had a bag."

Vidurr stood in the middle of the common. The giant wolf's coat was blood-caked, and his lips curled up in a snarl. Several of the townsfolk nervously watched him with weapons clutched in white-knuckled grips.

"Karl's son, Fjorn, Hakon's Bane. After all you have done, it shames me to ask this, but my people are concerned about your wolf." Gaut approached from the hall.

Fjorn glanced at Vidurr and rolled his eyes.

"He is good with children." Sigurlina's grin hid her fatigue and put lie to the blood and filth spattering her clothing.

"And housebroken." Ragna laughed, then shivered violently.

Sigurlina opened her cloak and enveloped her friend in its folds.

Fjorn sighed, then called, "Vidurr, could I have a word?"

Vidurr howled, taking on his human guise. His clothing and all he carried on his person returned from the place between the worlds that the form he wasn't currently using rested in. The weapons fell from the townspeople's hands as the big Ulfhednar strode by them.

"Surt's flaming nuts!" Gaut clutched the Mjolnir pendant around his neck.

"Yes," demanded Vidurr as he drew near.

"I... I wanted to thank you," blurted Gaut.

Vidurr dipped his head in acknowledgement.

"One of your kinsmen was my war chief. The trolls took him, but not before he laid two of them low. Let no one speak ill of you in this village, Ulfhednar, lest they answer to me." Gaut held out his remaining hand.

Vidurr took the offered hand. "So, it is spoken."

"So, it is spoken," echoed Gaut.

Munin flew out of the smaller hall and alighted on Fjorn's head, staring at Sigurlina.

"Munin says that the fire is set, and the door is fixed. Ragna needs to get out of the storm," said Sigurlina.

"As should we all," said Fjorn as falling sleet turned to blowing snow which drifted against the village's leeward wall.

#

Harr and Jolnir trudged through the thickening storm.

The path down to the beach had become treacherous with ice. Moving slowly, they reached the pebbly shore and found Daldis and Sigurd huddled under a blanket beneath the Apenhet's hull.

"We won. There is a warm hall to weather the storm in," greeted Jolnir.

"Thank you," said Daldis as she rose.

Sigurd stood, his eyes fixing on Harr.

"Young Lord." Harr knelt in the snow and held out the sheathed, bejewelled sword in both hands. "It is a symbol of your house. I thank you for its loan."

Sigurd stared Hel's servant in the glowing, blue eyes. Taking a deep breath, the boy stepped up and took the sword. "Thank you for your service, Hel's warrior."

Harr dipped his head, stood and walked into the storm.

"Where is he going?" asked Jolnir.

"His service to me is finished. Hel may have need of him, or perhaps he does not wish to be amongst the living. It may pain him to be reminded of what once was. I doubt I will see him again before I stand with my Lady," explained Daldis.

"We should get out of this storm." Jolnir led the way, following his fast disappearing footsteps to the trail that led to the village. By the time they reached the barren in front of the village, Jolnir couldn't see beyond his arm's reach. A dim, orange glow pierced the blizzard to his left. He made for it, finding the remains of the trolls' bonfire. A troll turned to stone lay in the middle of the hot coals and dying flames.

Daldis and Sigurd rushed to the fire's edge, allowing it to warm them.

"Hhhhh how mmmuch fffurther?" asked Daldis.

"Just a few strides," answered Jolnir.

"I'm cold," stated Sigurd.

"It's almost over," comforted Jolnir.

"For some. I think not for those who walk between worlds. You should rest while you are able." Daldis rubbed her leathery age-spotted hands over the fire.

"We should move on." Jolnir's voice held nervousness.

In minutes they entered the crowded hall. Ship's crew and villagers huddled around a young fire in the fire pit. The back of the hall, where private chambers would normally have been, was occupied by farm animals. A pig was spitted by the fire waiting for the coal bed to be ready to cook it. Someone had found some mead kegs that the trolls hadn't breached; one sat open by the door.

Jolnir, Daldis and Sigurd pushed through the crowd to the huddle of the Apenhet's crew at the far end of the fire.

Audun sat bare-chested, holding the blade of his battle axe and staring at the broken handle where it came out of the metal. "It was the finest oak. I don't know where I'll find its like. Look at the blade. Not a nick. Even a troll's thick skull couldn't hurt my beauty."

"They'll be a smith fit to put a new shaft to the blade in Jorvik. Maybe we can find someone there that can get the stains out of my dress." Ragna huddled by the fire, wrapped in a blanket. Her wet clothing was set to dry on an impromptu frame.

Fjorn looked up from where he sat snuggled under his cloak with Sigurlina, "Jolnir, Daldis, Sigurd, join us. It is better than a storm at sea by a long measure. Audun, now that everyone's here, tell us what you found."

Audun opened a large sack that sat on the dirt floor beside him. "I only took that which was human-made. The dead have no right to that which they stole." Audun paused to accept a horn from a flaxen-haired woman who blushed prettily when he smiled at her.

"I see you've made a friend," snipped Ragna.

Audun smiled. "I don't even know her name...yet."

Ragna went red-faced and sniffed.

Sigurlina leaned into Fjorn, half dozing. Outside the wind howled.

"Did you find anything interesting or odd?" asked Jolnir.

"Every troll had a bag of skatt."

"Was it struck in Wessex?" asked Fjorn.

Audun reached into the sack, pulled out a smaller pouch and opened it, extracting a silver coin. "Aethelstan's ugly mug on every coin."

"Odd."

"I also found this." Audun pulled out a roll of hide and spread it on the ground by the fire.

"We have to do something," demanded a shrill female voice in the background.

"Yifa, sit down. There's a storm out there, and nought a one of us has the strength for another fight. My Ragnar was taken. Don't you think I be wanting him back? We can't be following them in this. Even if we did, what could we do? I'll send to Jorvik for help as soon as the storm breaks," soothed Gaut's voice.

"Too late by then." Daldis rubbed her withered hands together over the fire. "I can feel my lady's presence. Some of those taken have already knelt before her. As for the others," she shrugged. "It is but time."

"Be silent, woman," snapped Obasi.

"Show respect," growled Jolnir.

"Trolls like their meat fresh. The folk they took are their larder. Easier to make them walk than to carry the dead," said Daldis.

"Thor protect them," whispered Audun.

"We can't just be letting the trolls eat them," gasped Kjorn.

"When the storm lets up–," began Fjorn.

"It will be too late!" Vidurr stood up. The fire cast a flickering glow over him. "The storm will cover even a trail like the one the trolls left before much longer."

"He's right. Overtaking the trolls without a storm would be easy enough. They have to push through the snow, and that will take time. Anyone chasing them will have an easy path to follow, but with this storm, it will be filled in," agreed Jolnir.

"Then it's pointless to worry about it." Obasi drained a horn and moved to the keg to get another.

"They'll have to make camp," said Sigurlina. "Nothing can keep moving in a storm like this."

As if to make her point, the wind gusted, driving a spray of snow in around the cracks where the roof met the walls.

"But how would we find that camp?" asked Audun.

"You'd need a guide," Vidurr's voice rumbled.

"No, Vidurr. It's too dangerous. Alone out there with no shelter. And what would you do?" asked Fjorn.

"We could find the trolls' camp and make a shelter in sight of it. Then when the storm breaks, we can come back to the village. Build a bonfire at the gate. We should be able to see that in the darkness," suggested Sigurlina.

"It's too dangerous!" Fjorn fell silent as a grey-haired woman appeared on her knees before him.

"Please, I couldn't help but hear. They killed my husband and took my son." She turned to Vidurr and extracted a preserved wolf's paw on a leather thong from around her neck. "My husband gave this to me when we wed. He left his pack to be with me. I was his bitch for twenty years. Please, my cub is all I have left. If he has not been eaten."

Vidurr closed his eyes as a cold as harsh as the icy wind outside clutched his heart. He remembered his bitch and their cub before the Crusaders came. "For the cub, for the pack, we are Ulfhednar by blood or choice." He took a step toward the hall's door.

"Wait!" Sigurlina stood up. "We will do this, but not without thought."

Fjorn stood up. "What must be—."

"NO!" Vidurr and Sigurlina spoke in unison. They shared a look then Sigurlina continued. "Fjorn, Vidurr and I can keep ourselves alive out there. Looking after others as well, in this storm, it would kill us all."

Jolnir placed a hand on Fjorn's shoulder. "She's right. Vidurr is a trapper; Sigurlina lived in a barrow for three years. I survived alone in Halogaland for a time. We will go while the trail still exists. You prepare the townsfolk to join us. Gather the equipment for an overland journey and be ready when the storm breaks."

Sigurlina and Vidurr had already begun preparing packs.

"When did I stop being the captain?" Fjorn whispered to Kjorn as he took a seat.

"You haven't. Sometimes you have to let those as know lead." Kjorn watched Sigurlina's slender form. "With that one, never oversteer the tiller. She has her own wind to drive her, and that's for sure." He sighed, regretting nigh on forty years.

#

Daldis slipped from the crew and moved amongst the people, quietly speaking to any and all she came to. She was guided to a skeletal woman sitting on the edge of the wood platform surrounding the dirt floor in the structure's middle.

"I am told you are a herb wife," stated Daldis.

The woman looked up. "Please, death mistress, call me Jora. And yes, I have some skill in the ways of healing."

"This is good. I have need of your stores, and quick, before the Seithkona and the wolf depart."

"There is little left of any virtue." Jora rose to her feet.

"What I require is of little virtue to the living. Show me what you have."

Nodding, Jora led the way to a corner of the hall where several crates were stacked. Calling a nearby man for help, she uncovered a crate and opened it. Inside were bags of dried leaves and berries. Daldis reached in and took a bag opening it.

"Too weak," whispered the Angel of Death.

"What is it you need? I know my wares," remarked Jora.

"I will know it when I see it." Daldis opened another bag. Then another, with the next bag, she paused, staring at the dried, white berries it contained.

"Yes, if she is quick and clever. The druids would approve." Daldis took the bag and marched over to Sigurlina, who was preparing her survival pack. Leather bags containing dry kindling, jerky, extra socks and slow-burning tallow candles lay around the young witch.

"We're going. There is nothing you can say," greeted the Seithkona.

"And nothing I would, my dear. I do not seek to take any before their time, and I trust in you and your companions' skills."

"I'm sorry." Sigurlina hung her head and bit her lip every inch the shy teenage girl.

Daldis smiled. "I remember when I could do that. Now my dear, take these. Do you know what they are?"

Sigurlina took the sack that Daldis held out and looked into it. "Mistletoe berries. They will kill you after they give you the trots and make you mad."

"Do you know how to use them?"

"Use them?"

"We don't have much time, so listen. First, you have to make a paste, then...."

#

Vidurr, Sigurlina and Jolnir, dressed for the cold and carrying packs, opened the hall's door and pushed out into the storm. The door was closed. Fjorn watched it for a moment before Audun called him over.

"Fjorn, you should see this."

Fjorn gave himself a shake and moved to where the big man was examining a scroll by the fire. "What is it?"

"A map, I can tell you that much. I took it from one of the trolls." Audun traced a line. "This is a coast. I'm not sure which one."

"What do the symbols mean?" asked Ragna. "Could they be treasure?"

"I don't know. It's not in any script I've seen," admitted Fjorn.

46

Ragna pushed her way in between the two men. "Some of it is thieves' code."

"And where would a respectable woman like yourself learn thieves' code," snipped Kjorn with a wink.

Ragna stuck her tongue out at the old sailor. "You pick things up."

"I know you do." Kjorn winked.

"What does it mean?" interrupted Audun.

"The drawings that look like wooden chests mean rich pickings." She pointed to two clusters of symbols. A blood-red line cut through the cluster on the coast, then turned west and inland before coming to the second cluster of symbols, which was surrounded by blood-red arrows.

The wind howled outside, and everyone tried not to think about those facing the storm without the protection of walls and fire.

Gaut joined his guests. "Your people are the bravest I've known, Karl's son."

"Thank you. Can you raise a force to follow them when the weather clears?"

"Everyone we can arm will be with you." Gaut looked down at the map. "That's the coast roundabouts. I've sailed it often enough to know. That place with the picture of the box and arrows near the bottom of the map is us. And this here at the bottom is the Humber River." He traced the lines of the inlet with his finger to the second collection of arrows and boxes. "This here must be the fort of Lax Bay up where the river narrows." Arrows and treasure chests surrounded Lax Bay.

"Where exactly is Jorvik," asked Fjorn.

Gaut tapped an area off the map to the northwest of Lax Bay. "Right about here."

"Why are the trolls raiding a nowhere fort? I could see raiding Jorvik. There has to be some good skatt there, but a harbour fort? I mean, trolls don't care who wins a human war," remarked Ragna.

Gaut glowered at the small woman.

Fjorn reached into the troll's skatt bag and let a handful of coins trickle through his fingers. "They care about skatt. Lax Bay is in trouble."

"Why?" asked Audun.

"Look at the number of arrows around it." Fjorn half-whispered.

Audun turned to Gaut, "I need someone to fix my battle axe. This just got more complicated."

#

Hours had passed, and Sigurlina still wondered if she could be as dishonourable as Daldis suggested. Of course, the old Angel of Death's plan might save human lives. There was honour in that.

The wind whipped over the sides of the compacted trail that the trolls had left. Vidurr had been right; already the way was difficult to follow. He had had to use his wolf form to catch traces of scent. Sigurlina and Jolnir watched for signs of their quarry's passage that hadn't yet been buried. No words were spoken against the howl of the wind, arm pointing sufficing. Ice crystallised on their cloaks and eyelashes as the snowshoes they had taken from the village crunched across the frozen terrain. The glimmer from the candle lanterns the humans carried barely pierced the darkness. Time passed as they trudged forward from windbreak to windbreak, pausing if there was any chance that they would begin to sweat under their layers of clothing. Munin tried to fly up and look around but was driven back to the safety of Sigurlina's cloak by the freezing winds.

After hours of trudging through the snow, an orange glow pierced the darkness. Vidurr howled, taking on his human guise. "They are there." He pointed to the intermittent spark of light.

Sigurlina dropped her pack and pulled out a small, wooden shovel with an iron-edged blade. Testing the hard-packed snow at the side of the trail, she found a spot that suited her and began digging. Jolnir found a place where fallen trees blocked the wind from three directions and started breaking off branches. After a time, he set a pile of dry kindling and sparked it with a taper lit from the lantern. Vidurr shucked his pack and cloak, howled as he took on his wolf form, and left to scout the troll camp.

A short time later, Vidurr returned to find a warm jerky stew on what remained of the fire. His cloak was spread over the bottom of a snow shelter dug into the side of the trail. Jolnir dished out a bowl of the stew for him. The big wolf lapped it up, allowing its warmth to chase the chill away from his insides. The bowl was stowed and the fire left to be buried by the snow and ice.

Sigurlina was the first to slip into the shelter, then Vidurr with his furry back pressed tight against her, then Jolnir with his back pressed into Vidurr's front. Munin perched on top of the huge wolf, nestling into his fur. Two cloaks covered them, and the snow walls blocked the wind. The candle lanterns flickered at the shelter's mouth. Sigurlina pulled pine branches over the opening then the lanterns were covered, plunging them into absolute darkness. Minutes passed as the confined space warmed with the heat of their bodies.

"Sleep soundly, Vidurr. We are your pack." Sigurlina hugged his shaggy form.

Vidurr wondered how the girl could know his heart, his crushing need for a pack to call his own. Vidurr closed his eyes and let his breathing steady. The wind howled outside the shelter. Inside he lay nestled between his pack mates. He knew their secrets. Humans were nose blind to so much, but the foolishness of human ways didn't matter, and what they did was their concern. What he knew was that in the company of his companions, the gaping hole left by his wife and son could, for a moment, be set aside. He slept in that primitive hole in the snow and, for once, knew peace.

Sigurlina lay with Vidurr's furry body next to her. She remembered her father's hunting dog, Pointer, and her mother's cat, Stealth. They had been lost in the Crusader's attack. She remembered her grandmother in the barrow, teaching her, protecting her from spirits too powerful for her to control. She remembered her mother and her father. Her family lost to Crusader blades. She felt the warmth of Vidurr, man, wolf, friend, brother. She loved Fjorn, but she felt such a kinship with Vidurr. His pain ran as deep as her own, perhaps deeper. They were both outcasts, even in a crowded room. Not just because of their losses, everyone had losses, but because of what they were. The Ulfhednar, wolfman, and Seith, mistress of death, both human and something other. She loathed sleeping in great halls with people milling about. On the ship, it was as bad, crowded in with others. Here, with only two friends, she could find peace. Let go of the sorrow and simply rest. She drifted into slumber, lulled by the sound of the big wolf's heart.

Jolnir lay with the wolf's legs around him. The wolf knew. He had to know. He must smell it, but he never said a word. As a member of the royal guard, Jolnir had camaraderie, but with Fjorn's band, there was something more. They were a family. Jolnir pondered the last time he had known family. The wedding day had been a thing of dread, arranged to bind two strong houses so they could stand against the Crusader raids. A noble reason to ruin a person's life. If only Anina had run away with him. He'd loved her. She had taught him what he was, and they had explored each other, but when the final test came, she had betrayed him. A tear formed in Jolnir's eye. Eir, Lady Frigg, how he loved her from the moment he saw her. And then to discover that she was a mirror to himself. Womanly in every way but one, and that one a match to his own needs. Fjorn had told him of Jarl Erik's permission to wed, and his heart sang. It would be perfect. His beloved and his newfound family. He could but hope they wouldn't reject him if and when they learned his secret. He snuggled into the wolf, who rested his chin on the top of Jolnir's head. The steady sound of his companions' breathing lulled him to sleep.

CHAPTER 5: MONSTER'S WAR

Fjorn huddled under his cloak. The wind howled, but he was so exhausted he was oblivious to it. His companions formed a little clump of bodies by the fire. Sleepy villagers had raked the hot coals to one end of the fire pit and set the pig on a spit over them. The other end of the pit flared up with young fire lending light to the hall.

In his dreams, Fjorn was fifteen again. Fimbulwinter had only gone on for a month, and his mother yet lived. Word had come that Jarl Harold Fair Hair had died the very day that Skoll and Hati had devoured the sun and moon. Fjorn stood in the town's common, the chill biting his cheeks, snow falling. He sang a dirge for the Great Jarl. He had sung for the father he had never seen, the father he didn't know was his. Geldnir and Kjorn grasped hands with a man who looked like Jarl Erik Bloodaxe, Fjorn's secret half-brother, but older, and formed a triangle around Fjorn.

"Most have but one to lose," said the man Fjorn took to be Harold Fair Hair.

Fjorn woke with a start and lay still, thinking for a time before the smell of roasting pork caused his mouth to water.

"How long have we slept?" Audun's voice came from Fjorn's left.

"Long enough for it to cook. All I need to know," said Kjorn.

Fjorn opened his eyes and saw his mentor, eating dagger in hand, closing on where a woman was doling out cuts of meat to those gathered. A large cauldron sat beside the fire pit. As Fjorn watched, the carver dislodged a mostly denuded leg from the carcass and dropped it into the pot. He knew it would be pork stew for dinner.

"Better get moving, or the best of it will be gone." Audun stood and strode towards the carcass.

Fjorn sat up and was preparing to rise when a pretty, dark-haired girl appeared at his side with several cuts of pork. "Please, it is only fitting that we serve Fjorn Hakon's Bane."

Fjorn smiled and took the wooden platter. "Thank you."

The girl smiled, blushed, bit her lip shyly, then moved away.

"You shouldn't let things like that go to your head." Ragna walked up and plucked a slice of pork off Fjorn's platter with her eating knife.

"Little risk with my crew. Besides, I've found the one I want. I hope she's all right." Concern clouded Fjorn's features.

"You're pretty smart for a man." Ragna snagged another slice of pork.

"Did you want something other than my breakfast?" Drawing his belt knife, Fjorn speared a slice of meat and popped it into his mouth.

Ragna sat down on the dirt floor beside him.

"Have you taken a good look at the skatt we took from the trolls?"

Fjorn savoured the juicy meat before he swallowed and replied. "I'm sure you have. Skatt is skatt. Better we have it than Aethelstan and his ilk." He took another mouthful of meat and moved his platter away from Ragna as she prepared to stab another slice.

Ragna let out a 'huff' sound and shook her head. "Spoken like a Karl's son. Look at this." She held up one of the coins.

"It's a coin."

Ragna shook her head. "Where would Aethelstan get enough skatt to hire troll mercenaries?"

"The White God's church." Fjorn used his hand to cover his full mouth as he spoke.

"Is interested in taking gold, not on spending skatt. And they hate everything that isn't human more than they hate us."

Fjorn swallowed. "You don't have to like your mercenaries. Truth be told, my father says it is better if you don't. Do you think Aethelstan has found a new silver mine?"

Audun took a seat beside Fjorn, being careful to balance a wood platter full of meat. "There's not going to be anything left of that pig in a few minutes."

Ragna moved to the big man's side and deftly speared a large slab of meat off his pile. "Then I should get in line for seconds. After I convince the Karl's son that we need to talk."

"About what?" asked Audun.

"The skatt is wrong."

Audun nodded. "Been thinking bout that."

"If Aethelstan has got a new source for silver, it could be bad for Jarl Erik. Skatt can win a war." Fjorn chewed slowly as he pondered.

"I'm thinking it's not so bad as Wessex finding a silver mine. He might be shaving the coins, but that wouldn't save him much," remarked Audun.

"Finally, a man with a thought to call his own," breathed Ragna. "Look."

The diminutive woman reached into a belt pouch extracting a small metal box. Opening it revealed a scale that was two brass trays suspended from a rod that hung from a chain.

"A merchant's scale? Where'd you pick that up?" asked Fjorn.

"A friend gave it to me," Ragna smiled.

"The runes on its side say that it belongs to Brunn. Is that the Brunn from Orkney?" asked Audun.

"Oh, I remember now. I found it in the snow. Brunn must have dropped it. I was going to give it back to him, but we set sail before I saw him." Ragna smiled.

The men rolled their eyes.

"We'll give it back to him when we get home. I'm sure he'll be thrilled," said Fjorn.

"Well, of course. What I always intended." Ragna patted her belt pouch, then turned to Fjorn. "I need a silver skatt struck anywhere but Wessex."

Fjorn reached for his belt pouch, which sat with the small collection of possessions that had served as his pillow. In seconds Ragna had Fjorn's coin, which she placed in one of the trays.

She then placed a coin from the Wessex skatt in the other tray. The scales tipped down on the side with Fjorn's coin.

"You see, all coins should weigh the same. The skatt from the trolls is too light," observed Ragna.

"Ivaldi's tongs! I was looking forward to spending that skatt. Jorvik is quite the place, or at least it used to be when there were sun and moon." Kjorn sat down beside Fjorn and started eating. "I remember this one time we made port just as they were starting the festival of the Peco. Some of the oarsmen and I decided to join in. I can tell you, them Jorvikians know a thing or two about brawling. I'd almost won the day when, well... Let's say; she were a lovely distraction. Couldn't see busting up me knuckles over a wooden statue when there's a maid right, ready and willing for the taking."

Fjorn smiled, then the words of his dream echoed in his mind. 'Most have but one to lose.' "So Aethelstan hired the trolls with fake coins. I've heard of shaving. Who hasn't, but how do you make fake coins? A coin is a coin." Fjorn looked perplexed.

Audun took the Wessex coin and looked around the room. A grinding stone sat at the edge of the raised platform around the outside wall. Moving to the stone, he placed the coin on a flat section, then put his eating knife on the coin. He gave the back of the knife a quick rap and the coin split in two. He carried back the two parts of the coin and passed them around. The centre of the coin was a different colour than the outer part.

"Had a trader try to pay off a gambling debt with coins like that once. The core is tin with just enough silver on the outside to stand up to stamping. Worth about a quarter what the coin says it is." Kjorn eyed the coin. "Royal guards were none too happy about it when I tried to pay me keep with them, but they took me at my word that I didn't know when some other folk showed up with bad coins. Turned out there was a crooked smith in Finnmark making them by the bucket load."

Fjorn looked at the half coin. "Trolls aren't that bright. The Crusaders probably thought they would never figure it out."

"Or at least not until it was too late. You don't have to be paying a dead mercenary," observed Kjorn.

Fjorn nodded as he unrolled the map they'd found. The arrows around Jorvik were three different colours. About three of them were red like the line marking the trolls' path. "Red for troll companies."

"There are thirteen arrows but how many troops for each?" asked Ragna.

"The one that took this town started with about a hundred. It's a good guess that the others will be the same," observed Kjorn.

"Three hundred trolls, four-hundred, something, and six-hundred-something. At a guess," remarked Fjorn. "That's a large force since we lost the sun. Even with fake skatt, how can Aethelstan think to pay them all?"

"Like I said. You don't have to pay the dead." Kjorn shook his head.

"But you send the coin back to their kin. It's what's done," said Fjorn.

"Karl's son." Ragna rolled her eyes.

"It's what a man of honour does, lad. We've all seen what passes for honour with Aethelstan and his Roman ilk." Kjorn spat into the fire.

Fjorn stroked his beard. "This could work for us. I wish we could tell Sigurlina and Vidurr." The wind blew in a pummelling gust that made the great hall rock and the fire spark up while ice and snow pushed in under the eaves. All looked to the door with worried expressions.

#

Vidurr awoke to Munin pecking at him. He opened his eyes to blackness. The shelter was still warm, but Sigurlina no longer nestled against his back. Carefully, he extracted himself from Jolnir and Munin, pushed the brush out from the entrance with his snout and stepped into the storm. Snow and hail as large as a big man's knuckle pummelled down. The wind made the dead trees of the forest creak and sway. He followed a line of fast-filling tracks to where snowbanks blocked the wind from three sides. The sharp smell of urine filled the air, along with the sound of a sigh. Through the storm, he could see the orange glow of the trolls' fire. Vidurr waited until Sigurlina rounded the snowbank.

"Freya!" Sigurlina swore at the sight of the huge wolf 'smiling' at her. "Vidurr, you do that on purpose."

Vidurr ducked his head, then walked by her and cocked a leg in the relatively sheltered spot. When he came out, he was surprised to find that Sigurlina hadn't returned to the shelter. Instead, she sat working with a mortar and pestle. She'd dropped several white berries into what appeared to be urine and was crushing them.

Vidurr sniffed and didn't like what he smelled. Howling, he resumed his human form. "Poison?"

"Daldis's idea. Mistletoe berries. If I can shadow step close enough to the fire to... I'll have to get a good coating on my dagger then stab their meat...." Sigurlina swallowed convulsively. "Wipe the coating off inside the flesh, then when the trolls eat, they will get sick. Maybe even go mad and...."

Vidurr silently watched the girl in her turmoil.

"I... I know poison is dishonourable. It's like something a Crusader would do, but what am I supposed to do? If we can make the trolls think the food is diseased, or even kill some of them, it could save some of their captives. How can I do nothing if I can help?"

Vidurr tipped his head. "You'll need a distraction. I will scout the troll camp again." Howling, Vidurr became the wolf and bounded into the storm.

Sigurlina added more berries to her mix and began crushing them.

Jolnir felt a chill down his spine and opened his eyes. He could feel Munin perched on his side.

"Pardon me, mistress bird, but I need to get up."

"Pretty bird, pretty bird," said Munin.

"I don't want to hurt you by accident. So move."

Munin jumped down in the darkness of the shelter as Jolnir exited into the slightly less black world beyond. Sigurlina huddled over something in the lee of a snow embankment. A deeper shadow in the night, identifiable only because she moved.

Jolnir pulled his cloak from the shelter and donned it before joining his comrade. "What are you doing?"

Sigurlina looked up from crushing the white berries into a paste. "Jolnir, you scared me. I... I'm going to do something bad for a good reason."

Jolnir nodded. "How do you intend to give them the poison?"

"How do you know?" Sigurlina hung her head.

"It's the only thing that makes sense. I know what honour says about poison, but the trolls have no honour. Eating their victims like cattle. Stabbing them won't work. You may kill three or four, but the others will kill you."

"I was going to smear it into the flesh of a roasting body with my knife."

Jolnir nodded. "I'm sure the dead will understand. Are you sure there isn't a better way?"

"What?"

Jolnir smiled. "The village they raided had a lot of mead. I'd wager the trolls have brought a few kegs along. If you slip your poison into those kegs, you might get them all."

Sigurlina smiled and nodded. "And that might just make them sick. At least it would leave them a chance at an honourable death." Reaching into her pack, Sigurlina pulled out a wooden bowl. "Pee in this. I was making a paste to put on a knife, but if we do kegs, it will be easier to fill a skin with liquid and dump it in.

Jolnir took the bowl and bit his lip. "I'll be right back."

"I promise not to peek." Sigurlina smiled.

Minutes later, Vidurr returned to find Sigurlina pouring liquid from her pestle into a waterskin held by Jolnir. Munin huddled against a tree trunk watching for trouble. Vidurr howled, taking his human form and retrieved his cloak from the shelter.

"They have spitted two people. The other prisoners are huddled in a pit in the snow near the fire. They've spread cloaks over the pit's bottom. I couldn't get close enough to see how many there are."

"Help me," Sigurlina jerked around to see the translucent form of a powerfully built man in rich clothing. His golden hair fell around his shoulders, and he carried a battle axe. Vidurr and Jolnir didn't react.

"Spirit," said Sigurlina.

"It can't end like this. No honour. Eaten by a beast. No chance to enter Valhalla." The spirit turned to gaze at the distant fire.

Vidurr and Jolnir stared at Sigurlina.

"Vidurr, could you see any kegs near the fire?" asked Sigurlina.

"Couldn't get close enough," answered the Ulfhednar.

"They're on the far side just outside the heat of the fire. Help me," pleaded the spirit.

Long ago Sigurlina had realised it was usually best to ignore the overly friendly shades. Most times, they wanted more than she could give, but there were exceptions. She decided to take a chance. Sigurlina fingered her grandmother's gift in her pouch and faced the shade.

"I will do what I can if you help us." Sigurlina stared at the shade.

"Who's she talking to?" asked Jolnir.

"The dead." Vidurr shrugged and began collecting twigs for a cooking fire that he placed behind a deadfall that would block its light from the perspective of the trolls' camp.

"She did that on the ship, but it wasn't like this." Jolnir looked at Sigurlina curiously.

"This one was here already." Vidurr placed his tinder then, igniting a taper from the candle lantern, lit it.

"How are you named?" asked Sigurlina.

"Airic Golden Hair."

"How many trolls are there in that camp?"

"Eighty or so."

"Where are they?"

"The trolls are dug into the snowbanks around the fire. They set a watch, but he seems more concerned with how quickly I'm roasting than what is going on around him."

"How many mead barrels are there?"

"Four. One was newly breached when they spitted me."

"Why don't the humans sneak away?"

"Trolls took our cloaks, shoes and socks as soon as they made camp. You can't get far with frozen feet. Help me."

Sigurlina stared at the shade. "Come when I call."

Sigurlina turned to Vidurr and Jolnir. "I'm going to need a distraction to draw the guard's attention away from the fire."

Vidurr smiled. "I can do that, but if the trolls have a tracker, they'll hunt us down."

Sigurlina bit her lip in thought. The cold was seeping through her clothing, and the pummeling of the hail was bruising her. "I have an idea. First, I need to see something."

Kneeling in the snow by the fire that Vidurr had kindled, Sigurlina spoke in a near whisper that sent a shudder up the spines of the living.

"Come hither servant, durable symbol of our ending. I summon thee who was Airic Golden Hair in life to be my black one. To do my bidding. To the pain of the borderlands, I summon thee. Not alive, not dead, and by my will be bound. Thou art my black one!"

Sigurlina heard something like a scream. Vidurr and Jolnir cringed.

A black skeleton emerged from the ground and seemed to glower at Sigurlina.

"Airic Golden Hair, you asked for a chance to show your worth. This I give thee. Now let me see your feet," ordered Sigurlina.

#

Audun worked the smithy's billows while an elderly smith watched Audun's battle axe heat in the forge. The wind howled outside the small building, and the big man couldn't help but think fondly of the hall, come barn, where his friends slept. The smith picked up the weapon with a pair of tongs and used an iron rod to push the shattered wood out of its socket. He then put the axe head back amongst the coals. Taking a rough-worked, oak staff that leaned against the wall, the smith eyeballed the width of one end, then, using a knife, shaped it to the socket in the axe head.

Outside the smithy, the wind howled as snow blew into the structure, only to be melted by the heat of the forge.

The smith took a twist of iron out of the coals, put its looped end on a spike and added a couple more twists as the axe head reddened.

"You can stop pumping now." The smith pushed the metal twist back into the coals.

Audun let go of the billow's handle.

The smith used tongs to pull the axe head from the coals and thrust it onto the oaken shaft. The wood charred and smoked from contacting the hot metal. With a small hammer, the smith tapped the axe head onto the wood until it came up tight. Then he took the axe and thrust the head into a bucket of fish oil that burst into flames.

"This is a master's trick," explained the smith.

Audun watched, fascinated. "Should the shaft stick out on top like that?"

"I'll trim it and smooth the shaft to fit your hand. No to worry. I'm as good or better than any you'll find in them big cities. I've forged the weapons of jarls and karls. Comes a time when a man wants a quiet life. I've seen enough of battle and blood. I'll go to Bilskirnir when my time comes and forge for great Thor with my Ingrid by my side. I'd rather shoe a horse or mend a cauldron than make another blade, but you've earned me best work and no lie to that. Now turn the wheel on the grindstone. I'll put an edge to this axe you could shave with. Fine metal here."

Audun moved to the grinding wheel as the smith dampened it with water from a bucket.

#

Ragna, Fjorn and Kjorn piled wood into the trolls' fire pit that sat outside town. By the time Fjorn had thought of the crippled troll that the flames had turned to stone, the fire was out. When they checked, the beast had reverted to its fleshy state and crawled away.

Thrusting the torch he'd brought from the hall into the set wood, Fjorn ignited it.

"Stay in sight of the flames. I doubt the troll has gone far." The wind caught Fjorn's cloak and sent it flapping.

"Never thought I'd see the day I'd want to find a troll. And with me bad knee acting up," griped Kjorn.

"Feeling old," teased Ragna.

"More 'en feeling. But I'm betting yea could be making me forget the years." Kjorn leered playfully.

"You wouldn't survive it, you old goat." Ragna teased.

"Worse ways to go, harlot." Kjorn smiled with mischievous warmth.

Ragna grinned back at him. "Let's get started."

The three humans spread out and started inspecting the area where the barren met the dead forest. The fire provided a beacon in the storm and dark for their return.

After what seemed a long time, Ragna called, "Over here."

Fjorn and Kjorn raced to join her, drawing their weapons. A dark gap loomed where trees had been pushed aside to make way for something large.

Flanking the small woman, the two men stared into the gap.

Ragna cleared her throat and spoke in Orse. "We seek parley. We swear by Gungnir, no harm will come to you if you take no action against us." Ragna repeated the message in Pictish, then the tongue of the White God's church, followed by Gaelic. She'd finished the sentence in Sami, the language of the Finns, when a deep, guttural voice returned a halting reply. A moment later, a troll crawled out of the woods. The stump of its leg looked red and blistered.

Fjorn held out a bony piece of meat he'd salvaged from the stew pot.

The troll eyed the humans suspiciously, then took the meat and grunted.

"What did he... she...?" began Kjorn.

"Hard to tell with trolls," observed Ragna.

"It doesn't matter. What did it say?" asked Fjorn.

"Why?" Ragna translated.

"Tell it that they were cheated, then show it this and explain what it's looking at." Fjorn held out a piece of the counterfeit Wessex skatt that was cut in half.

Ragna released a series of Sami words and cautiously held out the broken, counterfeit coin to the troll.

The troll grunted, then screamed, grabbed a dead tree in one hand and tore it out of the ground. Fjorn, Kjorn and Ragna leapt out of the way as the tree fell, sending a shower of snow into the air.

When the air cleared, the troll was pounding its head into another dead tree which looked like it was about to drop.

The three humans moved closer. "Ragna, tell it that we think all the trolls were paid with bad coins and that if it will tell its people about this, we will take it back to its tribe."

Ragna translated. The humans waited as the troll seemed to ponder. It grunted two words.

"How walk?" translated Ragna.

The troll pawed at its leg, which was cut off mid-calf.

"We'll make it a leg out of wood, iron and leather," offered Fjorn.

Ragna translated. She had to try several times before the troll understood.

"I also told it that it could crawl over to the fire while it waited," remarked Ragna.

"This be all fine and good, so long as it doesn't try to eat us," observed Kjorn.

"Are you ready to face three hundred trolls?" asked Fjorn.

Kjorn sighed heavily. "Fine, but I'm not expecting the villagers to like it."

"Which is better, vengeance against mercenaries or victory over the monster that hired them?"

"Just hope the people see it that way," remarked Kjorn.

Fjorn and Kjorn each took one of the troll's arms and helped it to the fire.

Fjorn paused to inspect the amputated stump.

"This won't do. Even with a peg, the end is raw. It will hurt too much to walk on and likely get infected."

Clearing his throat, he began to sing.

"Youth to the Gods, golden apples of grace.

Indun's power heal mortals of faith."

The stump sealed over as a light dew covered the troll.

#

Jolnir couldn't stop snickering as he donned the extra socks he'd packed in case his feet got wet and pulled on his boots.

Sigurlina knelt in the snow, securing a pair of dirty socks over her skeleton's feet and cinching them tight against its leg bones with a bit of cord braided from their rope.

The skeleton stood up and took several steps.

"Vidurr?" asked Sigurlina.

The tracker moved to look at the footprints and grunted. "If they're in a rush, or don't know tracking, it might be enough."

Sigurlina looked at her skeleton appraisingly. "We're as ready as we'll ever be."

Vidurr's reply was to howl, taking on his wolf form. He led Jolnir and the black skeleton towards the trolls' camp. The storm was beginning to abate, but the wind still screeched. They skirted the slope above the trolls' camp, staying behind the line of dead trees. Vidurr stopped them at a point where the snow had piled up on a collection of deadfall trees. He began digging out under the deadfall while Jolnir looped a rope around several supporting branches and trailed it into the woods. The skeleton ran away from the troll's camp, leaving a trail of footprints leading to a frozen stream. It then walked back, leaving a trail to the deadfall. It repeated this three times, then pulled off its socks and gave them to Jolnir, who cringed to accept them. Slipping behind a tree, the skeleton stood perfectly still with the magical replica of Sigurlina's staff held at the ready. Vidurr and Jolnir crept behind the cover of the trees, trailing one end of the rope behind them. Vidurr pressed his cold, wet nose into Jolnir's face.

Jolnir nodded, stood up, braced himself against a tree and pulled on the rope. Vidurr bit into the line with his powerful jaws and added his full wolfen strength to the effort. The branches supporting the deadfall pulled out. The overburden of snow careened down the embankment burying several of the trolls' snow shelters.

The guard troll leapt up, shouting. Soon the encampment was rushing to dig out their comrades.

Sigurlina stepped into a shadow, appearing from another shadow by the fire. The body of Airic Golden Hair was spitted on a slender tree trunk and hung close to the flames. A pit had been dug close to the fire and lined with several cloaks. Humans slept in a miserable pile within it. Sigurlina felt awful as the energies of Svartalfheim were slow to leave her, and she had to harden her heart to the villagers. All the trolls' attentions had been diverted to the snow slide. Three steps brought her to the mead barrels. The open one was nearly empty. She ignored it and pried at the wooden bung at the top of the second barrel until it popped out. A layer of ice still blocked her access to the mead. She thrust her eating knife through the bunghole. The ice cracked. The smell of thick mead poured out. She drained her skin containing the poison into the barrel, then slipped the bung back into place.

"Brakoop ugla troll, bulot!" A guttural voice broke through the sound of the storm. Sigurlina threw herself into the new-fallen snow by the barrels and swept snow over herself.

There was a grunting sound, then the voice spoke again, "Faplat." There was a sound like an enormous fist slamming into wood.

"Croppot," said the voice. There was a gulping sound, then a loud belch and a sigh.

Sigurlina risked moving enough to shift the snow away from her eyes. The guard troll was back. It towered against the starry sky, a deeper shadow in the night, holding the silhouette of an enormous tankard in one hand. Shifting her gaze, she could see the first mead barrel amongst the flames.

"Bulots!" grumbled the troll as it moved to where the snow had been piled into a crude seat and settled itself.

Sigurlina waited, barely daring to breathe. She was at least feeling better as the energies of Svartalfheim left her. She felt a surge of energy and knew that Airic, her black skeleton, had been destroyed.

Time passed as the troll continued to grumble to itself. Finally, it stood up and lurched over to Airic's body. It reached to tear an arm off the roasting corpse.

Sigurlina took her chance and sprang from her hiding place. Thrusting her staff between the troll's legs, she drove her shoulder into its back, causing it to stumble into the fire. The bright light and heat from the fire acted as the sun once did and turned the beast to stone. Being sure to stay on the icy, compacted ground around the fire, Sigurlina moved to a shadow and stepped through it, emerging from a shadow nearly thirty strides away. She felt sick but managed to glance over the troll camp. Dark shadows moved, digging out other dark shadows. The sound of a wolf howl echoed over the land. It had an edge to it that sent a shudder up her spine.

#

Airic Golden Hair longed for release. The Seith hadn't told him it would be so cold. It was a cold worse than any he'd known before or after Fimbulwinter, but strangely, it did not stop him from moving or performing his lady's bidding. He knew he was her thrall. Where her command left space, he had some freedom, but he dared not think of going against her intent. He held up a black, skeletal hand and looked at the bones. How he longed for the flesh that roasted on the trolls' fire even as he huddled behind a lifeless tree. The tree and he were both shadows of what they had been.

The wolf and the warrior pulled on the rope. The deadfall gave way. They slunk into the ruined forest, erasing their tracks as they went. He... could he even make that claim when all that had made him a man now roasted on a spit? In any case, he had a different role to play. A, hopefully, finite one. The cold and the burning. No lungs to breathe with. His chest burnt like he'd held his breath too long. Still, it did nothing to weaken him. How strange.

In the darkness, he could see trolls scrambling up the embankment; tearing into the snow to free their trapped comrades. Such vile creatures, yet still they fought for their own.

Time passed, seconds or an age? He could not tell. One of the trolls pummeled another, then pointed to the slope and grunted what seemed to be a command.

Twenty trolls left the efforts to save their comrades and moved to investigate the snow slide's source. They found the rope. That couldn't be helped. They soon discover the tracks from Airic's stocking-clad feet. That was intended. His lady is clever. The echo of the man he had been wished he'd met her in life. Still, a witch woman, that would have been nothing but trouble.

The trolls close on him. Hulking brutes.

A babble of noise came from the trolls as they conversed.

Now is his moment! The second chance the Seith promised.

He sprang into view, then raced along the trail left by his previous passage. The trolls follow him, pushing through the snow that his lighter form barely dents.

Airic reached the snow and ice-covered stream with the trolls three strides behind him. The ice gave way under the trolls' pounding feet. The first troll fell into a hollow, slamming his face into the ice. The stream was long frozen, but as it froze, it formed layers of air and ice. Other trolls lowed the first troll's example. Soon the rest fell back. Now was the time.

Airic Golden Hair, son of Halfdan, turned. Empty chest burning, icy cold, death given form. With a silent scream, he charged the closest of the ice-stuck trolls and swung his staff to flatten the troll's nose. He swung again, crushing its throat.

Airic raced to the next troll and drove his staff butt first into the beast's groin. The troll clutched itself in reflex. Airic struck it across the eyes. A third blow finished the beast.

Other trolls closed on Airic, following the stream's edge.

Airic longed for them to come. He longed to end the tortured half-life the Seith had granted him. He Smashed a troll's knee. A club sweeps low. Airic feels his legs being torn away. His chest and arms fall to the ice and snow. There can't be more pain, but somehow there is. He drives his staff between a troll's legs. He feels his shoulder grabbed and pulled away. His arm spirals through the air to lodge in the branches of a dead tree. Swiping with his remaining arm, he grabs the troll's leg and drags himself towards it, sinking his teeth into the tough flesh. The troll kicks, and Airic's neck and chest fly into the cold and dark. He bites harder as liquid heat washes into what once supported his throat. Before all is over, he hears one of the trolls howl like a wolf.

"Airic Golden Hair," spoke the woman. She was flaxen-haired, shapely and armoured in silver chain mail with a face that was perfection itself.

Airic looked down at himself. He was all there. It was him, except... He looked at his left hand. The skin was the same ebony black as his skeleton form.

"What?"

"You fought to the last. The Seith gave you a second chance. You bear that mark, but it need not be one of shame. The feast will soon be laid. Come."

Airic Golden Hair took the Valkyrie's hand and left Midgard behind.

#

Vidurr and Jolnir moved cautiously, sweeping their tracks away as they went. The weather was helping. The snow now fell in big white flakes, and the wind, while strong enough to sweep snow from the surrounding dunes, was more apt to fill in a footprint than reveal one.

The lack of trolls told them the beasts had fallen for the skeleton's ploy. Vidurr and Jolnir had circled around and were halfway back to their shelter when they heard a wolf howl.

Vidurr's lip curled at the sound, and a deep growl escaped him.

"Was that howl like yours?" asked Jolnir.

Vidurr looked at his companion. Even through the canine features, his offence was apparent.

"Like yours but not like yours," Jolnir whispered.

Vidurr howled, taking on his human form. "What comes is only the form of a wolf. I have heard of trolls that have mastered the transformation. They have nothing of the nobility of wolf kind."

"We should go."

"He will track us. I must face him. Tell Sigurlina from me that she is a true bitch, no matter her form, and tell Fjorn, I will keep my word on the plain of Vigrid."

Vidurr howled again, taking on his wolf form.

"I'll go once I know where you'll be, but only to fetch Sigurlina. She can heal. When you win the fight, you may need that."

Vidurr nuzzled Jolnir in agreement; both knew his victory was far from assured. He let the stalo ruffle the fur around his neck, then led the way through the ruined woods to a clearing.

Vidurr walked the clearing's edge, pausing to pee on a tree every few strides, then he curled up at one side of the clearing as if conserving his strength.

Jolnir watched him for several moments, then returned to their shelter.

#

Audun worked with the old smith who told him of the ways of metal. The head of his axe held tight to the oaken handle and was sharp enough to shave with. It was like he was a boy again, learning of the sea and ships from his father and grandfather. It would take him years to master the art the old man offered, years he couldn't spare, but what he gained he knew would aid him in repairing his gear in future.

Audun rubbed the handle of his axe with a piece of hide he'd dipped into a sand bucket. The wood slowly grew smooth and splinter-free. A teen boy now worked the bellows, and the old smith had shaped the twisted metal into a sword.

"The trick is to get the temperature right. Too hot, and the blade will snap. Too cold, and it is soft as butter. Look to the colour of this blade. This is right as it's like to be." The smith pulled the blade from the forge and thrust it into the quench bucket. Smoke billowed into the air. The boy had already stopped pumping the bellows.

The smithy door opened, allowing the smoke to billow out. Fjorn appeared in the clearing air.

"Have you got it?" asked Fjorn.

"I'm not too fond of it, given what them beasts done," snipped the smith.

Fjorn sighed. "I can't disagree, but what else can we do?"

"Those filth ate me apprentice. He were nought but a boy." Tears trickled from the smith's eyes, turning black as they flowed over his sooty cheeks.

Fjorn nodded and stayed silent.

"I'm hoping them beasts aren't in a mood to listen, but here it is." The smith lifted an iron frame with a spiral spike on its bottom from a corner of the smithy and passed it to Fjorn. Fjorn grunted as he took the weight. "Thank you. If it helps, if this works, many apprentices will be saved."

The old smith nodded. "Aye, just not the one as worked me forge."

The teenage billows boy moved to the smith's side. "You still have me, grandfather. Biffindi would want us to go on."

The old man hugged the lad. Fjorn and Audun left the smithy, closing the door behind them.

"He is a master of his art." Audun swung his battle-axe experimentally. "The balance is even better than it was before."

"Good. I..." Audun walked beside his friend towards the fire outside the gate. "Am I a fool thinking I can bargain with trolls?"

Audun considered. "Can we kill even the band that attacked this village with the people we have?"

"Probably not. When we saved the village, we had surprise on our side, and there were fewer of them."

"And you're sure the arrows on the map are trolls being used to attack Jorvik?"

"It makes sense."

"Then you don't have much choice. Fjorn, it's the same as at sea. If a storm blows in, you try to make port. If you can't, you tie down and do your best." Audun paused to inspect the village gates. "Odd that the gates aren't broken. How'd the trolls get in?"

"I noticed that too, the hinges are intact, and the crossbar is in one piece. I've tried talking to some of the villagers, but none of them wants to talk about the attack. And what happened to the watch? A place this size not setting a night watch makes no sense."

"Maybe ask our troll friend out there," suggested Audun.

"Ragna will love that. It barely understands enough Sami for her to get simple ideas across. We'll have to try."

Fjorn walked towards the fire outside the village. The snow had thinned to big fluffy puffs and intermittent gusts of wind. If he squinted, he could almost imagine it was a normal winter's night from a time when the sun would rise.

The troll sat by the fire, picking its nose. Ragna sat upwind of it, out of reach with her hand on her short sword. Kjorn sat with a man on the other side of the fire. Kjorn had his hand on his sword hilt. The other man held a two-man bucksaw and eyed the troll with malice. A log lay on the ground before them.

"What took so long? If I miss dinner because of this, I'll..." began Ragna coming to her feet.

The troll looked up and saw Audun emerging from the blowing snow. It screamed and tried to scramble away.

"What's it saying? What's going on," demanded Fjorn.

"It... something about finishing the job," translated Ragna.

Audun stared at the troll and spoke a few words in Sami. The troll quieted.

"I didn't know you spoke Sami," commented Fjorn.

"Just a few useful phrases," Audun smiled.

"Bet I know what they were useful for." Ragna rolled her eyes.

"What's it mean?" Kjorn glanced from the big man to the troll.

"Take it slow; it won't hurt. Really, and what other phrases do you know?" commented Ragna.

Audun released a series of words.

Ragna blushed and shook her head. "You can't tell me that worked?"

Audun shrugged.

Fjorn took a long, slow breath. "Tell her she needs to screw the metal mount into the log." He held out the metal and leather mount to the troll. Kjorn collected the log and handed it to the troll.

The troll stared at the pieces, then looked up, confused.

"Hel in a hot bath. It can't figure it out," griped Kjorn. "How dim is it?"

Fjorn slowly moved to the troll and guided it so that it held the screw end of the metal bracket against the top of the log, then he showed the troll how to screw the one into the other. The troll grunted and nodded with each stage. Fjorn pushed the bracket against the troll's stump and did up the leather straps that cinched it tight.

"The lad has it for sure," whispered Kjorn.

"What?" Ragna watched in awe as the troll stared at Fjorn first with confusion, then doubt, surprise, then an expression of wrapped devotion.

"By the end, the troll will be thanking us for attacking it. I've seen its like, but never this strong," remarked Audun.

"The lad's blood father had it. If you met Harold, you'd follow him into Jotunheim with nought but a sock to cover your dangle," observed Kjorn.

With the brace attached, Fjorn helped the troll to stand. The troll took a couple of hesitant steps and grunted a sentence.

"She says it's too long," translated Ragna.

"Then bring the saw, and let's get this right. The storm is letting up. I'll be expecting Vidurr and Munin soon."

The man carried the saw over. The troll looked startled. Fjorn stroked its arm, and it settled. The man's eyes darted from Fjorn to the troll and back again.

"About the width of my thumb." Fjorn laid his thumb against the stump of the log.

"I reckon that will about do it." The spot was marked with a knife, then Fjorn took the other side of the saw, and they shortened the enormous peg leg.

#

Vidurr lay in the snow waiting. The forest was quiet except for the occasional howling gusts of wind that sent snow skittering across the clearing. The storm was almost spent. He sniffed. He could smell his enemy approaching. All that was worst in troll and wolf was coming to do battle. No loyalty, no love of pup and pack. Savagery without constraint. His father had told him what to expect. He remembered the old Ulfhednar, the hours of training. Learning how to hunt and track. Learning how to harness his rage and direct it for the good of the pack. The images all ended in the same place. An old Godi, with hands, feet and tongue cut away, eyes gouged out, waiting to die before a broken statue of Surt. Whether these trolls knew it or not, in attacking the towns of Northumbria, they served the Crusaders who did such things. This false wolf that stank of filth and death was the worst abomination of them all.

Vidurr built his rage. His burnt village, his murdered wife, his cub. His cub! He would make them bleed for that. The way they imprisoned animals to fight for their Pope's pleasure.

The filth they spewed into Midgard.

He let the rage take him. He forgot himself, focussed solely on his revenge. Solely on the abomination that came. He quivered with anticipation.

Then it was there. A black wolf, neck and shoulders larger than Vidurr, burst into the clearing. It paused to sniff a scent marker, then howled a challenge.

Vidurr held himself in check. He wanted to, needed to, lunge, but he couldn't give this foe any advantage.

The black wolf sniffed the air and stalked towards where the falling snow buried Vidurr. It grew closer. Vidurr inhaled, his blood pounded in his ears, his senses narrowed. In all the world, there was only him and his foe.

The black wolf drew nearer. Vidurr exploded out of the snow, a blur of red fur and teeth. He gripped the throat of his foe and bit down. Rage took him and fired his strength. The surge of force toppled the black wolf. The red wolf landed on the top of the canine pile, his teeth clamped tight on the enemy's throat. The black wolf used its superior size and weight to roll, crushing the red wolf on the ground then the larger beast pulled away.

The red wolf felt the flesh in its teeth give as blood showered him.

Vidurr sprung onto his paws, spitting fur and flesh. The wolves circled each other looking for an opening. Blood dripped from the black wolf's throat. Vidurr's paw found a depression in the ground, and his shoulder dipped down. The black wolf lunged. Vidurr tried to evade but his paw caught in the deeper snow allowing the black wolf to slam into him. The two wolves became a snapping and snarling ball of fur and teeth. Snow compacted under them and flew up into both their eyes. Vidurr felt his claws dig into flesh but also felt teeth tear into his side. Stretching, he snapped at where he thought his enemy's hind legs might be, and a bony, fur-covered shaft fell into his mouth. He bit down hard, and there was a crunching sound. He felt his enemy tear at him, leaving wounds under the fur of his chest. Kicking, he opened the flow of blood from his enemy's throat and felt himself healing as he sucked the life force from his foe. Vidurr knew he was failing as the two wolves tore at each other. His enemy's strength was too great, and Vidurr's healing could not keep up with the damage he was taking. Rage drove him, but deep in his mind, he heard his father's words.

"You will not always be the strongest. When you fight a stronger opponent, keep your distance. Use your speed and agility. Make them come to you and force them to be reckless, then strike at a moment of your choosing. Do not match strength with strength when your opponent is the stronger. Find where they are weak and strike there."

Bracing his legs against his foe Vidurr pushed. He felt his flesh tear where his rival had locked its teeth against his back. Landing on his paws, he used the time it took for his foe to right himself to run. Vidurr stopped at the edge of the clearing. His sides heaved. One of his forelegs hurt, and blood dripped from him.

The black wolf stood. Blood dripped from its throat, staining the ice and snow; its left hind leg turned at an odd angle. It charged Vidurr, using an awkward three-legged gate. Vidurr raced away, circling the clearing, ignoring the pain from his foreleg. The black wolf followed, paused, threw its head back and began to howl.

Vidurr turned and drove himself towards his foe. Sharp teeth encountered the flesh of the black wolf's shoulder. Vidurr's claws raked down his enemy's side. The black wolf bit into Vidurr's neck, hauling him up like a disobedient pup, tearing a chunk out of its own foreleg where Vidurr's teeth had sunk in as it did so. The black wolf shook Vidurr, then threw him into a nearby tree. Snow fell out of the branches burying the red wolf.

Vidurr let the blood in his mouth heal some of the damage. He was nearly spent. Rage had taken him as far as it could.

The black wolf howled, thinking it was victorious. Vidurr sprang from the snow and raced forward, catching the larger animal by the throat. This time Vidurr shifted position so that he was a weight dragging his foe down, forcing it to lean on its injured shoulder. The black wolf's howl cut off as it struggled to break free. Its good leg kicked, leaving bleeding wounds on Vidurr's chest. Vidurr held on, biting into the arteries and veins his previous attacks had exposed. The black wolf managed to get its hind leg into a gutting position and tore down Vidurr's abdomen. Vidurr held on as his life's blood fell into the snow.

Vidurr twisted his head and pulled. Blood pumped out of his foe's throat, showering him. He stumbled as he tried to heal. The black wolf pounced on Vidurr, blood still pouring from the black beast's wounds. Vidurr managed to thrust out a paw, tearing deeper into one of his foe's wounds. A crimson tide covered the red wolf as everything went black.

CHAPTER 6: COLD AND WET

Sigurlina watched as the trolls in the camp finished digging out their comrades and huddled by the fire. When they found the guard troll, that Sigurlina had pushed into the fire, they laughed and took turns relieving themselves on him. Wood was added to the flames around the stricken troll as they passed around the mead barrel. Several of them tore off sections of the roasting corpses and ate them. Then the effects of her potion struck. First one troll vomited over the one sitting beside it. A second followed its example. Soon they were all up lurching around. Troll bumped into troll, and fights began. Weapons were drawn as they lurched about. One troll tripped over a roasting spit and landed in the fire on top of the guard troll turning to stone. The sound of guttural shouting filled the air.

Sigurlina looked up and saw some stars at the eastern edge of the sky. The snow fell in large flakes, and the wind had lessened. She crept to the shelter she had dug.

"Munin," she called in her mind.

"Pretty bird," replied the raven from inside the snow shelter. 'I needed to get warm,' explained the familiar's mental voice.

"I understand. Do you think you could show Fjorn and the others the way here?"

Munin stuck her head out of the shelter. 'I thought I was supposed to go with the wolf.'

"I know, but he should be back by now. If something has happened, we may need help." Sigurlina glanced around with a mix of nervousness and hope.

'It's still a little windy, and there might be hawks or eagles around. Some of them have survived. The queen's familiar warned me. I miss him.'

"We can visit when this is over."

The sound of crunching snow reached the ears of bird and girl. Sigurlina readied her staff. Jolnir burst out of the dead forest, his chest heaving.

"What happened? Where's Vidurr?" demanded Sigurlina.

"He, hu hu, troll wolf, hu hu, fight. Probably…" Jolnir paused to swallow, then continued. "He might be hurt."

'I'll get Fjorn and the others to help.' Munin leapt into the air.

"Munin, wait. Help us find Vidurr first," Sigurlina screamed in her thoughts, but the raven was already gone. Sigurlina reached into the shelter and pulled out her travel pack and the veiled candle lantern. "How far is he?"

"What about the trolls?" asked Jolnir.

"Last I saw, they were doing our work for us. Vidurr comes first." Sigurlina started back along Jolnir's tracks.

Jolnir took a deep breath and followed.

#

Fjorn passed the troll a bowl of the thin pork soup that was the villager's dinner. The troll paced around the fire, becoming accustomed to its peg leg. Ragna sipped at her own bowl of soup and watched the behemoth with wary eyes. The troll sniffed the soup, then took a long swallow and grunted out a sentence.

"She says it's good," translated Ragna.

"I'm glad she likes it," replied Fjorn.

The troll let out another series of words.

Ragna set her soup aside before she spilt it as she laughed.

"What?" asked Fjorn.

Ragna replied to the troll in Sami. Fjorn could make out one word, "Seithkona."

The troll looked disappointed but nodded and replied.

Ragna formed another sentence.

"What are you talking about," demanded Fjorn.

"Just girl talk. It seems that Nose-Crusher, that's her name, is taken with you. She says you are nice nice. The type that makes a good, second husband to look after the children."

Fjorn tried not to grimace. "You have told her...."

"I told her you are first husband to a powerful Seithkona. She said that's too bad because she'd like a softy man in the house, but she wouldn't challenge a Seithkona because they have big magic and make the dead fight for them."

"Thank you." Fjorn released a breath he hadn't realised he was holding.

"Thank Sigurlina."

"I will. The storm has just about let up. It shouldn't be long now."

Ragna stared at Fjorn, her sarcastic demeanour slipping away. "Do you really believe they are alright?"

Fjorn stared at the small woman. "I have to, Ragna. I have to."

Fjorn bent to put another log on the fire and straightened to find himself staring straight into Munin's eyes where she had landed on the top of Ragna's hood.

"Get off me, you black chicken," snapped Ragna.

"Yura bitch, yura a bitch," spoke the raven as it danced from one foot to another.

"Ragna, stand still. Something is wrong. Where's Vidurr? They were supposed to come to get us together." Fjorn looked into the raven's eyes as if he could read its mind. "Is Sigurlina alright?"

"Good Bird."

"Is Vidurr?"

"Yura bitch."

"Is Jolnir?"

"Good bird."

"Can you lead us to them?"

Munin danced from foot to foot, then let out a squawk.

"What in the names of the Aesir does that mean?" demanded Ragna.

"Have they been captured?"

"Good bird," the intonation was hesitant. Munin danced in a circle on Ragna's head.

"It doesn't matter; we need to go, and what we find, we find." Fjorn started towards the village gate.

Nose-Crusher asked a question, and Ragna replied.

Nose-Crusher nodded, then said something else.

"You're right. Not a soft man, not when it counts." Ragna followed Fjorn to collect the others.

#

Jolnir led the way to the clearing's edge and froze when it came into sight. Near the middle lay a troll. Jolnir drew his sword. Sigurlina, seeing his action, readied her staff. They crept into the clearing. The troll didn't move. They moved closer.

"Could it be dead?" asked Sigurlina.

"But where's Vidurr?" Jolnir scanned the edges of the clearing as if she expected to see the big, red wolf pop out of the shadows.

"Lady Freya, protect me!" Sigurlina raced towards the troll, pausing the length of her staff away to poke the beast. When it didn't move, she rushed closer. "Help me. He's under it."

Human legs sprawled out from under the troll carcass. Digging in the snow, Sigurlina uncovered Vidurr's face.

Jolnir came up beside Sigurlina. "Is he alive?"

"I can't tell. We need to get this off him." Sigurlina stood and planted the base of her staff to act as a lever and started pushing. Jolnir added his strength to her efforts. The troll carcass shifted, leaving a smear of bodily fluids in its wake. Vidurr's form came more into view. Sigurlina shifted her staff's anchor point, and again they heaved. This time the troll moved completely off Vidurr.

Sigurlina fell to her knees beside her friend. Gaping wounds oozed blood into Vidurr's clothing. Closing her eyes, Sigurlina mustered her power and cast her spell. Several minor wounds closed on Vidurr, and the black frostbite on his fingers turned to red, swollen skin. Sigurlina cast the spell again. Then another spell. The dew that came with each spell soaked Vidurr's clothing.

His chest rose and fell. Sigurlina sat back, tears trickling down her cheeks. Standing, she passed Jolnir her cloak. "Wrap him in this. Keep him warm. Try to dry him out."

Jolnir nodded. "Will he be alright?"

"Probably, in time. We need to set a watch." Sigurlina knelt in the snow and focused inward. The cycle was all. Each moment brought her closer to death; each death fed new life. The wheel turned. It could be fast or slow. The turning was all. "Come hither servant, durable symbol of our ending. I summon thee black one!"

The ground erupted up into a black skeleton.

"Patrol the border of the clearing and warn me of any who approach. Defend me, Jolnir and Vidurr from harm if it is necessary and wait for further orders." Sigurlina looked at the skeleton as it nodded and shambled off to walk around the clearing's edge.

Sigurlina moved back to Vidurr and cast another healing.

"I'll make a fire. He's going to need warmth." Jolnir moved to the edge of the forest and started breaking off twigs.

Sigurlina cast another healing. Vidurr opened his eyes and focused on Sigurlina. He smiled, "Good bitch!" He closed his eyes in exhaustion.

Sigurlina breathed a sigh of relief, then cast another healing. Vidurr's clothing was soaked with the magical dew that accompanied the healing spells, and her cloak was fast following. The cold would kill as certainly as wounds in this situation.

"Vidurr, if you can hear me, you need to change so we can dry you off. The cold could kill you." Sigurlina stroked her friend's forehead.

Vidurr tried to howl, but it caught in his throat.

"One more." Sigurlina did another healing; water started to puddle on the snow.

Vidurr sat up with Sigurlina's help. His breathing was ragged with pain. He fought his way to a standing position. Taking a deep breath, he managed a weak howl. Seconds later, a woozy-looking wolf stood on the snow with dry, if blood-matted, fur.

Minutes later, Jolnir's fire burnt in the corner of the clearing where the wind had drifted the snow into a windbreak. Vidurr lay by the flames as the skeleton patrolled around them. The snow had stopped, and the world was quiet. Sigurlina performed another healing on Vidurr, who seemed to be regaining some strength.

Jolnir walked to the troll's body.

Vidurr howled, taking his human guise and stood warming his wet clothes by the fire. "Thorough." He commented as he watched Jolnir decapitate the troll.

"You killed it," observed Sigurlina.

Vidurr grunted. "We must go. The trolls will track us."

"I know. As soon as you're dry."

"Sooner." Vidurr stumbled, and Sigurlina rushed to support him. "I can dry a little first."

Jolnir returned to the fireside. "A bag of skatt struck in Wessex, one of those tree trunks the trolls use as clubs, a human-made short sword it was using as a dirk and this." He held up a scroll.

"What does it say?" asked Sigurlina.

"I never learned to read," Jolnir passed over the scroll.

Sigurlina looked at it. "It's not runes. I think it's the script the White God's church uses. This at the bottom is in runes."

Sigurlina sounded out the words. "'Berkano, Claguz othala othala dagaz dagaz raidho isaice naudhneed keaz ehwo raidho.' B l oo d D r I n k e r … Blood Drinker."

"A troll name." Vidurr stirred the ashes of their dying fire.

Sigurlina rolled up the scroll and put it in her pack, then felt Vidurr's tunic. "You're still damp."

"Matters not." Vidurr stepped away from the fire, this time keeping his balance.

Sigurlina and Jolnir fell in behind him.

"I hope Munin is all right," whispered Sigurlina.

#

Fjorn led a party, composed of the crew and oarsmen of the Apenhet and a dozen armed villagers, through the cold and dark. Nose Crusher, the troll, hobbled at Fjorn's side using a spade that consisted of a slab of wood fixed to a wooden shaft to make a path for the humans. Fjorn and Audun worked smaller spades clearing the snow that fell into the passage. Munin kept leaping from her unwilling perch on top of Ragna into the air, then returning to point the way with her beak. The sky had cleared, and stars twinkled in the blackness. After several minutes Fjorn ordered a change. Six oarsmen armed with spades took the front of the line.

Audun passed his spade to an oarsman and leaned against the snow wall of the trail. Towards the village, people worked to widen the path and pack in its sides so it wouldn't collapse. "This is taking forever."

"It can't be helped. We'll need the trail clear if we have to retreat from the trolls," observed Fjorn.

Nose Crusher looked up at the mention of trolls. Fjorn smiled at her and nodded. The troll donned a missing tooth grin and settled against the side of the trench.

"Ragna," Fjorn turned to the small woman who held one of the party's torches.

"The arm. Perch on the arm. Not the head, the arm. The arm." Ragna held her free arm out while Munin stood on the top of her hood and ignored the gesture.

"Ragna," Fjorn repeated. "I need you to ask Nose Crusher how the trolls got past the village gate."

Ragna turned to look at Nose Crusher and translated the question.

Nose Crusher seemed to think, then answered.

"She says that the gate was open. The slimy man opened it and killed the guards so they could get in. Then the slimy man left. The chief said to let him go."

"What did the slimy man look like?" Audun pushed away from the snowbank.

"Munin, I swear if you dirty my cloak, I'm going to find something to stuff you with," cautioned Ragna as the raven walked a circle on her skull.

"Ragna… Munin, please perch on Audun for a bit. You'll have a better view," said Fjorn.

Munin looked at Fjorn with her beady, black eyes, then squawked, "Pretty bird, good bird," and leapt off Ragna landing on Audun's shoulder.

"Hello, my dark beauty." Audun's voice was amused.

"Pretty bird," replied Munin.

"Good riddance," snipped Ragna.

"Ragna, ask Nose Crusher if she can describe the slimy man." Fjorn watched as the oarsmen struggled to move the snow, a harsh expression crossing his face. "Obasi, you aren't here to lean on that shovel. Get to work."

Ragna moved to Nose Crusher's side and asked a series of questions before returning to Fjorn. "She says she can't tell with humans. We all look alike, small and squishy. He was about your height, skinny, even for a puny man, and dressed all in black. When he left the village, he pulled a cow bone out of his bag and kissed it. At first, she thought it had meat on it, but it didn't."

"Ask her to draw the cow bone in the snow," said Fjorn.

Ragna relayed the message. Nose Crusher drew the White God's cross in a snowdrift.

Fjorn sighed. "A spy. There's probably at least one in every village on the routes marked on the map." Pushing away from the trail's edge, Fjorn picked up his spade and led his team back to the front of the trench. Munin leapt into the air to check their progress.

#

Sigurlina led the way into their shelter overlooking the troll's encampment. Creeping forward, she looked down at her foes. Half a dozen bodies littered the snow. Other trolls were still retching while several squatted on the snow and ice. The bodies on spits were charred. No new victims had been added to the grizzly kitchen.

"Your plan worked," whispered Vidurr from directly behind her.

"You need to get in the shelter and stay warm so you can dry out." Sigurlina pointed to where their snow shelter was hidden under a brush pile.

"We must go. Not all the trolls were poisoned." Vidurr hugged himself.

Sigurlina reached under her cloak and fingered Vidurr's tunic. It was damp, as was her cloak, which he wore over his clothes. Ice had formed on the outside of the cloak, making it rigid. Sigurlina touched Vidurr's cloak, which she wore. It too was frozen solid, but her clothes beneath it were dry.

"Jolnir," she whispered.

Jolnir and the skeleton gazed along the path they'd left through the woods. He moved to Sigurlina's side.

"We need to move," said Jolnir.

"Trade cloaks with Vidurr. He can have at least one dry layer." Sigurlina stared once more into the trolls' camp, shaking her head. "It will take another blizzard to hide this mess."

Soon they were heading towards where they thought the village would be. The stars were apparent enough to show north, so they struck a course east.

They set a fast pace for Vidurr's sake, allowing the Ulfhednar to build up body heat under their last dry cloak, at the risk of Sigurlina and Jolnir working up a sweat. Their camp had vanished behind them when they heard a scream followed by a guttural voice snapping out what seemed to be orders.

"Keep mmmmmmoving." Vidurr spoke through chattering teeth.

"You should become the wolf and run ahead," suggested Sigurlina.

"Wolf wet to skin," replied Vidurr.

"I know, but it's faster."

"I think we can stay ahead of them." Jolnir pointed to his snowshoes. "They're so heavy, they have to plough through while we can walk on top, and there is no point in hiding our trail."

Sigurlina nodded. "As long as we hold out. Skeleton, stay back and do anything you can to delay the trolls that follow us."

The skeleton stopped walking.

Jolnir paused, and it was like a light came on in his eyes. "Skeleton, make a false trail into the woods. Make it look like we dragged something heavy that way. Sigurlina, help me brush out our tracks. Vidurr, keep walking. We'll catch up."

"Skeleton, do as he says. Jolnir, we can't do this for long. They'll overtake us." Sigurlina cut a branch off a dead pine tree and used it to brush out their tracks as the skeleton grabbed a larger branch and dragged it towards the dead woods, leaving a depressed track in the snow.

"We don't need to do it for long. Just long enough so that our trail is out of sight. They have to know there are three of us. And anybody that can track could tell one of us is injured."

Sigurlina smiled. "Make them think Vidurr collapsed, and we dragged him off the trail. They'll stop and search the woods."

"Exactly."

Sigurlina and Jolnir brushed out their tracks for twenty strides before dropping the branches and hurrying to catch up with Vidurr. They slogged on in the approximate direction of the village. Their candle lantern, a dim light in a dark world.

What seemed a lifetime later, Sigurlina gasped and stood a little straighter. "Skeleton's gone."

"They'll be coming then. It won't take much to find our trail," said Jolnir.

Vidurr grunted.

Their legs burned from walking in the snowshoes and their bodies felt chilled. Sweat impregnated Sigurlina and Jolnir's clothing, allowing the cold to bite through. They were near collapse when Jolnir pointed out distant lights forward and to the left of them. A moment later, Munin landed on Sigurlina's shoulder.

'I found them, and I brought them. They have a pet troll now. Ragna threatened to stuff me for no reason. No reason at all. I'm so glad you're safe. Vidurr doesn't look good. He should know better than to get wet and cold. I...' Munin's mental voice rattled into Sigurlina's thoughts.

"Munin, you are a very good bird, and you did very well. I'll make sure you get extra liver the next time I can. Right now, Vidurr needs to get warm and dry. Fly back to Fjorn and bring him to us. Tell him that there are trolls following us." Sigurlina spoke aloud as well as thinking the message to help her focus.

'I'll do that. I like the wolf. He slips me meat when he thinks no one can see.' Munin leapt into the air.

Despite the trembling in her exhausted legs, Sigurlina moved towards the lights.

Vidurr collapsed, shivering violently. Sigurlina and Jolnir hoisted his arms over their shoulders, and the three stumbled on. One step then another, the lights grew nearer.

#

Munin landed on Fjorn's shoulder.

"Is the dot of light them?" he demanded.

"Good bird, Good bird."

"Are they injured?"

"Yura bitch."

A snarl came to Fjorn's face that made Nose Crusher take a step back as he drove his shovel into the drift in front of him. Snow flew before him. The rest of those with shovels joined in, creating a small blizzard. Obasi stood back and sneered.

"You might like to try using that." Ragna pointed to his shovel.

"Mind your own business, wench."

"If you're not going to use it, give the shovel to someone who will." Ragna shoved her torch into Obasi's hand, snatched the shovel away from him and began clearing debris that fell back into the trench.

Fjorn's arms ached, and his back felt like it was on fire. How long the frenzied shovelling had gone on, he couldn't say. The dot of light had grown so that he could make out three figures leaning on each other against it. He leapt onto the snow, sinking to his waist, and pushed through. Audun came beside him with two of the oarsmen. Sigurlina fell into Fjorn's arms. Vidurr found himself picked up like a child by Audun while the oarsmen collected Jolnir.

"You, you, you." Fjorn pointed out oarsmen without releasing Sigurlina. "Build a fire."

"Gaut, set your people in a perimeter guard."

"Trolls chasing us. There are people alive in the troll camp. We poisoned their mead to make them sick, but it won't last," Sigurlina half-whispered.

Fjorn nodded. "Your trail will lead us to them, but for now, we need to look after you."

"We need to rescue my people." Gaut moved to Fjorn's side, fury in the townsman's eyes at the thought of delay.

Fjorn looked at the village leader grimly. "We will. Tell your people to extend three trenches along the line of my people's trail in front of us for thirty strides. Have Nose Crusher dig the central trench. That will be fastest. Undercut the snow on the central trench's sides. Dig the flanking trenches a stride away from the central one and only a shoulder-width apart. Position men in the flanking trenches. When the trolls run into the central trench, we can collapse the walls onto them. They'll be half-buried, and we'll be in a better position to... negotiate. They either listen to what Nose Crusher tells them, or we do what we have to before they can dig out."

Gaut stared at Fjorn. "Hakon's bane, that royal bastard doesn't stand a chance." Gaut left to order his folk.

The fire was laid well up the human trail and sparked with a torch. Soon Sigurlina, Vidurr and Jolnir lay on and under dry cloaks around the fire. Sigurlina and Vidurr's damp clothes were spread over crude drying racks near the flames. Jolnir refused to be stripped so vehemently that they left him his undertunic and trews while pressing a pair of dry socks on him. A small cauldron was filled with snow and dried meat, then set by the flames to heat.

Vidurr's shivering subsided, and he dozed in the borrowed cloak.

Ragna stood by the fire turning the clothes, so they dried, and watching her friends. Munin landed on her head. "Skuld's scissors! Bird, will you stop doing that!"

"Yura bitch." Munin dropped down to land on the cloak covering Sigurlina.

Ragna looked at her friends and whispered. "I'm not the mothering type."

"You shouldn't be closing any doors," observed Kjorn's voice. The old sailor stepped into the light of the fire.

"I thought you'd be waiting to ambush the trolls."

"Fjorn sent me to fetch you. We've spotted a torch heading towards the trail. He needs you to translate for Nose Crusher. He's going to try to show the beasts that Aethelstan cheated them." Kjorn shook his head. "He's a smart lad, but I'm thinking this might be a bit too much."

"Worth a try, as long as they're up to their waists in snow." Ragna pulled her cloak tight and stepped away from the fire. "You coming?"

"Nay. I'm to watch here. Fjorn is less than trusting of some of the folk. He wants a watch kept on these three."

Ragna smiled her approval and vanished into the dark.

CHAPTER 7: DIPLOMACY

The lumbering figures of twelve armed trolls, illuminated by two torches, came into view. They were all breathing heavily as they pushed the snow in front of them to either side with crude shovels leaving an untidy trench through the frozen landscape. They came to the human-made trench and surged forward. The narrow path forced them into a single file. A horn sounded, and men heaved, pushing the undercut walls of the trench inwards. The snow buried the trolls waist-deep. Before the trolls could react, a voice bellowed a sentence in trollish.

The lead troll bellowed back. What sounded like an argument ensued. Humans surrounding the half-buried trolls readied their weapons.

Fjorn stood in front of the collapsed trench with Nose Crusher, Ragna and Audun.

Nose Crusher turned to Ragna and spoke in Sami.

Ragna rolled her eyes. "He wants to know why he should listen to a 'soft human'."

"Tell her to tell him that this human could kill him and his group before they got out of the snow." Fjorn's voice was sharp. Nose Crusher seemed to understand the tone. Her eyes went wide.

Ragna translated, then Nose Crusher spoke to the troll leader. The troll leader grunted something, then Nose-Crusher spoke to Ragna.

"Nose Crusher says it is too bad you have a Seithkona. She didn't know you could be soft and hard. Arm Ripper, the troll captain, says he will look at your proof if his trolls aren't harmed."

"Agreed," said Fjorn.

The message was relayed. The troll at the front of the line pushed through to the clear passage. Under torchlight, Fjorn laid out the counterfeit coin. Arm Ripper pulled a coin from his skatt bag, snapped it between his huge, calloused fingers, and then examined his own broken coin. The troll sneered, sending a shudder through everyone present. Turning to Fjorn, Arm Ripper spoke in halting Orse.

"You... no kill troll... anymore."

"For this fight, if you release the humans you took." Fjorn did his best to look the troll in the eye.

Arm Ripper pondered for a moment. "Me talk... chief back camp, no promise, bad sick there."

Fjorn smiled. "My Seithkona did that to your band so they wouldn't eat my people before we could reach you. I can have her take away the curse if you let the humans go."

Arm Ripper went pale and thumped his chest three times. "Powerful death witch. Chief, do listen. Wolf troll dead. Trolls human place dead, outside Nose Crusher. Stupid fight, pay fake. Chief listen. No good fighting strong punies."

"Then we have a truce until I can speak with your chieftain."

Arm Ripper looked confused. Ragna translated for Nose Crusher, who translated for Arm

Ripper, who grunted, spat in his enormous hand and held it out to Fjorn. Fjorn spat in his hand and locked grips with the troll. Fjorn's face went red as he gritted his teeth, but he didn't cry out. The troll let go and nodded before moving to dig out its comrades.

Fjorn walked back along the human passage until he was out of sight, then shoved his hand into the snow at the side of the trail.

Audun walked up behind him. "Broken?"

"I don't think so." Fjorn half-whispered. There were tears in his eyes.

"Good, you'll need it. Why didn't you tell him the whole plan?"

"He's a troop leader. He can't make that kind of decision. The chieftain is who I need to talk to. Now I have an introduction." Fjorn pulled his hand out of the snow. It was turning purple, but he could flex all his fingers.

"You're the Karl's son. How soon do we leave?"

"As soon as we can. I'm going to check on Vidurr."

There was the sound of a wolf howl.

"I think he's awake," observed Audun.

Fjorn softly sang a healing song as he moved up the trail to the fire. Vidurr, in his wolf form, was shaking himself. Water flew off his coat, hissing when it met the flames. Sigurlina stood on a cloak in her undercoat. Kjorn was helping her don her strap dress.

"Looks like the cloaks have shrunk from the wetting, but they'll do in a pinch." Kjorn took a little longer than he needed to drawing Sigurlina's hair up from the back of her dress. The old sailor let the loose strands flow through his fingers with a look of sad resolve.

Jolnir took his cloak from the drying rack, threw it over his shoulders and did up the jewelled c pin that marked his rank in the Jarl's guard.

"You're up. I'm glad," remarked Fjorn.

"Why are you bargaining with the trolls?" demanded Sigurlina.

"Because it is better to win a war than a battle," answered Fjorn in an even voice.

"They ate people." Sigurlina started putting on her boots.

"And they will eat more. It is the way of trolls. All I can do is try to keep them from eating our people. What they do to Aethelstan's troops will be their concern."

Vidurr looked up as his lips pulled back from his teeth. He shook again. Only a fine spray came from him. His fur puffed out in a thick, damp halo. He howled, and stood up, a naked man on the snow. Two steps, and he was standing on a cloak beside his dry clothing. Sigurlina's eyes scanned up and down the Ulfhednar's lean, wiry form.

Vidurr began to dress as images of his mutilated father filled his mind. "The trolls can feast on Crusaders. Crusaders have no honour. They are less than men."

"Aethelstan seems to be intent on taking a fort called Lax Bay. We found a map, and it seems to say that a huge force is closing on it. If I can prove to these trolls that they have been cheated, they may prove it to the others. Then as the attack starts, they can turn on Aethelstan's regular troops," explained Fjorn.

Vidurr smiled and grunted.

"Sigurlina, I may have given the impression that you cursed the trolls back at their camp. I'll need you to do something that will make them think you ended the curse," Fjorn continued.

"It wasn't a curse. It was mistletoe berries in pee." Sigurlina blushed.

"Maybe it would be better not to tell the trolls that you peed in their mead," suggested Audun.

Sigurlina chuckled and blushed. "I've, at least, done that much."

"You may have done a lot more than you think!" observed Fjorn. "Are you all up to walking?"

All three nodded.

In minutes Fjorn walked beside Arm Ripper along the trolls' trail at the front of the humans and trolls. It soon became apparent that the trolls had pushed through, leaving an unstable passage. Humans and trolls alike worked to clear snow and reinforce the passage's walls as they went. It was quicker going than cutting through virgin snow.

Sigurlina trudged behind Fjorn. Her legs ached, and she wanted nothing more than to sleep. The nap she'd had while her clothing dried had barely scratched the surface of her fatigue.

Munin circled overhead. She swooped down, landing on Ragna's hood.

"Siggy, if this black chicken lands on me one more time, it's a roasting spit!" Ragna tried to shoo the bird away.

"She likes you," commented Sigurlina.

'No I don't. She's a bitch,' commented Munin in Sigurlina's thoughts.

"It's one-sided," snapped Ragna.

Sigurlina rolled her eyes. "Why have you landed, Munin?"

'I saw the trolls' campfire. It looked like the guard troll was the only one awake, and there were no humans roasting.' Spoke the bird's mental voice.

Sigurlina considered her words. Her grandmother's voice seemed to whisper in the back of her mind. 'Much can be made of little if you play upon what others don't know. The ignorance of fools is a Seithkona's greatest power.'

"Fjorn, we near the trolls' encampment." She half shouted, then threw her arms up dramatically. "My ire is slacked, so ends my justice." She dropped her arms and addressed Arm Ripper. "I have lifted my curse. There will be lingering effects. If I am forced to cast the curse again; it will kill you all." Sigurlina spoke loudly and slowly for Arm Ripper's benefit.

The big troll watched slack-jawed. Sigurlina was pleased to see him swallow convulsively.

"Thank you, my lady. Preserve your strength for now," Fjorn replied.

Sigurlina watched a smile twitch at the corner of his mouth.

They came to where Sigurlina had dug the snow shelter and looked down at the trolls' camp. A lone guard stood by the fire. Dark, frozen puddles littered the ground. The humans still occupied their makeshift shelter. Stone-trolls were heaped in the centre of the flames.

"I show coin. You wait... Ready to run," instructed Arm Ripper.

"No run without people!" Fjorn patted his sword.

Arm Ripper gave Fjorn a gap-toothed smile and slapped him on the shoulder, making him lurch to the side.

"Hard, punie." Arm Ripper walked into the troll camp while Fjorn rubbed his shoulder.

"I'm confident you can survive being their enemy. I'm not so sure you'll survive being their friend," remarked Audun with a smirk.

"I'm not so sure about the friend part." Fjorn surveyed the surroundings. "I want a fire there." He pointed to the middle of the trail.

"That will melt the ice and flood the trail," cautioned Audun.

Fjorn smiled. "Yes. Once the fire is started, have our people find things that slide on ice and water. If the trolls charge...."

Audun looked down the slope into the trolls' camp and smiled. "Makes me almost hope they try it. It would be a sight." He left to order the humans on the trail.

Sigurlina pulled the brush away from the front of her snow shelter and climbed inside. Moments later, a slightly-damp, huge wolf slipped in beside her. The sounds of the humans and trolls gathering wood outside were almost soothing. Exhaustion pulled at her, and the air in the shelter warmed quickly. She plummeted into sleep.

The logs for the fire were set, and the centre of them lit. It would only be a matter of time before a steady stream of water washed down the slope into the trolls' camp. Light and warmth from the fire reflected off the fresh snow, reminiscent of the days when there were sun and moon.

Fjorn sat on a log and watched the slope. After a time, Arm Ripper walked up the slope accompanied by a massive troll who cradled its bulging stomach with one hand. Fjorn stood on the log, which brought him to the trolls' eye level. The trolls glowered at the growing fire, then looked to Fjorn.

The sickly troll spoke Orse with a thick accent. "Your Seithkona powerful. I not so sick since pup. I Eye Biter, chief fire river trolls. Aethelstan's mouth tells lies. We go back north. We keep this many humans for eating." Eye Biter held up eight fingers.

"No, you will release all the humans," Fjorn's voice stayed even and firm.

"Need humans or starve! This many humans or fight." Eye Biter raised five fingers.

Fjorn let his fingers touch the hilt of his sword. "There is a way you may have different things for eating, and the silver you were promised."

Eye Biter set his club on the ground like a cane and leaned on it, clutching his belly with his free hand. "I listen." Eye Biter's beady eyes went wide. "Soon!" The big troll lumbered into the woods knocking over several medium-sized, dead trees in its haste. A moment later, a horrible groaning sound echoed off the snow-covered landscape.

Arm Ripper looked at Fjorn and shook his head. "You mate gold-hair Seithkona. Brave, stupid, not sure."

Fjorn shrugged. "I try to keep her happy."

"You better!" Arm Ripper nodded emphatically.

Eye Biter lumbered out of the woods, looking haggard. "How get food, go home?"

Fjorn smiled. "You and the other bands have all been cheated by the mouths of Aethelstan. In a battle, you have to trust the troops you think are on your side. That will make Aethelstan's troops easy prey. There is no shame in betraying one who seeks to cheat you first."

Many explanations later, Fjorn once more had his hand thrust into a snowdrift and was murmuring the words of a healing song.

Gaut led his people into the troll camp as Eye Biter threw a sack containing cloaks, shoes, and socks into the makeshift prison that held the captured humans. Moments later, Gaut's people helped the captives back to the human's fire. Several had to be carried, and two were dead from the cold.

The fire on the trail that the humans had set still burned, but much of the wood had been pulled away so it wouldn't get out of control. The air warmed around the blaze, and soon the ground was littered with humans.

Gaut knelt, clutching a teenaged man's hand. The teenager spoke softly. Gaut stood and moved to Fjorn.

"Thank you for this. We...Well--."

"Get your people home. You are their leader. That is your first responsibility." Fjorn gripped the other man's shoulder.

Gaut smiled. "I don't think it would be good for us to be around trolls right now. With all you've done, I hate to ask for more, but many of my people have frozen feet or fingers. They can't walk, and we can't carry all of them."

"I'll ask her. Can you think of why Aethelstan would want to invade you and Lax Bay?"

Gaut looked surprised. "For us, I'm thinking we were a supply stop, not more 'en that. Lax Bay, it doesn't take much to see it. If Wessex takes control of the Humber, Aethelstan can cut Jorvik off from the sea."

Fjorn startled. "Are you saying that the Humber still flows? I thought they just moved Jorvik when the rivers froze?"

Gaut laid a finger beside his nose. "Not all rivers froze, Karl's son. Leastways, not on the Great Island. The Ouse still feeds the Humber. It's said that King Cuaran has traded favours with some of them Celtic Godi. What you call 'em?"

Fjorn thought. "Druids."

"Right you are. In any case, they keep the river flowing, so Jorvik don't die for lack of it."

"It makes sense now. If Aethelstan can block the Humber, he will have as good as won the war for Northumbria."

"Aye."

80

"Gaut, when you go back to your village, I want to send some of my people with you to bring my ship to Lax Bay." Fjorn closed his eyes in thought.

"Well, and good. There's some of mine who'd be liking a turn with Aethelstan's men. They're none too fond of trolls, as you can imagine, but they know who really did our village and want a piece of him."

"One for one."

The two leaders shook hands then Fjorn moved to a nondescript hole in the trail's side. Inside, Sigurlina slept curled up with Vidurr in wolf form. A wave of jealousy swept through Fjorn that he forced down. He gently shook Sigurlina's shoulder. Her eyes snapped open as her hand strayed for her dagger before she was fully awake. Her scowl turned to a smile as she saw Fjorn's face.

"Are the trolls attacking?"

"They've agreed to my plan. The prisoners are by the fire. Several of them might lose fingers or feet if they don't get help."

Sigurlina nodded. "When we reach a place with a good inn, I want to sleep in a private room until I can't sleep anymore and wake up to warm mead and roasted meats."

"I'll be right there with you." Fjorn smiled.

"I'd like that." She pulled him half into the shelter and kissed him before crawling out. Vidurr opened one eye, looked at her, then scuffed around and went back to sleep.

"Is he?" began Fjorn.

"The three of us didn't get much sleep and got chilled. It takes a toll. We'll be alright in time." Sigurlina moved to the liberated prisoners. Kneeling by a man whose fingers were black, she laid her hands on him, closed her eyes, and chanted softly. A thin dew fell on the man, and the black fingers turned pink. Sigurlina moved on to the next injured person as the first one dried by the fire.

Later she sipped at a bowl of hot broth and watched as Gaut led his people towards their village. Most of the ex-prisoners walked. Three were on makeshift stretchers. The dead lay on pyres that still burnt around the human camp. Audun, Jolnir and the Apenhet's oarsmen walked with the villagers.

"I don't like it," grumbled Kjorn.

Sigurlina turned to look at the old sailor. "What?"

"Them larking off." He pointed to the villagers. "If them trolls turn on us, we'll need every sword we can find. And I don't like losing Audun's axe and Jolnir's sword at me side." Kjorn shook his head.

Sigurlina sipped her broth. "The villagers had to take their injured home, and someone needs to fetch the Apenhet now that we know the river is open."

"Aye, I know. I still don't have to like it. You no can trust a troll."

Sigurlina chuckled, then finished her broth.

"What's funny?" Kjorn relished the young woman's smile.

"Do you think I trust them? I've watched them for two days. The best I can say is they look after their own."

Kjorn stroked his beard. "Aye, we'll both keep an eye on them."

"Trust me, Kjorn, Vidurr, Ragna, and Fjorn, whether you believe it or not, will be watching as hard as us. Fjorn is doing what he thinks he has to, but he is no fool."

"Aye. His choice in women would tell anyone that."

Sigurlina blushed and gently kissed the old sailor's cheek.

"There you are." Fjorn walked up to them. "Those that stayed back are making a shelter. We all need some rest. The trolls that didn't 'fall under the curse' are digging the trail forward. Eye Biter says it should be one sleep and one waking before we reach Lax Bay. A sleep after that before the other groups arrive for the siege. Eye Biter has told me that a 'slimy man' is supposed to open the gate when they give the signal."

#

Sigurlina walked through the trolls' camp. The stench was incredible, and she had to be careful where she stepped. The six trolls that had killed each other during the mistletoe's effect were laid side by side at the edge of the camp. Each had a club in its hand but had otherwise been looted by their fellows.

"You do?" grunted a deep voice behind her.

Sigurlina spun around to find herself staring into the chest of a troll. She stepped back so she could look the troll in the eye.

"You do?" repeated the troll pointing at the bodies.

"I cast the curse. They," she pointed to the bodies, "did the killing."

The troll stood silent, then knelt and caressed the brow of the corpse on the end. "Bone Snapper, mother."

"I'm sorry," Sigurlina spoke, not knowing what else to say.

"Why?"

Sigurlina pointed to the human's fire. "Humans mine. Mothers, fathers, sisters, brothers, sons, daughters."

"Food yours." The troll nodded. "Mother mine." It sighed. "Want home. Tired! Middle place not home. Jotunheim home. Big ice. Middle place too hot. Always sweat. Good for punies. Mother said come." The troll began to weep.

Sigurlina tentatively reached out and touched the troll's shoulder. The big body shook, and a deep rumble of sorrow escaped it. The huge hand clenched into a fist. Sigurlina backed away. The fist slammed into the mouth of the corpse. The troll reached into its mother's mouth and pulled out a canine tooth. Turning, it held the tooth out to Sigurlina. "Take."

Sigurlina took the tooth.

"Remember." The troll walked away.

Sigurlina looked at the tooth in silence. "Did you tear the flesh from someone's mother? Did you kill for money? I will remember. I will remember it all! And I won't need a tooth to do so, but my Queen may have a use for this." She slipped the tooth into her belt pouch and left the bodies behind.

#

Fjorn waited with Arm Ripper as the trolls' fire burnt down. The human fire on the slope above still burnt brightly, a beacon in the cold and dark.

"Where are you from?" asked Fjorn.

"North," grunted Arm Ripper. "You special man you tribe?"

Fjorn considered. "Karls' son….Chief's son, and captain… hunt-party leader."

Nose Crusher released a sigh and eyed Fjorn.

Arm Ripper pointed at himself. "Chief's son, third wife mother." He made a dismissive wave of his hand. "Too much tell. Too much never right. Too much stupid troll. Come middle place be free."

"Came to Midgard to get away from your title. I wonder if they have any need for a bard in Alfgard." Fjorn pocked at the snow.

Arm Ripper nodded and grunted.

"Before the middle place where?" Fjorn stared into the fire.

Arm Ripper made a gesture to include the troll camp. "Jotunheim. M-m-m . Bigger than fingers tribes, extra trolls come when Skoll eat sun. Good time for trolls."

"Bad time for humans," remarked Fjorn.

Arm Ripper nodded. "See that." He smiled. "Good for trolls."

The conversation was interrupted by one of the stone trolls in the fire waving an arm. Arm Ripper grabbed the appendage by the wrist and dragged the troll out of the fire. It stayed stone as it melted a hole in the compacted ice, then it opened its eyes.

Arm Ripper spoke to the partially revived troll, hoisted it up and threw it in a snowbank.

"Make cold." Arm Ripper settled to wait for the next troll to cool down enough to touch.

CHAPTER 8: CALL OF THE DEAD

Audun lay by the fire in the village. The prisoners had been reunited with their loved ones, and the faint hopes of too many dashed. The quiet sound of sobbing was the song of the village. Daldis moved amongst the people. She would perform her rites after all those who went to rescue the prisoners had slept. Audun knew that her duties reached further than ritual. She gave comfort when no other could. She reached into the darkness of despair and reminded the living that they yet lived.

Gaut sat beside him. "It's a sad lookout."

"At least you have Daldis." Auden stared into the fire.

"I suppose it makes it easier." Gaut picked up a stick and poked the logs sending sparks into the air. "My gran always scolded me for doing that when I was a lad. I guess there are some advantages to being the head man."

An elderly woman shuffled over and glowered at Gaut. "Stop poking it. Do you want to set the thatch on fire? Honestly, men, you never grow up!"

Auden snorted with laughter.

"Or maybe not." Gaut put the stick down.

"Daldis does make it better. My mother's parents died when she was not more than eight summers. Our village's Angel of Death took her in. She was my gran for all the things that matter. I remember how she'd speak to people. She served Lady Hel all the years of my life. She made the best honey cakes. I'd try to make port just to get a taste. People don't see death as they should. They see it as something to fear, not just another voyage. My gran taught me that as she taught me my letters. That and other things." Audun closed his eyes and dozed where he sat.

"You're leaving after a sleep?" asked Gaut.

"After a long sleep. It will take Fjorn days to reach Lax Bay. There's time for it. I need rest. There are things happening, and we're in the middle of them." Audun lay back wrapped in his cloak and was lost to the world.

"At least someone I trust is." Gaut grabbed a blanket and put it over Audun's feet, where they stuck out under his cloak.

#

Fjorn led the humans across the abandoned trolls' camp onto the new trail cut through the snow. Eye Biter's trolls had risen, mostly recovered from the poisoning, and moved ahead on the trail to reinforce the healthy trolls that had begun the excavation while the humans slept.

"It be a good thing that the trolls are ahead of us. I've heard grumbling from the villagers. There are those who'd like to settle the score. A sleeping troll doesn't seem such a problem to an angry man," observed Kjorn.

"Part of why I insisted we sleep the night." As Fjorn spoke, part of the trail left by the trolls collapsed.

"We'll have to shore things up unless we want our retreat cut off," Kjorn kicked at a clump of snow.

"It will keep us from overtaking the trolls before we reach Lax Bay. Probably for the best." Fjorn turned to the rest of his band. "Shovels to the fore. I want a clear path back in case our new friends change their minds."

Humans with spades stepped forward and cut into the loosened snow of the Troll's trail clearing the debris and reinforcing the way. After the better part of a day, the trail's surface shifted from compacted snow to sheet ice.

"We be moving on apace. From the map, I'm guessing this is the upper Hull River. Flow must of shifted with the earth shakes when the skies went dark." Kjorn strode forward at Fjorn's left.

"We can thank the trolls for the ground we're covering. Say what you will. They can dig even if they are sloppy about it." Fjorn looked at a brown pile in the middle of the path. "Though there are disadvantages to following them. Is it getting colder?"

Sigurlina shuddered and looked distracted as she walked at Fjorn's right. "Can we move faster?"

"Are you alright?" Fjorn looked at her.

Sigurlina moved close and whispered. "There was a village near here. The people died when the river flooded. There was no one to do angel of death duties. They are everywhere. They all want to get in. Fjorn, they're so cold. Men, women, children. A little girl is clutching a doll, sobbing for her mother. It's so much death and so little life." Sigurlina shivered.

Fjorn opened his cloak and pulled her to his side. She released a sob as she wrapped her arms around him.

Munin swept down, landing on Fjorn's head. 'I'm here. I'm here.' Sigurlina heard her familiar's mental voice.

"Munin, help me."

Under the shelter of her cloak, Sigurlina pulled a rainbow-hued ring from her belt pouch and slipped it on. Her thoughts focused. She began to push back against the tide of the dead that assailed her. Reaching back into her pouch, she clutched the stones that were her grandmother's parting gift.

Unseen, and barely felt by the others, spirits clustered around the Seithkona. A soaking wet man holding a splitting axe hovered in front of Fjorn, barely avoiding being stepped through. 'Help me build a barricade.' A woman with water frothing from her mouth as she desperately tried to talk appeared to Sigurlina's right. Dogs, cats, horses, cows, all the inhabitants of a barnyard swarmed around the trail. Sigurlina froze, staring ahead. A woman of late-middle years with sharp features wearing an expensive dress and amber jewellery stood in front of her.

"Sister," spoke the woman.

Sigurlina froze.

"I'll take that." The spectre charged.

Sigurlina mustered her defences and roared a single command. "BE GONE!"

The spectre shuddered and paused in its advance.

"Sigurlina?" asked Fjorn as she moved away from him and took a fighting stance.

"Impressive child, but you are still just a child. You cannot win. Surrender your body, and it will hurt less. I promise to take good care of that handsome man on your arm." The spectre spoke in almost mothering tones.

"It's a spirit. I think she was Seithkona. She wants to take my body."

"Will take your body, little sister. I have been waiting three years for this." The spirit charged again.

"BE GONE!" Sigurlina slammed the spirit once more. While she was doing this, the spirit of the drowning woman dove into her from behind.

Sigurlina's body took a deep, shuddering breath.

"Everyone needs an apprentice once you reach a certain age," commented the spectre.

Sigurlina focused her battle inward as the drowning woman tried to seize more control of her body. Arguments flashed, bits of memory were thrown between Sigurlina and the other spirit like weapons. Remembered sorrow became a sword that could wound the mind. Joy became a shield that would turn a blow. Sigurlina bargained, letting the other spirit sift through her memories in exchange for control of her mouth and tongue. "Fjorn, get me out of here. Hurry!"

The other spectre rushed forward, invading Sigurlina's body. Sigurlina was vaguely aware of her body being picked up and the jolt of someone running.

\#

"BE GONE!" Sigurlina spoke the words, then stiffened and convulsed.

Fjorn knelt beside her as the rest of the party crowded in.

Sigurlina gasped and shouted, "Fjorn, get me out of here. Hurry!"

Fjorn lifted her slender form and bolted along the trail. The others fell in behind. Vidurr appeared at Fjorn's side carrying one of their torches, and the two sprinted over the ice. The shattered remains of a village came into view. It had an earthen embankment around it that only the top of could be seen. Ice had enveloped the rest. The frozen roofs of various buildings and a great hall could be seen through its broken gate. The ice had filled in around the buildings to a depth where one would have to crawl on their belly to pass through the doorways.

The men kept running as Sigurlina screeched and gibbered in Fjorn's arms.

\#

It was like a battle against two swordsmen. Sigurlina held the staff of her will before her and strove to block blows that were, in fact, blasts of spiritual energy. It was taking all her concentration to defend. Then there was a light.

"This doesn't seem fair. Two against one."

Sigurlina felt her heart surge. "Grandmother," she whispered.

"Hello, dear." The image of an elegant woman of maybe thirty with long, blond hair that was a match to Sigurlina's own appeared at her right. The newcomer was clad in a golden-coloured robe and held an oaken staff.

"GO AWAY, THIS IS MY PLACE!" screeched the senior of the two spectres.

"I cannot believe your lack of manners. I am Inga, daughter of Asdis of the line of Jarl Ingvarr. In life, I walked the shadow road. The one you have attacked is my granddaughter and apprentice." Inga spoke with strained politeness, then her tone became threatening. "By what name, and by what right, do you seek to steal the form my kin calls her own?"

The older looking of the spectres seemed taken aback, then donned a haughty expression. "I am Frida, high mistress of the shadow road of the lineage of Anina, the dark spirit queen, handmaiden of Laufey. I seek this form by right of power."

Inga sighed and shook her head. "Then why do you attack with another. In a test of wills, it is quite clear. Would you face my granddaughter singly? Would you dare?"

"Grandmother--," began Sigurlina.

Inga raised a hand, cutting her off. "Would you?"

The senior spectre sneered. "Brina, leave this form. I will find a body for you to inhabit once I have crushed this upstart."

The younger-looking spectre bowed her head and vanished.

"Would you care to make your peace with Freya before we begin, child?" taunted Frida.

"Grandmother, I ca..." began Sigurlina.

"This is your fight, my dear. Remember what I always said about people who took titles to themselves. You will make me proud." Inga vanished.

#

Fjorn felt his chest burning, and his legs ached from running. The ice gave way under his foot, and he started to trip. Vidurr caught Fjorn one-handed and hauled him to his feet.

Sigurlina lay still, then her eyes opened. She stared up at Fjorn. "You can put me down."

Fjorn almost dropped her from the shock. "Sigurlina?"

"Not exactly," she sighed. So romantic being carried in a handsome man's arms again. "Sigurlina is a little busy. She should be along shortly. You must be tired of carrying us." Sigurlina's eyes shifted to look at the ground.

Fjorn set her down.

She brushed her dress straight and started walking. There was a subtle swing in her hips that wasn't Sigurlina. It riveted both men's gaze to her buttocks. She glanced back, "Coming?"

Fjorn and Vidurr looked at each other, then rushed to flank Sigurlina's form. "Who?"

"Have you forgotten already? I'm hurt." Sigurlina's finger trailed flirtatiously over Fjorn's chest as she shot him a smouldering look.

"You're Inga, Sigurlina's grandmother," gasped Fjorn.

"Smart and handsome. My girl is a lucky little minx. Though you should get on with it.

She is seventeen. Pretty soon, people will be calling her an old maid. And I'll tell you one thing, young Karl; no woman of my line has ever been an old maid."

"Sigurlina is sixteen." Fjorn focused on the inconsequentiality to ground himself in the strangeness.

Inga smiled. "Or so she thinks. My daughter was a touch reckless in her youth. She ran away with a sailor and came home months later with a black eye and Sigurlina in her arms. Birger had loved my girl since they were children. He took her on, babe and all. We let Sigurlina think he was her father. Truth to tell, he loved her as much as any father could, so it made no difference. Telling her that she was a year younger than she was helped the town and her believe it. None of us wanted her hunting out the fool that sired her after what he did."

"Why are you here?" demanded Vidurr.

Inga's expression became dark. "Because I will defend my kin. That hussy wants a new body, and she is arrogant enough to think she can steal from my lineage? I think she is learning what it is to challenge one of the line of Ingvarr. Honestly, I would have let Sigurlina deal with it herself, except for Frida involving her apprentice. Apprentice, if the woman had any gumption, she would have been off on her own years ago. That, and Frida being in her place of power, is just too much. It would be like entering into an honour duel and having your opponent bring his whole family armed to the teeth. There's no telling how many spirits that woman has ready to draw into her fight. My girl is stronger than she thinks, but there is reason in all things. Please tell her I said that when she comes back. She needs to know she can win her own battles."

They came to the edge of the flooded, frozen river, and Sigurlina's form stepped onto the hard-packed snow of the trolls' trail and stopped. "Never thought much of trolls, of course. I never had to deal with them before Fimbulwinter. I hear they have really small...."

Inga looked at the two men who stared at her. "Oh, the trollop's powers taper off away from the village. The edge of the flood marks the edge of where she has any special advantage. It was bad luck, and maybe some nudging by Frida, that the trolls came so close to the village. We can wait here for the rest of your party to catch up."

#

Sigurlina let her power flow. Frida was more experienced, but she was also dead. The dead were subject to the living in Midgard. The wave of emotional energy Sigurlina projected hit the spectre. Frida turned part of it away, but the force still drove her back.

Frida sent a blast of emotion towards Sigurlina, who sidestepped it.

Reaching within, Sigurlina touched her pain and sadness: her mother and father slain in a treacherous Crusader attack; the lonely years living in a barrow with only the dead and her grandmother for company; her grandmother's death. She sent the pain into the spectre.

Frida felt the blast of negative emotion. The pain was crippling. Everyone had loss, but this? She sought out her mother's death, but she had cared little for the woman. Her betrothed desertion, more anger than sorrow. How could he leave her? She was more than he would ever deserve. Her remorse at her own death. It had been hard, but she'd cared little for the living around her and most followed her into death as Ragnarok shook the land.

Sigurlina gathered her will and emotion: the sorrow of separation; the fear of losing those she came to love. She let fly with the emotion driving back Frida. Sigurlina could feel the connections between her body and mind and sensed that they were in friendly, if flirtatious, hands.

"Grandmother, if you take him before I do, I swear we are going to have words!"

Sigurlina reached inside. The joy of being held by Fjorn; the peace in the snow shelter with Vidurr's warm fur against her; Ragna's laugh; Audun's quiet strength; her mother teaching her how to make bread; the warmth and love of her parents in the time before the Crusaders. These became a shield that turned the feeble attacks of her opponent.

Sigurlina's mind opened. To know joy, you had to know sorrow. They were like life and death, like all things. The cycle was all. Wheels within wheels, turning. Yggdrasil would burn, but from the root, new life would spring. Those she loved would die, but in their living, they would be a source of joy and life.

Frida felt her hold on Sigurlina slipping. The blasts of sorrow had left the spectre dazed. How anyone could survive the pain. Desperately she reached for power and found there was none. She called to the spirits of those that died in her village, but they didn't come. The body she sought to take was outside her domain.

Sigurlina looked at the fading spectre and shook her head. "I pity you." With a thrust of will, she pushed the spectre out of her mortal form.

"Grandmother, you better not be doing what I think you're doing," snapped Sigurlina.

#

"Oh... She is a clever one." Inga stretched like a cat.

"Is she alright?" asked Fjorn.

"She's learning. Of course, I'm sure between you and Ragna, there are many things she could learn." Inga ran a finger along Fjorn's throat. "It is a pity I'm not sixty years younger."

Vidurr stared at the ground. Inga saw him out of the corner of Sigurlina's eye and left Fjorn. She stepped over to Vidurr and cupped the Ulfhednar's cheek. "It gets better, my wolfen friend. There is little I can say, but open your eyes and ears. Things may not be as black as they seem."

Vidurr looked up and saw nothing of flirtation in Sigurlina's form. What he saw was compassion and understanding, so much like his friend's that he could barely tell them apart. "For the moment, dear wolf, remember. Death is but a season. Do not begrudge the winter. Without it, there would be no spring." Inga pulled Vidurr into a hug.

Tears fell from Vidurr's eyes. When the hug broke, he saw Sigurlina gazing back at him. "From both of us, the seasons always change, even in Ragnarok."

Vidurr nodded.

Sigurlina released her friend, then turned and found herself caught up in her beloved's arms.

"Inga wanted me to tell you that she always knew you'd win. It's just that a mob against one wasn't fair." Fjorn kissed Sigurlina. "She also said we should get on with it before you became an old maid." He grinned rakishly.

"My gran would." Sigurlina smiled, shook her head, then kissed Fjorn. "But for now, we should build a fire. Your tunic is sweat-soaked."

The fire was barely kindled when the rest of the troop stepped off the river ice.

"What happened?" demanded Ragna by way of greeting.

"Two powerful spirits wanted my body," Sigurlina turned to face Fjorn and smiled, "And not in a fun way."

"Really, now? Are you safe? Are the spirits still here?" Ragna looked like a squirrel scolding someone who'd disturbed its lunch.

"Inga says hello." Sigurlina smiled sadly. "It would have been nice to visit longer." She sighed and held her hands out to the growing fire. "We should have something to eat while Fjorn and Vidurr dry their clothing."

Vidurr stood further up the trail, looking at a discoloured heap. "The trolls are close. Maybe an hour ahead of us."

"Then we'll make camp here and let them get further ahead," said Fjorn.

Kjorn moved to Sigurlina's side. "You were right, lass. I should have trusted him from the start."

Sigurlina smiled at the old sailor. "Just think of who trained him."

#

Audun manned the tiller oar of the Apenhet. Floating the boat and reloading the cargo had taken longer than he'd expected. The lack of tides since the moon had been devoured had made the process all the harder, but they were finally away. The coast of Northumbria sped by as a south-east wind drove them along. All six oarsmen and Obasi rowed on the starboard, countering the eastern airflow, driving them forward. Jolnir sat the ice watch.

"Light, port forward," called Jolnir's voice.

Audun strained to see in the dark. A fire blazed on a spit of land that partially blocked the entrance to the Humber River.

"Ship oars," bellowed Audun.

The oarsmen brought their oars aboard and sat watching the fire that marked the entrance to the river.

"Lights forward starboard." Jolnir's voice held concern.

Audun gazed into the dark. Like dim stars, he could make out lights in the distance. "Freya's tits," he spat. "Svafnir, take the ice watch. Balance the oar stations. Jolnir, get back here."

Jolnir moved from the bow as one of the oarsmen took his place. The other oarsmen and Obasi shifted, so they manned an equal number of oars on both sides of the ship.

"Are you thinking what I'm thinking?" Jolnir sat by Audun at the stern.

"Those lights." Audun gestured forward. "Could be nothing, could be an invasion fleet. Either way, I want to stay ahead of them."

"That won't be easy if they turn up the Humber. We need more oars in the water," Jolnir eyed the oarsmen.

"The Humber is a trickster." Audun smiled. "There were shoals and shallows before Fimbulwinter. What it holds now is the Allfather's guess. The Apenhet has a shallow draft. Add to that we're running light, and I know a few tricks."

"I'm glad you do. How long to Lax Bay?"

"A day's travel, more or less. It depends on the current and the wind." Audun stroked his beard. "I wanted to drop anchor when we reached fresh water and rest the men, but if that fleet turns up the river, that will be out."

Audun pushed hard on the tiller oar, cutting around the fire on the end of the spit of land that marked the mouth of the Humber. "Take your oar station."

Jolnir followed the order.

Audun glanced at the distant lights and nodded. "You want to race. We'll race, and Nidhogg take the loser. READY OARS."

The oars were extended and hung over the water.

"Stroke," ordered Audun.

The Apenhet made its way up the Humber.

#

Vidurr raced through the dead forest, paralleling the path of the trolls' trail. Munin flew above. They watched over each other.

Munin cawed and swept down to land on his back. "Yura bitch, Yura bitch," spoke the bird.

Vidurr wondered why humans had problems understanding the raven's meaning. He slowed and crept forward. A crowd of trolls stood on the trail holding torches. Others dug shelter holes into the snow on either side. Several trees had been suspended as deadfalls over the trail. The ambush was nearly prepared.

Vidurr crept closer and watched as a troll placed blocks of snow over the mouth of a snow shelter containing an armed troll. When the troll finished, it swept snow over the opening to complete the disguise.

Minutes later, the trolls that weren't concealed ran along the trail towards Lax Bay.

Vidurr growled. Munin flew towards the light of the human's fire. Vidurr cocked a leg against a tree and marked the spot, then ran back to the human camp.

#

Audun took a turn on an oar as Svafnir manned the tiller, and Jolnir stood the ice watch. Audun pulled with the steady rhythm of the other oarsmen and took the opportunity to think. The Humber's current was almost non-existent, and the inlet's water was still salt. Svafnir kept them to the south, middle of the passage and away from the silt flats that dotted the northern shore. By putting more oarsmen to starboard than port Audun had compensated for the wind direction and was still running sail.

"Ice forward port," called Jolnir.

"Ice forward port, aye," called back Svafnir, and the ship shifted slightly.

"Bloody stupid running from a bunch of merchants," muttered Obasi.

Audun pretended not to hear him.

"Pause," called Audun.

The oars went up and waited.

Audun called, "Shipping Oar." He drew his oar aboard before standing. "Resume stroke." The oarsmen resumed their steady rhythm.

Audun moved to the stern of the Apenhet and looked back. A collection of dim lights littered the river behind them. He scanned the northern coast. Forward of them, he saw light. "Steer starboard towards that light."

"But... Begging your pardon. I've sailed the Humber when there were sun and moon. There are mudflats up that way," objected Svafnir.

"Good man to know it and share it, but that's what I'm counting on. Our friends back there seem to be following our lights. If they are friendly, grounding in mud won't do nought but make for a longer trip. If they are Crusaders, it will cost them time that we can use. I'll drop a line to gauge the depth." Audun moved to the bow where Jolnir huddled in his cloak, shivering. "Take an oar. It will warm you."

Jolnir nodded. Moments later, the ritual of adding an oar was finished. Audun had used the time to tie a weight to a rope. He threw it over the side and measured a span of rope before the weight caught and dragged. He pulled the rope in, then dropped the weight again.

"Hand shorter," he whispered, then repeated the process.

What seemed a long time later, Audun dropped the weight and found it sank half a fathom. He pulled down the bow lantern and shuttered it, so no light escaped. Moving back on the ship, he doused the two midship's torches, then the stern lantern. "Steer port; get some water under our keel."

"What's this now?" demanded Obasi in a loud voice.

"Quiet. Just row and not a word," Audun hissed in a harsh whisper. He then went forward and manned the ice watch.

The Apenhet moved into deeper water. Audun reached down, dipped his finger in the flow and tasted it. The salt taste was fading but judging how far up the river they were, it told him that the flow was slow. The wind still blew southwest. He gazed into the dark.

Time passed. The lights behind them angled towards the light onshore then they stopped. If he listened carefully, Auden fancied he could hear angry voices that sounded like Anglic.

CHAPTER 9: TROUBLE WILL FIND YOU

Fjorn crept behind Vidurr, who was in his wolf form. The cold and dark of Fimbulwinter surrounded them. They had only a single candle lantern lit, and it was shrouded.

'They closed up the hole with snow blocks. I always thought a shelter made of ice would be cold, but the one you made was really warm, and it was nice to snuggle into Vidurr's fur. I always thought men looked good with a hairy chest, but he does carry it a little far.' Sigurlina absently petted Munin under her cloak as she half-listened to the raven's mental babble. Of all the people in their group, she was the one that would have appreciated silence the most, and she was the one that couldn't get a moment's peace. Vidurr, at the head of the group, at least didn't have a stream of chatter in his mind.

Everything went dark. Sigurlina was used to the dark of Fimbulwinter, but this was different. All light was extinguished.

"What?" she heard Fjorn's voice.

"Whose hand is that?" snapped Ragna in a harsh whisper.

"I, uggghhh. That wasn't funny," snarled one of the villagers. "Surt's flaming nuts, that throbs."

A child-like laugh sounded in the dark.

Something pinched Sigurlina's buttocks, then slapped her other cheek.

"Take your hands off me," snapped Ragna.

"Ow, weren't me, so watch where you're slapping, girl."

There came the child-like laugh again. "It's over there," remarked Ragna.

There was the crunch of snowshoes and a squeal and a splat.

"Where, it's as dark as Svartalfheim. I'll, arrrgh!" one of the villagers cried out, followed by the sound of a body falling into snow.

"Get off me," complained Ragna.

"Everyone follow my voice. If we can get out of this dark, we might see what's attacking us," called Fjorn.

Vidurr growled, then yipped. The party took a few steps then there was the sound of bodies falling to the snow amidst a series of "umps" and complaints. Again, the high-pitched laughter.

"What is this thing? Where is this thing?" demanded Fjorn.

Sigurlina closed her eyes, since vision was a useless sense, and remembered back. They had been in Diwon's house in Orkney. It had been a game. Blindfolded, then spun around; she had had to seek out the old man and wrap a ribbon around his neck. Ragna had laughed to see her stumbling around, bumping into things.

"My little Seith, you have more than eyes. See with your ears. They'll tell you true when your eyes lie or fail. Now come and get me," Diwon had taught her.

At first, she'd always failed, but with practice, she'd learned to listen for the scrape of his boots on the ground and the soft sound when he brushed against something. She'd even learned to ignore Ragna's voice and laughter as they played the game.

She gave herself to listening. There was a buzzing sound. Something groped her then darted away; the buzz got louder then softer.

"What the, oomph," commented Fjorn's voice.

"Get your foot out of my," snapped a voice.

"That's mine, and if you want to keep that hand, you'll move it," growled Ragna.

"Ow, you're standing on my leg," snipped another person.

"That's my hair," snarled yet another voice.

Vidurr stood in the black as the humans fell over themselves. He didn't know what was attacking them, but he knew the smells of his companions. There was an odd smell, sharp like sweat mixed with smoke from a driftwood fire. He waited as the scent grew stronger.

Sigurlina froze listening. The buzzing sound drew nearer. She could almost see it in her mind. It came closer. She swung her staff, clipping the creature. The impact felt like she was hitting fabric.

Vidurr snarled. There was the sound of him leaping, then a high-pitched scream. Sigurlina moved to the scream, bumping into the big wolf and following his body to his jaws. There she found a being no bigger than a toddler.

"Let me go!" demanded a high voice.

"Make the darkness go away," demanded Sigurlina.

The darkness vanished, replaced by the gloom of Fimbulwinter.

Through the shadows, Sigurlina could see Ragna and the villagers disentangling themselves from a heap in the snow. It looked like several of them had tripped over a buried branch. Fjorn stood forward, cupping himself one-handed while holding the lantern in his free hand. The small creature was held in Vidurr's jaws, and its shoulder was clutched in Sigurlina's hand. It looked like a small man with rust-coloured hair and jet-black eyes. He had grey and black wings that seemed to trail off into smoke and was dressed in fine-looking trews.

"Why did you attack us?" demanded Sigurlina.

"It seemed like fun. I don't get many visitors, you see. The trolls that came by yesterday weren't any amusement at all. They have no sense of humour. No appreciation for a good joke. Can you believe it? They threatened to kill me. I mean, really, I ask you?" The small figure spoke in a refined, if high-pitched, voice.

Vidurr growled.

"Please, madam, if you could discourage your wolf from eating me. I don't see why you're so aggressive. It was only a small joke. No one died. Just a little bit of fun. If you let me up, I promise to take no further action against your party."

Fjorn moved behind Sigurlina and un-shuttered the candle lantern. "Vidurr, please let him up, but be ready to bite his head off if anything strange happens."

Vidurr growled, then opened his jaws. Sigurlina helped set the small being on its feet and knelt in the snow so she could keep a hand on its shoulder.

"Well, my dear, the hands of a beautiful maid are an improvement over the mouth of a wolf." The small figure smiled.

"What are you?" demanded Fjorn.

"I'm a what now, am I? You mortals, no sense of humour, and you're rude." The creature made expressive gestures with its hands as it spoke.

"My apologies if the form of our introduction has left me lacking in manners. If I may, who and what are you?" countered Fjorn.

The small figure sniffed and inclined its head in a cultured acknowledgement. "Better. I'm Squee Squee Swikil, second son of Quee Squee Swikil Karl of the Shadow Mountains of Svartalfheim." The creature's voice was high-pitched enough to make the humans wince. "And I am a Skui."

"Like the one that helped us fire the port in Winchester?" asked Sigurlina.

"Please," Squee Squee Swikil made an elegant dismissive gesture with its free hand. "Those fire types are poor cousins at best. They completely lack breeding and are braggarts to boot. They're always going on about the things they burn. You may not believe this, but I met one who tried to take credit for the burning of Rome. Anybody who studies knows that Nero did that to make space for his palace.

"Say what you will about Nero. You can't deny that the man had a flair for the dramatic. I caught his performance in the Coliseum some years ago. He could never handle his props. My greasing his mask handle simply made the probable, inevitable. It was a good night. His reaction was the essence of a subtle act escalating into a magnificent joke. A few drops of oil and an emperor kills his empress. That is what a joke should be."

Fjorn cleared his throat.

Squee Squee Swikil looked at the young captain and sighed. "Oh, yes, of course. In short, I am a Shadow Skui, born and raised in Svartalfheim. May I ask to whom I speak, though judging from your attire, I must say, I am not expecting much."

Fjorn smiled and stood straighter, then bowed. "I am Fjorn, Hakon's bane, heir apparent to the Karl's seat of the Orkney Islands, distaff claimant to the throne of Norveig, Captain of the Apenhet, a longship in the fleet of Jarl Erik Bloodaxe, at your service."

"Oh! My Lord, it is such a pleasure to make your acquaintance. Had I known you were a man of breeding, I would never have assailed you with such an obvious trick." Squee Squee Swikil bowed as best he could with Sigurlina clutching his shoulder.

"Can I kick it?" asked Ragna, who had joined the group surrounding the Skui.

"Really," Squee Squee Swikil rolled his eyes.

Fjorn continued, indicating Sigurlina, "This is my betrothed, Lady Sigurlina shadow walker, dear as sister to Gunnhild Queen of Norveig. And these are the members of my house." Fjorn gestured to encompass the party.

"An honour, to be sure." Squee Squee Swikil bowed again.

"If you will grant us safe passage, we will be going. We can leave this incident behind us and part as friends." Fjorn smiled as his hand strayed to casually caress the hilt of his dagger.

"I will grant you safe passage, Karl's son. But I cannot speak for them." Squee Squee Swikil pointed into the trees and, when everyone glanced, pulled free of Sigurlina's grasp and leapt into the air.

Six trolls crashed through the forest from the direction of the trail. They paused, blinking stupidly at the humans.

"Because it was a pleasure to converse with a man of breeding, I will offer you my aid this once." Squee Squee Swikil's voice came from the treetops. The ground under the trolls' feet erupted into fire. Ice and snow melted in an instant as the trolls howled in agony.

"Oh, what fun!" Squee Squee Swikil flitted from branch to branch, pelting the trolls with bits of twig. Reaching one branch, he jumped on it. The branch broke from the trunk, landing directly on a troll's head as the troll danced from foot to foot on the near molten ground.

"Run." Fjorn led his group on a snowshoe sprint through the trees.

Behind them, the sound of troll screams and high-pitched laughter rent the air, followed by the sound of falling trees. Fjorn's group reached the trail past the ambush site and slowed to a walk.

"Do you think they'll follow us?" asked Ragna.

"They have to, but Eye Biter won't attack directly. He fears Sigurlina too much. An ambush before you could muster your magic is one thing. Facing you directly is too risky in his mind. If any troll asks, you called the fire," said Fjorn.

"Why did Squee Squee Swikil help us?" Sigurlina looked perplexed.

Ragna snorted with laughter. "You're playing with jarls and karls now, me lady."

"Ragna, I've asked you not to call me that." Sigurlina's voice held strained tolerance.

Fjorn smiled. "You'll have to get used to it. Ragna is right. There is that type in every court. Primping and preening and looking for any chance to show how superior they are. My rank is higher than his. Me owing him a favour gives him status and a story to tell."

"When you said you were in the succession for the throne of Norveig; I thought he was going to shine your boots," remarked Ragna as they followed the trail.

"But you're. Well... I mean... Jarl Erik hasn't acknowledged you." Sigurlina bit her lip.

"And I'd never make the claim to a human, but it is true enough, as much as I wish it weren't." Fjorn riveted his gaze forward.

They were looking for a good area to set up camp when they saw a fire in the distance. A short walk later, they came to the trolls' encampment. Arm Ripper stood up as they approached the fire. Fjorn could see that Arm Ripper's face was swollen, and there was a bandage around his chest.

"You alive. Arm Ripper band chief. Eye Biter cheat Fjorn puny. Me challenge, me win! Him banish, he take family. No stop, troll law. Me much happy you not food. Eye Biter still live?"

"I think so." Fjorn cleared his throat and sang,

"Youth to the Gods, golden apples of grace.

Idun's power, heal mortals of faith."

Arm Ripper straightened as the bruises on his face vanished. With a callused hand, he pulled away the cloth covering his middle and examined the healthy flesh there.

"Maybe you match death witch." Arm Ripper nodded, then slapped Fjorn on the arm, staggering him. "Come fire. Tell how beat Eye Biter."

Fjorn and the party followed Arm Ripper to the trolls' fire. A pair of dreyri were spitted on slender tree trunks over the flames, their huge bat-like bodies sizzling as they cooked. Nose Crusher sat on a compacted mound of snow, gnawing on what looked like a giant bat wing. Arm Ripper settled beside her. She pressed into his side.

"I send trolls other tribes. Chief meet after sleep. Me trolls tell Chiefs Aethelstan cheat. We talk, then make Aethelstan pay. Bad king cheat troll. Stupid king cheat troll."

"Thank you," said Fjorn.

"You puny, but you strong, you fight, no cheat. Troll like you. You tell how you beat Eye Biter. Story make laugh me hope."

Fjorn took a moment to think before he began improvising a ballad. A short while later, he stood by the fire with the camp crowded around. Half the trolls were lying on the ground gasping for breath as they laughed. Fjorn leapt from one foot to the other mimicking Eye Biter on the hot earth. When he told them how the branch came down, he hunched over and reeled drunkenly. All the trolls whooped with mirth.

Sigurlina stood at the edge of the crowd.

"The lads a Skald and no lie in it." Kjorn dashed tears from his eyes and stood beside her.

"I was there, and I can hardly recognise the story. It wasn't as much fun to go through it." Sigurlina stared at Fjorn. "I wish I could do that."

"What lass?"

"The way he can enjoy himself. Surrounded by trolls, facing a battle, and there he is, laughing and putting on a show."

"See through it, lass. See through it to him. We all gild the lily. We all sail dark waters. Skalds have learned to hide the shadows inside. Kraken lurk under the calm waters. I reckon you've seen a glimpse or two of the depths."

Sigurlina paused in thought. "Sometimes, when we're alone. When he's worried about his crew, his people, or his father. It hurts to see him fall into that dark place."

"And what do you do when he does?" Kjorn looked her in the eyes.

"I... I try to be there. Nothing really. I listen if he wants to talk. I make suggestions if it's something he can do something about. I stay close, so he isn't alone. I've learned not to talk about his mother. Doing that makes it worse."

Kjorn smiled and kissed her cheek. "I'm glad he didn't listen when I told him to leave you in Ekenas. Promise you'll look after him? He's dear as me own blood could ever have been to me. I want him looked after."

"Of course, but?" Kjorn placed a finger against her lips, then walked away.

CHAPTER 10: A RACE ON THE HUMBER

Audun steered the Apenhet and its exhausted crew into the southern channel on the Humber. The mudflats that had once dotted this section of the river were now islands. The water under them was brackish. They passed the river Ancholme, where it drained into the Humber and saw nothing but a path of ice and snow. No current pushed them as they passed the Ancholme's mouth.

Audun considered, then called out, "Drop bow anchor. Ship oars."

There was a splash, and the oars were drawn aboard. Audun stared astern as the anchor line pulled taught, and the ship stopped in the channel. There were no lights behind them. "Crack the food chest but keep it dark. Journey bread and water only. We'll feast when we reach Lax Bay."

Jolnir moved to the stern from his oar station. "Is stopping wise?"

"We're all for it. If they're in cogs, they won't be getting up this channel. Their draft is too deep. Even a skeid will be having a might of worry. We'll all be better for a rest and a bit of food. They won't be getting by us at any rate. If they tried, I dare say we could snag them by dropping a weighted sea bench over the side."

"The canal's that shallow?" Jolnir sounded shocked.

Audun held his hands a dagger's length apart. "That's what we have under our keel and less than the length of me arm to either side before we're into the mud. It's another reason to rest the men. Tired sailors make mistakes. We can't afford any."

"Aye." Jolnir rubbed his arms as if easing an ache.

"We best get midship afore they clean out the journey bread." Audun and Jolnir joined the men around the food chest.

Soon everyone huddled at their station, wrapped in blankets. Audun nodded at the tiller oar, occasionally jerking awake. The air grew still, and the silence of Fimbulwinter descended. The only sound was the slosh of the current against the hull.

Audun awoke when the stern of the Apenhet slammed into Read's Island on the north side of the channel. The small ship shifted to port, tilting across the channel and buried its bow on the muddy bottom to the south.

"What happened?" demanded Jolnir.

Audun felt the deck tilt against the current. The mud held fast before water topped the gunwale. Standing, he rushed to the front of the ship, where he found the frayed end of the anchor line. Jolnir appeared at his side.

"Cut," whispered Audun.

"Lights aft." Svafnir's voice barely carried over the ship.

Audun released a string of words in five languages that called into question the parentage of gods, giants and norns.

Jolnir couldn't help but be impressed. "What do we do?"

Audun stopped swearing. "We get off the mud." A moment of silent thought followed. Picking up an oar, he pushed against the mud at the bow. The oar blade sank into the riverbed. Next, he tried to free the stern. The flow of the water held them tight.

"We could be asking those coming up the channel for help," Obasi piped in as Audun tried to think.

"And if they are the troops we're supposed to warn Lax Bay about, then what?" demanded Jolnir.

"Like as nought just some traders," sneered Obasi.

Audun ignored them as they argued. He bit his lip, then went to the anchor rope. "Can't push against the mud, and stern's too wedged to shift. Nought but forward," he muttered.

"Right then. Obasi, spark the lanterns and torches. Jolnir, stop talking and do. I need you to feed out this line while I go ashore. Be sharp. The rest of you get ready to pull." Audun moved to the stern, pulling the front anchor line with him, as Jolnir rushed to the rope that was secured to the bow and fed out the line.

Audun stood on the gunwale as the torches cast a dim light over the snowbound world. With a stride that would have been a leap for most men, he stepped onto the frozen waste of Read's Island and followed the shore up current. He soon came to a frozen oak tree. Many of its dead branches had shattered, but the trunk still looked sturdy. Looping the rope around the tree, he dragged the free end of the line back to the Apenhet and leapt aboard.

"Jolnir, move the stern anchor forward and be ready to drop it on a short line. Two spans should be enough. Everyone else, grab the line I'm holding."

Jolnir positioned himself at the bow with the shot anchor line secured to the prow and the holed stone that made the aft anchor ready to drop. The crew lined up along amidships with the rope looped around the oak tree in their hands.

"Ready. Take tension. Heave," called Audun.

The Apenhet rocked against the force of the current but didn't come free.

"Once again, lads. "Ready. Tension. Heave." Audun felt his arms strain. The Apenhet shifted, then slammed back into the mud.

"Rest for a minute." Audun sat on a sea bench to think. For some reason, his thoughts took him to a day in Orkney when Diwon had joined him on his fishing run. He was taking the time between dropping nets and hauling them in to strengthen the runic magic on his battle axe.

"You've skill at that, but I dare say you're only seeing part of what the runes are about." Diwon's voice was soothing.

Audun had smiled. There was something about the old man that made him want to humour him. "Really, so what would you say they're about?"

"Everything. Yggdrasil and the void beyond. Runes of wind, runes of fire, runes of earth, runes of sea. If one were to truly master them all, then one could shape the universe to their will."

The old man traced a symbol in the air. The wind blasted over their boat, shifting their position and dragging the nets about. "The wind is just fire and air. The runes are marked with fire and air, earth and water. It's all in knowing which holds which mark and how to blend them. I think your nets are full."

"What? Can't be." Audun had looked over the side and seen the drag of full nets.

Audun focused, drawing the memory out, then traced a rune in the air. Nothing happened. He thought, closed his eyes and took a deep breath. He could see the symbol the old man drew. It glowed with golden light in his mind's eye. He traced the symbol again, letting his power flow into it. A blast of wind swept the deck.

"Thank you, Diwon. You're a crafty one. Hoist the sail." Audun leapt to his feet. Looking back along the channel, he could see that the distant lights were closer. There were at least five Snekkja. As many as two hundred and eighty-five men aboard.

"Sail? You're mad! There's no wind," objected Obasi.

The other crew moved to raise the sail.

"There will be." Audun smiled.

Moments later, the sail lay slack on the mast. The men were back, holding the rope tied to the tree.

"When I yell, pull; pull for all you're worth. When we are in the channel, drop the bow anchor and take your stations. Then we up anchor and row as if Grendel himself invited us for dinner." Audun stood behind the sail and focused his will, tracing the runes in the air. He felt the power gather, then he released it shouting, "PULL!"

Wind filled the sail, pushing the Apenhet forward. The oarsmen pulled, dragging the bow free of the mud. The ship moved into the middle of the channel. Jolnir dropped the anchor, and the ship bobbed at rest.

"To the oars," ordered Audun.

"What about the sail," Obasi pointed to the canvas, which now was slack again.

"Leave it."

"Oarsmen ready. Stroke. Raise anchor." Audun sat at the tiller and traced the rune in the air once more. Wind blasted into the sail, pushing the Apenhet forward.

There was a whooshing sound then something splashed into the water beside them. Audun looked back. The fleet following them had closed, so he could see the bow of the lead vessel. A torch burnt there, and a man was preparing a crossbow. He raised the bow to his shoulder and let fly. Audun ducked. The bolt sank into the sternpost.

"Friendly merchants, a cold day in Muspelheim. Svafnir, take the tiller oar. Wait for me at the point of the island." Audun let go of the oar and stepped onto the gunwale. Svafnir shipped his oar and rushed to take the tiller. Audun leapt, landing on Read's Island and raced forward to where a dead willow overhung the channel. The Apenhet pulled by him.

Unsheathing his battle-axe, he swung mightily against the tree's trunk. The tree shuddered as a hole blasted out of it.

Sheathing his axe, Audun braced himself against the landward side of the tree and pushed. A crossbow bolt skipped across the water nearby. Audun strained. The tree cracked and leaned, nothing more. Stepping back, he called the wind and focused it on the tree. With a tremendous cracking sound, it fell into the channel. Audun raced to where the Apenhet had anchored at the tip of the island. Leaping, he caught the gunwale; everything from his waist down submerged in the frigid river.

"ROW!" Audun ordered as Jolnir helped him into the boat. "I'll take the tiller oar. You take your station." Audun addressed Svafnir. Moments later, Audun cringed as another arrow sank into the gunwale by his hand.

Jolnir sat the ice watch, and the sail hung limp on the mast.

Audun looked back. The Snekkja were trapped in the channel behind the fallen tree. The crossbowman kept loading and shooting, but Audun knew that at that range, it was shots in the dark.

Mustering his will, he turned to the sail and called the wind. This time placing his concentration behind it so that it would hold. The Apenhet lurched ahead.

"Don't see why we can't ship oars. Not right the way he works us," grumbled Obasi's voice.

"Obasi, shut up about things you ken nothing about," snarled Svafnir.

"You want...?" Obasi fell silent.

"We're all about fed up with your griping. Now work yur oar, or you'll be finding out what's pressing into yur back," spoke the oarsman behind Obasi's station.

Silence descended except for the sounds of a ship on the move.

A little over an hour later, the Apenhet was tied to a solid dock that thrust into the river a short sail past where the Ouse and Trent meet to form the Humber. The Trent was solid ice, but the Ouse flowed around the pier's pylons. The pier nearly blocked the Ouse, leaving only a narrow channel for ships to pass through. Three other vessels were docked. Ashore was a circular earth embankment topped by a palisade made of logs sharpened to points at the top with a closed, wooden gate facing the pier.

Audun leapt onto the dock and tied off the stern line. Jolnir tied off the bow as six heavily armed men marched down the dock with weapons drawn.

"Who are you, who do you sail under, and what is your business?" demanded the most forward of the men.

Audun moved up the dock. "I am Audun Bear Friend. We voyage by order of Jarl Erik of Norveig, and I bear grave tidings for your head person."

"King Cuaran rules these lands, not Jarl Erik. You must have the King's permission to move through Northumbria." The foremost of the guardsmen spoke in a weary voice. Now that the guards were closer, Audun could see that their mail and helms were battered and their cloaks dirty and tattered around the hem.

"We were invited. My captain is Fjorn, Karl's son of Orkney."

"And where is he then?" demanded the guard captain.

"He's coming overland. It is a long story, and we have come with haste. Please grant me an audience with your leader." Audun looked down at the guardsman.

The guardsman eyed the Apenhet, and its crew, then returned his gaze to Audun. "Have your men tie off and set for port. I'll take you to see Lord Brendan. He's head of this fort."

"Thank you." Audun fell into step beside the smaller man.

"Don't be thanking me. Lord Brendan is none too fond of visitors out of season."

Coming to the gate, Audun noticed that men in battered armour armed with crossbows scanned the area around the palisade. At a signal from the guard captain, the gate opened, and Audun was escorted into a large yard. Various trades were arranged around the inner wall of the palisade. A smith's hammer striking steel could be heard. A cooper was shaving what looked like a cart axle to the right. Fires burnt by each shop supplying light. A square of great halls stood in the middle of the yard. Six horses cantered along a path that circled the fort's interior, their handlers jogging beside them, holding long tethers.

"Have to exercise them. Lovely to see, isn't it? Nought like a good horse. Breaks me heart so many have been for the block since the sun went dark." The guard captain's voice was soft and a little unsteady.

"They're beautiful beasts," agreed Audun.

"You a horseman?" asked the guard.

"No, but who couldn't see the beauty in them. They are the wind given form."

"Aye, that they are. I'm Gimnir. I'll speak for you with Brendan. A man who sees horses as more than dinner these days is worth a chance." The guard captain led the way into the largest of the great halls. Audun was struck by how few women there were. Maybe half a dozen female thralls moved about mending clothes and cooking food. A short, muscular man with a bald head, dressed in a heavy cloak and tunic, sat on a wooden bench at the end of the common room. He was looking over several skins, occasionally dipping a stylus into an ink bowl, and making a notation.

Gimnir led the way to the short man's feet. "Lord Brendan, this is Audun Bear Friend, the captain of the new arrivals. He says he has news," stated the guard.

Brendan finished noting something on the skin, then let his eyes track up Audun. "From the size of you, I'd say more bear's son."

Audun forced a smile. "My mother was always elusive about the circumstances of my conception."

The small man glowered at Audun. "What do you have to tell me?"

"There is a force coming this way. Troll mercenaries and Aethelstan's troops. The human part of the force is stuck in the channel by Read's Island the last I saw. At least five Snekkja, probably more. My Captain, Fjorn, son of Karl Geldnir of Orkney, is working to turn the trolls to our side, but it isn't a sure thing."

"Trolls. You expect me to believe that?" Brendan snorted. "And how did you come across this information?"

Audun took a deep breath, then briefly recounted the events of the last few days.

Brendan shook his head. "Bedtime stories to frighten children. We don't need children's tales here. We have held this channel since the darkness came. I know more men dead than you have met. The real world is frightening enough. Trolls and a pumped-up Karl's son." Brendan spat into the fire. "Where is your proof?"

Audun passed over a broken piece of Wessex skatt.

Brendan took it and fingered the coin. "This proves nothing. I—."

A guard raced into the great hall and ran up to Brendan. "My Lord, the signal fire is lit. A fleet is coming up the channel."

Brendan stared at Audun. "I will take you at your word about the ships. Bring your men inside the palisade. Take what rest and food you can. We prepare for battle." He turned to the guard that had brought Audun. "Gimnir, close the channel gate. Let's see how well a Snekkja sails in mud."

#

Fjorn, Sigurlina and Vidurr watched as the troll chieftains stood around a fire. The other two chiefs looked older than Arm Ripper, but no less powerful, and, if anything, they were more pungent. They grunted and growled at each other and repeatedly examined broken counterfeit coins.

One pointed at Sigurlina. Arm Ripper shook his head, repeating "Gump, Gump, Gump," over and over again. He grabbed his stomach, pointed to his mouth and backside and made an action like throwing a spear, followed by more grunting. The older trolls looked at the pretty teen. Sigurlina smiled imperiously at them, then knelt in the snow and chanted.

"Come hither servant, durable symbol of our ending. I summon thee black one." The black skeleton rose from the ground and stood regarding the trolls.

"Fetch me a hot drink from camp. These talks have become tedious."

The skeleton took off over the snow.

The three trolls looked at Sigurlina, then babbled at each other.

Vidurr nodded sagely. "This is taking too long. I'm going for a run." He howled, becoming the giant, red wolf and bounded into the darkness.

The three trolls babbled excitedly. After a time, one of the older trolls slammed his club into the ground, shouting, "Gump!" and walked away. The two remaining troll leaders spat in their palms and shook hands.

Arm Ripper turned to Fjorn. "Leg Smasher with us. He want Aethelstan pay. Head Crusher go. Leave punies alone. Too many her tribe die walk here. Aethelstan's slimy man, not open gate for food her tribe. Big fight, no food."

Fjorn nodded. "Then we're as ready as we'll ever be. When Aethelstan's men attack, you and your trolls will run up as if you're going to help them. When you get close--."

"Trolls make pay for bad skatt. We make pay big, and we eat."

Fjorn nodded. "But only Aethelstan's troops."

#

Audun stood by Gimnir on what appeared to be two piers facing each other across the Orse, leaving an open passage just big enough for a Skeid to fit through with oars shipped. There were torches on each pier. The trail from the far pier led nowhere. A horse stood harnessed on each side of the piers, and a hinged platform leaned into the air, ready to bridge the gap between the piers. After telling Jolnir to get the men inside the fort, Audun followed the guard captain.

"I'm sorry for my Lord's words. Hold this line and pull it when I tell you." Gimnir passed Audun a rope and moved to the harnessed horse.

"He's seen too much for too long," observed Audun.

"That's more than true, but not the half of it." Gimnir guided the horse along a trail leading away from the pier. A pulley made a grinding sound to Audun's right. When he looked into the water, he could see the shadow of a barrier moving across the current's flow. On the far side, a man was leading the horse up a path, and another barrier was moving across. The two barriers met with a bang.

"Pull and keep pulling until I tell you to stop," yelled Gimnir.

Audun pulled his rope, and the bridge-like construct folded down so that its lower portion braced the back of the panels blocking the river's flow. Its top made a bridge so the channel could be crossed. On the downstream side of the bridge, the river's flow had slowed to a trickle. On the upstream side, the water was building up against the barrier.

"What?" began Audun.

"Water's not as deep as before Fimbulwinter. Spring, summer and fall, a skeid can make it this far, then the Orse shallows out. By blocking the flow, we can get them past this set of shallows. Druids man other watergates further upstream. It's why we need the horses. They help us open and close the lock and pull the ships from the downstream to the upstream pier. The watergate also comes in handy for stopping anything downriver." Gimnir smiled. "It were Brendan's idea to use it as a weapon. He knows his business; he just goes about it in a bad way."

Audun nodded as they started walking back to the fort. "How many swords can he bring to the battle?"

"Fort has a hundred and twenty men fit to fight."

Audun shook his head. "If those ships I saw are full."

"I know. Four to one or more. I, for one, believe you about the trolls. Aethelstan wants our hides, and that's no lie. Take Lax Bay. You take Jorvik and all the lands between. Though I dare say, the druids would make the Orse run red before they'd let that Pope kisser claim a stride of their land. Still in all, cut off the sea, and you starve the land."

"We'll have to hope that Fjorn can bring the trolls." Audun's voice held doubt.

"Funny to be hoping to see a troll."

"You can't imagine." Audun suppressed a shudder.

Soon after, Audun slept with his crew in a corner of the great hall. A horn and the sound of guardsmen rushing to station woke them. The guardsmen moved with the numb determination of those who had seen too many battles. Brendan fell in with the men filing from the hall.

"Where do you want us?" asked Audun before the Lord could leave the building.

"Stay here. This isn't your fight, glory hound." Brendan sneered and pushed out of the hall.

Gimnir held back as the rest of the men cleared the building.

"Forgive him. Brendan's kept the path to the sea open, spilt blood and lost men. But no one thinks of him. Others go on raids and gain glory while he holds the path so they can return. His deeds are ignored. He fears that Odin himself will think nought of him. And maybe he will. We've never faced a force as large as the one that comes. Twelve Skeid, each fully manned! Something has set Aethelstan off, and that's for sure."

Audun nodded. "I'll set my men about the wall to watch for my captain and help as is needed."

"When it comes to that." Gimnir rushed to join the troops going into battle.

chapter 11: war

Audun gathered his cloak and ordered his crew to the fort's palisade, then moved to the archer's platform by the main gate. A man armed with a crossbow grunted at him when he ascended to the shelf that circled the inside of the palisade. Audun stared out. The lights of a dozen ships twinkled, forming a long line downstream on what had been the river and was now a strip of mud. Troops from the fort marched out of the gate and broke into smaller companies. Some companies moved to the path of compacted snow by the river while others disappeared into the snowy desolation away from the flowing water.

#

The invaders leapt from their vessels onto the path by the river. The first rank of defenders raced along the pathway, paused and loosed a flight of crossbow bolts. Distant screams reached Audun's ears. The invaders formed a shield wall across the path. A second flight of bolts flew from the men of Lax Bay before the invaders replied with bolts of their own. The defending troops fell back behind a shield wall erected by the second rank of their fellows. The Lax Bay crossbows loosed again, to little effect. The attackers moved forward.

Beside the ships, two companies of invaders pulled objects over the frozen fields on the fort side of the river, fading into points of torchlight in the dark, frozen forest. On the bank opposite the fort, a line of torches moved over the frozen wastes vanishing amongst the dead trees.

The main invasion force progressed unimpeded for several strides until the men in the lead screamed and dropped to their knees. The men behind them tripped over the front rank. The defenders from the fort let loose a volley of bolts into the hobbled invaders, staining the ice red. Yet another volley fell amongst the attackers. Then the invaders sent bolts of their own careening into the defenders. The troops from the fort moved out of crossbow range and re-established their shield wall. Some men left the defenders carrying their wounded back to the fort.

Aethelstan's forces removed their wounded to the mud-grounded ships. After a time, the invaders seemed to attack the forest, slashing at branches with their battle-axes. Gathering a branch each, five of their number moved to the front of the line and started sweeping the snow. The sweepers quickly fell to crossbow bolts. Other men took their place. Thus, the trail was cleared of the caltrops that the defenders had buried to guard their retreat.

#

Svafnir appeared on the ladder to the archer's platform below Audun. "Fjorn is coming from behind the fort. Jolnir's gone out the back gate to tell him the lay of things. The captain must have more 'an a hundred trolls with him."

Audun smiled in a way that made the crossbowman beside him step away. "This will be interesting."

108

A dark shadow flew over the palisade then a large raven landed on Audun's shoulder.

"Good bird, good bird," stated Munin.

"Yes, you are," agreed Audun. "Tell Sigurlina that two companies split away from the main invader's force and are cutting cross country. You can see their torches from here. A large group split away and went somewhere on the opposite bank. Fjorn will know what to do."

"Good bird, good bird," agreed the raven as she leapt into the air.

The crossbowman stared at Audun in shock.

"You get used to it." Svafnir slapped the guardsman on the back.

#

On the trail, the guardsmen fell back towards the fort as crossbowmen, from the shelter of their shield wall, continued to take out the sweepers. Flights of bolts flew from the invader's column, some finding their mark.

The rear of the guardsmen's column was emerging onto the open ground before the fort, where they would break ranks and file through the gate. Many rushed to bolster the crossbowmen on the palisade.

A war horn sounded four blasts. Fire erupted on an embankment above the trail by the river, then flaming logs rolled down onto the invaders, pinning men into the mud of the recently diminished channel. The defenders on the trail fired bolts as swiftly as they could load them. The men on the embankment fired down into the disorganised attackers.

Roaring, invaders from further back on the trail mounted the embankment and rushed forward only to tumble into a hidden trench, impaling themselves on the wooden stakes that lined its bottom.

The troops on the embankment charged the invaders that the logs had left standing, then joined the force that held the trail. The defenders pushed forward but were soon stalled by fresh troops from the ships. In minutes the battle had turned. The men of Lax Bay set up a shield wall and allowed themselves to be slowly forced back as other men carried the wounded to the fort.

Audun watched as more and more crossbowmen mounted the parapet and readied their bolts. In the distance, he could see the end of the invader's column that followed the path beside the river. The invaders marched in a line four across.

A company of defenders formed a shield wall at a spot where the trail swung away from the river before meeting the barren around the fort. Ice had been piled to the sides of the trail, forming a deep trench. Men behind the trench pushed blocks of snow and ice down on the attackers within it. The Lax Bay shield wall plugged the end of the trench. The invading troops were soon buried up to their knees as they tried to push through a bombardment of ice and snow. The Pikes and crossbow bolts of the defenders felled any invader who showed a vulnerable spot.

A group of Aethelstan's troops split away from those on the path behind the trench and scrambled up the steep embankment into the trees.

#

Audun could see Brendan in front of the fortress's main gate watch as the invaders topped the steep rise by the blocked river path. The Lord held a horn to his lips and released two blasts.

Men, that Audun had barely noticed, moved to the built-up sides of the ice trench, grabbed long branches and pulled. The trench sides caved in, burying the attackers at the front of their column and blocking the path. Brendan sounded three horn blasts. All the defenders raced into the fort and closed the gate just as the attackers that scrambled up the embankment charged, screaming, onto the barren.

"All bows to the parapet. Get the wounded into the healing hall. Light the cauldron fires. I'm in the mood to poach some Crusaders. But first, our guests look thirsty. We wouldn't be good hosts if we didn't give them a drink." Brendan held his horn to his lips and released six short blasts.

"This will be a sight." The guardsman standing beside Audun turned his attention to the river.

There was a rushing sound as water surged down the river's course, filling it to its pre-Fimbulwinter levels. The icy trail that the invaders were on was submerged. The water hit the invader's ships which were driven back, colliding with each other. One ship tipped up and rolled onto its side before jamming into the mud. The rush of water drove one ship's bow up so fast its stern jammed into the river bottom, and it stuck there as water topped its stern.

The men on the trail skidded and slipped, falling into the water. The flaming logs were extinguished, then driven back in the flood, smashing into men and ships as they went.

Then it was over.

Audun leapt down from the parapet and moved to Brendan's side. "That was incredible! Opening the watergate upstream was inspired. Odin himself could not have done better. You, sir, are a genius."

For less than a second, a smile played at the corner of Brendan's lips then he scowled. "We're still outnumbered." The short man stomped away. There was a cry, part terror, half hope, all surprise, from the palisade.

#

Jolnir fought beside Fjorn as he led a troop of twenty trolls against one of the bands of invaders that had split from the main group and cut onto the higher ground away from the river. They had been filling a sledge with kindling torn from the forest as they approached the fort. Ragna's voice echoed through the darkness.

"So Aethelstan and the choir boy.

"Did eat some nuts and know some joy.

"And this made his queen so gay.

"She, with her maids, did go to play.

"His troops took boys that very day.

"Out to the field to get in the fray."

Half of the invaders in the band were caught by the taunting song racing after the voice while the trolls fell on those remaining.

Fjorn started a song of his own.

"The shields of Asgard are shields of might.

"Turn the wrath of giants to flight.

"Shields to hold a warrior's might.

"The shields of Asgard are shields of might."

A shimmering dome covered Fjorn and Jolnir just as a flight of bolts came at them from two Crusaders that had stayed back from the main battle. One bolt pushed through the dome, nicking Jolnir. Jolnir lunged, dropping low so that he seemed to vanish in the snow. He came up beside one of the invaders and thrust his dagger under the man's mail shirt and padded gambeson, driving the blade into his groin, then vanished into the snow.

Sigurlina stepped out of a shadow cast by a torch carried by an invader. She traced her hand over the man to the right of the torchbearer, 'gifting' him with the taint of Svartalfheim, then drove her staff into the back of the neck of the torchbearer. Her black skeleton leapt onto the man to the torchbearer's left, driving its bony fingers into his eyes. Vidurr, in his wolf form, pounced out of the shadows ripping out the torchbearer's throat.

Trolls were everywhere, tearing into the invaders who weren't chasing Ragna's song. Two trolls grabbed an invader by the legs and pulled, splitting him like men might break a wishbone. Two invaders pounced on one of the trolls, driving their blades deep into the creature.

Fjorn felt all his training with Jolnir come together. In a fluid flow, he moved into the battle, drawing his blade across an invader's leg, then dancing to one side so swiftly and naturally that his foe's sword drove into the empty air where he had been.

In minutes, Fjorn's team and the trolls were victorious. They turned their attention to the invaders trying to reach Ragna, striking them from the rear.

"And so, the Crusader.

"Did try to invade her.

"But his lance was too short by far."

Ragna's voice carried through the darkness.

"You can stop now," called Fjorn.

"About time. My throat was getting sore!" There was a crashing sound, and Ragna, riding on Nose-Crusher's shoulders, appeared at the edge of the torchlight.

Nose Crusher spoke a short sentence.

"What did she say?" asked Sigurlina.

"She liked the song where Aethelstan had to squat like a lady because he's so small down there."

"How did she understand it?" Sigurlina grimaced.

"I translated. She likes to sing and wants new material."

Fjorn sighed in resignation. "Do you have this effect on every innocent female you meet?"

"What is that supposed to mean?" Sigurlina held her arm out, and Munin landed on it.

"Nothing! Who needs healing?" Fjorn wiped his sword on a dead invader's cloak.

"Munin says the other light is that way." Sigurlina pointed into the darkness. "There are about forty of them."

Vidurr growled and bounded into the darkness to scout the way.

Sigurlina grimaced. "Ragna, can we talk?"

The small woman clambered off Nose-Crusher's shoulders and walked with Sigurlina to the edge of the torchlight. A whispered conversation followed, then Ragna nodded and moved to one of the dead Crusaders. Using her dagger, she cut off the hem of his cloak and carried it to Sigurlina, who slipped behind a tree.

"What was that about?" asked Fjorn when Ragna joined him by the torch.

"Nothing you should worry about. Be nice to her. She isn't feeling well."

Fjorn's voice became gentle. "I worried that with getting chilled, she might catch a cold."

Ragna shook her head and sighed. "Men, even the nice ones, dead stupid."

"What?" began Fjorn.

#

Brendan stared out from the palisade. Shaking his head, he released a sigh and turned to Audun. "I don't often say this, but I was wrong, Audun Bear Friend. I can't think what else to call those... Well, they're trolls, just like in the stories, and it looks like your captain's got them right riled against Aethelstan's men. You know them. Should we go out and help?"

Audun looked where the trolls had attacked the wet, cold, disorganised invaders. At their first approach, the men had done nothing, undoubtedly thinking their allies were coming to their aid. Then the trolls had gone mad, slaughtering anything that moved. The invasion force was still trying to regroup along the trail while the reserves were trying to refloat their ships.

"I think I'd let them wear themselves out first. They might think all humans look alike." Audun noted that a half-dozen trolls had left the fight to build a fire at the edge of the barren surrounding the fort. Six of the invaders were spitted in preparation for the victory feast. His eyes strayed to a line of trolls laid out on the ice. Each had been stripped of everything but their battle club. Taken by surprise and disadvantaged as they were, Aethelstan's troops still had the advantage of numbers, and they were taking their toll.

"I don't know about that." Brendan pointed to the roasting humans.

"It's part of the deal. They are trolls, and right now, we need them."

Brendan nodded. "War...Maybe I'd rather go to Thorudvangar when my time comes. I've seen too much blood." The Lord slipped down the ladder.

Audun watched the battle.

#

Sigurlina watched as an invader's blade separated her black skeleton's head from its body. Jolnir danced in and severed the invader's left leg. Of the twenty trolls that had been part of their group, only ten remained, and three of them needed healing. Five invaders stood in a tight cluster with their backs to the barrel of oil that they had been transporting. Torches had been mounted in the snow providing enough light to fight by. Vidurr prowled around the edge of the circle of light in his wolf form, a snarl on his face.

Focusing her will, Sigurlina started syphoning the energies of the invaders' souls. As the energy flowed, she felt the deep gash in her side close, and the flow of blood from a wound in her arm ceased. The cramps eased, and she felt almost normal.

"Give up," commanded Fjorn. "I intend to send one ship back to Aethelstan with those I let live. You can be on it, or you can be troll food."

Three of the invaders glanced about with terrified eyes. A tall, lean man dressed in a brown tunic, trews and cloak seemed strangely calm. Another dressed in fine mail and wearing the cross tabard of the Crusaders scowled in defiance.

"I..." began the youngest invader who wore leather armour.

"Et te in inferno esse in aeternum maledictis flammis acribus!" shouted the man in fine mail. All the other men were dressed in the Norse style.

"What did he say?" asked Fjorn.

Ragna stood back from the battle, nursing a cut on her forearm. "Something like, you will cook forever! I think it's like going to Niphilheim, or Ekenas on a slow night. Take your pick."

"Look around you. We're already going to cook," snapped a young man in leather.

Fjorn looked at the young invader. The man was no older than himself. "By Gungnir, I promise safe passage if you surrender and lay down your arms."

"Paganus juramento." The Crusader spat.

"Don't be a fool. He swore by Gungnir. For them, that is as binding as swearing by the cross," stated the man in brown.

The young invader glanced from side to side, then leapt away from the barrel, dropping his sword as he did so.

"Proditor," snapped the Crusader.

"At least he'll be alive," snapped an invader, who threw down his long sword and stepped away from the barrel. "I never cared much for church. I came for the silver. A dead man can't spend skatt."

Fjorn eyed the remaining men. Sigurlina increased her spell. Her wounds were now gone.

"No king is worth dying for," stated the third invader as he stepped from the barrel.

The Crusader snarled and lunged at Fjorn. Vidurr leapt, caught the man's outstretched sword arm in his jaws and bit down. With a snap of bone, the Crusader dropped his blade. Vidurr released him. A troll stepped up and tapped the Crusader's helm with its club. The Crusader collapsed unconscious.

"This one trip home, yum," said the troll.

The brown-clad man eyed Fjorn. "You swear the trolls won't eat me?"

"I do so swear."

The invader dropped his mace and stepped away from the barrel.

"I hear that Jorvik is nice this time of year," commented the man in brown.

"Wouldn't know, never been," replied Fjorn. "Sigurlina, please help with the healing. Ragna, Jolnir, tie up our guests and give the trolls some rope so they can keep their travelling rations fresh without breaking his other arm." Fjorn moved towards an injured troll.

The brown-clad man sighed and allowed himself to be bound.

"Sometimes he is scary," whispered Sigurlina as she watched Fjorn heal the trolls.

"But only when he has to be," remarked Ragna from her side.

#

Kjorn and the folk from Horn Aegir and twenty trolls hid behind a mound of snow overlooking the invading ships that were piled against each other. A halo of torchlight illuminated the salvage efforts. Between the sailors that worked to float the ships and the men left to guard them, Kjorn estimated that there were a hundred men in this part of the battle.

"We fight now?" asked the troll leader, a large fellow, even for a troll, who was missing an eye. In typical troll fashion, he was named One-Eye.

Kjorn sighed. "Would you be throwing your life away? There be too many of them."

There was a raven's 'Kaww,' and Kjorn held out his arm.

Munin alighted and stared at the old sailor. "Good bird." Her voice was tired.

"I wish I could let you rest me fine, feathered lass, but I can't. There's too many here for me to handle. Tell Fjorn I need him as quick as he can make it."

Munin ducked her head. "Yura bitch, good bird."

"Bird funny," remarked One-Eye.

"Bird brave, with all the crossbows about."

"Good bird, good bird," agreed Munin, then she leapt into the air.

Kjorn scanned the scene, then bit his lip. "Right then, this is how it's going to go until we have more men... err, troops."

#

Aden watched from the fort's rampart as an invader snuck up on a troll's back only to fall with a feathered bolt in the invader's leg. The invaders had spilt onto the barren around the fort, ready for conquest, but now it was a melee as they tried to scramble back to the path that would take them to their ships.

The fort's gate opened, and Brendan led a force of fifty men onto the field, driving the invaders back towards the trolls, trapping them between the two forces, keeping the pressure on the invaders so that they couldn't organise into fighting formations.

A group of about twenty-five invaders, wearing Crusader tabards, had formed into a box formation and were cutting their way back to the river trail, gathering men to their number as they went.

Audun wanted to look away but couldn't. He had seen men die before, but the carnage here repulsed him. Scanning down the river's course, he could see that the invaders had freed one of their ships, and it was making its way towards the fort. As he watched, the men on the ship raised a device on a framework of beams. With a start, he recognised a ballista. The invaders lit the end of a bolt that flamed in the darkness and flew towards the fort. The bolt fell short but did skewer a troll and started a fire on the battlefield. Glancing along the palisade, Audun spotted two of his oarsmen.

"Men of the Apenhet to me," bellowed Audun as he bolted to the gate. The oarsmen fell in behind him.

"Let us out. They've floated one of their ships and are coming up the river." Audun addressed the guardsman standing at the gate.

"And what are you gonna do about it?" demanded the guardsman.

"Close the river off before they reach us. They have a weapon that could burn the fort without them even landing. I've seen its like before." Audun glared at the guard.

The guardsman pondered. "Be quick if you can." He lifted the beam barring the gate. Audun and his oarsmen raced out of the fort.

The path inland from the fort was still clear of the fighting, and they reached the watergate at a run. Two men guarded the horses on either end of the pier-like structure, but the torches had been extinguished.

"Close the river. The invaders have floated a ship and are coming with a ballista."

"Do it, man! This is Audun. He's a friend." Audun recognised Gimnir's voice. The men raced to lead the horses down the trail as Audun grabbed the rope that would drop the reinforcing bridge against the back of the floodgates. As soon as the gates were in place, Audun pulled the rope. The crossbeam under the bridge locked into place, giving the gates the strength they needed to hold against the flood.

"That won't hold it for long," observed Gimnir.

"Long enough, I'm hoping. Where do you keep the oil?"

"Leave your men to work the river gate, and I'll show you."

Audun gestured towards the oarsmen. "Stay here and get him to teach you what to do." His finger pointed to the guardsman that stood by the ropes.

Audun and Gimnir sprinted back to the fort. They arrived in time to see a ballista bolt plough into the palisade by the main gate. The pot of oil at the bolt's tip shattered, splashing oil over the logs that the flaming rags wrapped around the bolt's head set alight. On the river, the longship was mired in mud, but now its ballista was within range of the fort.

"Open the gate," ordered Gimnir.

The gate opened, and he and Audun slipped in.

"What's your plan?" demanded Gimnir.

"I've seen this ballista bolt before. That ship has to have barrels of oil on it. I'll need crossbowmen who know their way around an oar, oil, rags and firepots."

#

Kjorn and his troop crawled up to the edge of the torchlight illuminating the invaders' ships. The ship on the upriver end had been freed and was starting up the flow with a complement of men. The rest of the invader crews worked to free the next ship in the pile. Twenty trolls and six men scooped up snow and compressed it into balls of ice.

"Now," commanded Kjorn.

Twenty-six snowballs flew, striking seventeen torches, sending them into the snow where they fizzled and extinguished. Before the defenders could process the attack, twenty-six more snowballs flew, finding their marks, plunging half of the salvage operation into darkness. Invader troops scrambled towards the source of the assault as Kjorn led his team away in the darkness. By the time the site of their first attack was reached, Kjorn's team had launched another attack extinguishing sixteen more lights. They moved on as the recovery operation ground to a halt in the dark.

"Go now, fight," Kjorn whispered. One-Eye grunted and took fifteen of the tolls. In moments there was the sound of combat coming from the area they'd launched their second volley from. Kjorn took the men and the remaining five trolls and moved about the salvage area knocking out torches with snowballs.

#

Sigurlina held out her arm, and Munin alighted.

"She says that Kjorn needs help." Sigurlina heaved a heavy sigh and grimaced.

Fjorn pushed the torch he carried shaft first into the snow and paused to warm his hands against its flame. "Can she guide us?"

"She says it's that way," Sigurlina pointed into the dark.

Vidurr looked up from where he was breathing into the bound Crusader's face. The Crusader was whimpering in terror.

"If you could scout the ground, please." Fjorn addressed the wolf.

Vidurr wagged his tail and bounded into the darkness.

"I think he's enjoying this," observed Sigurlina.

"He's killing Crusaders. I know he's enjoying this," replied Fjorn.

"Fight more?" asked one of the trolls in enthusiastic tones.

"Fight more," agreed Fjorn in a resigned voice.

The ten trolls who'd survived the first two encounters stamped their feet happily. "Ragna, Nose-Crusher. I want you to take the prisoners to the fort. Nose-Crusher can take the Crusader. The men at arms can go with Ragna.

"But," began Ragna as Fjorn lit a second torch from the one he held.

"Needs to be done. Take lefty with you." Fjorn indicated a troll that was examining a stump where its right hand should have been.

"Sigurlina, have Munin fly to Audun to find out how things stand."

"Yura bitch, Yura bitch," stated the raven.

"After she's had a chance to rest and warm up. She's tired." Sigurlina tucked the raven into the warmth under her cloak.

Fjorn sighed. "If she needs to. Let's go. Kjorn needs us."

#

Audun sat at the tiller of the Apenhet. The kravi was mired in the mud by the pier. They'd loosed the bow-line, and fifteen men manned the small craft. His own crew had been augmented with warriors from the fort. The oars were shipped, and several small braziers burnt along the line of the midships. Each man had a set of bolts with the heads wrapped in rags, a crossbow and a pot of oil beside him.

A horn sounded from upriver then there was the sound of rushing water. The Apenhet rocked then swung around until the stern line pulled up sharply. With the small ship aligned with the rush of water, Audun cut the stern line. They raced towards the larger longship in the channel. As they sped along, Audun traced a series of the runes tattooed on his arm. His skin and the skins of nearly half the men on the Apenhet took on a sheen like iron.

The invaders' skeid rose on the water, but its bow anchor held it in place.

The Apenhet raced with the current towards the larger ship. Audun rode the tiller oar, then, as a man, the people on the small longship dipped rag-wrapped bolts into oil and lit them at the braziers. Crossbows were raised, and a rain of fire was sent onto the skeid with the ballista. Audun cut the Apenhet hard, keeping them to one side of the current as another volley was fired.

The crossbowmen on the skeid fired back, but the speed of the small ship's passage and Audun's protective spell largely defeated the invaders' attack. Only one forward crossbowman on the Apenhet toppled into the river.

The current carried the Apenhet at such speed that their third volley of bolts saw them beside the skeid. Fires blazed, and bolt-pierced bodies could be seen on the deck of the larger ship. A hail of crossbow bolts slammed into the Apenhet, and three more crossbowmen toppled into the water before they were past the skeid. They fired a final volley of flaming bolts onto the skeid. Another crossbowman toppled into the river from the Apenhet. Audun deliberately let the current drive the Apenhet onto the embankment, beaching the small craft before reaching the tangle of invaders' ships blocking the channel.

Audun and the crossbowmen leapt onto the shore and vanished into the darkness. Six strides back from the river where they landed, Audun stumbled onto a trail that started where the enemy ships had first off-loaded and vanished into the darkness inland.

#

Brendan ascended to the fort's palisade. The wound in his side throbbed. He was out of the fight, but he could still lead. The skeid with the ballista blazed, and he watched as the lights on the Apenhet were doused.

"Unclear on his conception." The Lord smiled. "Be well, Bear's Friend. This I will remember." He scanned the battle. The barren around the fort was littered with the bodies of men from both sides and trolls. The steady twang of crossbows as his men picked their targets made a backdrop to it all. The fire by the gate was extinguished. The crossbowman beside him sat on a barrel with a bandage around his leg. Over half his men were dead or too wounded to fight. Looking down, it seemed that even the trolls were tired. The field kitchen they'd set up was seeing a steady stream of trolls who had worked out an exchange where a raw human corpse would be exchanged for roughly a quarter of a cooked one. A pile of armour, weapons and sundry was growing at the edge of the fire's light. He could count forty-two troll bodies lying on the ground, and that was just the ones they had retrieved. He shook his head. They were beasts, he'd seen that on the battlefield, but this day they were his beasts. He mourned them as he would a warhorse.

The river's surge was finished. The upstream enemy ships were in a mire while it looked like one or perhaps two of the downstream ones had been knocked clear into the river channel.

#

Kjorn sat in the snow beside One-Eye. The big troll had a slash across his belly. Kjorn had backtracked when he heard the trolls bellowing. The invaders had sandwiched the trolls between two forces. Kjorn's counter-assault had driven the invaders back, but not before half the trolls in the rear guard had been slaughtered.

"Please let me remember it. The lad did his best to teach this old dog. Now how did it go?"

He sang in a rough baritone.

"Youth to the Gods, golden apples of grace.

"Indun's power heal mortals of faith."

For all his trying before this time, something shifted inside of him and energy coursed through his voice, surrounding him and the wounded troll with sparkling lights. One-Eye looked up at Kjorn and smiled a gap-toothed smile. "Me fight again."

Kjorn buried his surprise at his new ability by standing up and surveying the tangled ships. Two of the vessels had been washed back into the downstream channel by the last flood. One of the vessels had ridden up over another, nearly slicing it in half, while the foremost vessel looked to be in an open channel but completely full of water. The teams working on the ships were either swept away or dragging themselves out of the river.

A raven cried above. Kjorn uncovered his candle lantern. Munin descended to his outstretched arm.

"Good bird." She pointed with her beak to the tangle of ships. "Bitch."

"They do have a bit of a job, though I'd say that one upstream of the tangle will be ready

118

sooner than we'd like."

"Good bird." Munin leapt into the air.

#

Sigurlina trudged through the snow with her companions. Her feet were cold, and her cramps were back. Munin cawed, and Sigurlina held her arm out.

"I know. I promise. I'll get you lots of liver and kidney." Sigurlina paused.

"That is a very normal thing for ravens to do. I guess it's up to you. There's more than enough for the trolls. Only do it to Aethelstan's men, please." Pause.

"Where? Oh, I see him." Sigurlina pointed to a hulking form at the edge of the torchlight and announced, "Vidurr's found us."

The wolf howled, taking on his human form as he approached the torch. "Kjorn's near. He's lost two of his human troops and fifteen of the trolls. There was a second rush of water down the river. The Crusader scum are wet and freezing."

Fjorn nodded. "Good."

"Follow me closely. Someone has set traps and snares all along the river. I'll guide you around them." Vidurr snatched up the torch and led the way into the darkness.

After a short walk, Kjorn came into sight. He was in the middle of a group of trolls and humans performing the Apples of Indun spell song.

"You finally got it, old friend." Fjorn smiled.

"That I have. We'd best strike before they can organise."

"Aye. We should..." Fjorn trailed off as Sigurlina knelt on the snow and chanted.

"Come hither servant, durable symbol of our ending. I summon thee who was Bone-Snapper in life to be my black one. To do my bidding. To the pain of the borderlands, I summon thee. Not alive, not dead, and by my will be bound. Thou are my black one!"

The earth seemed to erupt beside her, and she was forced to step back as an enormous skeleton climbed from the ground and glowered around with its empty eye sockets. The top left Canine tooth was missing from the skeleton's maw.

The other trolls looked at Sigurlina with terror. "In case any of you were thinking of betraying us. Remember, even in death, there is no escape from me!"

"Bone-Snapper, kill those who serve Aethelstan," she ordered.

The skeleton took off at a run. The trolls looked at each other, then followed their undead companion's example.

"Warn me next time," said Fjorn.

"About the spell or about the troll sneaking up behind you with his club raised?" asked Sigurlina.

Kjorn smiled. "You'll make a fine Karl's wife. There is no doubting that."

"Keep this one close, Fjorn. I might be tempted to steal her," teased Jolnir.

"Thank you." Fjorn glanced around, seeing only friends, then quickly kissed Sigurlina.

"We need to end this."

Fjorn led the way towards the damaged invader's fleet. The trolls moved at will amongst the wet and freezing humanity, killing and maiming. The skeleton had charged into the midst of some of Aethelstan's men who'd managed to organise and was surrounded. It swung a tree trunk it had taken for a club, shattering two battered men. The others closed and cut it down. On the far embankment, a group of crossbowmen were pegging anyone that tried to reach the intact but flooded ship.

To the right, a force of Aethelstan's men were charging down the path from the fort.

"Munin, fly to the fort and find Ragna. You deserve a rest." Sigurlina held out her arm so the raven could launch.

"Good bird?" Munin stared into her mistress's eyes.

"Very good bird." Sigurlina kissed the raven's head.

"Good bird." Munin groomed the hair beside Sigurlina's ear, then leapt into the air.

#

Audun collected his extended crew and led them to a hillock overlooking the mangled ships. There they waited as the invaders lit torches and began to dry out. On the opposite shore, a group of trolls were picking off the easy prey. Bodies drifted down the Humber. He felt sick. Near seven-hundred men were dead this day. How many widows? How many orphans? He knew Valhalla awaited the children of the Aesir, but it was cold comfort. A man moved onto the flooded, but otherwise undamaged, longship and started bailing. Audun nudged the crossbowman beside him, who took aim and let fly. The invader slumped face down in the water.

#

Brendan stared at the diminutive woman with four bound men on a rope.

"Fjorn was going to help Kjorn stop them from refloating their fleet." Ragna eyed the Lord with an appraising expression.

"He sounds like he has some sense. I wish I knew how it stood there." Brendan paced back and forth in the courtyard.

A raven cried, and Munin plummeted out of the air to land on Ragna's hood.

"Listen you, black chicken, I'm sure I can find chestnuts somewhere to stuff you with. The arm." Ragna thrust out her arm.

"Yura bitch, yura bitch." Munin hopped onto Ragna's arm.

"The raven again." Brendan stared at the bird.

"She belongs to my friend, Sigurlina."

"Yura bitch," complained Munin.

"Alright, belongs may not be the right word."

"And you can understand... her...it." Brendan looked dumbfounded.

Sigurlina can, but Munin is good for some messages. "What do you want to know? I'll try to ask."

120

"How many troops are left by the boats?" blurted Brendan.

"More than a hundred?" asked Ragna.

"Yura bitch."

"More than fifty."

"Good bird."

"More than seventy."

"Yura bitch."

Brendan shook his head. "Between fifty and seventy. I can't believe I'm taking tactical intelligence from a bird. Then again, if it is good enough for the All-Father, who am I to say different." He turned to the prisoners. "Who wants to go home?" he demanded.

Three of the men looked up.

"I need a messenger. I'm told that this Fjorn wants to send one ship back to Aethelstan so that Pope kisser knows of his failure. I consider that a worthy idea and will even make it two ships. I need one of you to carry a message of parlay to your commander. Who will it be?"

"I'll do it," said the oldest of the three.

"Tell him I will let him leave with his men."

Ragna cleared her throat. "Trolls."

"Of course. The trolls keep the ones they've captured."

The man nodded and was shortly untied. As guards led the freed man to the gate, the man in brown spoke. "Excuse me, your lordship. I hear that Jorvik is nice this time of year."

Brendan eyed the man and replied. "The women of the capital are beyond compare."

"You'd recommend that I buy a house there?"

"When all is said and done," replied Brendan. "Untie him. Feed him in the hall. Then you can report."

"As you command, my Lord," said the man in brown.

Ragna rolled her eyes and sighed. "You could have told us. I would have untied you."

The man smiled. "You didn't say the magic words."

"Spies, all the same," muttered Ragna.

#

Fjorn leaned against a dead tree, breathing heavily from the effort of rigging a deadfall that would sweep over the path by the river at the pull of a stick. The trolls fell back before the troops that moved up the trail to reinforce those besieging the fort. A kind of compromise had been reached between the human combatants regarding the area around the stranded ships. So long as the invaders limited their work to the downriver vessels, they were left un-harassed by Fjorn's forces. Fjorn and the defenders held free reign over the craft trapped upriver, and the tangle of ships blocking the channel was a form of no man's land.

Sigurlina stepped out of a shadow cast by Fjorn's torch. She stumbled and leaned against a dead tree.

"Are you alright?" Fjorn stepped towards her.

"No." Sigurlina moved away from him. "If we touch, I'll pass the taint of Svartalfheim to you. It is Audun on the other side of the river. He has ten crossbowmen. They are running out of bolts."

Fjorn glanced across the river to where a torch had been stuck in the snow.

"He says that the local Lord Brendan feels under-appreciated in holding the fort and that they have seen many battles. He also says that this Brendan is a brilliant man."

"Are you feeling better now?" asked Fjorn.

Sigurlina moved close and slipped her arms around him. "Yes."

Together they sank to sit with their backs against the frozen tree, cradled in each other's arms, quietly watching the river and the mayhem of war.

#

Later a troop of men came down the path bearing a pole with a white shield on top.

A raven cried out. Sigurlina stood and held out one arm. Munin landed.

'It's over. They agreed to a truce. Aethelstan's men are leaving, taking as many as can fit on two ships. Anyone left behind can be ransomed unless the trolls have already claimed them. Or they become thralls. With the way people live under Aethelstan, that might be an improvement for them. I mean, the people in Wessex were--.' Munin spoke into her mistress's mind.

"Munin," whispered Sigurlina.

'Oh right. Arm-Ripper and Nose-Crusher are both alright. The other troll chief died. Arm Ripper has claimed rulership of the tribe, though that isn't much. There are only forty trolls left, and half of them are wounded. They've been breaking the arms of Aethelstan troops that they are taking for their trip home. Ragna has been pointing out Crusaders for them. She really doesn't like Crusaders. Not that I blame her. She cries in her sleep sometimes, you know. No little girl should be--.'

"I know. So, we'll be extra nice to her, but for now...." Sigurlina smiled indulgently.

'Right. The White God's Godis are staying long enough to do angel of death duties, then they have to leave. Brendan, who is very nice, gave me liver and said he wishes he had a raven as clever as me to fly messages and see things from the sky. He has very good taste, and I never minded bald men when I was human. I think he's rather handsome. He said he'd fill a basin with warm water for me in the great hall so that I could get my feathers clean. That is really good because I had an itch, and I'm afraid I may have fleas, and....'

"It's done. They've called a truce," relayed Sigurlina as Munin continued to babble.

Fjorn pulled her close, and they watched Aethelstan's men shuffle towards the ships. Many of them showed wounds or carried wounded comrades. A long time later, the two ships downriver from the blockage set off with full, if injured, complements. Fjorn and Sigurlina moved to the tangle of ships that partially blocked the river.

A shadow stood against the torchlight.

Fjorn projected his voice. "It's done."

Jolnir appeared out of the gloom. "About time."

Kjorn appeared from another angle with two of the Horn Aegir folk. "Cost more than anyone should ever pay."

Sigurlina nodded. "How many do you think...?"

"Too many. Far too many!" Jolnir touched her shoulder while Fjorn hugged her.

Vidurr, in his human form, picked his way through the wreckage of a longship to join them. "Too few Crusaders, but it was a start."

"Come to the far bank and wait there," shouted Audun.

Moments later, the Apenhet drifted down the current and anchored beside them.

"A few bolts as need pulling out, but I brought her back to you safe and sound," remarked Audun.

Fjorn and the others boarded and took stations. A short row later, they were tied up to the Lax Bay pier.

chapter 12: Rest Yea The Weary

Fjorn quaffed from a horn of weak mead, then turned back to the wounded men lying in a row in the healing hall of the Lax Bay fort. Of the one hundred and twenty guardsmen that started the fight, eighty-two were injured, and nineteen were past the skill of any mortal healer. Forty of Aethelstan's men also lay wounded in the hall.

"Youth to the Gods, golden apples of grace.

"Indun's power heal mortals of faith."

Lights danced about the wounded.

The injured stirred as their wounds closed. Fjorn looked to where Sigurlina stood among another group of injured men. She called her power, and several of them sat up, staring at her with adoration.

"Impressive," commented a voice from behind Fjorn. The young skald turned to face Lord Brendan. The man's left arm was in a sling.

"It is a skill to be mastered, but useful. I have to say. Your defence of the fort was incredible. Few could have held against such numbers." Fjorn extended his hand.

Brendan tentatively grasped Fjorn's wrist, trying to crush it in his grip. Fjorn exerted equal force and schooled his expression into one of friendly calm. A sneer touched Brendan's face, then he looked over at Sigurlina and let off his grip.

"Is that your Seith?" Brendan sounded incredulous.

"That is Sigurlina, my betrothed; she does walk the shadow road." Fjorn kept his voice neutral.

"I expected an old hag with missing teeth. Or a giantess the size of a house. The trolls are afraid of her. I've had some of my men strike up conversations with them. They are telling stories that seem more fancy than fact."

"All stories are more fancy than fact. Every good skald knows that. Take a village. Three or four retellings later, it was a city. Kill a Bondi that beat his ox; you will have slaughtered a jarl that whipped his Bondi unjustly. It is the way of stories."

Brendan stood back and examined Fjorn. "Odd truth for a skald to speak."

Fjorn shrugged.

Brendan watched as Sigurlina cast another healing spell. Several of the men around her shuffled away from the group she was working on.

"The trolls are asking for her to help heal them."

"I'll send her and Jolnir along. I can finish here."

"Youth to the Gods, golden apples of grace."

"Indun's power heal mortals of faith."

Fjorn sang, and the lights sparkled.

Brendan sighed and stopped cradling the wound in his side. "You're sending a guard with her? The way the trolls speak, I didn't think they'd dare."

"Trolls are not the brightest of creatures, and no one has eyes in the back of their head." Fjorn waited as those still wounded shuffled together.

"With that raven of hers, she near does. Fantastic thing that. If I had something like that watching the river." Brendan shook his head.

"Seek out a Seithkona. They have no love for the White God's tyranny."

"That I will. Though I doubt I'll find one as pretty as yours. I've ordered a feast. I have a few beef carcasses buried in the deep snow. We're breaking one out. You and yours are welcome to join us."

"Thank you. But we need to move on. We have a quest of our own, and I feel time is pressing."

"Why pressing?" asked Brendan.

"This attack. There is something Aethelstan wants in Northumbria, something worth spending a thousand men's lives to take."

"The trail your man Audun found and the troops that went on the opposite bank and vanished?"

Fjorn nodded. "It seems to make sense that they were supposed to complete the mission over land if the river attack failed."

"We'll have to flood the channel for you to get past the shallows anyway. That will take time. I'd say you have time enough for the meat to cook before you're going anywhere upriver. And son, you look like you could use a good sleep." Brendan's tone was paternal and only slightly condescending.

"In that case, I thank you for your hospitality, my Lord." Fjorn turned to the remaining wounded men on his side of the hall.

"Youth to the Gods, golden apples of grace...."

#

Sigurlina cast her healing spell. The trolls around her grunted and scrambled to their feet. Arm-Ripper and Nose-Crusher stood guard nearby. Jolnir didn't leave her side. A collection of humans were thrown together by the fire where bodies from the battlefield were roasting. The armour had been stripped from the human survivors then their underclothes and tabards returned to them. All of the men wore the Crusader's cross. Their broken arms dangled uselessly at their sides, and they were pale with pain and fear at the fate that awaited them.

"You no do this. It devil's work," pleaded one of the Crusaders in Orse when Sigurlina moved close.

"I know not your devil, but if you feel hard done by, Crusader, take parley with my father or mother. Speak to the head man of my village, or maybe his wife, who was with babe when Crusaders violated the obligation of the guest and slaughtered everyone I loved."

The Crusader looked to his feet and scowled. "Crusaders do God's will."

"Really? It must be his will that you end as troll scat on an icy trail." Sigurlina turned away and spoke as she left the troll's camp. "Fear nought. You will have your Angel of Death duties before the trolls take you away. That is more than your kind granted my family."

Jolnir fell in beside her. "Do you hate them that much?"

Sigurlina turned to face her friend. Jolnir could see tears trickling over her cheeks in the torchlight. "I have to, or I'd help them. That would start a battle with the trolls. Our people would die instead of them. There are good people that follow the White God, but Crusaders have made themselves my enemy. Would you have me betray the memory of my parents, my family, by sparing them from a fate they have earned many times over?"

Jolnir nodded. "As you say, it is a sad thing."

Sigurlina nodded and dashed the tears from her eyes. "As it should be." She grimaced.

"Are you alright?" asked Jolnir.

Sigurlina blushed. "Cramps."

Jolnir nodded. "Try a tea of red raspberry leaf, if you can find any. It should help."

#

Audun watched as guardsmen hoisted a cow's carcass onto a spit over the fire pit in the main great hall. The meat was frozen, but he hoped it would thaw and cook by the time he'd finished sleeping. For the time being, he held a loaf of journey bread in one hand and a horn of mead in the other. On all sides, men slept wrapped in cloaks and blankets. Fjorn stood in the corner of the hall, speaking to Gimnir. The guard captain laughed. Fjorn looked at his feet and smiled.

Audun decided he was too tired to do anything but mind his own business. Popping the last of his loaf into his mouth and draining his horn, he found a place on the platform, wrapped himself in his cloak and went to sleep.

#

Sigurlina sat on the edge of the platform with a loaf of journey bread and a tankard of weak mead, trying to ignore a spirit that regaled her with an outlandish story about how in life he had killed a hundred Crusaders. Now that she had a chance to relax, she had noticed the hundreds of dead clustered around the fort, and they had noticed her. It seemed like every one of them wanted something. They always wanted something!

Fjorn sat beside her and took a swallow from his horn. "I have a surprise," he said before taking a bite of bread. The smell of the cow cooking filled the hall, making his hunger all the more apparent.

Sigurlina grimaced. All the women she'd asked had given her advice, but most of it involved plants she didn't have access to or going back in time and not getting chilled when pursuing the trolls. "What's the surprise?" She leaned into Fjorn. His presence helped keep the spirits away and made her feel protected.

"I've got us a private room. Gimnir, the Guard Captain, wants to thank us for the healing we did."

Fjorn moved to kiss Sigurlina, but she pulled away.

"A private room? Now? How could you?" Sigurlina scowled at him.

"I... but you said... I thought." Fjorn looked shocked.

"Enjoy your room, alone." Sigurlina stood up and stormed off.

"What did you do?" Ragna adjusted her dress as she left a nearby semi-private corner where a handsome, young guardsman sat with a bemused expression.

"I, nothing. I, I got us a private room. I thought she'd be happy. She told me she wanted to. I thought we could, well... then sleep in peace and warmth for once. What does she expect?"

Ragna shook her head and rolled her eyes. "Men! Did you ever think that maybe she wouldn't want her first time to be today?"

Fjorn looked like a deer caught in the light of a ship's lantern. "I. We won. We survived. What better time to celebrate?"

"Idiot!" Ragna's voice dropped to a whisper. "The moon is dark."

"The moon is always dark." Fjorn matched Ragna's tone.

Ragna closed her eyes, took a deep breath, and spoke in a tone suitable for addressing a dim-witted child. "Her moon is dark, you idiot!"

Fjorn looked confused, then, slowly, his features cleared. "Oh."

Ragna shook her head. "I better go after her."

Fjorn stood. "No, I will."

Ragna stared at him. "I–."

Fjorn shook his head. "Thank you for explaining things to me, but we need to settle this if we are to have a life."

Fjorn moved through the great hall until he found Sigurlina huddled against the wall with her knees under her chin.

"I'm sorry," she said as Fjorn approached.

Fjorn moved slowly as if calming a skittish horse. "It's all right. Ragna explained."

Sigurlina blushed and looked away.

Fjorn took a seat beside her and put his arm over her shoulders. "Siggy, I love you, but I am a man. There are things I won't know unless you tell me. There are things I won't understand unless you explain them to me. Now, let's go to our room and sleep. I'll keep my leggings on."

Sigurlina stared at her betrothed and saw only the gentleness she knew he possessed. "That sounds nice."

Together they stood and moved to the private rooms at the end of the great hall.

\#

Audun awoke with the smell of roasting meat filling the air. Sitting up, he scanned the hall.

Guardsmen had breached barrels of mead and were allowing even the newly made thralls from the battle to fill their horns.

Lord Brendan sat at a long table at one end of the hall, sipping from a horn and looking sour.

Fjorn sat on the wood floor by the entry door with Sigurlina. Both held wooden plates full of roast beef.

Standing, Audun pulled his plate from his travel kit and joined the line by the firepit.

"You're up. I thought you might sleep through the feast." Ragna slipped into line beside him. From the staining on her plate, he could tell this wasn't her first helping.

"And you would have let me, wouldn't you have?"

"Not to worry. Only the outer bits were cooked fit for a man to eat when we had our firsts." Kjorn moved to stand with Audun and Ragna. There was still a little meat on his plate, and his drinking horn was looped through his belt. "I'd of wakened you before it were down to bones."

"I wouldn't have. The more you eat, the less for the rest of us," observed Vidurr as he joined the group.

"You're up. Fjorn said to tell you that the Apenhet is upriver, fully provisioned. He expects that the channel will be flooded shortly. He wants everyone ready to row, but he has a task to perform first."

Audun glanced towards Fjorn, who finished the meat on his plate, kissed Sigurlina then sauntered to the space in front of the head table.

"My Lord Brendan, might I entertain the hall?" Fjorn did a short theatrical bow.

"If it is your wish to do so, Captain."

Audun turned his attention to the older woman who was serving. The meat in the middle of the carcass was almost raw, but the outer cuts were well enough prepared, so he had her fill his plate. The others followed his example. Fjorn moved beside the fire pit. His voice sang out, first loud to still the chatter in the hall, then softer with melody. He beat a Bodhran in time to his words. The rhythm drew all into the cadence of his song.

"Of raids and battles, there are great tales.

Of Viking fleets unfurling their sails.

Of pillage and plunder, there are many lays.

Of Viking crews that fought all their days.

Of heroes aplenty, of strong men who fought.

I could sing stories of the wealth they have brought.

There are songs that I could sing.

But without a home, they don't mean a thing.

At the mouth of the Orse, stands a brave and true man.

Lord Brendan the cunning, who guards Cuaran's lands.

He holds the way from the land to the brine.

Without him, what home would raiders find?"

Brendan sat up in his chair at the mention of his name and scrutinised Fjorn, who continued singing.

"Wreckage and death, is what they would find.

If not for a man of bravery and mind.

Brendan, Lord Brendan Lax Bay did hold.

Gainst ten times his number, so it is told."

The song went on detailing the battle, always playing up Lord Brendan's cunning and the fall of Aethelstan's men. When Fjorn finished, the hall was hushed.

"He's got a thought in his head that one does," remarked Gimnir into Audun's ear.

Audun turned to face his friend. Gimnir's hair was shaved off on one side.

"Your hair...?" began Audun.

"Took a mace to the helm. Me old helm is a mess, and so was I. I was expecting to see Odin. Your captain sang his ditty over me a few times, and I started looking forward to the feast."

Brendan stood and raised his horn to Fjorn. "Hail the Skald, Fjorn, Hakon's Bane, heir to the Karldom of the Orkney Islands, Captain in the fleet of Jarl Erik Bloodaxe. I pronounce you and all that sail with you, friends of Northumbria."

A cheer went up from all present as Brendan drank from his horn and motioned Fjorn to do the same.

"I have information for you, but not where eyes can see, and ears can hear. Send your oarsmen to prepare your ship and gather those of your crew you'd trust with all that is dear to you," commanded Lord Brendan.

"As you wish, my Lord," agreed Fjorn.

"One more thing. Will you perform your song elsewhere? Maybe Jorvik?" Brendan blushed slightly.

"I intend to. Wherever I have an audience and leave to do so; I will sing the Lay of Lord Brendan." Fjorn smiled.

Brendan seemed to puff up. "Good. Good. It's not for me, you understand. The men get discouraged and start feeling that nobody appreciates the sacrifices they make. Knowing their story is being told will mean a lot to them."

"Of course, my Lord." Fjorn left to order his crew for departure.

Moments later, Fjorn, Sigurlina, Audun, Vidurr, Ragna, Kjorn and Jolnir stood in a small room with Brendan and the brown-clad spy.

"I believe some of you know Neese."

Fjorn eyed the spy with suspicion. "Ragna told me you were King Cuaran's eyes and ears amongst the invasion fleet."

"More than that. I have been hidden amongst Aethelstan forces for two years. I could be whipped for telling you what I'm about to, but much of it I think you already know, and we both seek the fall of Rome's puppet in Wessex."

"I will shield you. Tell the king that you spoke under my orders. Let his wrath fall to me should it come to it," said Brendan.

Neese nodded gravely. "Aethelstan has been seeking magic that he may wield to his advantage in the war. The horn of the kraken was only one such piece. He has also captured Ulfhednar and Selkie to try to find the secret of their transformation."

Vidurr looked up from examining the map on the table. "Captured?" His voice held shock, hope and dismay in equal measures.

Neese nodded. "Crusaders raided villages rumoured to house Ulfhednar along the coast of Gotland. They slaughtered the men but brought back the women and children. I spoke to women who were taken in the raids. The Crusaders spared their children if they took the White God's wafer. Crusaders took them as thralls. There are so many foreign men in Wessex that women are in short supply. The women endure all manner of abuse for the sake of their children." Neese looked to the floor, and his voice became strained. "I have never come so close to revealing myself to liberate a crusader's victim as when I heard how they used the wolf women."

"Surt! What were their names?" Red-faced Vidurr lunged towards Neese, grasping his tunic.

Neese leaned away from the crazed Ulfhednar. "I... I don't know. There were near a dozen enslaved Ulfhednar women in the village of Poole where I met them. Maybe twice that in children. They weren't my mission, and the names of thralls... You don't really try to remember, now do you?"

"I have to go." Vidurr turned to the curtained doorway. Audun's hand on his shoulder stopped him. "Think, friend."

Vidurr snarled at Audun. Sigurlina took his other arm. "How would you even get there?"

"But it might be her. It could be." Vidurr's voice cracked with emotion.

Fjorn moved to face his friend. "I know. And once we are done this mission, we will all go with you. We will free your people at the least and rescue your family if the Gods are kind. But we must not lose the war for the sake of a battle."

"So, you will only help me after you deliver the spear to your precious Jarl?" snapped Vidurr.

Fjorn smiled viciously. "A spear that will kill whatever it is thrown at and cannot miss. If we go into Wessex, we will need every advantage we can find. I want that spear with me. Once we know if your family lives and have rescued them; Jarl Erik can have the spear. Until then, he can wait. Since he set me this task, he expects me to die trying. We all know the truth of that, and we all know why. If you will but wait a few days; you will have us all at your back. Can you give us that long?"

"Swear it by your Gods." Vidurr stared into Fjorn's eyes, searching for any hint of deceit.

"I so do swear."

"Do you all swear?" asked Vidurr.

"We all so do swear," agreed the rest of the Apenhet's crew.

Vidurr closed his eyes and nodded. "A span of days, but no more."

"Now that that is over, it seems you already know what Aethelstan wants. He calls it the spear of Longinus. He sent an army of crusaders overland from where they offloaded the troops to attack a place called South Duffield. The spear and some other things are supposed to be there." Neese pointed to a spot on the map where the Ouse River looped north.

"It will take us about a day's sailing to make the trip. Overland in Fimbulwinter, with no trolls breaking a trail, at a guess, I'd say two days, maybe three. We can get ahead of them if we leave now," observed Audun.

"And do what?" asked Ragna. "There's an army of them."

"Some say the magic items are defended by the dead. There was a rumour that no man could breach the stronghold lest Hel take him. It could be that Lady Hel has taken the place as her own. The druids might know more," remarked Neese.

"The task remains the same. We will find a way," observed Fjorn. "If there is nothing else, our ship should be ready to sail."

Neese cleared his throat. "I need to get to Jorvik and report to the king. Any distance you can transport me would ease my passage."

"We've lost five oarsmen this voyage. We could use another oar in the water," observed Kjorn.

"I know," agreed Fjorn sadly. "Very well, Neese. But you'll work an oar."

"I would expect no less." Neese smiled and dipped his head. "I heard of your raid on New-Winchester. I'm beginning to believe some of the stories."

"I too must send a man to report. If you could use another strong blade in this endeavour, I would send Gimnir with you as my mouth to the King. If he should happen to stop for a few days to enjoy the pleasures of the druid lands, then that would be acceptable to me," offered Brendan.

"So it shall be, and thank you." Fjorn bowed in respect.

Chapter 13: The Druid Wood

Fjorn stowed his travel bag in his sea bench as the rest of the team boarded the Apenhet. The sea bench of one of the fallen oarsmen was made available to Neese. The items it contained were left with their owner's corpse.

The dock on the upstream side of the watergate was a long strip that projected off the shore, suitable for loading and unloading cargo. The water under them had swollen to the point where it filled the pre-Fimbulwinter channel and spilt out through a stone-lined cut on one side of the watergate behind them.

A breeze blew inland. Kjorn deposited Brendan's parting gift, a partially cooked haunch of beef with enough meat on it to make several ship's cauldrons of stew, amidships.

"At least we'll eat well." Ragna sliced off a strip of meat with her eating knife and popped it into her mouth.

Fjorn rolled his eyes. "Kjorn, take the ice watch and plumb the depths. From what Brendan told me, we could ground ourselves on this stretch. Audun, take the tiller oar. We should use the wind while we have it."

Audun took the tiller and smiled. "We'll have the wind if we need it, Captain. I'll promise you that."

Fjorn eyed his friend, shrugged, then called, "Cast off."

They made their way up the winding Ouse River towards Jorvik. The wind held. Safety dictated half speed, so the oars remained aboard. The river banks closed in as the channel grew shallow. They had barely exchanged the stories of their time apart when Kjorn pointed forward. "Look."

All eyes turned to the bow where a glowing, silver mist billowed over the river.

"What is it?" Fjorn squinted at the fog.

"It's pretty," remarked Ragna.

Vidurr sniffed the air. "I smell animals."

"There must be a town with some stock on the river," commented Jolnir.

"Wild things. Wolf, deer, badger, and others." Vidurr filled his lungs. "It is like before Fimbulwinter."

"Is that a falcon?" Sigurlina pointed to a dark shadow above.

"Maybe a Lord has kept some pets?" remarked Jolnir.

"I don't like it. We'll be sailing into that fog, and there's nought for it." Kjorn spoke from his station on the ice watch.

Fjorn considered. "Sigurlina, send Munin ahead and–."

"Munin doesn't want to go if there's a falcon up there, and I won't make her," interrupted Sigurlina.

"I..." Fjorn stroked his beard.

"It's just a bird. Send your pet, girl." Obasi's voice came from his oar station.

Sigurlina glared at him.

"No, Munin is right. I wouldn't ask any other crew member to take such a risk when we have no idea if the fog is even dangerous. I'm sorry, Munin. I didn't think."

"Pretty bird, pretty bird." Munin bobbed her head and hopped over to alight on Fjorn's arm.

Obasi snorted and muttered, "Tied in the wench's skirts."

Fjorn chose not to hear the comment. "Reef sail. We'll go in on oars. Have your weapons to hand. Vidurr, Sigurlina, go forward and keep a watch. Audun, stay on the tiller oar. Kjorn, take a depth. Make sure we have water under our keel."

"Now that's a sailor talking. Good lad," remarked Kjorn.

Minutes later, the Apenhet slipped into the fog. The world closed in, and it was like they sailed through a tunnel of silvery light.

"It's getting warmer," said Ragna.

"It can't be," remarked Kjorn.

"She's right. I'm sure of it," remarked Sigurlina.

Fjorn moved to the bow and dipped his fingers in the river. "Still cold, but I think the water's warmer than it was."

"It's the druids. They have their ways," volunteered Neese.

"King Cuaran made deals with them to keep the path to the sea open," added Gimnir.

"Surt's flaming nuts!" Vidurr's voice blasted from midship's.

Fjorn gasped. On both sides of the river was forest unlike anything he had seen since Fimbulwinter began. Every two hundred strides, a pole rose above the treetops supporting a wheel. The wheels glowed with silver light as bright as a full moon. There was only a thin dusting of snow on the ground. Holly, mistletoe and other evergreens sprouted amongst the deciduous trees. It was as if it were an ordinary Frer-Manudr without the accumulated death of the last three years. He could see clearly for a hundred strides. The mist gave way, and they sailed through a world that only slept in winter's grasp. The river was clear of ice.

"It's beautiful," remarked Sigurlina.

"Sorcery," muttered Obasi. "We can't trust it."

Fjorn ignored the man.

"It's the druids. I told you. Mastery over bough and leaf," added Neese.

Fjorn looked ahead. The river widened at one point, and docks were erected on either side. An open watergate spanned the river at the end of the piers. Another dock was built on the far side of the watergate. A fire burnt in a brazier on the pier. A man in a long, white robe stepped onto the pier and motioned for them to dock.

"What should we do?" asked Kjorn.

"We dock. We might learn something," said Fjorn.

Obasi grunted. "First, all in a hurry and now sightseeing."

Fjorn turned to Obasi. "Close your mouth. Nothing worthwhile comes out of it."

The Apenhet approached the dock.

"Ship oars," ordered Fjorn as he threw the bowline to the white-robed figure. The rope was secured, and the current pulled the Apenhet to parallel the pier. After the stern was secured, Fjorn turned to the white-robed man. He was young, with dark hair and sharp features. A sword and a pouch hung on the belt about his waist.

"Welcome, travellers. I must ask, who are you? Who do you sail under? And what is your business?" The white-robed man smiled.

Fjorn looked past the man to a small, square shelter with a thatch roof. Three other armed, white-robed figures lounged around one of the circle-topped posts that stood in front of the shelter. At this distance, Fjorn could see that the circle at the top of the post was divided into quarters. Each quarter was painted a different colour and contained a large ruby and emerald. The quarter at the top was black. The ones on the sides were green and blue, while the one on the bottom was red.

Returning his attention to the man on the pier, Fjorn smiled. "I am Fjorn, I sail for Jarl Erik Bloodaxe with permission of King Cuaran, and my business is grave. A troop of Crusaders comes this way overland. They seek a place called South Duffield."

"And you have graciously come to warn us," added the white-robed man.

"He's telling the truth," stated Sigurlina, who had moved behind Fjorn. Munin was perched obediently on her shoulder, and the young Seith's skin glowed like moonlight.

The white-robed man examined her. "Sister," he dipped his head. "I can see you are no minion of the Crusaders. I'll send word to the High Druid." Throwing his head back, the man howled.

Vidurr looked up with a shocked expression. A wolf bounded out of the forest and raced up to the man in white, who took a stick and, using a short knife he wore on his belt, scratched a series of lines along its length before giving it to the wolf. "Take this to the Myrddin." He ruffled the wolf's fur around the neck and laid his forehead against the animal's before kissing the wolf on the snout. The wolf raced into the woods.

"Your familiar?" asked Sigurlina.

"My friend. I am Dvyn of the Salmarshe grove. Come, we will take our rest as you tell me how you know about South Duffield and these Crusaders you speak of."

"Kjorn, Sigurlina, with me. Audun, be ready to sail."

"Efnisien, help them dock on the other side of the watergate. Then close the gate. If Crusaders are coming, time may be of the essence." Dvyn addressed one of the white-robed figures by the shelter.

Sigurlina shuddered as she climbed out of the Apenhet. "Dvyn, Gildas wants me to tell you that his skatt is in the hole in the old apple tree by the river. Take what he owes you and send the rest to his sister. Wynne in South Duffield, not Tahra. He's very insistent about that."

Dvyn paused, staring at Sigurlina. "It's about time you paid up, old friend. I won that race fair. I've missed you. Thank you, dark sister, for passing that message on. Gildas, your will will be done." Dvyn smiled. "It will be good to see Wynne again. Delivering the coin will give me an excuse."

Sigurlina stopped glowing. Fjorn moved to her side as they were led into the shelter.

"Nicely done with the glow," he whispered.

"Neece's idea. He told me that druids respect those who study magic no matter what names they call the Gods by."

They came to the shelter's only door. A sprig of mistletoe hung over the door jam.

"Enter here if thou would take the peace bond of mistletoe, and I will do the same." Dvyn led them into the shelter. The building had a small fire in its centre, and animal hides spread around the outer walls. A cauldron steamed over the fire.

"Sit." Devyn took a drinking horn on a leather strap down from a peg on a roof support and, using a ladle, filled it from the cauldron.

"Drink from the horn of hospitality and be known as friend." Dvyn took a sip from the horn and passed it to Fjorn. Fjorn drank, tasting apple cider, then gave the horn to Kjorn, who drank and handed it to Sigurlina, who, after drinking, passed it back to Dvyn, who drained it and hung it back up.

"I am sorry that there is no feast, but such is the world we now live in." Dvyn sat on an animal hide. "Tell me your tale. The Myrddin will be here soon. He'll want me to relay it to him."

Fjorn cleared his throat and related the story from their leaving Orkney on. Sigurlina was amazed. Where his normal tales had details and nuance that enthralled his listeners, this was concise, almost incomplete, yet supplying all the significant facts.

Dvyn smiled. "I should have recognised a bard in you. You can tell it to the Myrddin. I doubt I could match your skill."

The door opened to the shelter. "You must be talented for Dvyn here to admit that about flapping his lips." A bald-headed, elderly man in a white robe holding a gnarled staff stepped into the shelter.

"Myrddin," exclaimed Dvyn.

"Yes, yes, I am the Myrddin." He made a dismissive gesture. "Please call me Oscar. If somebody doesn't soon, I'm afraid I'll forget my own name. And you are?"

Fjorn stood as introductions were exchanged, then the story of their journey was told while the horn of cider was passed around again.

Fjorn finished speaking, and Oscar stared into the fire. "I see them as you describe." He shook his head. "I have feared this day. Dvyn, it is good you have ordered the watergate closed. The river is impassable to ships during the winter season if we do not flood it, and you, my friends, will have need of haste."

"If I may ask, why is it winter? I mean only winter, not Fimbulwinter, here?" Sigurlina spoke hesitantly.

Oscar smiled. "Do you ask for yourself or your queen? I know of Gunnhild's working."

Sigurlina looked distressed.

"I will say no more before others, but some of us know more than Gunnhild could dream. Whether her ambitions be madness or genius, time will tell. But to answer your question; my order draws on ancient powers to order the cycles of nature. King Cuaran has granted us protection in exchange for us keeping the land along the Orse living and the river open. Oh, that you had come during the green months, then these lands are rich. I am Myrddin of the grove that services this stretch of the river. There are thirteen groves between Lax Bay and Jorvik. It is all we can do to maintain them."

"Excuse me, but we should go," interrupted Fjorn.

"You have time. The water must accumulate before you can navigate the river. There are five more gates between here and South Duffield. You will have to wait at each. Do not worry. The Dryads of South Duffield have defences of their own. I will see to it that your stops are not wasted time."

Sigurlina touched Fjorn's shoulder and nodded as she asked. "What can you tell us about South Duffield?"

"As much as any man knows. It was years ago. The Romans had left the island, and we were once more a free people. Sadly, we proved free to fall on one another like savage dogs, petty kingdoms with no unity constantly fighting amongst themselves. The peoples to the north, no offence." Oscar shrugged.

"None taken," remarked Fjorn.

"In any case, the northerners saw our division for the weakness it was and were poised to sweep over us. Then the Great King Arthur rose, with more than a little help from the High Myrddin of the time. Arthur united the petty kingdoms and brought peace. He forged a land so strong that it drove back the invaders. A great man, but kings are by their nature arrogant. He ordered the treasures the Gods had left to protect the lands dug up. By his might of arms alone, would the south be held.

"The then High Myrddin saw the folly in this. He ordered the items brought to places of safekeeping. The dryad's grove and fortress at South Duffield was one such place. Treasures were hidden there, and great magics woven to keep them safe. No man may enter the sanctuary without being set upon by the dead. After that, there are other trials, but I know them not. What I do know is the gift of those treasures empowers us to keep this land alive despite Fimbulwinter."

"How can somebody be slain by the dead?" remarked Kjorn.

Sigurlina turned to look at him.

Kjorn blushed. "Errr. Forgive me, lass. Seen it, said a stupid thing."

Sigurlina patted his leg.

Kjorn blushed above his grizzled beard.

"How can we reach the treasures?" asked Fjorn.

"You cannot. She can." Oscar pointed at Sigurlina. "If the Lady of the Grove permits. No matter what you do, this is the tramp of doom for us. We cannot hold against all outer Midgard. If the Roman church knows where the magic is, they will stop at nothing to steal it. But without the magic of the cauldron and the sling, we cannot make the gems that maintain these lands. Perhaps your coming is planned by the few with many names to keep the treasures out of the hands of those who would destroy all."

"So, we may move your treasures?" asked Sigurlina.

"That will be up to the lady of South Duffield. As far as my authority extends, I will help you. Dvyn, you will sail with our friends. Let no watergate bar their way longer than necessity demands. Carry my bond of safe passage to the other groves." Oscar extended the fingers of his right hand and pulled off a ring. "If any challenge you, show them this."

Dvyn stood and bowed to the Myrddin before taking the ring. "As is your will, Oscar."

"On further consideration, you can call me Myrddin." Oscar rolled his eyes.

Dvyn smiled mischievously. "Whatever you say, father."

Oscar chuckled and stood up. "Go and be safe. Your mother would kill me if anything happened to you."

Father and son hugged, then Dvyn picked up a bag from the corner of the shelter and led the way back to the pier.

The water lever had barely risen, and the Apenhet rode low against the upstream dock.

"Will it be deep enough?" asked Fjorn.

"For a kravi, maybe by the time we reach the worst of the shallows," answered Dvyn.

"Can you work an oar?" demanded Kjorn.

"If you will teach, I will learn," replied Dvyn.

"You'll have to. Wind's dying," observed Kjorn.

"Then we'll use it while we have it. Stations everyone. Cast off," ordered Fjorn.

The bow and stern lines were loosed. They sailed slowly up the Orse, but soon the river began to meander, making the sail less effective in the weakening wind.

"Drop sail and ready oars," ordered Fjorn.

"Let me show you something new," offered Audun.

Fjorn shrugged. "If it saves rowing, I'm not one to object."

At the tiller oar, Audun traced a series of runes on his arm. Wind filled the sail. The Apenhet lurched forward.

There was a scream followed by a string of profanity drawn from seven languages. Fjorn glanced over to see Ragna with the front of her cloak soaked with stew holding a bowl she'd just filled from the ship's cauldron.

"Try warning a person first," spat Ragna.

"Still better 'en rowing," observed Kjorn.

"I don't row," sniffed Ragna.

"Exactly," said Jolnir with a chuckle.

The Apenhet sped along the river with a tailing wind. "Audun, this is fantastic. Kjorn, Vidurr, take the ice watch and plumb the depth. I don't want to run aground," ordered Fjorn.

"Seems too much of a risk to me," griped Obasi, just loud enough to be heard.

The river grew shallower until they pulled up beside a pier identical to the last one at the Salmarshe grove. This time the glow from the bejewelled circle on a post seemed dimmer. Dvyn jumped onto the pier, spoke to other white-robed figures, then returned to the Apenhet.

"They will pull your ship past the watergate and set the gate. It will be several hours before the channel is deep enough, and night is falling. A falcon delivered a message to them about us. They have prepared a modest feast."

"We would be honoured," Fjorn's smile widened. "And let us bring a guest's portion to the table. Ragna, please bring out the meat that Brendan gave us."

"What!" Ragna's voice squeaked.

"What good is a bounty unshared," added Audun.

Ragna grumbled as she hoisted what remained of the haunch of meat onto the pier.

White-robed figures appeared out of the gathering gloom to admire the beef.

"Thank you. Any guest that brings such a gift during these times is doubly welcome." A comely, dark-haired woman of early, middle years dressed in the white robes of a druid spoke. "I am Caoilfhin, High Dryad of this grove."

Kjorn stepped onto the pier and stood facing the woman. "Have you been forgetting your old friends?"

Caoilfhin stared at him, then smiled. Reaching out, she tugged his beard. "What do you expect when you grow a badger on your face." She grew serious. "You didn't come back."

Kjorn shrugged. "Ragnarok."

Caoilfhin smiled. "I forgive you. So now you sail with Hakon's bane."

"We do what we must. High Dryad, you've come up in the world."

"Ragnarok." Caoilfhin shrugged.

"You were never tellin' me much about druids and dryads," Kjorn ran a finger down the side of her arm.

"As I recall, we never had much time for it." Caoilfhin blushed like a maid.

"Maybe you could instruct me now. What be the difference?" Kjorn grinned rakishly.

Caoilfhin smiled. "There really is none. Druids are male and exemplify the projective force of nature; dryads are female and exemplify the receptive force of nature. For most things, it makes little difference." Caoilfhin reached out and gently tugged Kjorn's beard. "For most things."

"'Tis a fair thing you do holding back Fimbulwinter. I've not seen a sight so grand as your woods since before the sun went dark. I'd love to walk the trails if I had a guide, so I didn't lose myself."

Caoilhin slipped her arm through Kjorn's and guided him away from the docks. "Lincoln, see to our guests. I will be on the rock way trail if I am needed. Kjorn, tell me of the world outside my wood. I so seldom get to travel."

"Old sea dog still has a little life in him!" remarked Ragna making a lewd gesture.

Fjorn watched his mentor and friend walk away with a bemused expression.

"It's sweet," observed Sigurlina.

"Aye. And we should wish them joy in it," agreed Audun.

Vidurr stared at the deck of the Apenhet, pushing down against the pain that the image of the couple caused to rise inside of him.

"Fornicating like beasts in the field! It is an unsanctioned union. Disgusting," condemned Obasi.

"We sail from death to death. Why not taste of life when we can?" countered Jolnir. "You will say nothing within their hearing, or you will answer to me."

"Come, a warm fire and drink await." Dvyn led the way to a village surrounded by a palisade of sharpened logs. Inside the palisade was a yard with animal pens and craftsmen's shops around its outside edge. A circular house with a cone-shaped, thatch roof dominated the back of the enclosed area. A wreath of mistletoe hung over the roundhouse's door as a peace bond.

Dvyn led them into the roundhouse. At its middle was a large cauldron supported by a frame of iron bars over a fire pit. The outer sections of the circular chamber were separated into triangular-shaped duns, leaving a space around the fire. Each dun could be closed off by draped animal skins. Pegs were mounted on the inner support pillars that also formed the doorposts for the duns. Cloaks, tools, horns and all manner of the accoutrements of life hung from the pegs.

Ragna sighed and shook her head when she saw all that was left of the haunch of beef had been added to the cauldron's contents.

Animal skins had been laid on the floor around the fire to accommodate the guests.

"Welcome," A short, dark-skinned man with black hair and brown eyes approached them. "I am Lincoln, and it seems I am your host. Please sit." He gestured towards the animal hides.

Ragna had moved to where a belt, with a silver buckle, hung from a support pillar. Audun's hand landed gently on her shoulder. "The stew smells wonderful, doesn't it?"

Ragna looked up into the big, bearded face. "It should. That was good beef." She sighed. "We may as well enjoy it." Taking his hand, she moved to the furs by the fire.

The greeting horn was passed around, then the stew was served along with a ration of bread. Far from just the meat, the stew contained barley and vegetables unlike Fjorn had known since Fimbulwinter began. It tasted better than any food he could remember. Soon he was on his third bowl. Warmth spread through him as he ate, and the exhaustion instilled by the last week overtook him. He lay down, wrapped in his cloak, with Sigurlina nestled against him.

Fjorn awoke to Dvyn shaking his shoulder.

"The river section is full enough to give us passage." The Druid stepped back.

"How long?" asked Fjorn.

"Half the night. If we hurry, we can be at the next gate by dawn. Your man Kjorn went ahead to prepare your ship." Dvyn moved to wake Audun, who was curled around Ragna like a bear embracing a cub.

"Sigurlina?" whispered Fjorn.

"I'm awake. It just felt nice to forget everything for a few more heartbeats."

Fjorn kissed her. "Technically, we're in port and may Surt take anyone who objects."

Sigurlina smiled and sat up.

Moments later, they boarded the Apenhet. A clean-shaven Kjorn walked the deck, getting ready to sail and singing a seaman's song off-key and out of metre.

"You had a good night," observed Ragna.

Kjorn smiled. "Caoilhin says fair voyage, but she won't be seeing us off. Poor lass is tuckered out... from holding Fimbulwinter at bay, of course."

"Tell another one, Bragi," teased Ragna as she settled in the bow.

Fjorn gripped the old sailor's arm, smiled, and winked.

They were speeding up the channel with Kjorn sitting the bow watch when he shouted, "STOP!" and threw the anchor over the side.

Audun stilled the wind in the sail. All the oarsmen raced to put their oars in the water and backstroke. The Apenhet jerked to a stop. Fjorn lurched along the ship's length, catching himself on the bow post.

"What in the nine realms did we hit?" demanded Fjorn.

Kjorn pointed to a rocky outcrop in the channel.

Dvyn appeared at the bow. "They said it would be deep enough for a kravi. I knew we should have waited for the channel to fill."

"There's nought for it." Audun moved beside Fjorn. "We'll have to carry the ship around or wait."

Dvyn stroked his beard. "Won't that take a lot of time?"

"Do you have a better idea?" asked Fjorn.

"We're almost to the next watergate. If I can clear this section, we will have to stop at the gate anyway. Stand back." Dvyn closed his eyes and held his hands over the bow.

At first, nothing seemed to happen; then, the rock outcrop vanished under the flow. Soon the ripples indicating a shallow were gone. Sweat broke out on Dvyn's forehead as his breathing became laboured.

Sigurlina moved to the bow and watched with interest. Dvyn staggered back, and Audun caught the Druid before he fell.

"That was amazing," commented Sigurlina.

140

"Nicely done," agreed Fjorn after plumbing the river with an oar and finding it deep enough to pass.

"Good lad," echoed Kjorn.

"Can you move other hard things?" asked Ragna.

"More sorcery," muttered Obasi.

"We should be clear to the next watergate," observed Dvyn.

"We'll use the oars. Kjorn, good spotting. Keep it up. Audun, less speed in future. I'll not repeat my mistakes," said Fjorn.

"Dvyn, we should talk. It seems I haven't given you your due. I like to know what my crew are capable of."

Fjorn motioned for the Druid to join him and Audun in the stern. Sigurlina followed, assuming an invitation.

When they came to the next watergate, they were ushered through by the druids who took them into their roundhouse and fed them. This grove was in night when they entered the roundhouse. Sigurlina noticed a silvery light growing at the door as she sat on a bearskin and ate.

"Day and night are as important to nature's way as seasons. Thus, we have day and night as we have winter, spring, summer and fall," explained Dvyn.

Sigurlina swallowed her mouthful. "How did you know I was going to ask?"

"Because you always do. It is a virtue in my order. An open mind that seeks to know. You would have made a good dryad, had you been born amongst us."

"Thank you."

A tall man with red hair and chiselled features, dressed in a blue robe, stood by the fire gesturing for the group to quiet. When all were still, he spoke in a rich baritone. "My honoured guests. I am told of your quest. Moving forward, there is that you must know. It falls to me, the bard of this grove, to inform you, people of the north, of a great tale of gods and men and honour and death."

"A skald," remarked Jolnir from his spot around the fire.

Fjorn shrugged. "What matters a name? I just hope the story is one I haven't heard."

"It came to pass that Matholwch, King of Hibernia, did seek peace with Bran the Blessed, the divine, giant, King of Wales. To cement their bonds of friendship, it was agreed that Branwin, Bran's sister, daughter of the sea, would wed Matholwch as a peace bond. Truth to be told, this was a joining much desired by Branwin, for Matholwch was a comely man of seeming good manners, and in the joining, she would become the queen of a noble people much like her own."

The story continued telling of spiteful Evnissyen, half-brother to Bran, and how he mutilated the horses of Matholwch, violating the peace bond and bringing shame to Bran and his people. How noble Bran, in a bid for peace, did surrender to Matholwch as weregild, a cauldron that could return the dead to life, bereft of speech or reason but able to fight upon the command of the cauldron's owner.

All was well. Branwin took her place as queen of Hibernia. In time, Matholwch proved false and did cast his queen into thraldom. At this did Bran lead the men of Wales against Matholwch. In the battle, Matholwch used the cauldron. The men of Bran were hard-pressed in battle, facing both the living and the dead. In an act of redemption, Evnissyen hid amongst the dead to be tossed into the magic cauldron. Amongst the bodies, he braced his arms and legs against the cauldron's sides and pushed, splitting the vessel in twain even as he burst his heart with the effort. Thus, the author of all the sorrow and strife that had befallen two nations sacrificed himself to end the cycle of wrongs.

By the time the story was finished, the channel was flooded enough to allow the Apenhet to pass. Fjorn set sail once more.

The Apenhet came to the next watergate. The crew was made welcome in a roundhouse where a short, swarthy man told the tale of the sling of Lugh of the Long Arm, how the stone always hit its target, then returned to the sling. How the simple weapon could lay waste to armies if wielded with skill.

By the time the story was done, the channel was flooded. Hence, they proceeded to the next watergate where a tale was told of how Arthur sought to collect all the magic artefacts of Briton so his rule would be absolute, but the crafty Myrddin stole the treasures and hid them out of Arthur's knowledge, thus preserving the legacy of the great isle.

At the gate after that one, they ate and slept, then after a short journey, they came to a place where the river widened into a large pond. Mist shrouded the area as it had when they had entered the druid lands.

"This is where the Orse and Derwent rivers meet. We're almost at South Duffield. I don't know about this mist," remarked Kjorn. "The Orse is to the west."

Fjorn stroked his beard. "Dvyn, do you know about this mist?"

Dvyn joined Fjorn in the bow. "My father told me that a short stretch of the river was left in Fimbulwinter on either side of the South Duffle grove as a defence since it houses the treasures. Like a moat, only its ice, snow and cold. The stretch is short, and the river should be safe to navigate."

"Not much choice. Audun, steer for the western passage," ordered Fjorn.

They passed through the fog into the icy cold of Fimbulwinter. Less than half an hour later, they passed through fog again, reaching the South Duffield docks just as the glow of the magic disks was fading. At first glance, the area was like any other druid stronghold they had seen, except for a cut stone road leading to an upstream wooden bridge across the river channel.

Fjorn stepped onto the pier at the river's side and addressed an elderly woman with long, white hair. She was holding a hawthorn staff. She stood at the head of a delegation of white-robed women. "High Dryad, I presume." He bowed.

The elderly woman regarded Fjorn as if he was something she'd scraped off her boot.

"Myrddin, I bring greetings from my father, the Myrddin of Salmarshe grove, and grave tidings." Dvyn stepped onto the dock.

"Call me not Myrddin. I am Mother Superior. I can read, brother, and see in the flames. The messages precede you. I am considering their weight and taking appropriate action."

At these words, the hands of Fjorn and his crew grasped their weapons.

The Mother Superior scowled at them. "Have I offered hostility or yet refused your request for the spear? I hold no loyalty to the Crusaders or the false priests of Rome. I am wife to the Lamb of God. They have long since left his path. I despise the Crusaders, as I do any man that takes that which a woman will not freely give."

On the Apenhet, Obasi moved so that his crewmates formed a barrier between him and the Mother Superior.

"If it sets your minds at ease, over half my sisters bear the title Dryad, and the Druids hold the men's village fifty strides to the south. A name means little if the heart is pure. The Mother Superior looked over Fjorn's crew. "Come, girl, why don't you speak?" She gestured towards Sigurlina.

Sigurlina startled, then took a deep breath and stepped onto the dock. "Fjorn is my captain. It is meant that he should speak for the ship, as it would be for me to speak if I were captain."

The Mother Superior smiled as a hint of warmth entered her voice. "So, you bow to his position, not his gender?"

Sigurlina's face reddened. She heard her grandmother's voice in the back of her mind urging her forward. "I am Seithkona! I am owned by no one, man or woman. I let those best suited take the lead. To do less is to be a fool, but I rule myself."

The Mother Superior laughed. "The kitten has claws." She sighed. "Well said, girl. Let no one change you. And you, the small one. What say you of these men you voyage with?"

Ragna looked up from the boat and bit her lip. "I have known what I think made you, but I sleep well on the Apenhet amongst my friends."

"None could say more in praise of men they travel with. Although, none of you has a true understanding of the spear or the purpose for which it was made." She gestured at Fjorn. "I can still smell the God on you through all the mortal generations, bastard prince."

"I lay no claim to that bloodline. I am a loyal servant of Jarl Erik. I am the son of Karl Geldnir and no more. Nor do I wish to be more." Fjorn spoke with authority.

"Mayhap, you have some measure of your forbearer's wisdom. Frey is not the least in cunning, but still, for my comfort, I will not treat with you. Wait until it is full night, then send those who are of the cauldron of life up the stone road to the sanctuary. What you seek is there, and there mysteries I will reveal. If all goes well, later we can take counsel against our needs. I have already sent to Jorvik for troops, but it is unlikely they will arrive in time to be of use. None of us expected an attack across the icy wastes. As you rest, be warned, let none who bear the spear of life approach the sanctuary. Only death awaits them on the north side of the river." The

Mother Superior turned on her heel and swept up the path and across the wooden bridge. The women of her entourage fell in behind her.

An elderly white-robed man stepped onto the pier. "You must excuse the Mother Superior. She has reason to bear no love for men. Come, I am called Powell. I will guide you to the men's village where you can take your rest."

"Our ship..." began Fjorn.

"Will be treated with great care. You have my word. I'll order it pulled to the up-river dock and that the watergate be closed behind it. The Mother Superior is no fool. If we fail in our charge, the king will withdraw his protection. Part of our charge is to see that ships reach Jorvik," explained Powell.

CHAPTER 14: MOONLIGHT AND SPIRITS

A short walk later, Fjorn and his crew sat by the fire in a roundhouse. All was similar to the other groves save that here the men seemed to outnumber the women five to one, and there were no children or elderly. They had been served bowls of thin venison soup and given worn hides to sit on.

"What is this cauldron of life business?" asked Kjorn.

"She meant women," explained Ragna.

"What do women have to do with cauldrons? Aside from cooking." Kjorn scratched his chin.

Jolnir shook his head. "Try brewing up a baby in that gut of yours, and you might figure it out."

"What... Oh. And spears be long and straight." Kjorn nodded.

"Cauldrons are many things. The moon itself was said to be a cauldron," observed Fjorn.

"I haven't heard that one," remarked Dvyn.

Fjorn smiled, sensing an audience. He stood and spoke in a clear voice that filled the room. "My fair hosts, you have been generous, and, if I may, I would repay you with a tale from my northern land."

Powell dipped his head in acquiescence.

Fjorn continued. "This is a tale of the early days, a tale of light and a tale of dark. A story of the moon now lost to us and how its light came to grace the sky. In the early days of the nine realms, Great Odin became distressed by the randomness of day and night. Thus, he set a spark captured from Muspelheim, the realm of fire, into the skies. It was bound to a chariot drawn by the great horses Arvak and Alsvinn and driven by Sol, daughter of Mundilfaeri, over the realms of Vangard, Midgard and Alfgard. But this is not a story of the sun. Rather I speak of Sol's brother, Mani. For Mani too had a chariot, granted by great Odin, that he could be the light of the night. Unlike his sister, Mani would draw no fire, for his light would be cool as the waters of the world.

"Towards setting this light in the skies, Odin did summon the Dvergar, dwarf, named Vidfinn, who had insulted Odin in the past. Odin did offer to forgive the slight if Vidfinn would surrender his two children and his greatest treasure, the cauldron Saeg, unto Odin that he might share it with the worlds of light.

"Saeg was so massive it took all three Dvergar to carry it. Odin did take Saeg and mount it on Mani's chariot.

"Now, Mani, I charge you. Follow your sister's course. Your horses will never tire, and your chariot never fail. Grant the cool light of Saeg to the lands of Vangard, Midgard and Alfgard. Let your glow strengthen all magic and be a balm to spirits and souls. You are the silver to your sister's gold. Together you shall inspire rich harvests and mighty ocean tides."

"Mani drove his chariot into the sky, and all was well with the light of night following the light of day. But as we know; peace is not eternal. In dark Jotunheim, a witch named Angrboda did look upon the lands of light with envy. She swore that if the sun and moon did not grace her realm, no realm would know their blessing. So, she set her wolves Skoll and Hati to chase the sun and moon and devour them.

"Sol and Mani saw the wolves coming at their heels and did drive their horses hard, but even so, the wolves did slowly close the distance and threaten the light they brought to the realms. At times the wolves would overtake the chariot of the sun or moon. At those times, mighty Thor would charge to the defence of the light; beating back the wolves; allowing Sol and Mani to escape. Even so, in time, the chariots did slow, and not even mighty Thor's protections proved enough. On a dark day, Skoll and Hati did overtake the sun and moon, and with their powerful jaws did rend them asunder, devouring the sources of light and warmth, casting our world into Fimbulwinter."

Fjorn paused, letting darkness dwell in every mind, then spoke again. "I ask you, though. Cannot a thing once made be remade? Cannot the broken blade be forged anew? Do sparks not fly from Muspelheim still? Could not Vidfinn, or some other Dvergar of great skill, forge the moon anew? Is the darkness a passing thing? I know not; the future is veiled, but I can hope. We can hope, and so I say, hail Sol and Mani. Come grace the skies, rejoin your eternal race and let the light to shine."

"In truth, let the sun and moon to shine again!" called Powell. Other voices joined the chant. Soon all in the hall called out, "Let the sun and moon to shine again."

The sound crested, then stilled. The red flame of the fire seemed to turn golden as if in memory of a better time. Everyone returned to their hides.

"Nicely told," commented Powell. "It is full night. The women should go."

Fjorn looked out through the roundhouse doorway into the darkness beyond, then at Sigurlina and Ragna. "I don't like sending you two up there alone."

"The Mother Superior was insistent that it be only women, and the stories we've heard from the Druids say that men will be killed by the dead," countered Sigurlina between spoonfuls of soup.

"Aye. They could just be stories to scare men away. Like tales of kraken when it's really tricky currents and hidden rocks," observed Audun.

"There's nought for it," said Kjorn. "Leastways, unless one of us wants to take the chance."

Jolnir bit his lip. "Sigurlina, I have something in my sea bench that might help. Would you mind if I walked you and Ragna as far as the ship?"

"If it helps keep us alive, I'll carry you as far as the ship," agreed Ragna.

Sigurlina, Ragna and Jolnir donned their boots and cloaks, then, taking a candle lantern, headed into the night. They crossed the village's courtyard and passed through the gate in the palisade. The darkness closed in, making the light from their lantern a small puddle in the night.

"Jolnir, what do you have to help us?" asked Sigurlina.

"More what you don't have, am I right?" smirked Ragna.

"You know?" gasped Jolnir.

Ragna smiled. "I've known a lot of longship crews. It made for an interesting night, and food and a room is food and a room. It would never be my preference, but it was fun."

"What are you talking about?" Sigurlina scratched her head.

'I know,' Munin spoke into Sigurlina's mind.

"What?" Sigurlina was getting frustrated.

"I need your spare dress," stated Jolnir.

"I don't think that will work. It would be too easy for men to get past the defences if they could be tricked that simply."

"Yura bitch, yura bitch," commented Munin.

"Munin," began Sigurlina.

'I peaked when we were following the trolls. It was by accident, and Jolnir was making a privy call, and....'

They reached the Apenhet, and Jolnir began stripping. "Please get me the dress. It's too cold to stand around without a tunic and cloak."

Sigurlina collected the dress from her sea bench and turned around. Her mouth dropped open. "Freya's tits. You have tits?"

Where Jolnir had stood, there was a wiry, small-busted woman wearing only Jolnir's leggings and boots.

"Who... How..." Sigurlina stammered.

"Give me the dress, then we can talk." It was Jolnir's voice.

Sigurlina passed over the dress. The woman put it on, girthed on Jolnir's sword and put on his / her cloak.

"You look better as a man." Ragna settled on the deck, arranging her cloak around herself.

"I... but you and Eir, does she know? Does Fjorn know? Does Jarl Erik?"

"Eir knows. How could she not? Have you never wondered why a thrall put off the advances of a Karl's son? Fjorn would do any woman proud. Eir is like me, only she likes being a woman. I..." Jolnir sighed. "I was raised a Karl's daughter, but it never felt right. I hated weaving and grinding grain. And men... have you ever looked at a fine horse and seen how beautiful it was?"

Sigurlina nodded.

"Did you want to bed it?"

"That's disgusting," Sigurlina scowled.

Ragna considered her forearm, "And painful, I'd guess."

Jolnir ignored the small woman. "That's what looking at a man is like for me. Fjorn is beautiful, like a horse, but the idea of being with him makes my stomach turn. I look at Eir, and my heart races. Can you understand that? We aren't that different."

Sigurlina closed her eyes. "So, you went a Viking and never came back. You became the man you wanted to be."

"I became the man I always was inside. I am a man, in my heart, in my mind, in my soul. My body is a cruel mistake. And as for your other questions. Jarl Erik knows. As long as I live as a guardsman, he cares more about my sword arm than what is under my tunic. I don't think Fjorn knows. Obasi is too dim-witted to guess."

"Vidurr must know. He'd smell it," observed Sigurlina.

'I knew,' Munin's voice echoed in Sigurlina's mind. 'I just don't know how it would work. I mean without a....'

"Munin, please," Sigurlina interrupted aloud.

"Vidurr has been helping keep your secret. Things like distracting people when you washed," observed Ragna. "I think Audun suspects, but he minds his own business better than anybody else I know."

"And now you know, Sigurlina. I couldn't let you go unguarded into danger." Jolnir stared at her crewmates with pleading eyes.

Sigurlina thought back over the weeks since she'd met Jolnir, and a host of odd things made sense. "You are Jolnir, my friend. I'm glad to have your sword at my side. No wonder you knew about red raspberry leaf tea."

Sigurlina stepped close. "Can I hug you as a friend?"

Jolnir's reply was to hug Sigurlina.

"We should go," said Ragna.

"Just a moment." Sigurlina hopped aboard the Apenhet returning with three unlit torches. "We won't light them unless we need them."

"Good thought," agreed Jolnir.

The three walked to the bridge, which consisted of split wood secured to posts with ropes so it could be raised up to block those who attempted to cross it.

Ragna looked at a sign that hung on a rope spanning the bridge. The sign depicted a limp phallus with an arrow through it and a pair of testicles being crushed with a war hammer. "That's subtle."

Sigurlina slowly read the runes that formed one line of text on the sign.

"Death awaits all men who cross this bridge. The Mother Superior really hates men."

"Some women do, often for no more reason than they don't understand us," said Jolnir.

"And sometimes because they understand some men all too well," Ragna added in a sad voice.

#

Obasi slipped out of the roundhouse and made his way to the privy letting Sigurlina,

148

Ragna, and Jolnir get well ahead before following them, using the dark as his cloak. He neared the pier and hid behind the hut that stood there.

His heart raced to learn of Jolnir's secret. When he delivered the spear to Aethelstan, the king would probably give him his pick of rewards. He would ask that Johnir be part of that bounty. Then he'd make her take the wafer and marry him. As his wife, she would have no choice. He would drive the devil from her flesh. He groped himself in anticipation. The three women started along the stone path.

A wolf howled in the forest.

Obasi considered stealing the gems from the devil's wheel that the superstitious heathens claimed kept the seasons changing on their cursed land, but he couldn't risk letting the women get too far ahead of him. He glanced at the pole that supported the season wheel and decided it could wait, then followed the women, his mind afire with the things he would do to Jolnir. He crossed the bridge. The trees to either side of the stone road closed in, creating a tunnel of living boughs. The candle lantern the women carried was a distant glimmer.

A twig snapped in the forest to his right. He paused. Another twig snapped to his left. Taking a deep breath, he pulled a silver crucifix out of a secret compartment sewn into his pouch and hung it around his neck.

"I swear my fidelity to the Roman Church and its appointed ruler, the Pope. Let its light protect me. Let no spectre or spirit have power over me."

There was another snap. A desiccated corpse lurched onto the path. It was shorter than Obasi and armed with a short sword. It charged him.

Obasi drew his sword and swung, severing the corpse's arm, sending its sword flying into the trees.

The corpse clawed at him with its remaining hand.

Obasi severed the corpse's neck. The body fell to the ground.

Three other corpses leapt onto the trail.

#

Jolnir paused, listening. "I hear a battle."

"Wonderful." Ragna rolled her eyes and glared at Sigurlina. "Whenever I go anywhere with you, it's always the same."

"We should light the torches." Jolnir opened the door on the candle lantern. Using a taper, she produced from her belt pouch, she transferred the flame to her torch.

Sigurlina and Ragna lit their torches from Jolnir's, then the three women hurried back along the stone road. The light of their torches revealed a scene of horror. Thirty or more corpses clustered around Obasi, who fought like a demon. For every corpse he felled, two seemed to take its place, and more were crowding the trail with every second.

A corpse shuffled onto the trail behind them. Sigurlina turned, her staff ready to smash it. The corpse walked by her and joined the mob attacking Obasi.

"We have to help him," observed Jolnir.

"Do any of us even like Obasi? He was following us. I know Audun thinks he's a spy," remarked Ragna.

"Still." Sigurlina lifted her staff and smashed one of the corpses. The blow left a deep dent in its skull but did nothing to slow its attack on Obasi. Obasi screamed and vanished under a tide of the dead.

Before the women could do more, the corpses shambled into the surrounding forest, except for one who picked up Obasi's body and carried it up the trail. One of the corpses paused to regard Jolnir for a second before shuffling on.

Sigurlina closed her eyes and tried to speak with the spirits, but there was nothing there. The corpses almost hummed with magic, but, unlike her black skeletons, there was no soul.

"We should get moving," suggested Jolnir.

#

Fjorn stared into the fire. "Jolnir must have told her."

Audun nodded. "I wasn't sure you knew."

"The Apenhet is a small ship. Wave tosses you, hands go where you don't intend, and secrets are lost. Eir was a surprise, but it explains why she said me nay all those years." Fjorn sighed. "It would be a sight to see. Not that I'd ever."

"You'll let them be." Audun scooped a bowl of soup out of the cauldron.

"I love Eir. I just didn't realise it was, perforce, as a sister. Jolnir has become a friend in a short time. Who am I to say how another should live? Some would say that I should seek a Karl's daughter for a wife, not the daughter of a town guard. Same thing as I see it. It's what we're fighting for. The freedom to live and not be a slave to the whims of Rome."

Audun's hand landed on Fjorn's shoulder. "My Karl. On to other matters. Obasi seems to be taking a long time at the privy."

Fjorn smiled. "And Vidurr isn't by the fire. We both suspect Obasi, and I wanted to test the stories of the dead defending the sanctuary."

"You let him go?" Audun stared at his friend.

Fjorn shrugged. "His actions will prove him. If he follows the women, he is a spy. If he is attacked by the dead, he will do us the service of confirming the stories. If he doesn't follow the women, and is still in the privy, he has my sympathy. If he is attacked, Vidurr knows to follow well back and as a wolf. It is almost certain Vidurr will avoid Obasi's fate. Vidurr can tell us what happens when he gets back."

Audun nodded. "About the village?"

Fjorn sighed and shook his head. "I saw. I'd find it refreshing if it were another time and place."

"They aren't complete fools. Powell told me that when the hawk arrived warning of the attack, they sent the children and elderly as well as most of the food, livestock and treasures to the next grove upriver," remarked Audun.

"That is something, but I still fear for the village," said Fjorn.

"What about the village?" Dvyn appeared beside the two other men.

"The defences are a bad joke," explained Audun.

"Oh…" Dvyn looked embarrassed. "You must think us fools. You have to understand. We're under the king's protection. We haven't had to fight, and honestly, keeping the path from Jorvik to the sea alive and green takes all our energy. I wanted to learn how to fight, but my father insisted I study the magic of life. Most of the others here have done the same. No one ever thought that Aethelstan would send troops over the frozen wastes."

Fjorn closed his eyes and nodded. "I can't fault you. You did what you had to, but it has left you vulnerable."

There was the sound of a wolf howl then Vidurr entered the roundhouse wearing a grim expression. He moved to Fjorn's side and spoke softly.

"Obasi is dead. The dead guard the sanctuary from all men. I saw them attack from this side of the bridge. The women seemed safe."

Fjorn poked at the fire with a stick. "Obasi finally did something to help us. Do you think the dead can hold against an army of Crusaders?"

Vidurr blinked slowly. "We will hold. My mate and my cub demand it."

Fjorn nodded. "My word will be kept." He stood. "I need to speak with Powell. Dvyn, come with me, please. I'll need your support, and I need you to tell me what a druid can and cannot do."

"Kjorn, have an oarsman bring me my warhorn from the Apenhet. It's in my sea bench. Find someone who knows the river and, if it's deep enough, take the other oarsmen and move the ship to the western edge of the grove. It's too much in the centre of things if there is a battle. Leave Svafnir and Gimnir with the ship. I trust them not to run if things go bad. Svafnir knows the ship, while Gimnir is good with a blade. Bring the rest of the men back here."

#

Sigurlina, Ragna and Jolnir came to a place where earth-covered stone mounds loomed up on either side of the trail. A gate of split lumber blocked their passage, and torches burnt on a wood palisade, as tall as a man's shoulder, that topped the mound. The gate before them opened, revealing a rectangular area containing two roundhouses, one three times the size of the other, and a courtyard. Obasi's corpse lay on a wooden platform in the middle of the courtyard surrounded by white-robed women. One of the women seemed to be performing the White God's Angel of Death duties on the body.

The Mother Superior left supervising the group and approached Sigurlina's trio. "Welcome, sisters. I see you've added a third. No matter. Afrikaisi, Baird, attend us."

A short, dusky-skinned woman and a tall, red-haired woman left the group by the body and accompanied the Mother Superior as she led the way into the smaller roundhouse.

No walls divided the structure into duns, leaving it as one large, circular room. Sigurlina could see a cauldron big enough to easily contain a man set over a fire in the building's middle. The cauldron shone with silver light. Sigurlina could feel magic radiating from it. A spear of wood, no longer than her arm and as thick as her thumb, hung from chains over the cauldron. Living mistletoe leaves grew from the spear, and a droplet of blood hung from its tip. As she watched, the droplet grew, then fell into the cauldron, which hissed. A young woman in a white robe lifted what looked like a ruby out with a pair of silver tongs. She moved the gem to a clay jug and deposited the stone within. Three other clay jugs flanked the one she'd put the ruby in.

"What do you see?" demanded the Mother Superior.

"I..." Sigurlina considered. "I see the mistletoe spear that still drips with the blood of Baldur. The blood becomes a stone as red as its source and the cauldron Saeg, but that cannot be. Hati devoured Saeg."

"Baird, tell our guests what it is you see." The Mother Superior smirked.

The red-haired woman bit her lip, then spoke. "I see the cauldron of Bran the Blessed that brings dead warriors to half-life, and the sling of Lugh that always hits its mark and the enchanted sling stone that still drips with the blood of the giant king Balor who Lugh slew. The blood drips into the caldron forming emeralds as green as summer leaves. Each emerald holds the energy of the world of plants."

"Afrikaisi," the Mother Superior beckoned the short, dark woman forward. "Afrikaisi comes from outer Midgard, a place where a river flows through lands so dry that there is nought but sand. It is a place where the knowledge of the old ways has been nearly extinguished, but they continue like a flickering candle." The Mother Superior smiled at the dusky woman. "And in Afrikaisi, we have one of their brightest sparks. Speak, Afrikaisi, tell us what you see?"

Afrikaisi smiled. "I see the eye of the falcon, son of Aset, Horus, suspended over the knot of life twisted in silver, the tyet, the womb of Aset. The eye weeps tears of carnelian for the father it has never known in life. Those tears fall and harden on the tyet. They are the power of the life that comes of the union of man and woman."

"And I see a wicked Roman spear, long-bladed and cruel, that drips dark blood from its tip into a simple wooden cup. The cup fills with obsidian. The gems draw the evils of man as a poultice, clearing the way for new and better life to be born. I ask you, sisters, who sees true?"

"This is silly." Ragna inched towards the clay pots of precious stones.

Sigurlina bowed her head in thought, then half-whispered, "We all do, and none of us does."

The Mother Superior smiled. "But how, child?"

Sigurlina spoke softly. "It is none of the things we see, and all of them. The spear and the cauldron are divine. They are... Before the Gods, there were powers, older, greater, more primal and unrefined. The gods shaped them into what we know. But those powers are too much for any mortal to face in true form. They would drive us mad, so we dress them in a way that we can see and touch. It's like looking at a bright fire through a clear gem. It means nothing to the fire, but to the one who looks, the brightness is lessened, and the gem changes what you see as you look through it. What we expect to see is like the colour of the gem."

The Mother Superior smiled. "My dear, if you ever wish it, you will be welcomed amongst us. You grasp the core of truth. When the moon went dark, a fragment of essence, long bound, was freed and flowed back to itself like a cup of water poured back into a lake. The essence cannot be destroyed. The fragment of essence simply mixed with the greater power of itself. The cup is a fragment of that essence, of the cool light that is the healing and life-giving power of what I call the Holy Spirit, and you know as female or Goddess. The spear is the power of man to defend or oppress, to seek justice or injustice. It is an essence, and their union delivers life in a form based on what she who takes the gem from the cauldron expects."

Ragna yipped. All eyes turned to where she was pulling her hand back from one of the clay pots.

The Mother Superior chuckled. "That is not for you, my dear."

"I... I was just looking and... well." Ragna held out her hand, showing that the tips of her fingers were burnt.

"What?" began Sigurlina.

"This is part of the puzzle the Myrddin of Arthur's time left to safeguard the magics. He cast powerful protections on the items in this sanctuary. None save a maid may take the stones from the jars, but none who has not known the love of man and woman may use them. That much of the riddle is easy to circumvent. The rest is harder, for no man may enter the sanctuary, but no woman may touch the spear and keep her life. Only a woman who has recently known the love of man may move the cauldron and live, and the cauldron may not be moved until the spear has been taken down."

"It is a riddle that can't be solved." Jolnir shook her head.

"Mother Superior, the last rights are done," spoke a voice from the roundhouse's entrance.

"Then let the dryads bring in the corpse." The Mother Superior motioned for everyone to move away from the cauldron. Six women carried Obasi's body on a pallet into the roundhouse. Bracing the pallet on the cauldron's lip, they tilted it until the corpse slid into the vessel.

"This is the magic of Bran the Blessed," whispered Baird.

The cauldron glowed with a light like a full moon.

Sigurlina fell to her knees, clutching at the spirit stones that were her grandmother's final gift. "Stop shouting, stop shouting."

Munin left her perch on Sigurlina's shoulder and landed on the floor. "Yura bitch, Yura bitch. What's happening?"

Jolnir looked at the raven. Rising out of the bird was a ghostly image of a pretty, dark-haired young woman. "Who?" he demanded.

"I… I'm me again," said the girl that seemed to grow out of the raven.

"She is Munin as she was in her human life," observed a beautiful, thirtyish woman who looked enough like Sigurlina to be her sister.

"You again! What's wrong with Sigurlina?" Ragna put her hands on her hips and glared at the spirit of Inga, Sigurlina's grandmother.

"It is the cauldron. Near it, the powers of magic and spirits are increased. I should have thought that one who is sensitive might be overwhelmed. I will help her to leave." Afrikaisi moved to take Sigurlina's arm.

Other spirits began to appear, some wispy and indistinct, some almost solid in appearance.

Inga looked at Sigurlina with compassion. "Leave her. From pain comes learning. From learning, comes power. She will need power with what is to come."

"Look, you old biddy," began Ragna.

Ingvarr, Sigurlina's great, great, grandfather, materialised by Inga. The shade was of a warrior in his prime dressed in chainmail with a great sword. He smiled at Inga, then spoke gravely. "My little cat is right. For Sigurlina's sake, do not interfere."

A wild-haired crone materialised on Inga's other side, blocking access to Sigurlina. "She's done better than I would have thought, although she has only just begun," admitted the shade."

"Thank you, Katla. I'm quite proud of my girl," remarked Inga.

"It's killing her," objected Ragna.

Shades now filled the roundhouse, nearly crowding out the living. The women from the sanctuary stared wide-eyed, some seeing a loved one now passed, others seeing old foes. Teary reunions and long-dead arguments erupted all around the room.

"Does the forge kill the iron?" asked Inga.

"Enough," called the Mother Superior, who stood by the cauldron. "By the Lamb of God and the three that are one, I command you bothersome spirits of ill intent, return to your rest and trouble this place no more."

Ragna felt pressure like wind against her back as half of the spirits were driven from the room. The fights stopped, and loved ones continued to whisper words they'd longed to speak.

Sigurlina groaned and blinked.

Inga turned to face the Mother Superior. "Impressive, sister, but it changes nothing. She is my granddaughter, and she needs to be tempered."

"This is my sanctuary! You do not command me, but I concede to your request, within reason." The Mother Superior moved to stand in front of Inga.

"Fair words." Inga dipped her head.

Sigurlina whimpered, then looked up. Her skin glowed silver as her teeth clenched.

Her body trembled as she rose to her feet. "I... will... not... be... ruled!" Her voice was strained but clear. "I will rule!"

Her skin glowed brighter, rivalling the cauldron. "Kneel."

All the spirits in the shelter dropped to one knee. Inga, Ingvarr and Katla were the last to do so. Sigurlina closed her eyes and swallowed. "All save my grandmother, say your farewells and go thee to your rest until summoned."

The spirits dipped their heads, turned briefly to the living they knew then vanished. Sigurlina faced her grandmother. "Thank you."

"Could I do less, dear?" Inga smiled.

Sigurlina held out one of the two remaining witch stones. "I return that which was gifted."

"Are you sure?" asked Inga.

Sigurlina nodded, then grinned. "I don't want you peeking in on Fjorn and me."

"Cheek." Inga giggled and swished her hips. "I take your point. He is a fine example of a man." She sighed. "If I was sixty years younger and alive, I might make you fight for him. I'll still be about if you need me. I love you, child."

"I love you too, grandmother. Now I bid thee rest."

Inga vanished as the moon-like glow from the cauldron diminished.

The ghostly form of Munin sighed. "Well, the flying part is fun." With another sigh, she sank into the raven.

"I'm sorry, girl. Had I known how vulnerable you were–," began the Mother Superior.

Sigurlina held up her hand to stop the apology. "It was necessary. I–."

"Surt's flaming nuts!" swore Ragna.

Everyone jerked around to see Obasi climb from the cauldron and stand on the dirt floor. His skin was burnt red, and he gazed blankly ahead. The Mother Superior walked up to the ghoul. "I charge thee. Let no man come within a hundred strides of the sanctuary wall and live. Bring the corpses of all who die within a hundred strides of the sanctuary to the sanctuary's gate. These are your orders until the end of time. Now, go outside the sanctuary walls and perform your duty."

Obasi's corpse shuffled from the roundhouse.

"That isn't something you see every day," commented Ragna.

"His spirit has fled. Only the flesh remains." A war horn sounded in the distance interrupting the Mother Superior. "What was that?"

"The Crusaders have entered the grove," said Sigurlina.

"I did not know you had the sight?" said the Mother Superior.

"I don't need it. That was Fjorn's horn." Sigurlina's face was pale, and her voice strained.

Ragna moved to Sigurlina's side and placed a hand on her shoulder. "Fjorn is smart."

"If anyone can bring victory, it will be him," agreed Jolnir, then in a softer voice. "Whether he acknowledges it or not, he is his father's son, and there was never better in mortal kind at the art of battle than the Great Jarl."

'I could fly over and check.' Munin offered into Sigurlina's thoughts.

"No, Munin. Thank you, but there will be a lot of crossbows. I won't risk you for my peace of mind." Sigurlina faced the Mother Superior. "We need to get the treasures out of here before we are besieged."

"I have agreed to no such thing." There was heat in the Mother Superior's voice.

"Honoured, Mother Superior. Do you think you are safe behind your army of the dead?" asked Jolnir.

"They have never failed us."

Jolnir nodded. "I have lived as a man for seven years, as a king's guard for five of them. Your dead guards have never faced warriors trained to fight together. All the Crusaders will have to do is form an enclosed formation with shields to the outside, and they will cut through your dead protectors like wheat. You're mistaken to believe there is no thought in conducting a battle. The truth is, to lead men to victory, you must think. I can see a dozen ways to defeat your dead defenders, and once at the sanctuary, it would be an easy siege. Fire the palisade. Hack down the trees that grow close to your walls so they fall, smashing your defences. Do you have bows enough to make an attacker pay for closing on your gates?"

The Mother Superior gazed from Sigurlina to Jolnir. "You know that if we lose the cauldron and the spear, we cannot make the gems that maintain the groves. We have maybe enough stored in the other groves to last a year, but after that...."

"If the Crusaders steal the treasures, you won't have them anyway. At least with us--," began Sigurlina.

"With you, they won't be locked away and hidden in the hopes that they are forgotten so that some man may claim superiority to all. I know...I know. I must think upon this."

"You want to think? The Crusaders are coming! Don't you know what that means?" Ragna's voice squeaked.

"Better than most." The Mother Superior hugged herself. "Better than most. I still must consider. No matter my decision, there are things that must be done. Do you think I let the old Myrddin's protections stand alone? For three hundred years, I, and my predecessors, have woven spells on the house in which you stand. Do you think they can be removed in an instant? As things are, even if I let you take our treasures, and you could defeat the old High Myrddin's enchantments, you would be little more than empty shells bereft of spirit before you left the roundhouse. I will have your answer before dawn. If the answer is yes, I will have countered the enchantments on the house as best I can. I can promise no more than that. I give you leave to order the women of the sanctuary to our defence. I pray your skills may yet save us. Afrikaisi, attend to our guests. They are in charge of our defence."

Afrikaisi led Jolnir, Sigurlina and Ragna into the courtyard.

Turning, the small, dark woman asked, "How may we serve you?"

"We're doomed," remarked Ragna.

Chapter 15: Preparation

Fjorn stared into the fire. All was quiet, and the village seemed to sleep. He could feel something like a storm on the horizon.

Neese burst through the roundhouse door. He was clad in a grey robe and cloak. Coming to a halt by Fjorn, he spoke. "The Crusaders are coming. I saw their torches. Their column will be at the grove's edge before morning. I'm guessing that there are near two hundred of them. We underestimated back at Lax Bay, or more have joined them from someplace since."

Fjorn looked at Dvyn, who sat by the central fire with a slender, chestnut-haired dryad nestled into his side. "Wynne, please wake Powell. Neese, go back and keep an eye on the column. Leave an obvious trail. We'll find you. Dvyn, ready the druids."

"Right, I'll be up a tree with my crossbow. There are some good vantages just inside the edge of the grove." Neese bolted out of the roundhouse.

Fjorn shook Audun and Kjorn awake. "It's begun. Audun, help Dvyn and the druids. Kjorn, ready the crew. We march as soon as we are able."

Powell appeared from one of the duns. He was pale, and his voice shook when he spoke. "I'm still not sure about facing the Crusaders in the wilds. Wouldn't we be safer behind the village wall? The dead will stop them if they try to breach the sanctuary."

Fjorn moved to the village leader's side. "Powell, we discussed this. There are over a hundred Crusaders. From everything you've told me, the dead are a mob, nothing more. It would take thousands of them to stop a hundred trained, organised soldiers. And say what you will of the Crusaders. On the battlefield, they are some of the best in Midgard. We need to weaken them and split their forces. Even at that, we may not win. They outnumber us if we only count the living. And they are battle-hardened. We can die when they breach the town's barricade or fight them where your druids are strongest and maybe buy ourselves a chance by splitting their force. Those are our choices. You made me your war chief. You need to let me be your war chief."

Powell bit his lip and nodded. "I bow to your experience. Do what you must, but please, don't spend our lives if you can help it."

Fjorn looked grim. "I am in no rush to see Valhalla. I spend no life for little gain. Prepare your bowmen. When the town is besieged, they will be a true asset. Shooting a man takes no more skill than shooting a deer." Fjorn moved to join his crew, a group of five druids and Wynne, who'd agreed to follow Dvyn. With a silent prayer, Fjorn led them outside.

Vidurr howled, becoming the giant wolf. He sniffed the air, then followed a line of tracks through the winter woods.

"Are your people ready?" Fjorn moved to Dvyn's side.

"As we can be from training with wooden swords when the weather was good. I've 'played' at swordsmanship with most of them. We have a tournament every summer, grove against grove. To you, it would seem silly."

"At home, I train with a wooden blade. Don't count your people short. Much can be learned in friendly practice," Fjorn slapped Dvyn on the back.

"I told the council of Myrddins this would happen, but our need was for Earth shapers, so that is what we trained." Dvyn tentatively touched the handle of the short sword he wore on his belt. He had a battered round shield slung over his back.

Fjorn eyed Dvyn's followers, who were armed and attired similarly to Dvyn, then spoke in an even, reassuring voice that carried. "Used right, life can be a weapon. Do what I command and stay back from the fray if you are able. Our goal is to weaken the foe while keeping our strength intact. This is only the beginning. Be smart, and we may live to drain a horn and brag of our exploits."

Vidurr stopped at the base of a large oak tree and cocked a leg.

"Really, wolf." The voice came from a high branch. There was the sound of shuffling then Neese clambered down the trunk.

"Where are they?" asked Fjorn.

Neese pointed to a sloping wall of ice and snow that looked like somebody had cut semicircles out of it with a giant scoop. Mist hung over the icy escarpment. "A line of torches two hundred strides that way. They must be digging a road for themselves."

"Shoot one of them when they are about to break through, so we know where to strike." Fjorn turned to his team and pointed out two oarsmen. "You two are good with crossbows. Find a tree and take all the bolts you can carry. All you crossbowmen, when you run out of bolts, fall back to the village. I don't want to risk losing you to swordplay. We'll be right behind you."

The two oarsmen scrambled up trees flanking Neese's.

"Audun, take who you need and prepare your surprise. Everyone else, be quiet and take positions. Once you're set, cover the lanterns and keep torches handy." Fjorn moved to the edge of the grove, wincing at the noise the druids made and the amount of instruction his crew had to give to get them in position.

Then the waiting began. Cold crept into Fjorn's feet and hands. Kjorn shuffled away to his right, and there was the sound of water splashing against a tree trunk. One of the druids sneezed. Vidurr, in his wolf form, twitched and made a half whimpering sound, then seemed to chase after something. Audun pulled a wineskin from his shoulder, took a swig, then shuffled through the darkness to offer the skin to Fjorn. Fjorn took a swallow and almost gagged as the ice-distilled mead burnt its way to his stomach. He passed back the skin. Dvyn sat with his back to a tree holding Wynne's hand, seemingly lost in thought.

There was the sound of a twang followed by a scream. Fjorn's team threw the covers off their lanterns and ignited torches. There was another twang and a scream. Fjorn pinpointed where the scream came from and led his people to that section of the sloping ramp of ice and snow at the grove's edge. The frozen barrier opened, revealing a trail four could walk abreast, blocked by a long column of armoured men wielding spades.

Dvyn and another Druid spoke a sentence in Gallic and made motions with their hands. The ground under the first ranks of Crusaders on their trail turned into a half-frozen swamp soaking the invaders to the skin. Next, two other druids spoke a phrase and made a motion like an open-fingered punch. Thorny vines erupted into being across the trail's opening, spearing the Crusaders in the first rank, making a near-impenetrable barrier.

Fjorn put his war horn to his lips and released a blast.

Vidurr bounded forward, leading a group of four druids and Wynne into the mist topping the snows adjacent to the Crusaders' trail. The druids and dryad moved over the snow and ice with almost as much ease as the wolf. There was the sound of crossbows from the Crusader's trench. Neese and the other archers shot back and, judging from the screams, took a toll on the invading force.

The druids with Vidurr cast their spells; there was a shriek from the Crusader's force. Water sieved through the thorn barricade at the front of the invader's trench. The druids and Wynne raced further along the side of the Crusaders' trail and cast their spells again. More water sieved through the thorns as the sound of crossbows being released echoed up from the trench.

Wynne screamed. A second later, Vidurr howled. Moments after that, Vidurr, in human guise, stepped into the grove carrying Wynne with the four druids following moments later.

"Bring her here," ordered Fjorn.

Wynne was laid on the snow. Fjorn carefully extracted the bolt from her shoulder, then sang.

"Youth to the Gods, golden apples of grace.

"Idun's power heal mortals of faith."

Wynne opened her eyes and took a deep breath.

"Hang back while you regain your strength," ordered Fjorn. He turned to Vidurr. "How did it work?"

"We soaked maybe a third of them. There's at least two hundred in the column. Some are carrying large pieces of wood," observed Vidurr.

"Now, we let the cold work for us," observed Kjorn.

"The front ranks are falling back. The torches at the rear have moved into the dead trees. I think they're building fires." Neese called from above.

"Thor's hairy nuts! Their commander has sense," hissed Kjorn.

"They're cutting into the snow at the sides of their trench just out of crossbow range. I think they intend to exit at several points. They are leaving an ice shelf on the trail's edge so the crossbowmen can stand on it and see over the side. They'll shoot anything that approaches the trench."

Fjorn considered. "Spread the druids out. Audun, we'll likely need your trick sooner than expected."

"I'm ready, and it seems that Wynne can help with it." Audun pointed to the dryad.

160

"Good. Be ready." Fjorn watched the ice slope.

"Should we do another run?" asked Dvyn.

"They expect it now. Before, they were shooting blind. Now they'd fill you all with bolts." Fjorn bit his lip. "Still, it was a good trick. Here's hoping those bastards lose more than a few toes from it. Cover the lanterns and be silent. Heal any injuries and wait."

#

Jolnir walked around the inside of the palisade with half a dozen of the sanctuary's women focusing on his every word. In another time and place, he might have enjoyed it, but thoughts of Eir coupled with the impending threat told him those days were over. He missed Eir, the smell of her hair, her laugh. Like men in all times, it spurred him on.

"I will come back to you, beloved." His posture straightened, and he forgot the dress he wore. "Galvyn, I want pots and buckets of boiling water ready. When Crusaders close on the wall, I want them poached. Hot, cold and especially wet will be our allies in this fight.

"Cabe, we only have two crossbows and three short bows. We'll need to make every bolt and arrow count. Tell the archers to hold until they have a sure shot, and, by the Gods, tell them to keep their heads down. That goes for everyone. Do not give the Crusaders a target. Keep low. Oadira, collect a team. Cut branches from the nearby trees and fill the gaps in the palisade that a bolt could pass through."

A middle-aged woman with grey-streaked, dark hair in braids left the group to follow the order.

Jolnir nodded approval. "Afrikaisi, we're outnumbered, so I want a clear path to the healing station for everybody on the wall. Any injury is to be healed at once. I'm told you've skill in this area, so I'll leave the preparations to you."

"Yes, Jolnir. It will be as you say." The small, dark woman moved to the middle of the courtyard, where she was joined by several other women.

Jolnir turned his attention back to the defence. "When the enemy breaches the palisade, it will be hand to hand. That's when–."

#

Sigurlina stood by the stone path ninety-eight strides from the sanctuary with a group of six dryads. She had just strung a rope from the drawbridge into the woods. The rope was looped through the block and tackle that had once lifted the bridge. The pulley was now tied to a tree on the bank on one end and the corner of the bridge on the other. The pull rope was suspended in easy reach of her hiding place. The Orse River was at its pre-Fimbulwinter levels, and the securing lines on the drawbridge were cut so that the bridge rested loosely on its mounts.

Sigurlina turned to address her team. "We want to force them into the woods and break their formation. That will make them vulnerable to the dead."

The dryads nodded as one and dispersed into the forest. Baird remained by Sigurlina. Raising her hand, the dryad turned a section of the road five strides long into a half-frozen quagmire. To either side, thorn thickets sprang up, blocking the path between the trees, angling back to the river where a path of dry land, wide enough for one man to walk along, cut between the thorns and another frozen quagmire.

"Good." Sigurlina knelt on the ground. "Come hither servant, durable symbol of our ending. I summon thee black one."

The dryad gasped as the black skeleton rose out of the earth.

Sigurlina spoke. "Go to the watergate and stay hidden. Wait until the Crusaders are wading across the river, then pull the rope that lifts the bridge reinforcing the gate. Do not drain the gate first. Just lift the bridge. If the gate breaks, that is good. If it doesn't, open the side of the gate you're on. We want as many Crusaders as possible in the water when the watergate bursts. After the water level drops, kill the Crusaders that the current knocks over. Then, if you still exist, you may seek an honourable second death against the Crusaders. Do you understand?"

The skeleton nodded and walked down the road, barely noticing the quagmire it waded through.

"The dead can't follow such complex commands," observed Baird.

"The ones with souls can. We need to hide. Call your sisters."

"You...There is a soul bound to that? That is horrible!" Baird's features grew even paler.

Sigurlina sighed. "Baird, wasn't it?"

Baird nodded as she hugged herself.

Sigurlina fought to keep her tone reasonable. "If we do not use my servant to do this, one of us will have to. Being on the other side of the river is certain death. With this, I save one of your sister's lives."

"But..."

"Also, if you were trapped without a body, wouldn't you welcome a chance to earn a place in the worlds beyond?"

Baird bit her lip and exhaled noisily.

"My servant has a chance to die again. If they die well; they may pass to a realm where they belong. Should I be ashamed that I offer them that chance?"

"I... You are strange to me, woman of the north. I will think on your words."

"Good, now call your sisters. Munin, perch in the trees where you can watch the other riverbank. You are my eyes, my brave bird."

"Good bird. Good bird." Munin vanished into a tall oak.

\#

Ragna moved about the sanctuary's common, supervising a group of young women who were digging holes, placing sharpened stakes into the holes before refilling them with loose snow. Other women buried ropes that were tied to piles of firewood.

"Now, Leslie," ordered Ragna.

A woman with short, black hair cast a druidic spell. Water bubbled up, filling a low pond sided with logs in front of the sanctuary's gate.

"Put the ropes where I told you." Ragna smiled. "If we weren't all going to die, this could be fun. I need to make new friends!"

#

"They're breaking through twenty strides left and right of the original passage. They're clearing the original passage as well." Neese's voice called down from his hide in the tree.

Fjorn sounded a short bleat on his horn, announcing to his troops that the foe was coming once more.

The ice slope shattered as a flight of crossbow bolts flew into the grove. Druids gestured, and the first two ranks of Crusaders in each of the openings found themselves hip-deep in freezing water. The Crusaders behind them used their comrades as steppingstones and charged onto the shallower snows of the grove. Thorns erupted out of the ground, spearing some of the oncoming hoard. The Crusaders behind the thorns hacked their comrades free of the magical growth then, using sword and axe, continued the advance. A Crusader pushed ahead of his comrades and charged Wynne, who gestured in a near panic. The Crusader's blade turned into a venomous snake that bit him. He dropped the snake. It turned back into a sword as Wynne retreated.

The Crusaders continued to advance. The crossbows from the trees fell silent. Seconds later, Neese and the two oarsmen raced towards the village, bows slung on their backs. Fjorn sang as he fended off two Crusaders who were hip-deep in freezing mud.

"The shields of Asgard are shields of might.

"Turn the wrath of giants to flight.

"Shields to hold a warrior's might.

"The shields of Asgard are shields of might."

A sparkling shield formed in front of Fjorn, turning the blade of one of the Crusaders. Fjorn thrust into the other man, opening his throat, which showered blood into his remaining foe's eyes, allowing Fjorn to split open the second man's skull.

Crusaders poured into the grove. A Druid fell with a spear through his chest. An oarsman blocked a blade intended for one of the druids but exposed himself to a lethal thrust. Three venomous snakes crawled over the snow, biting Crusaders before turning back into swords.

Audun swung with his battle-axe, driving a Crusader back into a quagmire where he tripped and sank into the freezing mud amongst his mired comrades.

Three Crusaders closed on Audun like dogs worrying a bear. The big man swung his battle-axe back and forth, holding his assailants at bay until Dvyn came up behind them and gestured. Thorny vines enveloped the Crusaders, pinning their arms. Audun ended the restrained men.

Blood poured from Vidurr's wounds as he swung his sword as if it were a scythe, laying Crusaders low and driving others towards a field of thorns. A snake slithered amongst the

Crusaders biting one of their ankles before being stomped on and turning back into a sword.

Kjorn stood with a Druid and an oarsman facing seven Crusaders. Three of the Crusaders hung back and pulled crossbows from their shoulder harnesses. Kjorn and the oarsman parried the other Crusader's advance while the Druid fell back and gestured. A wall of thorns erupted around the forward Crusaders. Bloodied, the invaders fought on. Moments later, bolts flew through gaps in the thorns driving into Kjorn and the oarsmen. Both fell. The Druid cried, "NO," then gestured to the ground. Water jetted into the air covering Kjorn and the oarsmen. Both opened their eyes and grunting, pulled bolts from their wounds. The foremost of the Crusaders struggled free of the thorns as the crossbowmen came around the thorn barrier and prepared new bolts.

Fjorn could see that sheer numbers would overwhelm the defenders. Lifting his war horn, he sounded two blasts for the retreat.

Audun and Wynne fell back from their battles to stand beside mounds of loose snow they had collected earlier.

Kjorn, the druids and the oarsman scrambled away from the Crusaders, throwing themselves behind trees, barely avoiding the next round of crossbow bolts.

Vidurr swung with his blade, decapitating a Crusader. The Ulfhednar lapped at the blood that flowed from the stump of his victim's neck, healing the worst of his wounds before he howled, taking on his wolf form and bounded away from the battle.

Dvyn and the rest of the druids and oarsmen fell back.

Audun and Wynne called the wind. The piles of snow erupted into the air creating a whiteout, driving into the Crusaders.

The defenders ran into the woods and hurried towards the village.

#

Sigurlina heard two blasts of a distant horn from her position on the sanctuary's defences. The light from the season pole was beginning to grow. She shook her head and clambered down from the stone embankment into the sanctuary's courtyard, where several dryads waited. "Fjorn is retreating."

One of the dryads ran into the roundhouse containing the artefacts and emerged with the Mother Superior. She walked over to Sigurlina. "Dawn has come, and my acolyte tells me the grove's first defence has fallen."

"And," demanded Ragna.

"And, I would rather see the treasures used to defend the world than locked away by hypocrites that have left my beloved Lord's path. If you can find a way to free the treasures from the old Myrddin's enchantments; I will do nothing to hinder you taking them. I have opened the enchantments on the shelter that houses the treasures."

"Thank you."

"We'll need to tell Fjorn," observed Jolnir.

164

"He's trying to get to the village," said Sigurlina.

"How do you know that?" asked the Mother Superior.

"He's sounded the retreat, but he hasn't sounded the troops assembled. There are two things I know for sure. One, Fjorn won't enter the village until all his people do. Two, when he does, he'll announce it so that everyone knows to move to the next stage."

"Not that it matters," said Ragna. "We can't get to him, and what would we do if we could? We can't take the spear, and if we don't take the spear, we can't take the cauldron. We're a sheep on a boat that has been at sea too long."

Sigurlina crinkled her brow. "We're mutton stew?"

"No." Ragna rolled her eyes.

"What then?"

Jolnir shook his head. "You don't want to know."

"Lonely Shepherd's delight," remarked the Mother Superior with a twitch of her lips.

"Exactly," confirmed Ragna.

Sigurlina looked confused.

Minutes later, three distant horn blasts sounded.

"Fjorn and his team are in the village," announced Sigurlina.

"Wonderful. Now how do we let him know that we have permission to take the spear none of us can touch anyway?" asked Ragna.

"I'll send Munin when the time is right. For now, I need to go down the stone road. The dryads aren't used to fighting. Mother Superior, do you know the runes?" asked Sigurlina.

"No. I know Latin, but none of the men in the village do."

"So much for a message," snipped Ragna.

Sigurlina bit her lip and glowered at the smaller woman. "Mother Superior, could you please bring me ink and a thin hide. Fjorn and Audun can both read rune script. Once we decide what we're doing, I'll send a message to them with my raven."

"Oh, all fancy now, thinks she can write." Ragna crossed her arms and sniffed.

Jolnir smiled and nodded. "I hope she can. It might save our lives."

"I will have the hide and ink waiting when you return to the sanctuary," replied Mother Superior.

#

The freezing water around the Crusader's waist turned to earth. The cold bit into him, and the blizzard blinded him, filling his nose and mouth with snow. As quickly as it had come, the blizzard ceased. His comrades charged into the woods.

"Are you alive?" asked a gravelly voice.

"I am. Zenon was under the water when it turned to earth," replied the half-buried man.

"Then he is with the Lord. The Shepherd has ordered that we dig you out before joining the fray. Let's get this done before we lose out on the plunder. Rumour is the heathens have been hoarding emeralds and rubies that they waste on their profane, debauched rights. A handful of gems like that could set a man up for life." The second Crusader sank a shovel into the dirt around the half-buried man.

#

Verniamin sat as close to the fire as he could under a borrowed, dry cloak, and still, he shivered. Some Crusaders crowded around him while others gathered wood. His soaking clothes and armour hung on a polearm with its haft thrust into the snow. Wounds and scratches from the thorns covered his skin. He thought back to the olive fields of his home. His brother was probably sitting in the hall with his family.

"If only I'd let the bastard drown when he fell into the millstream, then I'd be the first son. Then I would have inherited the estate and wouldn't be freezing in some foreign ice pit." Verniamin muttered as his shivering grew worse. He reached to pull the cloak closer, then paused. The fingers of his right hand were black and wouldn't move. He hid them before the monk could see them. "If my choices are between dead and crippled, I will trust in the Lord to accept my sacrifice."

#

Theodosios stepped into the clearing around a log palisade that surrounded the village, only to throw himself back into the woods when an arrow whizzed by his ear.

Lifting a horn suspended by a strap on his chest, he blew four quick blasts.

"Good, assemble the men. No point in throwing lives away before we're ready for the assault," commented Oreste.

Theodosios looked at his Lord and older brother, who was clad in chain mail and held a longsword and shield similar to his own. "How many can we count on? We lost a lot of men breaking through the ice wall."

"We have an effective force. The leader of House Demoleon drowned. If we need men, I'm sure his house would join us."

"Might solve another problem too."

Oreste looked at his brother in confusion.

"Demoleon had a daughter and no sons. She's only eleven, but they'll need a protector with the world gone dark. The Pope did promise rewards if we capture the heathen treasures," explained Theodosios.

"In the middle of a battle, and you're trying to arrange a marriage?" Oreste shook his head.

"Spoken like a firstborn. I don't want to go from war to war all my life hoping to impress some duke or king with lands to give."

While the brothers spoke, several men gathered around them.

"I can't blame you, but let us win the battle first. Stay here and assemble the household. I'll search the area before we attack. Rumour has it that the heathens keep the women and men separate. Sounds like Sodom if you ask me, but we'll need to find both compounds."

"I'll have some of the lads build a fire away from the fort. Then we can assemble one of the ballista. Firebolts should make short work of that palisade," observed Theodosios.

"Good thought, little brother. If we keep using our heads, we may just get to go home." Oreste smiled. "Do you remember mother's baklava?"

"How could I forget? Something worth fighting for." Theodosios unconsciously licked his lips.

"From the looks of things, it shouldn't be hard to take that village. The Shepherds will be along as soon as they're done seeing to the wounded." Oreste turned to move away.

"Oreste, what about the devil spells?" asked Theodosios.

"I've not seen devil magics that cold steel and a brave heart couldn't defeat. We are the warriors of God. By his providence, we shall prevail. At the least, the Pope waved the tithes on our land for us joining the crusade. If it wasn't for that, we'd have lost the estate and mother and father would be on the street. We can't let that happen. We have to fight no matter the enemies' powers." Oreste strode into the growing light from the brightening season wheels.

#

Lucian strummed his lute and sang.

"Gentle lamb, oh son of God.

"Heal those whose faith is true.

"Let the wounds to close and seal.

"By your grace, their wounds to heal."

"I don't trust your magic, boy," griped a towering warrior dressed in chain, wearing a cap helm and carrying a broadsword and kite shield.

"I'm sorry I offend you, my Lord." Lucian bowed his head, his long, golden hair falling over his chest.

"Should have taken the cut like the other choir boys," griped the big man.

Lucian stood. He was slender and well-muscled, and, while not as tall as the other man, he was still taller than most of the wounded men who stood up after his healing. He wore an ox-hide chest plate that had scale mail sleeves attached. The armour looked like it was pieced together from cast-offs. "Then you would have no grandchildren to continue your line."

"Don't remind me, songbird! Get back to your duties." The big man stomped away.

"Do not pay Agis any mind. You do the Lord's work with your song. God has blessed you, and in time your father will see it." Babak, a short Crusader with a swarthy complexion, black hair and a scar on his jaw, comforted.

"Shepherd, I didn't see you there." Lucian bowed his head.

"It often happens when Agis is nigh. Heal those you can under my authority. I feel this may not be as easy a battle as we were led to believe. Whoever is commanding the heathens knows a thing or two."

"But we were told they were sorcerers. Dealers in dark arts who knew nothing of battle." Lucian moved so that he was in the midst of another group of wounded.

Babak shook his head. "That is your father speaking. We've both seen that the Pagans are not fools. They must still be brought into the Lord's house, but I do not think they are as black of soul as the priests tell us. And there is something familiar about the way this battle has gone. Heal all you can. When they are healed and warm, send the first ten to me and the rest to Agis." Babak walked away.

CHAPTER 16: DEAD MAN'S BATTLE

Sigurlina moved up the road. Looking ahead, she could see Crusaders mustering across the river. She reached the dryads hiding behind the trees, checked that the rope from the block and tackle was ready, and then hid. The silver light of the grove cast long shadows in the woods.

Ten Crusaders in a box phalanx crossed the bridge.

"Why can't you just leave us alone?" muttered Sigurlina.

The first rank of men found the road blocked by a quagmire. They spread out and began looking for a way past the obstacles. There was the sound of snapping twigs on all sides.

\#

Diocles crept along the edge of the thorn thicket. He missed his home, but as the third son of a count, he was lucky to be allowed to join the crusade and avoid the priesthood. He thought of his Agape. So beautiful, well above his station, but if he could win glory, perhaps her father would accept him. He came to a path of solid ground between the thorns and another swamp. Creeping forward, he moved into the forest behind the thorn thicket.

"I've found a—." He called before it leapt upon him. An old woman, her skin burnt red, a dagger in her hand. He fended her off, then screamed as he realised it was a corpse brought back from the grave. He tried to back away. The men crowding the trail behind him formed a barrier. He slashed out, removing the ghoul's arm. It kept coming for him. Two other walking corpses blocked the trail. The old woman's corpse clawed at his eyes, pulling off his helm. He stabbed at the horrid thing as the larger male corpse brought its sword down on his head. Diocles fell to the ground. Before the undead could drag Diocles away, the foremost Crusader on the dry path was pushed past the thorns by his fellows crowding behind him into the hands of the re-animated, dead defenders.

\#

Sigurlina listened as the Crusaders screamed. The second organised formation crossed the bridge and fell to hacking at the thorn bushes. A third crossed onto the stone road, but instead of diverting around the quagmire, they charged into it. The first men sank to their waists. Their fellows used them as stepping stones to cross the icy waters.

Undead corpses shambled onto the road, grappling the Crusaders into the quagmire.

"Baird, end your spell," ordered Sigurlina. "The rest of you get to the rope and pull when I tell you to."

Baird made a dismissive gesture. The freezing water turned back into stone, trapping the Crusaders and the dead who still clawed at them. More of the dead came. A fourth formation of Crusaders marched onto the bridge.

"NOW!" yelled Sigurlina.

The dryads pulled the rope. The bridge pivoted, dropping into the river, spilling the Crusaders into the water.

Crusaders' bolts flew at the dead who were finishing off the invaders trapped in the road.

"Baird, turn the ground back into water so our protectors can get out." Sigurlina watched with a sick fascination as the ground turned into icy slush. The undead dragged themselves out and shambled towards the Crusaders on the road.

"We're winning." Baird let her spell slip, returning the road to stone.

Of the thirty Crusaders that had crossed the river, thirteen remained alive. They had formed into a circle, shields to the outside. The dead were breaking against the shields like waves on the shore. Bastard swords and polearms thrust out of the defensive formation. The Crusaders quickly learned that decapitation was most effective against the dead. They began mowing down the undead horde. Beyond the river, another group of Crusaders was wading into the flow. Their heavy armour held them to the bottom, and the water was no deeper than a man's breast. The latest force was emerging on the sanctuary side of the river when there was a sound like breaking wood and rushing water. The current caught most of the men, toppling them and sending them careening down the river.

The front rank of Crusaders fell back to collect their comrades and add them to their formation. They then pushed ahead against the mob of the dead.

As Sigurlina watched, the corpse of Obasi shambled into the fray. He hooked the shield of one of the Crusaders with his sword and pulled him out of formation. The other dead fell on the displaced man tearing him apart. Obasi's body rushed the gap in the line. It looked like the formation might break until a Crusader decapitated Obasi's corpse. The shields closed in, sealing the formation.

Three horn blasts sounded, then a voice bellowing in a foreign tongue. The attackers fell back and spread out into a shield wall, using the river to protect their back as the rest of their comrades waded across the now shallow flow.

"Fall back. Break up the road. Force them into the trees. Munin to me," ordered Sigurlina.

Munin leapt from her perch and landed on Sigurlina's shoulder.

'There's another group of Crusaders attacking the village. They've got one of those big crossbow things and are trying to set the roundhouse on fire.' Munin spoke into Sigurlina's mind.

"They have ballista. How did they get ballista here?" Sigurlina followed the road. The dead still attacked the Crusaders by the river, but against an organised assault, the dead mob was ineffective and would soon be annihilated. Corpses shambled by her, carrying Crusader corpses back towards the sanctuary.

'I'm sure I don't know. My father would carry heavy things back on the farm. This one time....'

Sigurlina felt a tension in the back of her mind release. Her black skeleton had fallen.

She looked back at the Crusaders. "Freya's tits!"

The Crusaders in the centre of the front rank of the shield wall dropped to their knees, and a flight of crossbow bolts flew over their heads. Several bolts lodged in the ghouls. Others flew along the stone road's length. A bolt grazed one of the dryads, and the woman screamed.

Sigurlina pulled in her will and called the shadows around her to darken and lengthen, obscuring her and the women. "Baird, fill the road with thorns. We need cover."

Baird gestured, and the road turned to a thorn thicket as the next flight of bolts flew towards them.

"Back to the sanctuary now!" ordered Sigurlina.

chapter 17: siege

Fjorn stood on a barrel and looked over the palisade.

"What are they doing," demanded Powell from below.

Fjorn jumped down, allowing a crossbowman to take his place. "They're mustering and giving their reinforcements time to dry out and join them. There are too many trees too close to the town wall for me to see much."

Powell looked at the ground. "Maybe the troops from Jorvik will come before they attack."

"Not likely." Fjorn moved to where a shaved skin with a map of the grove hung from the inside of the barricade wall and examined it.

"If we're lucky, they won't know where the treasures are. Then, if they are stupid, they will split their forces and try to take the town and the sanctuary at the same time. If they are smart, they'll attack the sanctuary and leave a small force to keep us trapped."

There was a crashing sound. The men standing on tables and barrels, so they could see and shoot over the palisade, started screaming.

Fjorn raced to where the sound had come from and vaulted onto a table beside a crossbowman. Fjorn popped his head over the palisade. Flames licked up the gate, and a ballista bolt stuck out of it. Three flaming crossbow bolts flew over him, landing in the thatch of the roundhouse.

"Retrieve those bolts. Add them to our stock. Put out the fire." Fjorn leapt down.

A Druid ran behind the gate and pressed his hand into the ground. Water geysered up, hitting the underside of the gate and splitting into two pillars, one on each side of the gate. The water doused the flames and washed off the oil.

Another ballista bolt crashed into the roof of the roundhouse. The oil pot shattered, dosing the dry thatch and the smouldering rags caught.

"In the name of Tyr, get that fire out!" bellowed Fjorn.

"What are we going to do?" Powell clutched Fjorn's tunic.

"I didn't think they'd have ballista. They must have carried them all this way. We have to destroy that machine before they torch the village." Fjorn lifted his horn to his lips and blew five quick blasts. "I'll lead my people on a sally from the gate. We'll hit the ballista and its crew, destroy the weapon, then try to fight our way back to the gates."

Another bolt hit the roundhouse. Water was geysering up, turning the courtyard's ground into freezing mud and wetting the defenders.

"You'll be killed." Powell looked horrified.

"Probably, but what else can we do?" demanded Fjorn

Powell took a deep breath. "Where exactly is this ballista?"

Fjorn jumped onto the table, then popped his head over the palisade. The trees obscured the ballista, but he could make out the bolt they were loading. He pulled his head down, avoiding a crossbow bolt that flew into the fort and punched through the roundhouse's wall. A Druid staggered out of the roundhouse with blood on his tunic. The man fell into one of the geysers holding the fires at bay. His wound healed.

"We need to end this, or we'll be hip deep in freezing mud," stated Fjorn.

By now, Audun, Vidurr, Neece, Kjorn and Dvyn were gathered around Fjorn and Powell.

"If you can get me close, I may have a way to smash the weapon," said Powell. He was pale, and tension nearly radiated off him.

"Are you sure?" demanded Fjorn.

"If we die, we die together. This should give us a chance to get back to the village." Powell hugged his own trembling body. The loose, decrepit, leather armour he wore would have been comical if it wasn't for the pale-faced determination in his features.

Fjorn nodded. "I will sing the shield. The rest of you do what you can."

The men formed into a living arrowhead, shields to the outside with Powell in the middle. They waited behind the gate as Fjorn cleared his throat, then bellowed, "OPEN THE GATE." He began singing,

"The shields of Asgard are shields of might."

"Turn the wrath of giants to flight.

"Shields to hold a warrior's might.

"The shields of Asgard are shields of might."

Audun traced symbols on his arm, and the skins of the group took on a sheen like iron.

Vidurr bared his teeth.

Neece hoisted his shield higher.

Dvyn gripped his sword.

Powell hoped he could get through the next few moments without wetting himself.

The gate opened, and Fjorn's team charged. The sparkling lights of Fjorn's spell song came up, diverting crossbow bolts. A bolt got through and struck Fjorn, but the magically hardened skin from Audun's spell deflected it. Audun's spell faltered under the onslaught. Kjorn traced a line of symbols on the back of his shield, and the effect grew again.

Crusaders charged the open gate and were met by bolts and arrows.

Fjorn and his people mowed down any that dared cross their path. They reached the ballista, and the Crusaders there drew blades. Powell threw himself against an oak tree that overhung the area and screamed a string of Celtic words.

The tree glowed, seemed to sway in a wind that wasn't there, then swept down with a mighty branch smashing a Crusader into pulp.

"Destroy the ballista… that thing." Powell pointed to the weapon and the small pile of oil-tipped bolts beside it.

Fjorn sang as he pushed his attack against a Crusader wearing a horn similar to his own.

The hrokkvir, tree raised its roots and stepped on the ballista, shattering it.

"Back to the fort," ordered Fjorn, then he gasped as a longsword drove deep into his side. Grimacing with pain, he sang.

"The shields of Asgard are shields of might.

"Turn the wrath of giants to flight.

"Shields to hold a warrior's might.

"The shields of Asgard are shields of might."

Vidurr snarled, allowing rage to take him. He became a wild thing. Crusaders fell before his reckless furry, and as he drank their blood, the wounds they gave him healed.

Dvyn cast a wall of thorns that blocked six Crusaders closing on them. Powell gripped Fjorn on his good side and helped the skald to stand. Audun swung with his enchanted battle axe blasting a Crusader into two of his comrades. The three invaders fell in a tangle of arms and legs. Kjorn swept low with his blade removing a Crusader's foot, causing him to topple to the ground.

The men, except for Vidurr, formed a wedge and fell back towards the gate. The area before the gate was now flanked by thorns, while the path to it was a quagmire half full of armoured bodies. When the defenders approached, the quagmire became solid ground. The gate opened. A volley of crossbow bolts combined with the ground behind them becoming a thorn thicket guarded Fjorn and his people's return to the village. The gate was closed. Powell half-dragged Fjorn to one of the geysers and soaked him in the water. Fjorn's wound began to close.

"Vidurr." Fjorn gasped.

Audun gazed over the gate. The thorn thickets and quagmires were gone. The hrokkvir continued to fight, crushing Crusaders under its massive feet. Vidurr stumbled onto the path before the village. Blood dripped off him, and he swung his sword viciously. A crossbow bolt hit him in the shoulder.

Vidurr howled, becoming the giant wolf, and then bounded into the woods. A group of Crusaders chased him. Three horn notes sounded. The Crusaders returned to the cover of the trees. Other Crusaders attacked the hrokkvir with axes and torches. The living tree swung at them. For each Crusader it struck, it seemed like two took their place and soon, the creature was felled.

Powell gasped and hung his head. "Goodbye, old friend. I will miss your shade and the wind's song in your leaves."

Audun moved to Fjorn's side, pausing to splash enchanted geyser water onto several of his own wounds. "Vidurr escaped. Powell, I am sorry. Your tree creature fought bravely."

"The wheel turns." Powell stood. "What now?"

Fjorn rose and tentatively touched his side where the wound had been. The spot was tender but otherwise seemed healed. Water dripped from his clothing.

"Stop the water and dry out. Cold is as much an enemy as the Crusaders. Hopefully, they only had one ballista." Hugging himself, Fjorn headed for the roundhouse with Audun in his

174

wake.

Powell nodded. "Getting people warm and dry, I can manage. Thank you, war chief."

Fjorn paused at the roundhouse's door. "Thank you. Your hrokkvir turned the tide." Fjorn scanned the compound. Kjorn stood beside a crossbowman, seemingly helping the Druid to un-jam the reloading pulley of his weapon. Fjorn entered the roundhouse.

#

Theodosios gazed at the bloody pulp that had been a member of his household and wondered what he would tell the man's wife. Stepped on by a living tree. He glanced at the now inert pile of wood.

"My Lord, the heathens have barred the town gate. The wolfman is in the woods. What are your orders?"

Theodosios turned to look at a guardsman. He knew that under his helm, the old family guard's hair was more grey than brown. "All we can do is keep the men trapped inside the town. This is not the fight we were told to expect. The men who stormed us were as fine a group of warriors as I have seen."

A teenage youth in light, leather armour bearing a short sword raced up the path from the dock and came to a stop in front of Theodosios.

"Report," ordered the commander.

"We have crossed the river. The dead fight on the other shore. It is dark magic. A bevy of witches retreats along the road blocking it with devil's swamps and thorns. The shieldmen hold the dead at bay. Lord Oreste orders you to send him the second ballista."

"It would appear that Oreste will have to make do with the one he has," a deep rumbling voice sounded behind the messenger.

Theodosios dropped to one knee and bowed his head. "Shepherd," he breathed.

Agis looked down at the commander. "Rise. What has happened here?"

"Dark magic. They called a tree to life. It smashed our ballista before we could fell the creature. I've lost four men, and another dozen are wounded."

"We have moved the relief camp onto the field of shallow snows just past where we pierced the ice wall. Send the wounded there. I have the reinforcements recovered from the first battle. Do you need more men to hold this town?"

Theodosios stood resolutely. "My house can hold them, Shepherd."

Agis smiled gravely. "Then hold them. I will lead my troops to reinforce the band that fights the dead. Clean iron will defeat devil's magic."

Agis gestured, ordering his troop of forty men to follow him.

Babak stayed behind with a group of ten men. "We will take your wounded to the healer's camp. Then we will see about this town."

Theodosios swallowed noticeably. "Yes, Shepherd. But don't you want to go with Agis to seek the treasures?"

The small man laughed. "I doubt that Agis will find his conquest quick or easy. I have time and other tasks that are in my charge. It would seem that keeping our forces strong has fallen to me, as, I fear, will commanding the final battle. Agis is careless with the lives he shepherds. I would preserve the Greek contingent. My men and I have a task."

#

Sigurlina watched the sanctuary's gate close, then vaulted up the embankment and peeked over the palisade. The Crusaders marched forward, the dead hanging off their shields. Every once in a while, the dead would manage to pull a man from the formation, but for every Crusader they killed, six or more of the ghouls were decapitated. The Crusaders stopped, then spread into the trees around the roadway, expanding the clear area in the centre of their formation until it took up the road's width. Several warriors moved to the middle of the open space and dropped large pieces of wood. Several others pieced the wood together and positioned ropes on the frame.

Sigurlina jumped down with a worried expression. "They are setting up a ballista, and it looks like they have fire bolts."

"Wonderful." Ragna followed a marked trail over the courtyard.

"Stay on the snow we've marked in yellow." Jolnir approached along another trail. "I warned the women that were with you."

Sigurlina nodded. "What can we do about the ballista?"

"If we could reach it, the dryads could sink it then let the ground turn back into stone," observed Jolnir.

"We can't get a dryad close enough." Sigurlina scrambled up on the embankment and peeked out over the palisade.

She ducked so fast that she fell off the embankment and landed in the courtyard with a thump. A crossbow bolt flew into the courtyard while another smashed through the wall of the larger roundhouse.

Jolnir helped Sigurlina to stand. "Crossbows." Sigurlina blushed as she needlessly explained. "They've cut down all the ghouls. The ballista is almost assembled. They're kindling a fire beside it."

"We're cooked," said Ragna.

Sigurlina's eyes strayed to a line of dead Crusaders in the courtyard. "Can we use them?"

"The Mother Superior says the dryads can only revive one at a time, and each one takes half an hour. They're working on it." Jolnir bit his lip. "Sigurlina, do you remember when you had your skeleton wear my socks to trick the trolls?"

"Of course, but...."

"I have an idea."

#

The Crusader swung with his axe against the pole supporting the season wheel. The

176

wood splintered. The pole gave way. Ropes tied to the surrounding trees caught it before the wheel could hit the ground.

Babak lifted the wheel from the bracket that held it in place. The temperature in that section of the grove dropped. He passed the wheel, which was the size of a round shield, to one of his men. "Take this to the sledge. Be careful with it. The pontiff wishes these enchanted disks brought to his treasury."

"Why do you think that is, Babak?" asked a burly Crusader who had the gold trim of an officer surrounding the cross on his tabard.

"It is not our place to question that. God has chosen the Pope. It is for us to obey." Babak hugged himself against the growing cold.

"Like it is for us to obey catamites like Hakon and blustering fools like Aethelstan? How many men must we lose?"

Babak stared at the snowy ground. "As many as it is the Lord's will that he calls unto him. We should find all the posts. Once we have taken this territory, we will need to collect them. Maybe if we erect these wheels on the lands back home, we can drive back this eternal winter and feed our families."

#

Agis kept his men in a shield formation. The few dead that struck at them were no more than an annoyance. To his eyes, the devastation by the river was an example of weak leadership. The back of the first wave came into view. The Crusaders paused to dismember the ghouls caught between the two forces, then merged into one. Agis estimated his current numbers at eighty men. With the twenty-five keeping the village contained, and the thirty or so wounded, then the ten healers. He knew he could decimate this devil's temple. Looking forward, he could see that the ballista was nearly assembled.

"At least that fool Oreste did something right. Let the heathens have a taste of the fires that await them." Agis strode towards Oreste, who stood by the ballista.

#

Sigurlina held the bag of kindling inside her black skeleton's rib cage while Ragna tied it to a rib. Clay bottles of lamp oil hung inside the rib cage filling the space. Jolnir wrapped the cut-off fabric from a Crusader's cloak around the skeleton's neck until he could fasten a gorget around it.

"This is disgusting." Ragna started folding up the rest of the cloak so they could secure it where the stomach should have been. Inside every fold was a strip of white pork fat, drawn from the sanctuary's larder and slender twigs.

"Where did you get the idea?" asked Sigurlina.

"I was at a harbour siege. The town leader was a learned man. He said the Romans used to do this. He picked the oldest and leakiest ship in the harbour and filled it with wood and oil like a funeral barge. Then he hoisted its sail with a seaward breeze and let it ram the other ships.

It spilt burning wood everywhere and set the ship it hit on fire. We attacked in the confusion."

Sigurlina wrapped dry straw with cloth around the skeleton's legs.

"That's as good as it's going to be." Ragna finished securing the belly roll.

There was a whooshing sound, and a flaming bolt landed on the larger roundhouse.

Baird rushed up and summoned a geyser to douse the thatch.

"We need to do this now," stated Jolnir.

"Dress yourself as a Crusader," ordered Sigurlina.

Clumsy from all the wood and folded cloth around it, the black skeleton pulled on a dead Crusader's leggings, armour, tabard, and helm. Sigurlina and Ragna busied themselves with stuffing cloth into hollows to complete the disguise while Jolnir picked up a bottle of oil and started dousing the material.

"This better work the first time. I don't think there is any more oil in the sanctuary," Jolnir put the empty jar down, then thrust a reed-light into the folds of the cloth. "Ready."

"Good luck, Blaze." Ragna slapped the skeleton on the back, then wiped her oily palm off on her cloak.

"Blaze? Really?" Sigurlina shook her head while the skeleton stared at Ragna from its empty eye sockets.

The Mother Superior appeared from the smaller roundhouse with a ghoul in Crusader's armour beside her. The ghoul shambled to the sanctuary's gate and paused.

"I've instructed it as you commanded."

Jolnir hoisted one of the dead Crusaders and dragged it to the ghoul at the gate. The skeleton walked stiffly to the gate and took one of the corpse's arms. The ghoul grasped the other arm.

Clear the courtyard," called Jolnir.

A flaming bolt impacted the roof of the larger roundhouse, driving into the interior. Jolnir trusted the dryads to handle the fire as he used a taper to ignite the reed-light on the skeleton.

"Open the gate," he ordered.

The gate opened. The skeleton and ghoul stepped forward, dragging the corpse between them.

"We return your wounded," bellowed the Mother Superior from behind the palisade.

The battlefield seemed to still as the skeleton, the ghoul and the corpse moved from the sanctuary to the attacker's formation.

The Crusaders in the shield wall parted to admit what they thought were three of their own. The shield wall closed behind the trio. The ghoul attacked the closest Crusader. The skeleton ran towards the ballista, dodging past startled men. The air blowing onto the oil-soaked cloth caused the flame from the reed-light to spread, enveloping the skeleton in an inferno. At the ballista, a Crusader caught the skeleton's leg with a polearm, but the rolls of cloth and twigs protected the bone beneath. The skeleton threw itself on the ballista. The oil bottles in its chest smashed and leaked out. Crusaders stabbed at the skeleton, which dripped flaming oil onto the weapon like sweat. Seeing the pile of bolts by the ballista, the skeleton leapt on them, smashing the oil bottles on their tips.

The ballista burnt. Swords slashed and tore at the skeleton, but the cloth defeated most of the thrusts. It threw itself back at the ballista, seized a polearm, and parried blows as the flames grew. Crusaders stood on all sides of what was fast becoming an inferno. A polearm caught on the skeleton's cloak tearing it away. The helm fell away, revealing the skull beneath. The skeleton, now naked save for a chainmail tunic, stood on the ballista, slashing with its polearm. Flames wreathed it, and its mouth was thrown open in a silent laugh. It caught a Crusader in the throat and dragged him into the fire, where the man's flesh sizzled like roasting pork as he screamed.

#

Sigurlina filled the area in front of the gate with shadows allowing Jolnir to lead a group of dryads into the woods unseen. The ballista blazed, and Crusaders crowded around the fire. The ghoul had been cut down, but the skeleton still fought.

Beads of sweat formed on Sigurlina's brow. Maintaining the skeleton and the shadows was almost too much for her.

With a splashing sound, the Crusaders along the front right side of the defensive formation fell into freezing water. Half of them grabbed the man beside them and threw him onto solid ground. This first group scrambled around and offered their hands to help their comrades out of the quagmire.

Sigurlina jerked. "My skeleton is no more."

The quagmires that the Crusaders had sunk into turned back to earth and rock, trapping the legs of the slower men. The dryads Jolnir had led ran towards the sanctuary's gate. Jolnir and Sigurlina fell in behind them. A crossbow bolt caught one of the dryads, and she fell. Jolnir grabbed her by the back of her robe, hauling her with him. Sigurlina called the shadows to fill the path behind her, which was also filling with thorny brambles. Bolts flew. One caught Sigurlina's shoulder. She stumbled onward. Unsure moments passed. She felt hands grab her, then she was behind the sanctuary's gate, and it was closed and barred.

"This way." Afrikaisi half-carried Sigurlina to a place where a geyser of water gushed. The small, dark woman bathed Sigurlina's wounds which began to close.

Jolnir stood up from where he had been resting with his back against the wall. There were rents in his chainmail where bolts had pierced it.

"How many?" asked Sigurlina.

"We lost two of the dryads. The wounded are being cared for. I have to get back to the battle."

#

Agis stared at the fire that had been his ballista. Behind him and to his right, men struggled to free their comrades who were soaked to the skin and trapped in the earth. Other men huddled by the blazing ballista, trying to get warm in wet clothing. "The heathens have the devil with them, to be sure."

"Gabor, take Taavi and Rab, collect dry cloaks and blankets and bring them by the fire. Men, if you are wet, strip and set your clothes to dry. Borrow a dry cloak to wrap yourself in. Remember, cold will kill. Uday, Wagner, and Caden cut wood to keep the fire going. Watch for the dead. Keep the shields in place. The polearm men can dig out the trapped men," commanded Oreste.

"Cancel those orders," snapped Agis. "We will attack and take the heathen stronghold. Those fool enough to have gotten wet can stay warm by killing devil worshipers."

"But Shepherd, what of the dead warriors? If we break formation," began Oreste.

"The one thing you accomplished is you rid us of that annoyance. You've heard my orders. God's providence will guide us to victory." Agis looked over his men imperiously.

Oreste hung his head. "Yes, my Lord." Raising his voice, he bellowed, "Assault formation. Surround the fortress. Attack as ordered." His voice dropped. "And may God have mercy on us all." He lifted his horn to his lips and sounded a long blast.

CHAPTER 18: CALL TO VENGEANCE

Jolnir strode to the sanctuary's palisade, keeping to the yellow snow. Peeking over the barrier, he saw that the ballista blazed, but no dead worried the Crusader force. Turning, he saw that there were scorch marks on both roundhouse roofs. A fire burnt in the courtyard with bubbling cauldrons tight around it.

A horn sounded, followed by a flight of crossbow bolts. Three of the defenders were struck.

"Collect those bolts. Get them to our crossbows." Jolnir leapt from the embankment to the ground. "Crossbowmen..." He paused for a split second. "Crossbows, let fly. If our guests are kind enough to give us bolts, we can at least return the favour."

The dryads on the raised inner embankment flanking the gate shot into the charging Crusaders, but between shields, haste and inexperience, their crossbow bolts accomplished little.

"Thorn the gate," ordered Jolnir.

Dryads cast their spell on the ground under the gate. A thorny barrier grew around the gate, reinforcing it and making it harder to reach.

Jolnir moved to the compound's centre, scanned the parameter, then bellowed, "Bows, the trees."

Crusaders were scrambling up the trees beside the sanctuary. Bolts and arrows flew towards the trees. Two Crusaders fell screaming.

Moving back to the palisade, Jolnir looked over. Crusaders were scrambling up the embankment. The first rank knelt in the snow, forming a stepping platform for the second rank. Other Crusaders were chopping at trees around the sanctuary.

A line of dryads holding steaming buckets and cups waited at the base of the embankment.

"Hot water," ordered Jolnir.

The dryads passed the vessels to their comrades behind the palisade, who dumped boiling water onto the Crusaders. Bolts flew towards the defenders, most missed, but not all.

The shadows around the gate deepened, making it harder for the enemy to target them, and Jolnir knew that Sigurlina had recovered.

"Jolnir!" bellowed the Mother Superior from the far side of the courtyard.

"Keep the water flowing. Make them pay for the embankment." Jolnir leapt to the courtyard and raced to join the Mother Superior. "What?" he remounted the embankment.

"They are piling dry wood against the defences. We don't have enough bows to drive them off, and if we change the earth, we could topple the palisade." The Mother Superior wrung her hands.

Jolnir glanced over the palisade. Crusaders had piled wood as high as the embankment and were throwing wood onto the narrow track next to the fortification.

A dead Crusader lay under a tree not five strides distant with a crossbow across his chest. Other Crusaders appeared with helms in their hands that they'd wrapped in their cloaks. The helms were full of hot coals, which they threw onto the woodpile.

"We've run out of boiling water," Baird called from the courtyard.

Sigurlina lurched into view carrying four crossbows and a pile of bolts.

Jolnir leapt down. Sigurlina held up a hand to forestall him touching her.

"How?" demanded Jolnir.

Sigurlina dropped her burdens to the ground. "They do call me Shadow Stepper. The dead Crusaders don't need them." Sigurlina dropped to her knees and vomited.

"Let me," began Jolnir.

"The taint will transfer to anyone that touches me." Sigurlina sat weakly in the snow.

"Baird, get these to anyone who knows how to use them." Jolnir gestured to the crossbows.

The smell of wood smoke filled the compound.

The Mother Superior leapt from the embankment and stroked Sigurlina's cheek. The older woman gasped and fell to her knees.

"Why?" asked Sigurlina as she stood.

"My people need you more than me." The Mother Superior slowly stood and staggered towards the roundhouse.

"Look out." Ragna's voice caused Jolnir to jerk around to see a Crusader clamber over the palisade. Drawing blade, Jolnir closed on the man. A dozen Crusaders were topping the barrier, and licks of flames could be seen over the area he was defending. A tree fell, smashing through the palisade. Crusaders swarmed up the impromptu ramp it formed.

Glancing over the yard, Jolnir could see wounded women everywhere. The thorn barrier in front of the main gate turned into regular ground.

"My turn," whispered Ragna. There was the chill of Jotunheim in her voice.

A Crusader raced to the gate, driving back the women defending it, then threw up the bar that held it closed. Crusaders charged in.

"And now," whispered Ragna.

A rope swept across the Crusader's legs. The ice pond in front of the gate gave no traction, and the men flew into the air, landing hard on their backs. Before they could rise, a dryad turned the ground into a swamp. Five Crusaders sank under the surface, which turned back into earth, ice and snow entombing them.

Other men dropped over the barricade driving the defenders into the courtyard. Crusaders leapt to the ground only to fall screaming when their feet met hidden spikes.

One Crusader charged at a group of women. There was a cracking sound as a bundle of firewood secured around a palisade post dropped. A rope swept up, catching the Crusader between the legs with enough force to lift him off the ground. He fell into the snow, impaling himself on spikes.

Another Crusader caught up with three of the women. Two tried to fend him off while the third cast a spell. The Crusader's sword turned into a venomous serpent. Without pause, he threw it at a woman. The snake bit her, then turned back into a sword. The Crusader picked up his blade and pressed the attack.

Jolnir threw himself against two Crusaders who were fighting a dryad barely into her teens. His skilled blade made quick work of what would have overwhelmed the untrained girl.

"To the roundhouse. Swamp the compound. Thorn the threshold," bellowed Jolnir.

All the defenders fell back, turning the land in the compound into a quagmire. Jolnir raced to the smaller roundhouse, driving his blade into a Crusader that sought to mount the narrow strip of dry land the dryad spells left around the structure. Thorn thickets grew up around the roundhouses making a barricade to the quagmire's mote, blocking his view of the battlefield.

Sigurlina appeared by his side. "Munin is perched on the roof. She says that the Crusaders are falling back behind the embankment."

"That won't last." Jolnir sighed, "How many?"

"Most of the sanctuary's women have wounds. Afrikaisi is seeing to them. I've healed much of what the dryads couldn't. We've lost a dozen women. Cabe took a sword to the belly." Sigurlina swallowed hard.

Munin cawed.

"What!" gasped Sigurlina. "The Crusaders are using pieces of our palisade and tree trunks to make a bridge over the quagmire."

Jolnir closed his eyes. "If I do not survive, and you see Fjorn again, tell him to look after Eir for me, and... tell her I love her."

"What are you--?"

Jolnir gripped Sigurlina's arm. "Just do it."

"I will."

Jolnir strode into the smaller roundhouse.

As he entered, a ghoul emerged from the cauldron. Before any of the dryads attending could speak, Jolnir ordered the undead thing. "Enter the quagmire inside the embankment, grab Crusaders that attempt to cross the waters and hold them under until they drown. Stay under as much as you can. Do this until you no longer can."

The ghoul shambled from the building.

"Go to the other roundhouse and heal people." Jolnir strode to the chamber's centre as the women left the room.

"I am a man. I live as a man. I love as a man. I do the duties of a man. I do the work of a man. I am Jolnir, captain of the guard of Jarl Erik Bloodaxe, and I am a man." With a swift, decisive action, Jolnir grasped the spear and lifted it from the chains that held it. Fire danced around his hands. He cried out, then the spear was down. It rested in his hands which were burnt red and blistered.

"I am a man," he whispered.

Sigurlina and Ragna raced into the roundhouse. "What?" They spoke in unison.

"Freya's tits! Of all the stupid things! You must be a man. You're as silly and reckless as any man I've ever met! What were you thinking?" scolded Ragna.

Sigurlina knelt by Jolnir and performed a healing. "Bravely done." She kissed her friend on the cheek and performed another healing.

Jolnir felt his pain lessen. He flexed his fingers and found that they would move. "Write Fjorn, tell him we can move the treasures if we can escape."

"I will, but first, you need to get to the healing spring. The Crusaders have almost finished making a bridge."

#

Fjorn stared at the map of the grove hung on the village palisade. He was healed, and his clothes dried.

"Maybe they left," remarked Powell, who stood beside him.

"No. They are being smart. Leave a force to pin us down and use their men to take the sanctuary. I wish Sigurlina were here. She could ask Munin to fly up and tell us what's going on."

"That would be useful."

"Of course. You have to know what the enemy is doing to counter it." Fjorn looked surprised at the question.

"I am a man of peace. I've never thought of things in this way." Powell turned to the crossbowman leaning against the palisade. "Kane, please fetch Wynne." Turning back, Powell continued. "Fjorn, sit with me and ask your questions. I can tell you about the land up to a hundred strides from the village."

Powell sat in a chair that was against the palisade as an archer's perch, closed his eyes and breathed deeply. "I am one with the land. I see what the land sees."

"What are the Crusaders doing?" asked Fjorn.

"I cannot see so far as the sanctuary. "Twenty. No, twenty-five men wait around the village. Each has a crossbow and shelters behind the trees. I can show you on the map." Powell moved to the map of the grove and pointed out eight points around the village. "They have fires that they are clustered around."

"Good." Fjorn nodded. "Very good."

Wynne walked up to the two men. "You wanted me."

Powell nodded. "Wynne, would you be willing to fly over the woods and see where the Crusaders are?"

"You had someone that could do that all this time..." Fjorn buried his forehead in his hand.

"We are people of peace. War is foreign to us."

Fjorn looked up. "Right. Wynne, please check the docks and my ship. Then see where the Crusaders are gathered."

"Of course." Wynne closed her eyes, and, after a moment, a snowy owl stood where she had. She spread her wings and leapt into the air. As she gained altitude, a crossbow bolt barely missed her. She drove her wings hard and was out of range before another bolt could be launched.

"That was close," remarked Fjorn. "Now tell me, what would happen if the season poles were taken down?"

"Fimbulwinter would rush in."

"And if they were put up again?"

"It would take time, but Fimbulwinter would be driven back from where they stood."

"Audun, Kjorn," Fjorn bellowed.

The huge man strode up from where he had been conversing with a dryad. "Here."

Kjorn raced out of the roundhouse, a bowl of steaming stew in one hand and a wooden spoon in the other. "Yes."

"You two know the course of the Orse. Is there another way it could reach the sea from Jorvik?"

Kjorn sucked his cheek. "There was that daft plan to dig a channel between Hemingbrogh and Long Drax, but nought ever came of it."

"Heard about that. I liked the thought," agreed Audun.

Fjorn turned to Powell. "How many season poles do you have in this grove?"

"Twenty-six. Ten along the river and eight north and south."

"Is it the pole or disk that holds the magic?"

"The disk." Powell looked saddened. "To move them would mean the death of the areas we take them from, but with the treasures gone, there is no need for the Orse to loop up to South Duffle."

Fjorn smiled. "I think I have a way to win this now."

Several minutes of the men poring over maps ensued before Wynne plummeted into the compound and returned to her human guise. "They've taken down a season wheel. They shouldn't do that!"

"The docks and my ship, what are they like?" Fjorn bit his lip.

"The watergate is smashed. The river is no more than a trickle. Your ship is grounded but undamaged. The men there told me that the Crusaders haven't found them."

"Anything else?"

Wynne wrung her hands. "A large fire burns to the south in front of where the invaders entered our grove. I didn't want to get too close because of crossbows. It looked like there were injured men around the blaze. A man carried a season disk into the camp."

"They can't be fools enough to burn them, can they?" asked Powell.

"Not all Crusaders are fools. They need the season disks more than we do. I'm guessing they were testing what would happen if they were taken down." Fjorn stroked his beard.

"The sanctuary gate is open, and the Crusaders are building a bridge or a raft or something." Wynne finished her report.

"Yes, this could work well for us," stated Fjorn.

"How," demanded Powell.

#

"Push it forward," commanded Oreste.

The bridge consisted of two long, pine trunks with pieces of the palisade strapped to their tops to form a platform that men could walk on. The inside of the Pagan fortress was a swamp from its gate to a small island encircled with thorns that he could see two conical roofs over.

"What's taking so long? We're losing the light," snapped Agis.

"My Lord, the men are unwilling."

"WHAT?" bellowed Agis.

"We lost thirty-five men in taking the outer walls. Another thirty were wounded. Perhaps, we should move the wounded to the healers and attack in the morning with greater numbers. As you say, we are losing the light." Oreste silently prayed that his superior would listen to reason.

"Cowards! I will not go back to Rome and tell them that we were defeated by a gaggle of women. Prepare to lead the charge." Agis strutted away.

Oreste rubbed his forehead. "If I could taste her baklava one more time." He sighed. "Uday, tell the crossbowmen to fire their bolts. Use rags torn from the dead's clothing. Maybe we can ignite the thatch of the houses."

Uday shuffled uncomfortably. "My Lord, most of our crossbowmen have no more than three bolts left. We'd have none but for the ones recovered from the wounded and missed shots."

Oreste shook his head. "Tell the men to launch one flight of flaming arrows, then hold back the remaining bolts until they have a clear shot."

#

Jolnir sat with the spear in his lap, his hands bandaged in front of him.

Baird worked her magic, calling on the earth's healing power. The dirt floor of the roundhouse erupted into poppies. She selected a petal. "This contains the focus of the spell's power." She fed the petal to Jolnir. The pain in his hands eased. Sigurlina performed a healing as the poppies vanished. Baird cast the spell again and fed Jolnir another petal.

His hands were now simply red.

"Munin says they're coming," stated Sigurlina.

There was a crashing sound as flaming bolts smashed through the roundhouse roof. Fires started, and the temple women rushed to extinguish them.

Jolnir stood, gripping the mistletoe spear. "Let them come." He strode through the doorway. The wall of thorns blocked his path.

"Where are they coming from?" Jolnir clutched the spear. Blood dripped from its tip, and the living vines of mistletoe writhed like tentacles.

Sigurlina pointed to the section of thorn wall Munin indicated.

"Drop the barrier."

The thorns vanished as the dryad maintaining them relaxed. Revealed were the quagmire and a bridge, wide enough for two to cross abreast, that extended from the shattered sanctuary gate to touch on the land around the roundhouses. Crusaders charged onto the bridge. Jolnir stepped forward to meet them. He thrust, impaling not only the first Crusader but the one behind him. Their mail was as nothing, and no parry could stop the spear.

#

Oreste charged the champion that blocked the bridge. His enemy's first thrust killed the two men to his left. He sought to strike the heathen warrior. Something grabbed Oreste's leg and pulled him into the water. Icy limbs dragged him under. His chest burned. He thrashed in panic. Driven by the need to breathe, he drew freezing water into his lungs. A light appeared before him. He felt himself float towards it.

"Come, child. I'm the one who taught your mother to make baklava," spoke a woman's voice.

"Grandmother?"

#

Jolnir thrust, splitting a Crusader's shield and driving the links of his mail through his heart.

A black skeleton appeared to Jolnir's left, guarding his flank. Bolts whistled past the guardians. One drove into Jolnir's shoulder, but it mattered nought. The spear hungered. Blood flowed from its tip, staining the quagmire red. Another Crusader fell screaming into the icy waters. Jolnir pushed forward.

Blood. Blood and vengeance. They had wronged him! All the woe they had wrought, he would revisit on them. Children lost and enslaved, men and women unjustly bound. He would make the oppressors pay. The spoiled child would pay for the eyes cruelly taken. Hod would have his vengeance against his brother, Balder; Loki would be avenged for the slights done him and his children. Hel, Jormungand and Fenrir all would be avenged. The children slain in the White God's name would be avenged; the mothers, the fathers, the good men and true. All would find vengeance through him. He was forged by magics both fell and cunning for this day. Vengeance was his name. And now awake, his will would be done!

#

Sigurlina stood on the shore as Jolnir drove back the Crusaders. He was magnificent. He seemed as tall as a giant and blazed with a red-hued light, making him almost blinding to gaze upon. Her skeleton needlessly guarded his flank, for Jolnir's wounds healed as quickly as they came. Blood flowed from the spear's tip, bathing Jolnir and the skeleton. A bolt struck Jolnir's shoulder. He paid it no heed.

"What's he doing?" demanded Ragna.

Sigurlina focused her will on Jolnir. "The spear has him. He won't stop. I don't think that even the spear can protect him when he's attacked from all sides. Get ready to throw the bridge into the water and put the thorns back up. Get dryads who can perform swords to snakes ready to block the way."

Jolnir had reached the end of the bridge. Fifteen dead Crusaders bobbed in the water. The men in front of him sought to clear a path for the crossbowmen that stood ready at a distance.

Sigurlina raced onto the bridge as the black skeleton vanished into smoke. She pointed at Jolnir and paused for a half-second in thought. "By Loki, thy creator, by Freya queen of Seith, by Odin whom you hate, by Surt who will fire all. I command thee leave this stolen form. Remember your task completed.

"Remember the taste of Baldur's life. This form is not yours. Your task is done. I command thee back to the wood that is your own. Be gone!"

Jolnir turned. His eyes blazed red. He stepped towards Sigurlina, brandishing the spear.

"Jolnir, I'm your friend. You want to return to Eir, don't you? Help me take you back to her." Sigurlina backed away as hastily aimed bolts flew through the gate.

"Eir." Jolnir grimaced and looked about himself.

"By Loki, thy creator, by Freya queen of Seith, by Odin whom you hate, by Surt who will fire all. I command thee leave this stolen form. Remember your task completed.

"Remember the taste of Baldur's life. This form is not yours. Your task is done. I command thee back to the wood that is your own. Be gone!" Sigurlina repeated the spell.

Jolnir lurched onto the solid ground and threw the spear to the earth. Two Crusaders tried to rush the bridge. One was caught by a hand that rose from the quagmire. He tripped and fell into the water. A crossbow bolt struck the second Crusader as a group of women tipped up the bridge and threw it into the water. The gap in the barricade of thorns sealed.

Quiet filled the air.

Jolnir groaned.

"Heal him, get that bolt out of his shoulder," ordered Sigurlina.

"What was that?" asked Ragna with a quaver in her voice.

"The spear is a tool of vengeance. It is a thing of the Gods; too much for any mortal to control. It tried to take Jolnir, and almost succeeded." Sigurlina sat with her back against the wall. The incoming crossbow bolts had ceased, and the silver light of the grove was descending into dusk.

"But you saved him, right?" Ragna asked.

"We forced the spirit of the spear back into its wooden shaft. It's still there, waiting.

We can't let the Crusaders take it. In their hands...." Sigurlina shook her head. "I need to get a message to Fjorn."

#

Agis tossed Uday to the stone road and bellowed. "ONE MAN. ONE MAN did all that." He took a deep breath. "I will leave those of able body here to hold the siege. The devil lights are fading. We will heal the wounded and come back in the morning. When we do, the heathens will burn! Oreste, you useless wastrel, where are you?"

"My Lord," spoke Uday. "He died on the bridge."

Agis scowled. "It is God's will. I always liked Theodosios better, and now he is the first-born son of that house. That should make him happy."

#

"And you should tell him all about Jolnir and the spear. He might know what to do. I mean, skalds are supposed to have...."

"RAGNA," Sigurlina shouted. "Please, it's hard enough to do this as it is." She examined the jagged lines of runes she'd inked onto the shaved sheepskin.

"Most people who can read and write don't have problems like this." Ragna stared over Sigurlina's shoulder, where she sat on the dirt floor of the smaller roundhouse. A ghoul was in the cauldron, but other than the dryad attending it, they were alone.

"They probably did when they were first learning. I only started three weeks ago. It's not like banishing a spirit. This is hard." Sigurlina rubbed her forehead, leaving an ink mark behind.

"Sorry." Ragna patted her young friend's shoulder.

Sigurlina sighed. "It's as good as I think it can be. Munin."

The raven hopped over from the corner of the room where she was pecking at a plate of raw pig's liver. 'Say what you will. These dryads know how to eat. I'm glad they decided that keeping that pig just wasn't practical. It is so good. I know we have pig sometimes in Orkney, but I hardly ever get any, and then only the bits that people don't want to eat. That is so unfair.'

Sigurlina smiled at her bird. "Yes, it is. I'll do what I can. For now, I need you to take this to Fjorn or Audun in the village. Wait for them to send you back with a message."

'Will you be alright without me?' Munin spoke into Sigurlina's mind.

"I'll do my best."

"What's she saying?" asked Ragna.

"She was wondering if I'd be alright without her."

"I'll look after her, black chicken," said Ragna.

"Yura bitch." Munin hopped over and groomed the hair by Ragna's ear before picking up the scroll and flying out of the roundhouse.

"Now what?" asked Ragna.

"Now we need to find a chalice, a Crusader's spear and as much gold as we can." Sigurlina smiled at her friend.

"And I would know where these things are because?" Ragna spoke in indignant tones.

"Because we've been here for a full day, and I know you."

Ragna chuckled. "The Mother Superior has some nice things for a holy woman."

Chapter 19: Scorched Earth

Fjorn sat by the fire in the roundhouse as people removed anything useful from the structure.

"We've put all the food we kept back from the evacuation in the packs." Powell looked around sadly. "This is the third time I lost everything. I will miss my home here."

Fjorn spoke softly. "Your people will build a new grove on the Orse's new course. A place is just a place, the people, the memories, that is what makes it something."

"Do you really think this will work?" Powell sat beside Fjorn.

"Our chances are better than if we do nothing. I need to ask you. Is there a way to fill the river channel faster?"

"There may be. We can hasten the seasons. The channel is fed by the melt. To do so will be an affront to nature and will cost the season disks, but it can be done."

Fjorn took a deep breath. "Tell me how?"

The door flap opened, and Audun entered with Munin on his arm.

"Pretty bird, pretty bird." Munin took flight, landed on Fjorn's shoulder and began grooming the hair around his ear.

"I have never been so happy to see a bird in my life," commented Fjorn. "How are Sigurlina and the others?"

"Good bird. Good bird," squawked the raven.

Audun squatted by the fire. "It's almost full night. Munin was carrying this." He passed over a hide scroll. "Wynne left to scout the grove again. She should be back to report before we're ready to go."

"Wynne is a good scout." Fjorn unrolled the scroll and looked at the scraggly uneven symbols on it.

Ragna Jolnir Sigurlina good

Can move spear / cal... big pot

Sank... place bad in def... safe - not long.

Trick crusa...crusd... bad men.

Bad men dis... kill... stop ded men. Safe men near Sank....place I am.

Run away to nite.

Spear dan... bad. No use.

Where meat?

Sigurlina kiss kiss Fjorn.

"I need to spend more time teaching her how to write," observed Fjorn.

"For three weeks. I think she's amazing," remarked Audun.

"What does it mean?" asked Powell.

"That we proceed as planned with a minor change. Munin, tell Sigurlina to meet us at the western end of the grove by the river. Tell her to let the cold be her ally. Powell, we'll start with the disks on the other side of the river. Fimbulwinter will force any guards they've left to watch the sanctuary's north to reveal themselves or freeze."

"But the dryads," objected Powell.

"Will have shelter and fire. Until they leave." Fjorn smiled.

#

Sigurlina sat in the triangular dun that was the Mother Superior's dwelling space and looked over the contents of the old woman's personal chest.

"I ordered this made in the years before Fimbulwinter." The Mother Superior lifted a silver goblet with gold trim around its brim. Rubies and emeralds were mounted at the centre of golden cross patterns around its circumference. "When I took charge of this grove, people would come to us for healing. We did our best, but with none of us being able to move the grail, it was never enough. I commissioned a smith, and together we made this. The power of the grail and the spear rests in the stones. Any draft drunk from this cup will be healing. It will cure all conditions and neutralise all poisons, but its power is finite and can only be replenished by replacing the enchanted stones. With us needing the stones to maintain the groves, it has sat idle."

"It is perfect," remarked Sigurlina.

"Couldn't we use this one?" Ragna held up an unadorned silver goblet. "It seems a pity to let the Crusaders have something so useful and...." She trailed off as Sigurlina and Jolnir eyed her. Ragna slipped the silver goblet into her carrying pouch.

The Mother Superior shook her head. "The only gold I have is this." She extracted a golden torc from her chest. "It is from a time when a young girl thought too much of how she looked and too little about what really matters."

"It will be enough," said Jolnir. "I'll start beating it onto the spear." He left the dun.

"I want you to give this to Powell when you see him." The Mother Superior extracted a silver cloak pin. The useful tools of the good wife hung from it. She caressed it. "Tell him I'm sorry. It never should have been what it was. I...." A tear trickled down the old woman's cheek. "He knows the words. Just give him the pin."

"You can give it to him," stated Sigurlina.

"No. Your ruse is clever, but only a fool would fall for it if no one offers a defence come morning. I, and the three oldest sisters, will stay. We will make the Crusaders pay just enough so that they believe they have earned this victory. In any case, I will need time to reactivate the spells on the temple building."

"But–." began Sigurlina.

"This is my home. If sacrificing four of us can save the rest, there is no question." The Mother Superior reached into her chest and extracted a silver inkpot and stylus. "I want you to have this. May they serve you well." She turned to Ragna. "And you, young woman, have already helped yourself to a trinket. Sigurlina, I trust you to give this to Jolnir for his lady. It will speed the way for them should they ever choose. One born to the spear will still be required, but only once. Finding a spear is rarely a problem." She passed over a silver ring with a carnelian stone. "Afrikaisi will tell you of its use."

Sigurlina took the ring and put it in her pouch.

"Gather the treasures and position the replacements. Send in my sisters as you depart."

#

Jolnir beat the gold onto the iron of the spear blade. The two metals resisted the union. The soft gold eventually formed along the edge until it stuck.

He then walked into the smaller roundhouse. Sigurlina knelt by the clay pots containing the emeralds, rubies and carnelians. She reverently placed them into a leather pouch as Afrikaisi conversed with her in whispers. Ragna stood by the cauldron. The fire under it had been doused, and she was waiting for it to cool. A closed, wooden chest to one side held the mistletoe spear. Another box waited beside it.

Gritting his teeth against a remembered pain, Jolnir suspended the Crusader's spear over the cauldron.

"I'm going to regret this," said Ragna.

"I'm sure Audun has no regrets about his part," remarked Jolnir.

"Men never do." Ragna rolled her eyes, then gripped the cauldron. Silver light seemed to flow into her body. Using all her might, she hauled the pot away from its spot over the burnt-out fire. "We'll never be able to carry it."

Afrikaisi walked up and smiled. "You do not listen. Now that it is free of the old Myrddin's enchantment, I will deal with it." The small, dark woman knelt and seemed to reach into the cauldron. She stood holding a silver Tyet, the stylised image of a womb and its connecting passages. "The power," she whispered as her body began to glow.

"Afrikaisi," said Sigurlina.

"I, of course." Afrikaisi carried the Tyet to the box awaiting it, and laid it inside before closing the lid.

Jolnir collected a flat-topped chest that had been left in the chamber and placed it under the spear's point. He then draped the box in a cloak, arranged it to look like an altar cloth, and set the Mother Superior's cup under the spear's point.

"Caw, good bird, good bird," sounded from the doorway.

"Munin." Sigurlina raced to the bird, which hopped to her mistress's outstretched arm.

'Fjorn said to warn you it will get very cold, and you should use the cold as your ally. He also says that everyone from the Apenhet is alright and that you are to meet him at the grove's western edge by the river. Did I do good?' The raven spoke into Sigurlina's mind.

"Very good," said Sigurlina.

'I'm glad. I want you to know I try really hard, and I wouldn't want anyone to take my place because I'm your raven, and I think I've done good things for the crew, and I'm sorry if I

193

talk a little too much, it's just--.'

"Munin, you're my good bird. No one could ever take your place." Sigurlina stared at the raven.

'That's good because I wouldn't want you to go and do something like getting an owl to scout for you. I blend into the darkness better. Owls may blend into the snow, but they show up against trees and things, and well. I just wouldn't want you to make a mistake because owls aren't as good as ravens and--.'

Sigurlina kissed her bird's head. "I won't get an owl. I promise."

"We need to let the Mother Superior in here so that she can reset the spells on the building," said Jolnir.

#

Fjorn pulled down the section of the palisade they had cut away opposite the main gate and motioned Neece, Audun and ten druids forward. The men slipped into the dark. A few moments later, there was a sound like a hooting owl.

Powell, who sat beside Fjorn with his eyes closed, nodded. "The Crusaders haven't moved away from their fires. The first teams are in a position to attack if they do."

Fjorn motioned with his arm, and Dvyn and Kjorn moved through the gap with seven of the druids. Minutes passed then another group of five led by his oarsmen left the village. Minutes later, another group followed. The final group gathered by the impromptu gate. Powell looked over his home, then slipped into the night with his fellows and Fjorn, emptying the village.

Inside the houses, a trail of wood chips led from the fire pits to a pile of kindling set to ignite the thatch.

#

Audun listened to the last group pass his location. Through the trees, he could see six Crusaders huddled around a fire. Slipping away with his men, he came to the trail left by the escaping villagers. Neese and his men already followed the footsteps in the snow ahead of him. Calling the wind, Audun buried the trail behind him under a blanket of snow. Audun's team moved to the west of the others.

#

Dvyn and Kjorn guided their team to the north-northwest. When they were away from the village, Kjorn uncovered a candle lantern and, holding it low, led the way until they reached the river bank. The channel only carried a trickle of water down its centre.

"Your turn, my fine lads," whispered Kjorn.

Dvyn and the other druids focussed their minds. Stone moved on stone, creating a barrier, blocking the flow of the Orse. Kjorn kept watch as sweat formed on the druids' brows. Soon a wall of rock a stride wide blocked the river channel up to the level of the pre-Fimbulwinter embankment. A puddle formed at the stone wall's base and slowly crept up the channel.

#

Fjorn winced at the noise his group made as they followed Kjorn's troop. They passed the other team and crossed the river. Cleared of the dead guardians, the woods around the sanctuary were like any other. Fjorn stopped at the season pole north of the sanctuary.

"Quietly," he whispered.

Powell stroked the bark of a tree and murmured his incantation. The hrokkvir awoke.

"Please, pick me up." Powell waited as the hrokkvir set him on its shoulders.

"Move to the season pole." Powell rode the animated tree to the pole and reverently lifted down the season disk. "Gently pass this disk to the men below."

The hrokkvir passed the disk to the men around its feet. Fjorn accepted the disk and gave it to one of the druids. "Take this to the Apenhet. After that, join those making the escape path." The Druid took the shield and vanished into the woods.

"Now number two," hissed Fjorn.

Powell spoke softly to the hrokkvir, and it strode through the woods towards the next season pole. Fjorn and his team hurried to keep up as the temperature plummeted around them.

#

Audun guided his team to the base of the most upriver season pole of the grove. Bracing himself, he stood by the pole while the shortest of the druids stood directly behind him. A third man knelt in the snow behind the second. The tallest of the druids mounted the three of them like a living staircase. At that level, wooden pegs had been left in the pole. The third man caught them and climbed to the season wheel, which he turned until the green quarter was at the top.

#

Neese guided his team around the outer edge of the Crusaders' convalescent camp. Voices speaking in a foreign tongue penetrated the trees. He shrouded his lantern while his team hid.

"Enas nekros den borei na xodepsei chryso."

Two Crusaders carrying a torch came into view.

Neese touched the Druid to his right. The man crawled closer and whispered an incantation. The ground under the Crusaders turned to swamp. Immediately one Crusader hoisted the other out of the water. The Crusader on land reached back to help his comrade only to have a massive wolf charge into his buttocks, driving him headfirst into the water. The upright Crusader cried out and scrambled to get to land as crossbow bolts slammed into him. The water turned back into earth. Neece drove his blade into his upright, trapped enemy.

The wolf howled. Vidurr appeared by the kicking legs of the upside-down Crusader.

"Fjorn told us to keep an eye out for you," Neece sheathed his sword.

"The Crusaders have been sending men to scout the grove. I've counted six. Some of them have woodcraft." Vidurr curled his lip. "These ones didn't."

"If a patrol gets back with what we're doing...."

"We will hunt them." Vidurr nodded. "What is Fjorn doing?"

Kane moved through the forest. When his team had been put under an oarsman, he had thought that it was an insult, but now he understood. They had split up as soon as they were away from the village. Since then, he had been setting traps and snares. If the Crusaders came after them, they would be carrying their crippled home. He brushed snow over a spike trap, then froze.

"Oi iereís léne óti eínai láthos."

"Eínai lígo diaskedastikó. Ta korítsia ton Saxónon den noiázontai."

Voices came from the nearby woods, followed by a scream.

Kane smiled and crept away, leaving the Crusader to care for his stricken comrade.

#

Theodosios stared into the fire. Since the word of his brother's death had reached him, he had done little else.

"My Lord," spoke one of his men.

"Oreste was a good man. He always saw to it that the house guards were fed. He joined the crusade so that our parents wouldn't lose their lands. How am I going to tell our father? I... I should have taken the assault on the sanctuary instead of sitting here nursemaiding a village of devil lovers."

"My Lord, the village."

Theodosios looked up. "A rickety bundle of twigs. Why can't these Northmen build in proper stone? Savages I..."

"My Lord. Fire, the village is on fire," blurted the Crusader.

"What?" Theodosios leapt to his feet. "That was supposed to be our supplies for the trip back. Muster the men, charge the gate. Send word to the Shepherds. We need men to fight the blaze. Move, man, move."

Theodosios strode towards the village. A sane part of him noted that no bolts met his advance.

#

Fjorn hugged himself as the temperature plummeted. The eight season wheels north of the river were down. His group was hurrying towards the river to start on the other side.

"What's that," hissed one of the druids, pointing to a light in the woods.

"Ready blades." Fjorn hid his lantern.

"Hakon is an oath breaker," whispered Kjorn's voice.

"And a catamite to boot," replied Fjorn.

Fjorn sheathed his sword and approached the light. "All well?"

"The dam be made, though it will be days at this rate afore we'll float the ship," Kjorn spoke softly.

"Audun will do his job. Wynne said that the Crusaders were camped by the docks. We'll have to leave that season wheel and the one by their convalescent camp. Powell tells me that only half the sanctuary will be in Fimbulwinter. They may need help breaking the siege."

Kjorn chuckled. "When will you stop underestimating your lass, boy?"

Fjorn blushed. "Still, if you could reinforce her. I can get more runners at the ship."

Kjorn nodded. "We'll clear any scouts that could warn the main force."

Fjorn moved south with the hrokkvir picking its way past the trees with Powell in its branches.

#

Agis lay beside a fire in the dock shed, mentally reviewing how Oreste had set up the campaign for failure. He would strike tomorrow when the troops were healed. He sniffed, thinking how his useless son was proving to be of value after all.

A knock sounded on the shed's doorpost. One of his guards shoved his head in. "My Lord, the heathens have fired their village. I am concerned that we may not have enough supplies for our return home."

Agis sneered. "You sound like Babak. Once we take the spear, we can raid for supplies. Do not bother me unless something of merit happens."

#

Sigurlina crossed an invisible line on the walkway around the larger roundhouse. In the space of a step, the temperature went from cold to bone-numbing. A caw sounded from the roof. Stepping into the warmer area, Sigurlina held up her arm, and Munin landed.

'All the ones north have built up their fires. You could see them if you took down the thorns. Of course, I know why you can't, something I don't think an owl would understand.' Munin spoke into her mistress's thoughts.

"Good bird." Sigurlina straightened the feathers on her raven's neck.

"Is it time?" asked Jolnir.

Sigurlina nodded. "Now is the time."

Two dryads relaxed their concentration, and the quagmire and thorns to the northwest of the roundhouse turned back into snow and dirt.

Sigurlina picked up a small bench and walked across the compound. Reaching the embankment, she used the bench to stand on and look over the palisade. Red dots blazed in the forest.

'Munin, were either of the Crusaders at those fires alone?' Sigurlina spoke into her thoughts.

'This is why ravens are good. I notice things like that, and, I'll tell you, an owl just wouldn't. Owls are all about catching mice. It's all they think about and--.' Munin rambled.

'Munin, the men,' thought Sigurlina.

'Oh, yes, they both were. Sorry.'

"Were either of them asleep?" thought Sigurlina.

'The one on the right, and he snores.'

Sigurlina scanned the area around the Crusader on the right. His fire cast a shadow where it hit a tree trunk. That shadow was large enough to serve her. She raised a hand. Jolnir lit a torch and held it up while Ragna positioned a wood pole, casting a shadow on the embankment beside Sigurlina. Sigurlina took a deep breath and stepped into the woods beside the snoring Crusader. She shuffled close to him and lightly brushed the skin of his cheek, imparting Svartalheim's foulness to the man. She slipped into the night and knelt in the snow, whispering.

"Come hither servant, durable symbol of our ending. I summon thee black one."

The skeleton rose. Sigurlina motioned for it to follow her. Moments later, Sigurlina drove her staff into her enemy's throat while the skeleton smashed its staff into his knee. The two pummelled the man until he was still.

"Munin," whispered Sigurlina.

Munin landed on her arm. "Let them know the way is clear."

Sigurlina fed a piece of wood to the fire and looked at the corpse beside her.

"I wonder if you had a daughter?" she whispered, then she called on the shadows to blanket the area between the fire and the embankment so the others could join her.

Moments later, the dryads walked into the light cast by the fire. Two of them were carrying the box containing the mistletoe spear. Soon after, two more appeared, with the case containing the tyet/cauldron. Over several minutes, the sanctuary's population gathered around the small fire. After lighting a torch, they headed towards the river. They'd barely left the fire when they heard a voice to their rear speaking in a foreign tongue. The voice began shouting.

"Run," ordered Jolnir, who turned to face the foe.

Two Crusaders appeared on their trail and froze, facing Jolnir and the black skeleton. The four stared at each other, then the Crusaders took a step back. Jolnir held his ground. The Crusaders babbled to each other, then slowly sheathed their weapons, held their palms out, and took another step back.

Jolnir nodded once.

The Crusaders backed out of sight.

Sheathing his sword, Jolnir followed in the footsteps of the women from the grove.

Sigurlina hugged herself against the bitter cold of Fimbulwinter as she walked. Without warning, the air felt warmer, and she stepped into slush. A light was visible ahead. She braced for battle until Kjorn came into view.

"Good to see you, lass." Kjorn motioned with his torch for the druids with him to help with her dryad's burdens.

"Is everybody?" began Sigurlina.

"Last I heard," said Kjorn.

The groups folded into one and moved towards the Apenhet.

#

Babak sat by the fire with his wounded men. Of all those who assaulted the grove, there were now less than seventy. Fortunately, because of Lucian, most of them would be healed by morning. Babak stared at the disk on the sleigh. If only he could gather enough of them. Grow crops, feed his people. If only the heathens would see the error of their ways. He looked at the fire. The error of their ways. He asked himself whose ways were in error. Being a Godi of the false Gods was a death sentence in Aethelstan's land, while the heathens were open to letting all priests speak. Babak shook his head. He had a duty.

"Shepherd," shouted a teen wearing light, leather armour who raced into the convalescent camp.

"What is it?" demanded Babak.

"The village. It's on fire. Theodosios is trying to put it out."

"God's teeth, no! Run back. Tell Theodosios that he is not to enter the village. There won't be anything there anyway." Babak stroked the length of his scar.

"I'm sorry, Shepherd. Weren't we relying on the village's stores to get us home?" asked Lucian.

"Lucian, come with me and bring your lute. Your voice may be all that can save us." Babak strode towards a red glow that was topping the trees.

CHAPTER 20: A VICTORY OF SORTS

Audun's team adjusted the last of the disks along the river.

A shadow appeared. Audun barely had time to draw his axe before he heard a familiar voice.

"Hakon is an oath breaker," said Fjorn.

"And a catamite to boot," replied Audun.

"We've taken the disks north of the river. The ones by the Crusader camp and the docks are out of reach," explained Fjorn.

A candle lantern was uncovered, and Audun looked at his captain. Fjorn looked tired. Audun knew how he felt. "We can join you."

Powell had the hrokkvir lower him to the ground. "We all need sleep."

Fjorn snorted. "Captains never sleep. It feels warmer."

"The disks are set to summer. It is an abomination of the cycle, but we have little choice if we are to fill the river," observed Powell.

"A lesser evil to halt a greater evil," observed Audun.

Fjorn eyed Audun's group. "Do you have a Druid that can make a quagmire in your group?"

"Iden can." Audun indicated a slender man wearing cloth armour.

"Get some more men from the Apenhet and go to the season pole one west of the Crusader camp. I want you to take it, pole and all, and follow the river west a hundred strides, then mount it and set it to summer."

Powell gasped. "It will break the season wheel."

Fjorn stared into the dark. "If we don't float the Apenhet, we'll lose all the wheels."

"We'll do it." Audun motioned for his men to follow him.

\#

Babak raced to the village. The buildings blazed, and several men clutched their feet in front of its gate. Theodosios stumbled out of the gate carrying another Crusader. Babak could see blood dripping from the man's feet.

Theodosios stepped forward and addressed the Shepherd. "My Lord. The heathens fired their village. When we broke in, we found they'd put traps on the ground."

Babak looked at the burning village. "Lucian, heal the men. Theodosios, no one is to enter that place. Did you see a gap in the village wall?"

Theodosios shook his head. "I... I wasn't looking."

"Walk with me." Babak led the way around the village until they came to the hole Fjorn had made in the palisade.

"Your men were sleeping." Babak sighed. "I heard about your brother. I should have thought. Take some men and your peoples' ruined boots. Look amongst the dead for good boots and swap them. We can do that much."

Babak looked towards the season pole where the silver light was growing.

#

Vidurr sniffed the ground. The grove by the Crusader's convalescent camp was bordered by a line of traps. Some of which he respected as adequate examples of his profession's art. He could smell that Audun had been there. A deer bounded out of the forest, avoided a leg trap and raced through the snowy woods. He could smell summer. Looking west, he saw a glow coming from the season disks by the river.

He turned to where a Crusader lay with his leg in a snare. Vidurr howled, taking on his human form.

The Crusader saw Vidurr approach. "Please." He spoke in badly accented Orse.

Vidurr was a trapper, a hunter, a killer, but what he looked upon sickened him. Death should come quick. Leg snares were a disgrace to his trade.

"Grasp your sword. Close your eyes." He beheaded the Crusader, uncovered the trap and disabled it before moving to the warmer lands under the summer disks.

#

Sigurlina inhaled, taking in the fragrance of summer. The disk up the river's course glowed golden like the sun. Under its magic, the trees raced into life. Animals crowded into the area by the river, and birds sang. Water rushed into the Orse's channel. She stirred a cauldron of stew that had been erected over a fire on the river bank.

The dryads from the sanctuary lay on blankets spread on the high ground. Most slept, some conversed in low voices.

Audun appeared, leading a group of ten druids and Gimnir, who were carrying one of the season poles parallel to the ground. They walked up to the Apenhet and set the pole down. Audun pulled Sigurlina and Ragna into a hug. When the embrace broke, he slapped Jolnir on the arm.

"We need to place this pole upstream a hundred strides. My lot are all in from getting it here," observed Audun.

Jolnir smiled. "That we can manage." He recruited people from those gathered at the Apenhet. The group started up the river's course with the pole.

Audun sat on a hide someone had left against a tree and closed his eyes. A small body curled up beside him. They were both too tired to speak, and slumber took them.

Sigurlina stirred the pot and dished stew into the bowls Auden's group held out to her.

#

Agis stood in the middle of the road to the sanctuary. Everything was as he'd left it. Crusaders with polearms sought to catch a corner of the bridge they'd made the day before and pull it ashore. Two of the dead had attacked but been swiftly dealt with.

A bolt flew from the thorny barricade behind the quagmire, and one of the men fell into the water.

Babak and Theodosios moved to Agis's side.

"We should take some men and collect the season disks. The sanctuary isn't going anywhere, and the disks' powers are proven," said Babak.

"No! I will have the prize. We seek to liberate the spear that pierced the side of our Lord. To hold it is to be invincible. I will have it. None will gainsay me."

Agis strode to where his Crusaders had erected the bridge over the quagmire.

"Remember men, the riches they possess will be ours. Attack!"

Four Crusaders tentatively stepped onto the bridge. Bolts flew at them as the swords they held turned to vipers that they cast aside. They reached the end of the bridge and began hacking at the thorns with axes.

A gale-force gust of wind blasted over them, knocking them into the water. A horn sounded three long blasts.

#

Sigurlina lay curled in the bow of the Apenhet. Season wheels and the boxes containing the treasures from the sanctuary were stowed amidships. Oarsmen slept at their stations, ready to push off. The ship rocked, and she stood to look over the side. Water rushed down the river channel lifting the ship, which pulled against its mooring line.

Three distant horn blasts sounded. She glanced over to where several women from the sanctuary lay on blankets under an oak tree. They seemed to relax as if ending some effort, then stood and started moving upriver.

#

Agis watched as the quagmire and thorns that protected the roundhouses vanished, trapping four Crusaders waist-deep in earth.

"We have them. Their devil has deserted them. Charge," shouted Agis.

The Crusaders charged as two old women appeared in front of the roundhouse. One gestured, and wind blasted into the men's faces. The other called the quagmire, but the Crusaders forded it, leaving only four of their number behind.

Flames licked up through the thatch of the large roundhouse. An old woman threw herself through the doorway and drove her staff into a Crusader's stomach.

One of the women gestured, and the front rank of Crusaders was enveloped by thorns. Then the crossbowmen let fly, and the old woman died. The thorns vanished. The Crusaders charged on, striking the other women with spear and sword. In moments it was done. The larger roundhouse blazed. Agis strutted onto the sanctuary's compound. His men watched him with veiled contempt.

Agis paused beside the door of the smaller roundhouse. "You and you, enter and make sure the way is clear," he ordered two of the Crusaders.

Numbly the men entered. "It's only an old woman," one of them called out.

Agis straightened his cloak and pushed into the building.

The Mother Superior sat on a blanket. A reedlight was thrust into the ground beside her. The spear and the chalice were where Jolnir had left them.

"Where is your champion?" Agis demanded.

"No man is here to defend these treasures." The Mother Superior rose slowly to her feet.

"Your defender has died," Agis spoke in avaricious tones.

"I can assure you the last man to defend this sanctuary is dead." The Mother Superior locked gazes with the Shepherd. "I will warn you. Leave this place. What is here will bring you nought but pain. You pervert the teachings of the lamb. Go meditate on your sins."

Agis scowled and drew his sword. "Enough!" He decapitated the Mother Superior. Her blood fountained into the air filling the chalice.

Agis fell to one knee before the chalice and spear, motioning for the other Crusaders to do the same. Blood painted them all. They held their swords like crosses. After a moment of silence, Agis stood and took down the spear. Clutching it with one hand, he took the cup with the other and stepped towards the doorway.

Pain shot through his head.

He took another step.

His heart pounded as sweat poured from him.

Another step and his mouth went slack as drool fell from his lips.

He staggered into the compound, leaning on the spear. Blood dribbled from the chalice onto the ground, which erupted in flowers.

Agis pulled himself to his full height and brandished the spear above his head, slurring, "I ammmm invinccccable." He collapsed, the spear falling from his fingers, the chalice spilling its contents to the ground.

Babak walked up beside Agis and looked at him. Bending down, he picked up the chalice, then stepped back.

"Aren't you going to take the spear?" asked Theodosios.

Babak sniffed. "No soldier of the legion would have the wealth to gilt a spear, and why would they? These are not the prizes we came for. Although, this goblet is a prize." He caressed the cup.

Behind Babak, sparks from the larger roundhouse had ignited the smaller one.

"Lucian, take five men and bring the wounded to the healer's camp. We will muster there. Perhaps we can yet take the day. Theodosios, choose five men. Take the season disk down from the docks and secure it on the sleigh. It is a treasure far more valuable than the gems upon it. The rest of you, with me."

Babak led the way down the sanctuary road.

Left behind, Agis lay drooling in the dirt, lost in dreams of glory.

#

Fjorn watched with sorrow as Fimbulwinter claimed the strip of land along the river. It had been summer. Now the birds and animals fled west to the next disk. As he watched, a tree cracked apart from the water within it freezing. He marvelled at the power in the disk he carried.

Powell looked forlornly down from the hrokkvir's shoulder. As the three moved the final disk.

Fjorn heard a crash and glanced behind him. Bright spots of torches lit the dying forest.

"Run!" he bellowed, then put action to word.

#

Jolnir watched as the druids and dryads moved beside the fast-deepening river course. The Apenhet floated. Only her crew and Dvyn waited with the ship.

Neese and Gimnir had gone to help guard the druids and dryads as they walked upstream along a trail paralleling the river.

The world was filled with the sound of trees splitting. The hulking figure of the hrokkvir came into view. A small figure ran ahead of it.

"Sigurlina," Jolnir called.

Sigurlina stirred in her sleep, then opened her eyes.

"He's here," called Jolnir.

Sigurlina leapt to her feet and looked over the gunwale. Fjorn ran with a season disk in his grasp. In the distance, dark figures chased him.

The hrokkvir paused by the season pole, reached down and uprooted it, plunging the world into darkness. It then ran towards the Apenhet.

Sigurlina leapt to the shore, her chest tight. "Skeleton, protect Fjorn," she ordered.

The black skeleton raced towards the oncoming Crusaders.

Jolnir readied his blade.

"Dvyn, join me," snapped Sigurlina.

Audun leapt ashore, his battle axe at the ready. Ragna moved to his side. Kjorn flanked Sigurlina. Vidurr howled and leapt from the ship, a snarling wolf.

The skeleton crossed paths with Fjorn. The hrokkvir with Powell ran into the summer zone further upstream. The cold of Fimbulwinter swallowed the warm zone by the Apenhet.

The skeleton reached the Crusaders. It challenged the foremost man and was mown down. Sigurlina knelt, calling another skeleton, then snapped, "Protect Fjorn," and pointed to her beloved.

The water on the ground was fast turning to ice. Fjorn drew closer.

Munin dug into a bag on the ship, pulling out a wooden caltrop. She took to the air with it in her beak, heading for the Crusaders.

The second skeleton reached the Crusaders. It lasted longer than the first.

Munin dropped what she carried onto the snow. The first few Crusaders raced by it, but then one stepped on it and stumbled. Three men tripped over him and measured their length on

204

the icy ground.

Munin returned to the ship. 'I'd like to see an owl do that,' echoed in Sigurlina's mind.

"Dvyn, when I tell you, create a quagmire right in front of me." Sigurlina readied herself.

"Get aboard," Fjorn gasped as he skidded past his friends and slammed into the side of the ship.

"Now," snapped Sigurlina as she caused the shadows to grow in front of her.

There was a loud splash sound. Sigurlina and Dvyn threw themselves into the ship, which jerked ahead as Audun summoned the wind. The water in the channel held deep.

Sigurlina and Dvyn released their spells, revealing five Crusaders half-buried, with water freezing all around them.

Crossbow bolts zipped by the ship. All onboard were forced to duck.

"They'll come upriver," cautioned Ragna, who looked back at the Crusaders.

Kjorn, who'd taken the bow watch, smiled. "I'm thinking not."

"What's to stop them?" demanded Jolnir.

Kjorn pointed forward. At the extreme end of the season wheel's golden light, the bow of a snekkaj could be seen. "The troops from Jorvik have arrived."

Fjorn collapsed onto his sea bench, breathing hard. A moment later, he found Sigurlina pressed into his side as they sailed up the Orse.

#

Babak saw the larger longship in the distance.

"My Lord?" asked Theodosios.

"Providence has not been with us this day. We will take what treasures and provisions we have and go back the way we came. If the weather holds, we may survive." Babak started towards the convalescent camp. "Hurry, or do you relish another battle?" he asked the other Crusaders when they were slow to follow.

The Crusaders glanced at the oncoming longship, turned and walked away.

#

Two days later, Fjorn held Sigurlina in a private room of King Cuaran's great hall. They were both light-headed from the king's finest mead. The room reflected their status as heroes of the land. The work on the Orse's new course was well underway, and the passage to the sea would be open in days. Then the next quest would begin, but tonight was theirs.

Fjorn kissed Sigurlina. She kissed him back, as together they explored the mystery that is the spear and cauldron in love and honesty.

Fate of the Norns: Ragnarok
SAGA - FAFNIR'S TREASURE

Fate of the Norns: Ragnarok
CORE RULEBOOK

CHILDREN OF ERIU

Fate of the Norns: Ragnarok
LORDS OF THE ASH

PENDELHAVEN PUBLISHING

www.ingramcontent.com/pod-product-compliance
Lightning Source LLC
Chambersburg PA
CBHW051107030726
47504CB00006B/1830